Fanny Howarth

the

Journey

of a Lady

D J Prewer
and
Jacqueline George

Book Data

Title : Fanny Howarth the Journey of a Lady

Copyright © 2016 by J.E. George & D.J.Prewer
ISBN: 9798365566279

Cover design by Jacqueline George
All cover art copyright © 2022 by J.E. George
Cover material courtesy Daniel Eskridge
Printed and bound in Australia.

PUBLISHER
Q~Press Publishing

Contents

Foreword

Debbie,
I've been sitting at my computer all morning editing, but I have to say my heart's not in it. I'm having a Why Bother? morning. I've checked my sales on Amazon and nothing's happening. Nothing. All those lovely books I've written are going nowhere.

Yes, yes, I know, they'll start selling again sometime soon, but nothing like the way they should. They are good books, interesting stories and reasonably well written (although I say it myself) but somehow, they are just not reaching the right people. Or perhaps they are just not the right books?

You know what I think the problem is? Most of my books are romantic and women are the ones who buy romance. If they think that I or any other man can't write a romantic book, I suppose I shouldn't be surprised when they don't buy. I think they're silly. There just has to be a strand of romance that both men and women can read. After all, they make romance together in real life so why can't they do it together in a book?

Anyway, the cat woke me up early and I lay in bed thinking about things, wondering what is going on. Could it be that there are just too many romances out there? Everyone and her dog seem to be writing romantic ebooks, so perhaps mine (ours?) are just getting swamped in a pile of mediocre novels. Or even bad novels because, frankly, a lot of them are crap. We need something different, something to make us stand out from the crowd. Then I had this idea...

How about we write a book together? That could have so many benefits for both of us. You can help me answer the age-old question What do Women Want? And we can edit each other's work as we go along (don't think you'll be allowed any of the purple prose you indulge in sometimes). You can make sure the heroine thinks like a real woman, and I can tell you what she looks like through male eyes. And having both male and female input for the sex scenes - it's giving me shivers already.

What do you think? And what sort of book would you like to write? We could share the settings between England and America - why not? At least we will be writing about places we know and that will be good. And what genre? I'm not going to do horror - I scare too easily. Fantasy would be OK. Or history, with courtesans and pirates. But no bloody vampires. I can't stand modern vampires - the whole idea of them is just stupid. Come on, let's do it. It will be great fun.

So, let's get down to business. Can we sketch out the plot line we will use?

It never occurred to me to ask how you, Debbie, go about writing a book. Do you plan carefully, write notes, have a time-line, that sort of thing? I tend to have an idea for characters and their main interaction, and then just start the ball rolling. So I might want my heroine to head in a certain direction, looking for the love of her life (that's what heroines do, you know) but if something comes to mind as she travels, I like to be free to let it happen.

I had an experience once – a character (a heroine, as it happens) who was a nun. She was meant to jump into bed with a man – any man – early in the novel and generally go to the Devil until she had her just punishment at the end of the book. It didn't happen. No matter what I did, she just refused to cooperate and did not disgrace herself until the last page, by which time she had decided it was no disgrace at all. She wrote her own story and when I mentioned that to an experienced author, he said – I bet that's a good book. When characters write their own stories, you know you have a good book.

Anyway, I am happy to go along with however much planning you want to do. Right now, I am thinking about 18th century England. The heroine is living with her uncle on a country estate when something makes her run away to London. As we are talking sexy romance, I think the event that drives her away should be an attack by Fanny's uncle. On the other hand, I don't want a rape because there is nothing sexy about that. I suggest the uncle and his housekeeper, a strict and very proper woman, are running a private BDSM cellar where the old man abuses the servants, with the active help of the housekeeper – even though she looks as if she sucks limes for fun. Our heroine is forced downstairs, stripped, spanked and forced to watch as the old man services the housekeeper in interesting ways. And is warned that when the uncle returns from a short trip the following week, they will celebrate the heroine's introduction to the Dark Arts.

The heroine and her Irish maid escape before the uncle returns and we follow them to London and eventually America. How does that fit with you?

What are we going to call the heroine? She can't have a servant's name like Meg or Polly. A more aristocratic one like Arabella, perhaps. Penelope would be possible – that's classical. Medea? How about Francisca? That would let us call her Fanny, and there's a very loaded word. Americans would be talking about her bum, but British English sees things from the other side and would be talking about her pussy (fine by me, although I am sure we will be writing her a pretty bum too).

Anyway, I'm getting ahead of myself. Please think about this scenario and, if you are happy with it, would you like me to write the first couple of pages of the book and we can argue about them? We have to get the beginning right, or modern readers won't bother to read further.

Well, do let me know what you think. I'm off to town because a valve on our water tank has sprung a leak and I have to be a plumber this morning,
Regards,
Simon

Debbie,
I am missing a reply from you but that's fine. I know you have had a lot on your plate over the last couple of weeks. I sat down and wrote a possible beginning – what do you think? It introduces Fanny and Bridget, and gets them out of her uncle's grasp. Is it too fast? Too detailed, does it dump too much information? Don't hold back because we definitely have to get the beginning right.
Regards,
Simon

Chapter One ~ Best Foot Forward

*Our heroine leaves home ~ Thomas Curmudgeon ~ the old priory at
Christmas time ~ Spring in the cornfields ~ a packed lunch ~ the
freedom to drink from the bottle*

Francisca Howarth tightened the reins and brought the trap to a gentle halt just before the gateway. A few moments, and she would leave the grounds of Langston Priory. A cold thought jumped into her mind; she might never return.

The old priory basked in the midsummer sun, all glowing russet bricks and creamy Purbeck stonework. It looked homely. It was home, and had been for years. When she first came here with her mother, when she had been too young to understand, it had seemed big and frightening. Now, well, it was home and she loved it. She loved the mossy roof tiles and its crazy chimneys. She loved the ruins of the Great Hall, destroyed by Cromwell's cannons, now covered in wisteria and awaiting the day when Uncle had enough money and enthusiasm to rebuild it.

Behind the house, The Woods, a glorious mature forest. Mostly oak with interlopers of beech and ash, now dark and secret under its summer leaves. She loved the gently sloping lawns in front of the house, and the view out over the fens. Out of sight in the blue grey haze, the North Sea lapped at the land and threatened the white woolly sheep grazing the lawns. She loved the walled garden behind, an island of warmth and stillness even on winter days, built in King Henry VIII's time and still putting vegetables and fruit on the Priory table. She loved the secret places in the debatable lands between the garden and the stables, where a little girl could hide and play until mother called her in for tea.

It was all hers, her childhood, and now she was leaving, perhaps for ever. She shivered and flicked the reins to start Thomas Curmudgeon on his way. He flicked his ears and shouldered his harness as if the trap was as heavy as a harvest wagon. For Thomas, everything was always too much trouble. She flicked the reins again and he reluctantly broke into a trot.

Bridget broke into her thoughts. "Are you sad, Miss Fanny?"

"What? Oh yes, I suppose I am. It's a nice old place."

"Oh well, and I'm sure we'll be back by Christmas. It'll all blow over, sure it will."

Christmas. That brought another flood of memories, of dark frosty nights, of carol singers, of the men bringing in the Yule log, and holly and fir branches. Singing Christmas hymns in a freezing church and returning to the rich warmth of the fireside. Of the special dinners, and above all, of the soft time when her mother was still alive.

She shook herself free. "Come on, Thomas. You can walk once we're through the village." She flicked the reins to encourage him and imagined she heard Thomas sigh.

They rattled over the village cobbles and onto the road beyond. It was a good day to be travelling with the warmth on their faces, and the wind just enough to send swaying waves through the cornfields on either side. Now the fields were empty of people as the corn was more green than golden. Another month and the harvest would begin. The fields would be full of men and women labouring from the moment the dew was off the corn in the morning until dusk, praying for rainless days and hating the sun that sent them out to work again.

Thomas was walking now and the trap swayed comfortably. They had time. The stage did not leave Langport until evening and they had only ten miles to go. Suddenly, Fanny felt hungry.

"It's time for lunch, Bridget. What did cook pack for us?"

Bridget brought out a lunch basket from under her seat and lifted one lid. "She told me the lunch was on this side, Miss Fanny. Bread, cheese and pickle. And some of her elderflower wine to cheer you up, she said. And if you could see your way to sending back the basket and cloths, she'd be grateful. And will we stop, Miss?"

No! Fanny's nerves screamed. Keep moving, don't stop, get away. The road was smooth enough; they did not need to stop. "No, Bridget, we'll keep on. Thomas is slow enough as it is, and I can eat with one hand and drive with the other. You can feed me a bit at a time. And we can pretend to be farmers and drink our wine from the bottle."

Bridget looked shocked. "We have cups, Miss Fanny. Cook has packed plates and cups. Along with knives and a pat of butter."

Fanny thought for a moment and said, "No cups. We are adventurers, eating and drinking as we can. No cups. But some butter on our bread would be nice." Thomas plodded on as Bridget prepared chunks of crusty white bread with Eaton cheese and pickle, and passed half of them over to her. They washed it down with sweet elderflower, passing the bottle between them.

Hi Simon,

Here I am! Finally recovered from a spate of migraines. Did you know that a migraine would drive a normally sane person to be willingly decapitated? True story.

I am really looking forward to this collaboration. As you know, writing can be a lonely time. The headspace of a writer, or any creative person, can be a very interesting place full of drama and mayhem coupled with muttering storylines to oneself at all hours of the day. My children often look at me and ask me who I am talking to. I am well past the stage of blushing at my embarrassing behaviour, "just going over a storyline," is my go-to answer. They don't need to know if I am plotting the slow, painful death of someone. Or, as is more my normal, an erotic sex scene that can actually be performed. No faking it here!

Yes, sales are a mysterious thing, aren't they? I wonder if it's just a sign of our overabundance-of-literacy times that a well written story can be ignored and something that is equal to a good story found within a high school student's note book, can become the next big thing. Society doesn't want to be enlightened; they want to be entertained, and with as little effort as possible on their behalf. Not to worry though, I'm sure even the literary greats would be bypassed if they were alive today. Could you imagine Shakespeare reading in the middle of Times Square on a summer's afternoon? People wouldn't have the time to stand around and listen to his worded magic, so they would pass him by. Perhaps in this fast-paced world it is better that the Greats are not of this century?

It is a short-sighted mind that believes men cannot write romance. Although the stereotype would have us believe it, it is not the domain of women. Love and sex and all the trappings in between are purely emotional responses that come from being human – not a gender or orientation.

I have read and watched romance and sex of just about every legal and consensual kind, and at the end of the day, the body parts may vary, but that is all. I cannot remember the name of a European movie I watched many years ago, but it had a male-on-male love scene (my first), and it was simply beautiful to watch. It was filmed in a way that transcended gender. Imagine being able to view the world through that lens every day.

So, write your stories, my friend. I for one, am interested in what your mind can create.

My writing style is … well … (warning: I'm going to purple prose any minute now), it's … scatterbrained until I have a definite idea, the initial idea tends to hit me out of the blue and is usually an inspiring sentence that won't leave my mind. Then it's time for a little plotting and a lot of plodding by way of scrappy notes written in pretty notebooks. And then, with pen to paper, the story starts to flow and I write from start to finish, before going back and researching what is needed. Is that prose purple enough for you? I blame the male part of my female brain.

Which brings me to What Do Women Want. I think the absolute answer to that lies deep within a book of worldly secrets, seated right next to 'how to make sales'. Most likely shelved next to the Akashic Records.

Perhaps it is a case of what women think they can have, not so much as want? Unfortunately, there is still a from-day-of-birth conditioning that takes place about what is sexually correct. Who is anyone to dictate what is correct in any consensual sexual act? Be it that all participants are legally aged.

Personally, I'm more of a deep-dark-caramel-swirl kind of girl. No vanilla here. So for me and my characters, sex should be enjoyable, and most definitely, consensual. Our heroine is in for a fun time. Love the name by the way. I have known two Fanny's in my time and they both had a delicious wickedness about them. Must be the name!

I love the initial storyline. I think the amount of detail is good. Paints the picture nicely. It clearly conveys her reluctance to leave but also the desire to return. Sexual freedom and its discovery in that era has me thinking Hellfire escapades. I may be salivating at this moment. Of course, that may be the wine I'm drinking as well.

I'm thinking after the initial shock wears off from what her uncle did to her, perhaps our heroine realises she may like what she has seen – just not with her uncle and the foul-faced housekeeper.

I'm wondering what kind of spin we put on the uncle. Is he a nice caring man who just happens to like kink with, well, anyone, or is he the deviant kind? The caring one lends itself to no one suspecting him for the person he truly is which is why he goes undetected. The deviant one conjures up horrible images and would most likely deeply affect our heroine. Is he in total control or does the housekeeper have the control? Perhaps this would delve into a story line where we don't need to go?

I'm imagining the dungeon to be comfortable (for its time), and etched in the wall is 'Fais ce que tu voudras' – do what thou wilt – the Hellfire Club motto circa Sir Francis Dashwood's clubs throughout the 1730s. Of course, our heroine doesn't know what this means.

I'm thinking the sex acts the uncle has with Fanny initially are tame, perhaps just a bit of touching and then he and the housekeeper go at it, hammers and tongs, in front of her. It could be an initiation of sorts to see if she is suitable for 'bigger' things? Perhaps she could be a virginal sacrifice to take place at the Hellfire caves in West Wycombe? The distance between Langston Priory (West Oxfordshire) and the Caves (West Wycombe), approximately 50 km, seems achievable, and believable, for our time period. Did Hellfire make it to the US at that stage? Perhaps Fanny has a 'reputation' that follows her to the US. Maybe her uncle is an honorary member of the scene there? Do we have him appear towards the end, claiming an errant bride (is he truly her uncle)?

Ah, my brain is in overdrive. I'm loving it. My only concern is my matching the Georgian style of the writing but I'm sure you'll be able to rein me in when needed.

I hoped you enjoyed your plumbing duties the other morning. Women like a man with good hands. I'm sure Fanny and Bridget would appreciate their men being just the same. I know you'll have pointers to pass on.

Cheers.

Debbie,

Debb,

Oh dear, I have fallen at the first fence. I picked the name 'Langston Priory' because it sounded comfortable and realistic, and set it in the western Fens somewhere. Probably Cambridgeshire which is not too far north of London. And you had to go and look it up on Google and found a Langston Priory in Oxfordshire, now acting as a seniors care home. Well, too late now, plus Langston is a common family name in England. Unless you insist, let's leave our Langston Priory where it is. The modern one is far less interesting.

Good about the Hellfire Club. I had not thought of that, but I suggest she doesn't learn about it from her uncle but is taken there from London by the aristocrats who visit her brothel. Apparently the 'nuns' were a mixture of professionals, wives and sisters – so why not? By the way, I have read that Benjamin Franklin was an invited guest – naughty boy!

I think the uncle should run his own household the way he likes, and he likes tying up the servants and doing whatever he wants with them. Of course, the servants don't want to participate but if that's what the Lord wants, they may as well enjoy it. I saw the housekeeper as playing second fiddle to the uncle - we definitely can't afford any affection to develop there.

Why are you asking me about the uncle's character? He's all yours and you can make him villainous or Mr Pickwick with an attitude, as you like. However he is, I suggest he takes Fanny a long way down the slippery slope, so she has something serious to run away from.

Personally, I am not sure about spanking. I can't imagine enjoying it myself and I have yet to find a lady who wants me to do it to her. On the other hand, I can certainly see the attraction of a lady tied over a table. Anyone would look desirable from that angle and if you add corset and stockings, it might make Donald Trump look like an angel. Ah well – it hasn't happened yet. I can only dream.

I took Jana to Lviv last year and they have a café there dedicated to a local hero, Leopold von Sacher-Masoch. They even have a full sized bronze statue outside for tourists to pose for photographs. We went in one evening after a very nice meal and found the entrance area blocked by one of the waitresses whipping a young client. He was without his shirt and she was dressed in stockings and corset (of course) and looked very pretty as she wielded her cat. Everyone was laughing and cheering but I admit she was doing no more than make his back slightly pink. All the same, my lady chickened out immediately and we went straight home instead. We did go another night and had a good time with strange cocktails. And at the end of the evening, Jana persuaded one of the waitresses to chase me out of the café with her whip.

I am REALLY looking forward to your scene in the uncle's basement. I suggest you start from a flash back for Fanny in the stagecoach as she sways through the evening on her way to London.

By the way, I am normally healthy and would like this state of affairs to continue. However, if you persist in using either one or two spaces between sentences, I see apoplexy on the horizon. One space is standard!

Regards,

Simon

Simon, Simon, Simon.

You must have a very large monitor to even pick up the whole one space, two space, issue. I can assure you it's not deliberate – wouldn't want to cause you any health problems – just a case of fast fingers on a small keyboard. I promise from now on I'll be a good girl and use one space.

I had a friend of mine once say that if you don't like being spanked, it's not being done right. Food for thought there. I love your memory of Lviv. Poor Jana, maybe she thought you had something in mind for her. The surprising thing that most people don't realise about whips is that, in a skilled hand, it can flay the skin to bloody ribbons or it can place feather-like welts upon the skin that can drive a person to orgasm. Fear and excitement is all part of the fun.

This chapter with the uncle and Fanny brought about days of procrastination and as a result my house is very clean. I wonder if all writers are as good at avoiding storylines as I am. I couldn't get my head around the uncle touching his niece in such an intimate way, molesting her, and make it enjoyable for the reader. Is this a difference between the male and female brain? Possibly. I know that in some periods of time, our setting included, this could have been considered somewhat normal. Eeek! But I could not do it here. So I came up with what I think is a nicer twist.

During my research of Hellfire, I discovered there are caves in West Wycombe, England, that were used by Sir Francis Dashwood and his wicked followers. They are open to the public. An absolute must-do next time I am on the mother-land.

I have to admit I am struggling with the period style of the writing. I'm sure I will improve with time but for now bear with me.

Hope you enjoy.

Debb

Chapter Two ~ Memories and Nightmares

*The mail coach to London ~ a dark dream ~ Fais ce que tu voudras ~
a beautiful pillory ~ Miss Hodges the housekeeper ~ the importance of
obsidian ~ passion and a stolen kiss ~ Bridget and sleeping late ~ the altar
at Medmenham ~ an unwelcome betrothal*

Fanny startled awake as her head bumped against the wooded shutter on the stagecoach. Could this night get any worse? Not only was she cold because her travelling rug made little difference, but the coach also contained a pompous little man, full of self-importance, and his even smaller servant. One of them was wearing enough rose scent to last a year. No prize for guessing who the culprit was. It made her gag. Hours earlier, Fanny had handed over the trap and a very tired Thomas to the manager at a coaching inn and paid for him to return them both to Langston within the week. They had arrived in time to buy the last two tickets on an unscheduled coach that was departing in an hour. With just enough time to freshen up and take a meal at the small tavern, allowing them to keep cook's leftover food for the journey ahead. Now wide awake, Fanny looked to her right to see Bridget still sound asleep, curled up in the corner without a care in the world. The two men were snoring in unison. Their coach was small and old, as if hurriedly found in a stable somewhere to make this rushed journey. With only a driver and an old man for a guard, who both stood by as the roof was hurriedly loaded with trunks, Fanny had watched on amused as the servant gingerly climbed atop to ensure the ropes were tight.

The metal tyres on the wheels crunched small stones, rolling over them with a gentle bump. The larger stones jolted the carriage causing a dry groan from the axle which did little to help Fanny relax. In contrast, the clip clop of the horse's hooves almost soothed her as they cadenced over the flatter stones. How on earth Bridget slept through all of it was beyond her.

Closing her eyes again, she rested her head against a softer section of the wall, hoping it would cushion any blow from the rough road they were traveling on. Never before had she hated anyone as she did her uncle at that moment. How someone as beautiful and gentle as her mother could be related to such a monster was hard to imagine. Tears pricked her eyes as the memory of a whispering voice crept into her mind…

She recalled lying on her bed and rolling towards the dark void of her hearth. She closed her eyes, hoping for sleep, willing her dream to return. She had had a glimpse of something ...exciting. She just couldn't remember what it was.

Sounds drifted into her slumber as she reached out for her dream again...

A raised voice mumbled sternly in the distance. Then the sound of a sudden snap, softening on impact, again and again. Near to her, a deep voice whispered quietly. This is what she remembered most from before. It caused a sudden warmth to spread through her limbs and pool deep inside of her. Never in her life had a voice affected her so much.

Gentle whispers encouraged Fanny to open her eyes. She lay on her back feeling the softness of a fur beneath her nakedness. Looking into the void above, she felt as if she was floating sleepily towards the ceiling and reached out to grasp the orange glow of light that was just beyond her reach.

One side of her face soon grew warm and she turned her head towards a hearth, it was very large, much more than the small one in her bedchamber. Her body was heavy and relaxed, and she smiled, watching with fascination as the bright flames licked high into the stone arch, drawing her eyes to an etching in the stone. *Fais ce que tu voudras*. She stared, not knowing what the carved words meant. She had learnt languages as a child but hadn't been allowed to continue once her mother had died. Firelight danced in and out of the deep etching of the letters, moving whimsically, as if inspired by invisible music.

Once again a whisper called to her, telling her she was beautiful, that she would soon be his. Fanny smiled, this disembodied voice spoke to her like no other ever had. It - no, he, made her feel like a woman.

His words reached deep inside her and told her she was no longer the child she had felt like for far too long.

Rolling to one side, she searched the room, desperate to discover if the whispering man was as enchanting as his words.

The room was very large, with a hearth at each side, both burning bright. No wonder she was so warm. So many candles lined the walls that it felt like daylight.

In the centre of the room was a narrow refectory table. The light from the candles shone upon the polished oak surface, highlighting the curves of its turned legs. Strong and stout, it reminded Fanny of one she had seen in church, only this one was covered in cloth and had straps and buckles attached at the sides.

Glinting on the wall behind the table, were hitching rings lodged high into the stone, some with rope hanging down. Nearby were stools, whips and a large, wooden cross with small hitching rings at each end of the crossbar

Loud moaning drew Fanny's attention to the far corner of the room. A shocked gasp lodged in her throat as she watched a man rubbing the naked behind of a woman. Her legs straight, she was bent at the waist, with her wrists and neck firmly encased in what could only be described as a pillory. Yet this pillory was beautifully carved and had space for two people side by side. Not at all like the old weathered one she had seen in the town square.

As the man stepped back from the woman, Fanny realised that the pillory had been raised on a dais and he was exceedingly tall. At least six feet, maybe even seven. His large hand swept through his black curls and he turned to speak to a silhouetted man standing off to the side. Shadows flickered over the long sideburns that curved towards his mouth. With a sinister snarl he growled out something to the woman in front of him, and then laughing at her outrage, began to loosen his belt.

A low moan fell from her lips as a belt was stroked slowly down her back to her feet. In between her legs the dull pitter patter of the leather rung out as it was flicked from side to side. Higher and higher it moved with a soft slap, slap, slap of the lashes against her inner thighs, coming to rest just beneath her bottom.

The woman's head toppled forward and golden-red curls fell almost to the ground. Fanny gasped, wide-eyed. Oh, she knew that hair! Knew how it looked on a daily basis pinned tightly to the head of her uncle's sour faced, no-nonsense, housekeeper, Miss Hodges.

On the housekeeper's feet were the strangest shoes Fanny had ever seen. They were boots made from a red brocade overlaid with a darker fabric and laced above the ankles with a ridiculously high heels. Her legs were covered in sheer hose secured by a lacy garters. Far too expensive for a servant.

18

A different kind of awareness seeped inside Fanny as she realised Miss Hodges was naked everywhere else. Her fleshy, white bottom glowed with red welts and she moaned deeply as a large hand rubbed over her flesh. That moan spoke straight to Fanny's soul. She wasn't sure why. Her heart raced, keeping in time with the husky whine emanating from the corner. She held her breath as the man raised his hand to strike the woman with his belt.

"Like what you see?" whispered the voice now at her side. Fanny absently nodded, watching the other man make his way from the shadows to the front of the stocks and stood there waiting, for what she did not know.

She stared, mesmerised by his bare chest, as the man unlaced his breeches. With his left hand he gripped his cock. Fanny had never seen a naked man before and had only heard a whisper of what a cock looked like. An ugly one-eyed, slobbering adder, Bridget had said. But this man was beautiful. Strong and lean. His cock was no different and it certainly didn't look like any snake she had seen. Warmth pooled between her thighs as she watched him briskly fist his hand up and down his shaft, all the while smiling down at the housekeeper.

He took a step onto the small rise of a platform and reached for a handful of Miss Hodges hair making her grin and open her mouth wide. She smiled and it was then that Fanny realised she had never seen Miss Hodges smile in the whole time Fanny had lived with her uncle. From her position watching them from the side, Fanny could see the transformation and it was shocking – the housekeeper was beautiful and vibrant.

Agony pulled the man's features tight as he thrust repeatedly into the willing mouth. He looked tortured and as his breathing became laboured, he closed his eyes. Soundless words fell from his lips. His jaw clenched and he threw his head back, yelling. His release came in harsh groans echoing through the room.

Oh, how would he taste, Fanny wondered, parting her lips and wetting them with the tip of her tongue to ease the sudden dryness. She had heard all the things that a lady should not do. All the things her husband might want. "A lady does not do what a harlot will," her nanny had said, over and over. But how could something so…pleasurable…be wrong? If it could make the housekeeper smile so much, surely it was not awful?

The groans of the first man soon captivated Fanny's attention. He was now positioned behind the woman, thrusting his hips against her. Fanny had once overheard the scullery maids talking about how it was possible for a man and a woman to do it the same way as horses but she hadn't believed them. Now she couldn't draw her eyes away. She could see the slick wetness of his cock reflecting in the candlelight as it surged in and out. How long could he do this for? Fanny tried, and failed, to steady her breathing. Her breaths were fast and dry, and she felt giddy. How would it feel to pleasure two men at once?

Miss Hodges moaned loudly as the man pounded into her faster and faster. His hands gripped her hips so tightly she hardly moved. Surely that would hurt, Fanny thought. But as the housekeeper's moans became a high pitched squeal of yes, she very much doubted it.

"Do you like that?" the voice whispered, closer this time. So close she could feel the heat of his breath on her neck.

Fanny turned her head and was struck by eyes of obsidian, surrounded by an ornate silver half-mask that held a single ruby in the center of the temple. A startled squeak embedded in her throat.

"Don't be afraid, Fanny. I'll not harm you." From behind, he leaned in and captured her lips with his, holding her to him tightly. She was so taken by the intensity of the kiss, she could not have moved even if she had wanted to. His tongue darted across her lips, making Fanny gasp, he then took the opportunity to thrust his tongue inside. She moaned, welcoming the invasion. "You taste so sweet. I knew you would be perfect for us."

Fanny leaned closer into him and opened her mouth, using her tongue in the same way as he had. She wanted something more but did not know what 'more' was. His hand touched her breast, strong fingers kneading the sensitive globe, and what a thrilling delight it was. She knew she should be offended. Yes, she definitely should. Those lectures she had had all her life about what her husband would expect didn't matter now. She never wanted this feeling to go away. "More," breathlessly tumbled from her lips before she could think to stop it.

"I can give you more, but not all, not yet." His voice was heavy with desire. He moved above her with ease and came to rest at her side. His back shielded her from the room. Strong fingers trailed down her neck, past her breasts and rested between her thighs. "Tell me what you feel."

Fanny stared into the darkness of his eyes. How could she possibly put into words how she felt? What experience in her life so far did she have to compare? She didn't. For the longest time she had been closeted in the home of her uncle. Her only true friend was her maid. Her only knowledge of men and women were the scandalous Irish tales that Bridget told her to educate her about what her future husband would want. Would he make her feel this way, too?

"I feel warm and fluttery ...down there. I like it." The last part was all but a whisper as her cheeks heated, remembering how mortified her childhood nanny had made her feel when she had caught a young Fanny touching herself in the tub one day. She could still hear the angry words that Nanny had told her, yelling that she had sinned and must ask for forgiveness.

"Don't be embarrassed, little one. What you are feeling is as natural as the air we breathe. Tell me more." He demanded softly, his fingers stroking the hair between her thighs.

His gentle command encouraged Fanny to close her eyes and feel what was happening to her body. "My skin is hot, prickly, as if I am ill. My heart felt like a too-fast drum beating in my chest. Not so much now. My breasts and my nipples are hard," she stated, staring trustingly into his eyes. "They almost hurt. I ache, down there. I want something, yet I don't know what."

"What you are feeling is your body's natural response to being aroused. Do you want to know what I see?"

With wide eyes Fanny bit her lower lip and nodded, watching as the most magnificent smile lit across his face. Surely, he was an angel.

"I see a beautiful young woman with lust drowning in her eyes from enjoying her first kiss. I feel the moist heat between her legs warm my fingertips as they delve into your wetness. And I hear her say she wants more."

"Yes, I want more," she begged, surprised by the depth of her neediness.

"Your passion is a rare jewel. Never be ashamed of it."

"Remember your limits!" A gruff voice yelled, startling Fanny with its angry warning.

"I know what I am doing. Her innocence will remain intact." Fanny's angel spat out harshly over his shoulder.

"Make sure that it does. Her husband has plans," he warned, unappeased.

The sinister threat sent a chill along Fanny's spine. The angry voice seemed familiar. She tried to look beyond the man in front of her but his shoulders were too wide. No longer feeling as sleepy, dread washed over her. What was she doing? Her body belonged to her husband. Panic rose fast in her chest, and she forgot to breathe. Is that what more was? Her virginity? Tears pricked her eyes.

"Breathe now, little one, he demanded through gritted teeth. "Nothing we have done has taken your innocence. Nor will I. Do you believe me?"

"Yes." Once again, her mouth answered before her brain could catch up. Slapping both her hands over her tender lips only reminded her how good it felt to have him kiss her.

He looked down upon her, his smile warm and comforting. The light from a nearby candle flickered in his eyes and she caught a flash of their true colour. Golden brown. Not black as she had first thought. "Relax and enjoy your passion. I promise you that you will remain intact. Let me love you."

A finger inserted down there stole all thought and speech from her. Without hesitation, Fanny raised her hips to meet the gentle intrusion. How would it feel to have a man inside her? How would he fit? Closing her legs against his arm she grabbed hold of his wide shoulders, lifting and rocking herself against him. Quiet moans filled the room and she soon realised they were hers. The ache between her thighs became a ball of tightness under his palm.

Scattered feelings of dread fled her mind and all she could feel was the sticky heat that made it hard to breathe.

Fanny sighed as he cradled her head in his palm and his lips punished hers much harder than before. A thumb flickered over that other part down there and she let out a jolted squeak which drew murmured approval from the others in the room. She did not care. She could not think. All she could do was feel.

"That is it, fly. I will catch you," he whispered breathlessly against her mouth.

As if his words had cast a magic spell, Fanny thrust against his hand, begging for something. She squeezed her eyes tighter and felt herself climb higher and higher until she toppled over into absolute bliss. A scream tore from her throat and a peaceful darkness engulfed her.

Sunshine filtered through the shutters alerting Fanny to the lateness of the morning. It was unusual for her to sleep so late. Perhaps it was all those tarts she had eaten at dinner last night? Why cook had left so many on the platter when she knew they were Fanny's weakness, she would never know. One thing she did know now was that too many tarts made her very sleepy.

The look on her uncle's face when she had asked to retire early still struck her as odd. He had been cheery all day, which was quite opposite from his usual dour mood. Yet, when she had announced that she was feeling tired, he looked positively happy. He even smiled. Strange man.

Reaching for the bell pull to summon Bridget, stiffness crept along her arm and into the rest of her body. A low groan grated against her sore throat.

"Good morning, Miss Fanny." Bridget bustled in, heading straight for the windows to allow the sunshine and fresh air to fill the room.

"Is it? Still morning I mean?"

"Only just. I tried to wake you at your usual time but you told me to go away. Said you needed to get back to your dream. Going by that smile on your face at the time, it must have been a good one."

The small gasp alerted her maid to the heat staining Fanny's cheeks. Her heart raced in her chest as memories flooded her mind. Oh, my! If that is what too many of cook's tarts did to her dreams she would have to indulge more often.

"That must have been some dream you had. Your cheeks are as pink as the dawn this morning. "

"Oh, Bridget. I dreamt of a man and a room with two large fires, other men were there and a woman, too, I think. And a mask with eyes so black they looked like nothingness. I let him touch me," the last spoken as a whisper.

"You let a mask touch you?" Bridget asked, confusion crinkling her brow.

"Yes. No. I don't know." Fanny groaned. "What does it all mean?"

"I think it means that you had too much wine at supper last night, that's what it means. Now come on, Miss, time to get up."

"But I didn't. I admit I may have eaten too many tarts, but I was feeling so sleepy and didn't drink more than one glass."

Bridget placed the back of her hand on Fanny's forehead. "You do feel warm and your cheeks are flushed. Perhaps you should rest in bed for the day?"

"No. I think I feel this way because I have already been in bed too long," she argued, lifting her eyes to meet her maid's, "No. The day awaits. The sun is shining. I think I will take a stroll around the gardens. That will make me feel much better than being cooped up in my room any longer."

With memories of a dream quickly forgotten, Bridget set about readying Fanny for the day. After a quick meal in the kitchens, they set out to walk around the priory. It wasn't until mid-afternoon that they returned to the house.

Raised voices drew Fanny's attention towards her uncle's study, a room she had never been allowed to enter. Peeping over her shoulder to ensure she was all alone, she quickly made her way to the small, curtained alcove opposite the study door.

Harsh whispers escaped through the small gap in the doorway. She wasn't sure who was in there, but they were obviously angry. A loud thump startled her. Oh, she knew that sound. Many times she had been the cause of her uncle slamming his fist against the table when she had angered him.

"Come Saturday, she will be ready for my virginal sacrifice in the caves, laid bare upon the altar at Medmenham for all to see. After that, she will be all mine. She will have no choice but to become my wife."

The angry voice spoke again and was as quiet as before. This person had more control over their temper.

Thump. Thump. The table rattled under the increasing anger of her uncle's heavy fist.

"Yes, she is still a virgin. I told him to remember his limits, that her husband had plans for her. Are you not listening? I have already told you everything that happened."

"You promised her to Dodington. He may be an old man of sixty, but he will not take this lying down. I beg you to reconsider."

24

"I don't care about that old fool! If you had been there last night, you would have seen the temptress that she is. I could have taken her then and there, and she would have begged me for more. My niece may look as innocent as a new-born babe but she has the mind, and body, of a whore. She will please me greatly."

Fanny gasped and covered her mouth, staying the sickness she was sure would come. Memories flooded her mind of her dream from last night. A pleasant dream that had made her yearn to be a woman in love. But it wasn't a dream, was it? It couldn't have been.

I told him to remember his limits, that her husband had plans for her.

The words echoed in her mind from last night. Her uncle had spoken them then, just as he had now in his study. A panic settled at the nape of her neck. He was going to make her become his wife.

A sickening fear ran up her spine with a speed that was breathtaking as Fanny ran back to her room, reaching it in time to vomit into the chamber pot. She had to leave! She had to get far away before her uncle made Fanny his wife.

Her mind raced as she nibbled on the dry biscuits Bridget had fetched from the kitchen to settle her stomach.

She watched Bridget paced back and forth, digesting all that Fanny had told her. With fists clenched at her side, mumbling in a language Fanny did not understand.

"We leave on the 'morrow, Miss. Before dawn. I will arrange everything."

It was still too dark to see clearly when Fanny turned her head away from the breeze. She no longer cared that it felt cold against her face, at least it would dry her quiet tears that were still falling. Thankfully everyone else was asleep when they has left. Her humiliation ran soul deep, carving its way into her heart as well. Not only had her uncle promised her to a man old enough to be her grandfather, but he had then changed his mind and was going to force her to marry himself. Her uncle! Was that even legally allowed?

The dawn finally broke and they quietly left the small town that they had waited in until light. It wasn't safe to travel too far in the dark. As they passed through another village, Fanny sighed; she already missed her home. No, her uncle's home. Although, all her mother's belongings were still there. Fanny couldn't bear the dispose of them when she died. All of Fanny's childhood memories were there, too. In the hurry to leave there had been no time for sentiment. She only hoped that one day she would return to collect them.

Debbie,

That was fun and leaves me waiting for more. I changed a couple of simple things – a pillory was an instrument of judicial punishment and usually set up somewhere public, like a town square. The person to be shamed would be locked into it for an hour or two and the crowd would add to their humiliation by throwing rotten vegetables at them. Or worse. Your private pillory is far more elegant, of course.

One thing that is going to take some getting used to – for me as well - gentlemen of the time would never be seen in public without a wig. They had short cropped hair and covered their bare scalps with wigs. All subject to fashions of course, so the lawyer sharing the stagecoach was likely to have a full wig shape and his servant would probably not have a wig at all, but would wear a hat of some sort. Does not sound attractive to me!

So you did not take to the idea of Fanny's uncle abusing her directly. Can't say it would be a very tasteful thing to do, but in those times a man could be a tyrant in his own home and do virtually whatever he liked to women, children and servants. It happened, but was rarely spoken of. Your way of skating around it looked fine to me, but can I make a suggestion? In real life, anyone playing with your pink bits without explicit permission would invoke an immediate and very negative reaction. On the other hand, if Uncle had put something into your wine at dinner time, you might find yourself in a dreamlike state between reality and fantasy – and that would make Fanny's tranquil reactions much more understandable.

You know, I was thinking about this sequence on the drive down to Cairns, and all the way back. It's really interesting and instructive.

I suppose we are writing for both men and women? Meaning we have to accommodate the things that both of them find romantic and erotic? Well, I don't think you were looking at things through male eyes (I'm sure you will criticize me in the same way when it's my turn.) Men really like visuals. They want to see EVERYTHING. You only have to look at their porn to realise that men and women respond to different things.

So – Miss Hodges. I imagine that she is a sour-faced individual, dressed strictly every day, with her hair in a tight bun. She treats the house staff mercilessly, and never smiles. No attempt at make-up, of course, and she probably sucks lemons every day to get the right expression on her miserable face. Now you have her bent over in the pillory, naked. Did she wear stockings and a corset – I will go back and check. I like stockings and a corset in a situation like this. Anyway, there she is, restrained and abused, except that it can't be abuse if she is enjoying it so much.

I don't know if you understand just how powerful an image that is. Any man is going to be stirred to the cockles of his primitive, sex-crazed soul. Really! A woman displayed like that probably calls out to their Paleolithic instincts and drives them to just, well, jump aboard. Or at least, to wish they could. I can just see those white curves, muscles stretched taut by her position and high heels. And half-hidden in the shadows, the most important planet in the male firmament... Oooh – I'm going to be forced to take a cold shower!

Anyway, with all that erotic beauty displayed just how we men like it, what do you write about? Her shoes! Now, isn't that female? Of course, that's good. We are working together to produce something that is romantic and sexy for both sexes, so I don't object to the shoes. But, my dear, have mercy on mankind and give us a little more of the rest as well.

And Miss Hodges' breasts! You didn't mention them at all. We LOVE breasts to the point of distraction, and there is a pair, perhaps an unremarkable pair, hanging freely and swinging with each stroke of the cock inside her... Do you have any idea how that image – it's no good. Cold shower time, and perhaps a coffee. See you-

Right, I'm civilized again. Where was I? Yes, how about some drugged wine allowing the heroine to wander in and out of reality?

By the way, I have not edited any of your sentences. We can get down to that level when we do the final edit, but I can warn you now, you will have to fight for 'obsidian orbs'. That is definitely too purple for me. I have made a sort of start on the next sequence, but I will wait for your comments on the above before I complete it.

All the best,
Simon.

Hi Simon,

Ahh, wigs. Specifically, men in wigs made from horse/goat/human hair, powdered with starch is almost as unattractive as men wearing sport pants without underwear (why do you guys do that by the way?). Add to that the very real reason for the shaved head underneath the long, flowing, almost white fashion necessity – lice – and I'm already starting to itch. Isn't it ironic that the government of the day thought to impose a tax on hair powder, thus starting the demise of the much loved periwig and powder. Who would have ever thought a government did something right?

I can envisage our lawyer's wig scented with orange flower or lavender, as was the norm. The latter truly being gag-worthy when confined in a stagecoach.

I read somewhere once that sex for women is about 80% psychological. Men not so much. Who am I kidding? Not at all.

I certainly missed the mark with describing the sex, didn't I? That is not like me. Must have been blinded by the beauty of the shoes. Perhaps I should have written about how the supple skin on Miss Hodges' bum rippled over the muscles in her bottom and along the small of her back each time the uncle thrust into her. How the sweat covering her skin shimmered in the candle light. And her breasts …Those small handfuls of lushness overflowing from the too tight corset, swaying into the hands of the man in front of her who delights in twisting her nipples painfully. Now I need a cold shower. Definitely need to add something more for you men. How is it a man can't find anything in the fridge but give him a woman half cloaked in darkness and his eyes become a million watt spotlight?

Whilst I admit I love men for the reasons they are men, there is something quintessentially more beautiful about a woman's body compared to a man's. All those smooth curves are divine. Oh, and you are so right about men and breasts. Evolution will never fix that.

I have alluded to our heroine being drugged via her wine and whilst it was clear in my mind at the time, it is not clear when rereading it. Something I shall fix.

I'm thinking of where our heroine is heading and how to take her down the path of debauchery. I think the girl needs to be spanked! Speaking from an experience or two, I may have once hired a Dom to educate me in the pleasures that come from flogger and hand. I think our girl would respond quite well to a slap on that rosy-pink rump of hers. I can almost imagine her naked, her posh little mouth running off until she feels the sharp, cold slap of a hand heat her ass with a tingling flame. The more she gets the more she wants.

But that is for you to decide and I look forward to where you take us next.
Please don't be too civilized.
Debb.

Debb,
Now do be reasonable. How can I possibly let you off with only a vague hint
of having been spanked? I demand More! Or should I say, our readers will
demand more and more realism. I'm sorry but I can't believe **Fifty Shades**
of Grey *and the amazingly tedious Anaesthesia Steele are reality. Please tell*
me (us) more.
Yes, it is chilling how men glance at a woman and make an immediate
assessment and – don't kid yourself – that assessment is always sexual.
Unless she is pointing a gun, of course. Any female gets instantly rated for
desirability. And availability, and in male eyes availability is far more
important. So in male eyes a flash of thigh trumps the most elegant model.
Oh – should we stop using 'trump' now? Oh bugger it, I'm not changing
the English language just for the Groper-in-Chief.
Back to business. I have run into a rock and I believe it will take a female
mind to get around it. Fanny's coach will be held up on its way to London.
The highwayman will be an attractive figure and it is essential that he makes
love to Fanny. Takes her virginity, in fact. Trouble is, how can he do that?
Realistically, he can't ask for her consent outright – any woman would
automatically refuse, given the choice. And if she is not given the choice, it
would be rape and there is nothing romantic or erotic about that. So one way
or another, he is going to have to persuade her.
He has already robbed the other passengers and sent them off. I want him to
drive the coach to a side road and wait for the dawn. While they are waiting,
he can send Bridget to hold the horses while he and Fanny get down to
business. How does he win her over – at least more or less? He hasn't robbed
her yet; would she consent to save her money? "Put out and I won't rob
you…" That doesn't sound very gentlemanly, and we want Fanny to
remember him fondly. Could he offer to leave her a little money in return for
a kiss? Perhaps they could make a game of it, leaving her more money in
return for more liberties, until it doesn't matter anymore and she lets him
take everything and he leaves the purse anyway.
What do you think? Legal consent with a signed contract is impossible, of
course, so how do we get her into the right frame of mind?
Regards,
Simon

OMG! Simon.

I should never, ever, ever open one of your emails in public, specifically in a quiet café. Your request for me to be reasonable had me laughing like a loon. I may have even snorted – in a ladylike fashion of course – my coffee. I'm pretty sure someone whispered, "I'll have what she's having."

So in the spirit of reasonability, I'll tell you a little more…

A while ago I met with a Dom several times, in the name of research, before taking a plunge. I have always found BDSM to be interesting, yep, I'm that person at dinner parties, not the hardcore stuff but I like to explore new things.

During the first meeting I also met my Dom's partner, who is a Domme. Now if I ever wanted to play in the middle of a man and woman, I'd want two people just like them. Damn, it was a hot night.

As with all these situations, discussions/negotiations are king. There is something so empowering when you can sit and talk with like-minded people about sex. It's a shame that not everyone has this option. And yes, we did discuss breasts and a male's preoccupation with them.

After a few weeks of meetings, discussions, visiting the dungeon, agreeing upon a scene and setting the parameters, including completing a detailed contract, off I went with eyes wide open.

The thing that most people don't realise is that a BDSM scene does not always include intercourse. It is so much more. A skilled Dom/Domme guiding their submissive into subspace is truly beautiful. The scene agreed upon was a Master/slave scenario. My Dom gave me a lengthy contract that listed what I could expect and allowed for me to indicate what I was and was not comfortable with. Total negotiation.

My wants included flogging, spanking and electroplay.

Flogging – imagine a soft brick being slapped against your back. Thud, thud, thud. That's how it felt. I didn't find it painful. I enjoyed it immensely. The continuous pressure of impact across my back became melodic and soothing. I stood there, naked, legs apart to bear my weight whilst I was flogged. I cannot tell you how long I stood there but it was a long while, something I would not be able to do without the distraction of the flogger.

Spanking – so not my thing, as I quickly discovered. Where the flogging soothed me and even scattered my brain, the spanking had the exact opposite effect. Perhaps it was the way in which it was carried out – bent over a table and having to count was, for me, not the same as an erotic smack on the ass. I could not focus enough to count properly either. I swear I can count to 10!

Electroplay – well, hellooo, Baby! Having used a TENS machine for pain relief for many years, I have always wondered what it would be like to have a gentle zing of electricity play on my skin. Now I am not a masochist, let me make that clear. Any pain I receive has to be erotic in nature. My Dom used a wand which delivered light, delightfully wicked zaps of electricity to my body, including my girly bits and I'll be damned if my body didn't hum its approval.

Have I fulfilled your, or rather, our readers', demand for more?

You had to mention it, didn't you! Naughty man. Yes, I am talking about 50 Shades. *It is wonderful that the author has had so much success but the story, for me, is a bit too clichéd. Throw in those talking bobbleheads on morning TV comparing the BDSM lifestyle to domestic violence and I want to slap them all.*

Soapbox please…

Fifty Shades *aside because I don't think it depicts a true BDSM relationship. But the process of negotiating a BDSM scene/relationship etc., is probably much safer than picking someone up at the pub on a Friday night for a quick fuck. Not even going to mention the online dating crap. BDSM is consensual – no matter the kink - and domestic violence is not. I know, I survived that life many years ago. There are no blurred lines!*

Now please pass me the ladder so I can get down.

The great thing about 50 Shades *is that it has encouraged people to explore their sexuality. That's truly wonderful. Oh, and I love the soundtrack although I would have preferred Bette Midler's version of* **Beast of Burden**. *You are a very naughty man! Were you not spanked enough as a child? I try not to mention the T word in polite conversation. Trump. It has the women grabbing for their crotch. But what amazing times to be alive and to view politics, even for someone as disinterested in politics as I am.*

Fanny and her virginity – damn that girl for being pure. It would have been so much easier for you if she was a hussy. As I have kind of gone down the whole 'suspension of reality' pathway in the dungeon, what about the highwayman being someone she is familiar with? Namely the masked man from her uncle's dungeon. You know, the one with those wonderful obsidian eyes! He did, after all, promise her more.

Perhaps she recognises him by his manly scent? Or perhaps her hands went a-wandering in the dungeon, and she got a good feel of his trouser snake?

Seriously, I don't envy you this chapter. I'm not sure how I would write it. How do you convince someone to have sex with you given that you are probably a filthy, smelly, robber, riding a nag of a horse and brandishing a weapon of sorts. Nothing sexy there. Us women folk have sex with our minds first and then if the body stacks up…well giddy up, highway man. Perhaps our Fanny likes to play the equivalent of strip-jack poker. Can't resist a bet or a dare.
Good luck!

Debb,
I am deeply shocked. I have always thought of Tasmania as polite and countrified. A sort of freezing version of up here, I suppose, but now it turns out you have been studying in a BDSM college. Wow! I thought you lot were boring and more like the banjo player from the film Deliverance. (I just pulled that up on https://www.youtube.com/watch?v=Uzae_SqbmDE and it really is wonderful.) Anyway, instead of playing the banjo it turns out you while away the winter nights indulging in some very sophisticated sex.
I feel terrible. When I look at the people in the supermarket here, I don't think they have a sexy thought from one end of the year to the next. All the kids must be imported from further south. The only time I remember any of the locals talking about sex was the old man who said he was not going to have any more prostate exams because he was getting to like them.
Now, will you be convinced by Fanny's seduction, or will it make your toes curl? It's very difficult for a man to write a scene like this because I have absolutely no idea what it feels like to have a cock inside you. I will have to lean on your guidance.
And the virginity thing. I remember as a teenager coming to the conclusion that virginity was just smoke and mirrors, set up to confuse randy boys. Yes, I can understand the absolute fear of pregnancy but in the era of The Pill? Still seems to me there is little moral difference between a truly passionate kiss and making love. Except that love-making is even more fun, of course.
I didn't mention pregnancy this time around, although it is something we will have to deal with as Fanny continues her career. Instead I tried to catch the experience of giving in – that wonderful point when you are so enflamed that nothing else matters, you just need a cock, no matter who it belongs to. Anyway, please tear this to pieces, and then we will have to decide what Fanny does next,
Regards,
Simon

Chapter Three ~ A Gentleman of the Road

*Stopping on a dark night ~ unburdening a lawyer
~ a dashing rogue steals Fanny's shoe ~ a skillful highwayman
~ your money or your life ~ how did
that happen? ~ Rob Longshot*

Fanny woke. A voice had shouted and the coach was slowing. It lurched to a stop and swayed as the driver climbed down from the box and Fanny heard his running footsteps fade into the distance. She strained to see out into the night. Bridget rolled on her shoulder. "Wake up! Wake up – something's happening."

Across the carriage, she could make out the two men stirring. One of them whispered "Oh no -" and the door was wrenched open and slammed back against the side of the coach. A strong male voice shouted, "Right, let's be having you. Anyone here feeling his oats and wants to make a go of it? Just step up if you do. I might make your evening. Or then again, I might just plug you where you sit. Saves time, even if it do make a mess of the upholstery."

A dark lantern was set on the floor and its shutter pulled up. Light showed the passengers, still in their seats. It also glinted on the large horse pistol their attacker was pointing, still and deadly. Bridget began to whisper under her breath *Hail Mary, full of grace, the Lord is with thee* over and over. Across the carriage the two men stared down at the doorway. "Two gents and two ladies. Ain't that nice? You all family? No? So let's take the gents first. You, Sir. What are you?"

"I'm just a clerk, Sir," said the lawyer, but the lie was not convincing.

The highwayman studied him and then turned to his servant. "And you, kind sir? You're just a clerk too, I suppose."

The servant was trembling, scared into foolishness. "In service, Sir. With Mr Higgins..."

"Higgins. Higgins the clerk. You know, Higgins is ringing some bells. A whole peal of bells. You're Higgins the courtroom rat, aren't you? You're a snivelling lawyer. A lawyer, for God's sake! I'm going to enjoy doing business with you, right enough."

He lowered his pistol and pressed it against the servant's knee. "Where does he keep his money? Speak up or I'll blow your damn leg off and you can hop home."

"His coat. Lord save me, he has a special pocket in the back of his coat."

The pistol moved to point at the lawyer's fat knee. "Jacket off, or you'll be the one hopping home."

The lawyer stood and shrugged off his coat. The lamplight glowed on his watch chain. The highwayman reached out for the coat. One handed, he bounced it up and down, and felt for the secret pocket. "Very pleasant. I believe I shall be taking a weight off your shoulders. Now hand over the watch." He tossed the coat onto the seat and reached out to take the watch and chain. "Now ain't that just so? I wonder how much I shall get for this on Cheapside? Or shall I wear it myself? I shall be a pretty fine gent with a watch like this."

He turned to the servant. "He got anything else? What? Speak out, man?"

"His box is on top, Sir."

"Good. I shall look at that later. What've you got in your pockets, then? No, don't fret. I doubt he gives you enough to bother with. Now you take your worthy master and bugger off. If you head back up the road, it's only three or four miles to Steadworthy and you can knock up the inn keeper. Get going!"

The lawyer's face showed nothing. No life, no fear, no concern for his money. Without looking at his robber's face, he allowed himself to be helped down to the ground. His servant whispered encouragement as he led his master away. Fanny pressed back into the seat. Now it would be their turn.

The lantern gave enough light to see the man's face, open and pleased, as if happy to meet Fanny and ready to talk. He was relaxed, fearing nothing from the two women, pointing his pistol at the sky. "Well now, two pretty birds in a cage. What shall we do with you? Pluck a feather or two, I expect. What's your name, my girl?"

"Bridget Malone, Sir." Bridget's voice betrayed her fear.

"Well now, Bridget, where are you coming from?"

"Langston Priory, Sir. We live there."

"The Priory, eh. Well, there's a spot of luck. For me, anyway. I've fleeced a fat lawyer tonight, and I know a lady from the Priory will not be travelling with just copper in her purse. What's your mistress's name?"

"I am Francisca Howarth, Sir, and I'll thank you to leave my maid alone." Now the shock had left her, Fanny's brain was whirling like a windmill. What could she do? What could she give him to make him leave? Her purse was safe enough, next to her skin, tied by a ribbon around her waist. She could feel the weight of it now. He would never see it. Not even Bridget knew it was there. How much money did she have in her pocket? A few shillings, certainly less than a guinea.

The man was watching her face, trying to read her thoughts. "Well, Miss Francisca, I think you and I will have to sit down and have a chat. But not here. So – the pair of you. Give me a shoe."

"My shoe?"

"That's right. We're going for a little drive and I want you to stay where you are. You won't be hopping through the woods with just one shoe. You too, Bridget. Hand it over."

Bridget bent to unlace her shoe and, after a moment's rebellion, Fanny copied her. The man stuffed Bridget's shoe into his coat pocket but he took Fanny's and looked at it closely. She drew her stockinged foot under her skirt for protection. "Ah, Miss Francisca, what pretty little feet you have." He sighed and gave her shoe a kiss on the toe before pocketing it. Then he looked up at her and winked. "You just bide where you are and I shall take us off the highway."

Abruptly, the lantern disappeared and the door closed. He had taken the lawyer's coat with him. In the darkness, Bridget was crying softly. Fanny reached out for her shoulder. Outside, she could hear the man and his horse. She supposed he was tying it to the coach. The coach swayed as he climbed up onto the box. They lurched forward and the noise of the wheels covered everything.

"Cheer up, Bridget. You're not dead yet."

Bridget snorted and wiped her nose on her sleeve. "There's worse than that, Miss."

"Get on with you! He doesn't seem too bad. At least he was smiling."

"Where's he taking us, Miss?"

"I'm sure I don't know, Bridget. It sounded as if he wants to hide the coach. I expect he wants to go through our bags. And the mail."

"The mail, Miss? He'll hang for that. Do you think he knows?"

"I'm sure he knows very well. He'll only hang if they catch him, and he doesn't seem to be worried about that. Do you have any money with you?"

"Six shillings, Miss. Inside my shift."

"Well, he won't be able to find it there. I'm sure that lawyer is really upset, especially after he'd gone to all the trouble of hiding his money in a secret pocket. Still, it's hard to feel any sympathy for lawyers. I shouldn't say that, should I? Not as a Christian."

Fanny stared through the window beside her, trying to make out anything she could recognise. She could see trees, nothing more. Trees against dark greyness. What time was it? She supposed it was after midnight and it would be two hours or more before she would see anything.

The coach slowed and turned off the highway. The sound of the wheels changed, no longer steel running on stone. They must be on a side road, hiding from searchers on the highway. The coach slowed and creaked to a halt.

"Oh God," whimpered Bridget. Fanny shushed her, and waited. The door swung open again.

The man set his lantern on the floor and struggled to pull a shoe from his pocket. He handed it to Bridget. "Get out and hold the horses, my girl. Your mistress and I are going to have a little chat. And don't think of playing no games, because Miss Francisca will be paying for them."

Bridget slipped on her shoe without tying the laces and left.

The man watched her go and then climbed up to sit opposite Fanny, closing the door behind him. He did not look at her. Instead, he searched for a lantern hook and hung his lamp above them, filling the carriage with a dim light. Now she could see more of him as he set down his tricorn hat and struggled out of his riding coat. Underneath he wore a loose linen shirt with no stock at his neck. His hair was his own, rich brown, swept back and gathered in a black bow. Fanny caught the glint of a gold earring before she was drawn to his face. It looked confident, tanned by the weather, and his dark eyes were ready to smile.

He took her shoe from his coat pocket and reached down to take her foot. It was an intrusion, a liberty she did not want, but she needed her shoe and did not fight when he lifted her foot onto his lap.

36

"Just so, Miss Francisca. As pretty as I thought." He put her shoe down on the seat beside him and, using both hands, began to gently squeeze and manipulate her foot. His hands were strong and she could feel the roughness of his skin through her stocking. The sensation was strange, intimate, and she felt herself blush.

"Do you like that, Miss Fanny? Isn't it fine?"

She said nothing, made no effort to pull away. The man reached for her other foot and, placing both feet in his lap, unlaced her other shoe. Now he was working on both her feet, strong thumbs running again and again up her soles. He smiled at her uncertainty and said, "And it gets better than that, my lady. Just wait." With both arms, he reached behind her calves and pulled her to the edge of her seat. Lifting both legs onto his lap, he began to massage one, squeezing and gently twisting her calf.

A stranger is touching my legs, Fanny thought. A strange man. Why is he doing that? I should stop him but – it feels so… good.

He put her foot on the seat beside him and started again with the other. As he worked, he kept his eyes on her and his knowing smile never changed. She closed her eyes and let his hands take her.

He set her second foot down and now he was kneeling on the floor, her legs about him. His fingertips brushed her cheek and she opened her eyes again. He was close, very close. "You are a beautiful woman, my lady. A wonderful woman." And he came closer, leaning to brush her lips with his. Eyes closed again, she felt his arms around her, pulling her upright. His hand was behind her head and they were kissing. She put her arms around his shoulders and returned the kisses.

Nothing else mattered. She kissed and met his tongue with hers. His hand had enclosed her breast, gently squeezing, and still she was kissing. She held him, feeling the size and strength of him, marvelling at the way he could hold and command her.

Something was touching her, between her legs, something warm and resilient, butting against her. How had that happened? She moved her hips to bring it to her cunny.

It touched her! She felt wet and it slipped between her lips. She clung to him, still kissing, as it slid into her, filling her with its welcome intrusion.

37

The man pulled his head back. "Oh, Sweet Jesus!" he whispered, and sought her lips again. Fanny did not understand, and she did not care. Her world had been reduced to the cock sliding steadily in and out of her, and the overwhelming confusion it was creating.

She did not know how long she had been under the man's spell. She knew she had been bad, but everything had felt... wonderful. When he stood and lifted her bodily to lie along the seat, she knew something powerful and different had come into her life. Nothing would ever be the same again.

"You just lie there, my dear," he said. "I have some bags to go through, and I'll be back before I go." Fanny felt the coach moving on its springs as he rummaged through the luggage, but her mind was on the wonderful feeling glowing inside her.

He woke her when he opened the door again. She sat up. The dawn gave some grey light, and she could see now that the man's eyes were tired. He gave her another smile. "I shall be off, Miss Francisca. You just bide here, and someone will come along soon. Meeting you has been something to remember."

"What's your name?"

"Ah – you may call me Rob Longshot. Most people do." Another knowing smile.

"Do you have nothing to leave me? Where can I find you again?"

He thought for a moment, reached into his coat. He held out a plain gold ring, a wedding band. "Here's something to remember me by. And it is mine. Honest like, not robbed. As to where you can find me, there's a lot of folk would like to know that. But I dare say I shall find you soon enough if you're going to London. Now, I am off, and good luck to you." He raised his hat to her, and shut the door. She heard him go to his horse behind the coach, and trot away.

She stepped down onto a cropped pasture. Bare and untended, it looked like a common. The coach stood in the open and had been hidden only by the night. She hurried to Bridget, still holding the horses.

"Good morning, Bridget. Have you prepared breakfast?"

Bridget did not smile but said in a low voice, "Are you well, Miss? He didn't rob you?"

Fanny looked out over the common. He did rob me, I suppose, she thought. But I don't feel sad about it. A lark shot up high over their heads with her liquid song blessing the world. Fanny smiled and said, "Well, he did steal a kiss, but that's a small price to pay for keeping my purse."

"A kiss?" She could see Bridget was thinking, perhaps too shy to say what was on her mind. "Was it – was it..."

"It was fine, Bridget. Just fine. Now, we'd better see about getting along. I'll drive, and you can ride inside like a queen." Bundling up her skirts, Fanny climbed up to the box. The driver had left the reins hooked about the foot board. The whip stood in its holder; she hoped she would not need it. Carefully she slotted the reins between her fingers just as Fearnley, her uncle's coachman, had taught and pulled them through until the horses could feel her. "Let them go, Bridget, and jump aboard."

Bridget came back but stopped below her and asked, "May I ride beside you, Miss? Please. I've always wanted to do that."

She scrambled up and settled, bracing herself on the foot board. Fanny flicked the reins. "Walk on, boys. Let's go and look for some breakfast."

My Dear Simon,

Have you overcome your shock yet? Haven't you heard it's always the quiet ones you have to watch? And whilst I may look rather innocent, as if butter wouldn't melt in my mouth, I can assure you, some days it sizzles. Now enough about me, let's get back to the topic at hand...sex...or more specifically, virginity.

I poked around the internet searching virginity and OMG! I am so pleased I am not a child of today, especially one that has to rely on the net for sexual education. It's frightening the misinformation that is out there. It ranges from being airy-fairy (all sweet and magical and painless) to conditioning (religious bullshit citing touching oneself as sin) to practical, common sense. Although, this was a rarity. I did find this article, http://www.seventeen.com/love/a30103/things-no-one-tells-you-about-losing-your-virginity/ and it was one of the best that I came across. I particularly like the analogy, "Guys are like microwaves and girls are like slow cookers." How perfectly true is that!

I had some older teenagers I know read it …and in typical young people fashion I am still waiting their response. I'm sure it will happen when the power goes and the batteries in their devices go flat.

A couple of years ago I had the privilege of meeting a sprightly, older lady whose happy energy was infectious. We got to talking about writing and my Five Delights *and sex. Then she told me her story. This lady was raised in a strict religious household, (I want to say Catholic, but I don't clearly remember), and was taught that touching herself was sinful. She married a man of the same faith. Up until his death – they had been married for 50 years – she had never enjoyed sex. Never! So it was wonderful to hear her talk about being in her 70's and finally discovering her sexuality.*

It was a sad situation but one I find that is all too common, still. Sex is always something I have discussed openly with my children. I have always been of the opinion that if you don't know what pleasures you, how can you expect someone else to?

Sex is not a one-size-fits-all situation. I'm sure there's a pun in there somewhere. I'll let you find it.

I do like Fanny's seduction. Honestly, you had me at the foot rub. Good hands on tired feet and just about anyone will topple over into blissful arousal. Well, except for the petaphelaphobics of the world. The whole seduction was simple and easy. Nice. Consensual. No drama, and she got to keep her purse! Bonus.

It is true, though, that sometimes it just kind of slips in. Let's face it, those slippery little slugs have an inbuilt tracking beacon. Over the years I have had numerous conversations about this exact thing. Under the steamy, hot blanket of passion, things always just happen. A passionate, mind-numbing kiss would even lead the Pope astray, I'm sure. Pregnancy is something that may or may not happen, we'll have to decide.

As for her knickers…please…it was the 1800s…what knickers! Ahh, those were the days, weren't they? Did you know that it was once considered hygienic for a woman's private bits to be well ventilated? Hence up until approximately the mid 19 century, female underwear was open at the crotch. Some garment's openings extended to the thigh. Now that is a bit breezy. All in the name of cleanliness as they wouldn't have bathed very often. I'm not even letting my mind linger on what the natural body odour, of both men and women, saturated in the scents of the day to disguise what a daily dip in the local creek could wash away, would smell like. The open crotch was also the reason women had to ride side-saddle. It also made it easier to toilet as the women needed both hands to hike up all of those skirts. Sounds a bit laborious to me. Just go naked, I reckon.

Ladies everywhere today can thank the Parisian Can Can dancers who apparently, and somewhat ironically, helped close the crotch.

Not to leave you men folk out with all this women folk talk, here's a titbit for you. Men's briefs were invented in 1935. Randomhistory.com lists a contemporary magazine ad touting that the briefs offered "scientific suspension" and "restful buoyancy." Now, I'm not a man therefore I don't know what that means. So, in the infamous words of a certain Australian politician, "please explain."

Recently I had the pleasure of visiting the National Museum of Australia and on display were two vastly different coaches. The first, I fell in love with and my imagination ran wild to days of romantic, long drives in the countryside enclosed in a horse drawn carriage. The inside, boxy and small, reminded me of the closed confines of a lift. That's one thing 50 Shades *got right, there's certainly is something about being enclosed in a lift with a lover. Anyone who has exchanged something as simple as a kiss in a lift (or should I say elevator?) will know what I am talking about. Anyways, I am rambling. Back to the stagecoach.*

It is masculine and beautiful! Studded leather panels, fold down steps with red rungs, silver, ornate handles and fixtures, the whole carriage is black with red paint detailing, even on the wheels and undercarriage. The very clever thing about this particular coach is that it is a 'landau', basically a convertible in a carriage. Top up, top down? The choice is yours.

This amazing piece of history is coming up to being 200 years old. It was once owned by George and Janet Ranken of Scotland, who in 1821, travelled with it to Australia. There's nothing romantic about that. Upon the death of George Ranken in 1860, the coach was sold to Sebastian Hodge. He was the person responsible for painting it black and using it as a mourning vehicle for the next 65 years. You can find it on the museum's website.

The second coach is nothing if not practical. Ugly even. Owned by the Nowlands Family and used for mail and passenger services in the Liverpool Plains area of New South Wales in the 1880s. It also has a stellar movie career staring in two movies, The Man from Kangaroo *in 1920 and* Robbery Under Arms *in 1957. It is painted a khaki green colour, not original, and houses a thorough-brace suspension system which was originally designed in the US and was suitable for the rough road conditions in Australia. Updated suspension or not, this coach in all its wooden, steel and leather rustic glory, would not have been comfortable.*

I think our Fanny may have found herself in a coach similar to that of the mail coach above. Nothing luxurious there. Can you imagine the groaning and rocking of the carriage as Fanny and her seducer 'kissed'? I bet Bridget, diligently holding the horses with a still-unlaced shoe, knew what was going on.

Where to next for our heroine, after breakfast that is, because who doesn't want a jolly good feed after a jolly good rogering? Can I say that these days? Is it PC? Who cares!

With kind regards,

Debb

Debbie,

I like the pic of the landau you sent. Of course the upholstery looks a bit tired now, but in its day it would have been really comfortable. I can just imagine Rob Longshot kneeling between the two seats with Fanny's legs around him. An 18th century mail coach would have been bigger and certainly heavier as it would be carrying 6 people inside and more on top. Plus the mail, of course. And it would normally have 4 horses. The stages they rode might be 10 miles, then they would change the horses. They had worked out a way to do this really quickly. Four horses would be hitched up to a pole that ran to the front of the rear pair. They would have everything in place, collars, reins, everything, and then they would wait for the incoming coach.

When the coach arrived, the stable hands would pull the pin that fastened the pole to the front wheels and walk the tired team away. Turn the front wheels to the side so that the pole of the waiting team could be pinned into place, and off you go again. Apparently the first stage out of London went to about Heathrow, and the companies always used their smartest, most expensive horses because everyone could see them. I have read there was a holding area in Croydon with about 4,500 horses waiting for their turn to go out of town. That's a lot of horses. It was all very efficient and they really kept to their time tables. London to Exeter (about 275 km, 175 miles) in only 17 hours in the high days of coach travel.

Mind you, the passengers must have had a pretty uncomfortable 17 hours even when the roads were in good shape. And with 6 people inside I suppose you got to know each other very well...

Anyway, do you know how old the British Royal Mail is? Hard to believe – 500 years old this year! Founded by our old friend Henry VIII. Interfering with the King's Mail was a very important business and warranted an automatic death sentence, so our randy highwayman will be dancing on air if he is ever caught.

Enough about stagecoaches. I suppose it was much easier to avoid getting your novel writing side-tracked in pre-internet days. You only asked questions you really, really needed an answer to, and your resources would be limited to the village library. Nowadays, you start off innocently wondering how exactly a young lady would travel to London and you end up with a heap of very interesting but totally useless information.

I am glad you are happy with the seduction of Fanny. I am not completely happy about a couple of things. Firstly, what do we call her pussy? I checked in Teesa Mee's Thesaurus Erotica *and she has literally hundreds of alternatives for pussy, but I can't say I liked any of them. (That is, the words. I like pussies very well indeed...) I chose cunny as a word that an educated girl of Fanny's time might use. What do you think?*

Also, I have been looking again at what I wrote for the critical moments:-

Something was touching her, between her legs, something warm and resilient, butting against her. How had that happened? She moved her hips to bring it to her cunny.

It touched her! She felt wet and it slipped between her lips. She clung to him, still kissing, as it slid into her, filling her with its welcome intrusion.

The man pulled his head back. "Oh, Sweet Jesus!" he whispered, and sought her lips again. Fanny did not understand and she did not care. Her world had been reduced to the cock sliding steadily in and out of her, and the overwhelming confusion it was creating.

That does not seem to do it justice. The highwayman's handling of Fanny has won her over and she is certainly ready. Sizzling, to use your own terminology. But what does she feel? It is her first time and, for argument's sake, I am not going to introduce any discomfort – she is too ready for that. What does it feel like? Bigger than she had anticipated? She must have speculated about that with her girlfriends. Smaller? Harder? What thoughts sprang into her mind? What surprised her?

I have absolutely no idea how to fill this gap. We are meant to write about what we know, and I lack the equipment to ever know for sure. What would you add to the sentences above?

I'm sure you are right about the knickers. There was a fairly recent television series about a middle class family who tried to live exactly like an equivalent family would have lived in an Edwardian house in London before the First War. The production company found a house that had hardly been modernised at all – solid fuel cooker, antique plumbing, toilet in the back yard, and moved the family in. The man was a Royal Marine working at the Admiralty, so things were not so very different for him. He just had to wear a uniform from 100 years ago, and very smart he looked too.

His wife and daughter had much more trouble. They got out of their leggings and sweaters into layers and layers of dresses, petticoats and pinafores, and got to work cooking and cleaning. Tough life!

Yes – they had drawers rather than knickers. Knee-length and made from cotton. The audience did not see if they were split or not, but the ladies did say they were a real pain. They tied at the waist – no knicker elastic then – and they quickly found that, within the confines of the back yard toilet, bundling up their skirts and petticoats in order to reach and re-tie their drawers was really difficult. They quickly decided not to bother. After all, no-one would ever know what they had under their skirts unless they did cartwheels in the yard.

I'm told it's pretty much the same up here. We dress baggy and no-one wears their shorts two days running, so why bother with panties? Anything to keep cool! Perhaps when Fanny is a kept woman she will be asked to parade in her underwear, and then we will see what she chooses to put on.

What else? Yes, looking for breakfast. Fanny will drive the coach to its next stopping point. She will be light-headed from lack of sleep and general excitement, and she will have plenty of time to examine her feelings about making love. What will she be thinking? If you help with that, I will take her up to the next coaching inn, and then we will have to decide what she will be doing when she gets to London.

Regards,
Simon

Hi Simon,
I do like the use of cunny to describe Fanny's lady bits. I know it's used a lot in literature but it would have to be one of my favourite words. Sounds naughty and sweet all at the same time. Very much like the body part itself.

I must admit when I first read the seduction scene I had a clear mental picture in my mind of good 'ole Rob on his knees, Fanny poised on the edge of the seat, more than ready to receive him. Unfortunately, I do think our heroine was left hanging. Waiting for the big O that never came. How women can relate to that! Did you do this deliberately or is it as simple as the interpretation of my female mind?

As to how it felt, well…I don't want to crush the fragility of the male ego, but size does count and, more importantly, so does skill. Not sure our highwayman has much of either.

A woman's first time is something she will remember forever. Be it good, bad or somewhere in between. Not sure it's the same for men. You boys are nothing if not randiness on two legs. Do you ever grow out of this?

I've never known a man want a woman to 'examine her feelings about making love'. Is this just for your characters or do you ask your wife this as well? I bet she would slap you up the side of the head with a frying pan if you did. Now it is time to examine what Fanny was feeling and it leaves our girl wanting more. Can't say that I blame her.

Cheers!

Debbie.

Chapter Four ~ A Breakfast to Remember

Thoughts while driving ~ interrogating Bridget ~
how Miss Hodges enjoyed herself ~ riding into town ~
Old Fearnley's training pays off ~ ordering breakfast and peace

Fanny relaxed the horses into a slow walk. Surely they must be as tired and as hungry as she was. She knew she should hasten. After all, the coach hadn't arrived and people would be searching for the mail. Wouldn't they? She was happy to bide her time, swaying along with the gentle cadence of tired horses and the jolting rattle of a stagecoach.

Warmth bathed her face and neck and, closing her eyes against the bright morning rays of sun, she felt relaxed as she cast her mind back to him. Her heart quickened as she remembered all that she had felt and tasted of...Rob Longshot.

He had smelled of the cool summer night and horses. No overwhelming scent for him. His hands had been strong and a little rough as they squeezed her travel weary feet and legs. But, oh, it had felt so good.

His kiss, powerful and hungry, had claimed her mouth without hesitation. The growth of his beard had scoured her skin. She could still feel the heated rash as it prickled the tender skin around her mouth. He had tasted like a fine, aged brandy. Perhaps he had found a flagon in the lawyer's trunk.

And when he had made his way between her legs, the cool air was shocking on her uncovered thighs. Her skirts had bunched high on her hips and she knew she should not be allowing him such liberties. But her mind was elsewhere, too lost in the passion she felt from his closeness. It spread quickly through her body, weakening her lady's resolve. Something that felt so wonderful could surely not be all that bad.

When he had nestled into her thighs he stared into Fanny's eyes, possessing her, and that is when she felt... it. Oh, she knew what 'it' was. She had never felt a cock before but had heard all the stories, even though ladies should not know such things. She had seen the stallions, long and thick, as they readied for their mares. Once she had even heard the upstairs maid whisper about one of her uncle's footmen being the size of a horse. Back then, Fanny had not understood why someone would say such a thing.

Her breath had caught as she felt his cock press against her thigh. It felt heavy and...soft...against her skin. Oh, how she would have liked to hold it in her hands. To feel it, and see what it looked like. "No two are the same," she had once overheard.

He had moved in closer and rested the blunt head of his cock against the wetness of her cunny. With a steady hand, he had steered the head along her slit and probed a tender spot causing Fanny to whimper and grab at his shoulders. Holding on tight, her breath stuttered from her open mouth as he rocked himself against her. She moved closer to him, desperately wanting more. And then he was inside her.

Although she winced at the intrusion, her mind was already floating towards the heavens.

How wonderful it felt to have him inside her. The pressure of being so full caused her cunny to ache. She could feel every stroke as he moved in and out of her. Heat gathered between her thighs as he pushed his cock in hard and deep. He was speaking to himself but Fanny was too deep in her pleasure to understand what he was saying. At that moment she didn't care. What could be so important that he needed to speak?

His weight pinned her against the seat, and she found it harder to breathe. With her mouth against his chest, she gasped between gritted teeth when he pumped faster. She had almost reached something wonderful when he had suddenly stopped, grunted and then collapsed against her.

Fanny had closed her eyes to the wonderful serenity that flowed through her as he gently laid her on the seat. It was a good thing that he had thought to do so as she could not move at all. She should have felt ashamed – she knew she should. As she played her feelings through again, only defiance. Not shame. It had been... exciting.

A jolt of the carriage startled Fanny back to the present, reminding her that she held the reins. She frowned, feeling the ache of need still deep inside her. Surely her body could not want something more so soon. What else could there be? Rob Longshot. His name echoed through her mind. Squinting as the sun glinted off something, she looked down to see the small band of gold circling her finger and smiled.

As they passed another copse she looked around and realised she had no idea where they were. Or if they were even going the right way. A distant yap from a dog carried on the breeze from up ahead, encouraging Fanny to speed up the horses.

"Look, Miss Fanny." Bridget yelled excitedly, as she pointed towards the distant smoke rising in the air.

Fanny looked along the road far ahead of them at what seemed to be a town. The mumbled hum of busy life became louder the closer they got. The faint smell of cooking awoke her hunger and all thoughts of Rob Longshot were quickly forgotten.

In the dawn light, Fanny saw tendrils of smoke rising from the houses and cottages they passed. In each one, some woman would be stoking the fire and getting ready for the daily round of cooking and cleaning. Bridget would be used to that, she supposed. In fact, being a lady's maid must have seemed like a release from prison. She still lived under Miss Hodges' eye, but with Fanny's protection to keep her safe. She wondered if Bridget had ever caught her uncle's eye.

"Are you having a good trip, Bridget?"

"Surely, Miss, surely. I never thought to see myself sitting up here. Isn't it grand? And isn't it grand that you have the learning to drive the horses? I could never do that."

"Oh, I'm sure you could, given the chance." Fanny looked at Bridget's face, alive and full of the joy of the morning. She showed no worry for the future. That was frightening; Fanny would have to care for two people when they reached London.

She thought of home and asked, "Bridget, did you know what my uncle does with... I mean, with Miss Hodges. And other women, I suppose."

Bridget retreated back into a servant's shell. "No, Miss."

"Nothing? Nothing at all?"

Colour was coming to Bridget's cheeks. "I heard stories, Miss."

Fanny chuckled. "If you heard stories, I'm sure all the girls were talking about it all day."

"Mmh, yes, Miss."

"So, tell me. Who else did my uncle take downstairs? Miss Hodges and who else?"

Bridget had shrunk in embarrassment. "All of us, Miss."

"What – everyone? Why didn't I know? Why didn't you tell me?"

As Bridget cringed, they came back to the highway and Fanny turned in the direction of London. The noise of the wheels grinding on roadstone and the clip-clop of the horses' shoes became louder.

"So?" she demanded, "Why didn't you tell me? I might have stopped it."

"The Master said we were to hold our tongues, Miss, or he would send us away with no letter."

That sounded true enough. A servant who crossed her master would be sent away with no reference at all, and no hope of a future position.

"And they took you too? Why?"

"I dropped a cup from your breakfast tray, Miss, and Miss Hodges said I should be whipped for it. And I was, too."

"Whipped?" She thought back to Miss Hodges, with welts across her naked bottom. "Who did it? My uncle? Did he take you down to – to his special room?"

"Miss Hodges did, Miss. She bent me over a table and tied my hands on the other side. Then she lifted my skirts over my back and pinned them there. And left me. Left me for ages, and when she came back, she was near naked. As shameless as a bitch on heat, that woman. Showing her teats and cunny for anyone to see.

"And then your uncle came. There was nothing I could do. He didn't say nothing, just stood there behind me. I could smell his wine and snuff. He was looking at me, playing with my… thing."

"Oh, you poor thing. I can't imagine how-". But she could imagine. She remembered very well just how things went.

"He had Miss Hodges whip me, Miss. Six strokes of his belt. That got him going, so he put Miss Hodges across the table across from me and gave her a dozen or more himself." Bridget had tears on her cheeks but did not stop. "He was all fired up, Miss. He had his todger out and it was bouncing around as he laid into Miss Hodges' bum. Then he threw the belt on the floor and stuck it into her. She liked it! Really – I could see her face. He didn't stop in her long because he came around the table and stuck it into me. It hurt me.

"But he didn't do me properly, thank God. He was off around the table and back into Miss Hodges. He did her proper then, and she was moaning like it was the nicest thing that had ever happened to her, the sour bitch. Then he buttoned himself up and he was gone."

So; right under her nose, her uncle had taken Bridget and – used her. Her own personal maid, and her uncle had done that to her. Poor Bridget, stretched across the table with her skirts thrown up over her back. Uncle playing with her bum, and with her... Fanny shook her head to get rid of the picture.

Bridget had said 'all of us'. All the serving girls, Fanny guessed, and some of them were married women with children. How could he do that? Power and privilege. And shame, as well. No woman would want to advertise what had happened to her. Tongues would be wagging in the village, and none would be as sharp and wicked as the old women. They would know where to put the blame – on the girls themselves.

Fanny slowed the horses and swung them wide to climb over a stone bridge. In the shadow of pollarded willows, the stream wound away deep, cool and inviting.

"Miss? Can I ask a question?"

"Of course, but I can't promise to answer it."

"When your uncle took you down there, did he do you too?"

Fanny swallowed. Bridget could ask because Fanny had let her down. And besides, the Priory lay in the past. In a way, they only had each other now. But she couldn't share the whole story.

"No. He didn't. He just, um, looked at me. And I saw Miss Hodges. I don't understand that woman. It looked really painful."

"She was really sweet to me when she came to untie me. Honestly, she brushed the hair out of my eyes and called me a good girl. She said I was to hold my tongue and your uncle would be kind to me. My maidenhood, it was, and who will want me now?"

50

Two farm hands, grizzled men in smocks, were walking along the road. They stood aside and took their hats off as the coach passed, staring openly at the sight of two women driving.

"Don't worry about that, Bridget. I shall take care of you when the time comes, and my uncle will give you a dowry too, or his friends will hear of it. Now, enough of that. We're coming to town."

The road came out of the trees and on either side they were passing gardens, rich with fences of peas and beans, and dark rows of potatoes. Already people were hard at work, hoeing, weeding and watering. Beyond the gardens, the buildings of the town crowded around the church spire. The clatter of the wheels changed with the cobbled town streets. Whealdon. Fanny had been here once before and thought she remembered a coaching inn on the main street.

People were staring openly at them now, and two young boys ran beside them. One of them called out "Madam, Madam, are you driving the coach?"

Bridget was quick to answer. "You mind your manners, lad, and you can be sure the horses are not driving themselves. Do you know where we are going, Miss?"

"I think so. The main street should be just here… yes." As they turned, the wide main street opened up for them. Thank goodness it was not market day, and driving was no challenge. A young man standing outside a butcher's shop ran up to them calling out, "Miss, good morning Miss, shall I drive you?"

"I believe we are managing very well, thank you. We don't have far to go."

More people were staring at them now. Perhaps they were the most interesting thing that had happened in Whealdon all year. "Pull up here, Miss," shouted the young man, "and the George will send out to help you."

Fanny felt her worm turn and, rather than let the staring and shouting upset her, she decided to show the townsfolk not every lady was helpless. She could hear old Fearnley teaching her on her uncle's landau. "When you come to an entry, Miss Fanny, do you go right on. Right on, until your back wheels have near gone past it. Then you may turn the horses, and they'll take you through as sweet and nice as you could wish. But if you turn early, you may take a gate post with you. Or you could lose a wheel, and that would be a pretty mess. Now, slowly does it…"

The George stood on the other side of the road, an imposing stone building with an arched entrance to the stable yard behind. She slowed to a stop, just as Fearnley taught, and flicked the reins to turn the horses. They shuffled sideways, turning the front wheels below her, until the four of them were square off the side of the coach. She eased them on and they threaded the archway. As sweet and nice as you could wish for. Fearnley would be proud of her.

As soon as she pulled up, people were everywhere. Men appeared from the surrounding stables to take the horses' heads, servants and the women from the inn's kitchens came out to see the show, and the innkeeper was there, helping first Bridget and then Fanny down to the ground.

"Where is the coachman, Miss? What happened, if I may ask?" The inn staff crowded around to hear.

"Rob Longshot happened, Sir. He sent two passengers and the coachman back to Steadworthy on foot. Now, if you will permit me, we would like some peace, and perhaps some breakfast."

Debb,

Well, that was… interesting. Very interesting, in fact. I try to imagine how a lady feels but, although I might be on the right track, you do it better. An unfair advantage, I think. And I am never going to get a chance of pretending I know more than you because Fanny will remain a woman right to the end of the book, and we will never be looking at sex from the other end of the stick (as it were!)

Such a difference between men and women. I mean, we don't need a mirror to see what's what. We're obvious, and that's the whole point. It sticks out and does things. I also get the impression we are much more curious about pussies than you are about cocks. We can't help ourselves. We get the chance to look up a lady's skirt and we're going to take it every time. We love a woman who confidently wears a mini-skirt and live in hope we might just get a peep… Never happens, of course, and we know it will never happen (at least, intentionally) but we still live in hope. On the other hand, a lady only has an equal desire to see a cock if she is feeling receptive and if it is attached to someone stimulating.

Another difference is that men are comfortable with their cocks. I'm not saying they are in love with them, although when they are naked their hands seem to naturally find their way down there. I mean, they treat it like an old friend. I have noticed women are often much more uncertain. They just can't imagine anyone liking their pussy as much as men really do. Even after a brief trip around the galaxy from oral sex, they still ask, 'Do you <u>really</u> like doing it to me?' Are they crazy? Is this a trick question?

I am working on the second edition of my How to make Wild, Passionate Love to your Man *and came up with this scenario to display a difference between male and female desire: imagine a TV games show and the presenter is saying to an average man, 'Behind that door is a beautiful, horny, naked lady who would really like to make love to you'. Now, what would the man say? Nothing, of course. He would just hurry to the door.*

Now imagine the presenter saying to the average woman, 'Behind that door is a handsome, horny, naked man who would really like to make love to you'. What would the woman say? Well, there would be A LOT of questions before she even gets close enough to the door to open it and have a quick peep. Oh well, vive la difference, I suppose. Sometimes I really envy gay men. At least they communicate on the same wavelength.

Back to the book. I am bothered about the ring. I wanted Fanny to have a keepsake, and Rob's mother's ring seemed sensible. But she had to ask for it, and I'm not happy about that. I am also unhappy about her wearing it. For sure, Bridget will <u>know</u> what had happened, and I'm sure Fanny does not want to share that with Bridget yet. I would be happier if she kept it in her pocket and just thought about it.

I had not meant that you would write that last bit; I was going to do it with your advice. Never mind. I shall take the girls into town where they will breakfast on devilled kidneys and go on to London later. That will be fun because I do not have a feel for London in the late 18ᵗʰ century. I'm sure there will be lots of stuff on the web.

We need to get Fanny to the point where her money is running out and she has to trade sex for money. I would like to make her into a more or less independent courtesan, a kept woman rather than a prostitute, so she can move freely in society. And explore the Hell Fire Club, of course. She can't do that if she is on her back in Soho turning five shilling tricks. We need sex with some class, as befits an educated young lady.

Christmas is just days away, and we will be visiting our daughter in Townsville. When we are not eating or pouring beer down our necks, I might get time to sit and write. Otherwise, it will have to wait until I get back and, as it is wet season, that could take a while. Have a good and suitably

debauched Christmas!
Regards,
Simon

Dear Simon,
Happy New Year!
I hope you thoroughly enjoyed this festive season. My NYE was spent quietly with jazz music from the beer garden across the street, softly lulling its way into my life via the open balcony door. Coupled with this the sounds of crashing waves from the beach, the hot, yes hot! weather, a few glasses of wine and it was the perfect way to spend an afternoon up until the cricket commenced on TV. Then it was veggie lasagne and coffee (so very classy), whilst the 20-over big bash game slogged it out. I must admit I didn't see midnight in at all. I woke to hear a rather piss poor effort of celebration from inebriated souls in the garden. They didn't even do the countdown to midnight. How rude! If they're going to wake me up with a celebration, at least do it properly.
I very much agree with men being comfortable with their cocks. After all, you guys were born with your first play toy. And play you do.
Women, however (generally speaking because I am an exception to this rule), are not comfortable with their body. Sexually or otherwise. I do wonder if it stems from evolution and the whole baby-maker-by-default situation. As we moved through the decades and centuries when a woman's worth was dictated by her dowry, family connections, looks, body type, etc., and still are. Long gone are the days when the width of a woman's hips determined if she was a good breeder and suitable mate.
Let's raise a glass to simpler times, shall we?
Was it the church who took all the fun and enjoyment out of having sex for sex sake? Why can't people have sex just because it feels good? I mean it is as natural as breathing and probably the second thing mankind did after drawing its first breath. So why not?
It is true about your game show lady. I recently watched a movie called He's just not that into you, *and one of the age-old scenarios addressed is where a boy hits a girl because he likes her. I even remember being told this. But what a croc of shit. That boy hit the girl because he is a little brat. It is actually worth watching, or reading, because it makes you think about the crap we were told as kids. Different generations have different ideas, but are we evolving any? Back to your lady, we live in a media-driven-social-perception*

of what our perfect mate should be. Hence all the questions that your lady, us ladies, have.

Perhaps it should be 'let's have sex and discuss things later'? Because if you are not compatible sexually, you are left unfulfilled, and how else do you make up when you have an argument? Gifts? Flowers? Pfft!

Wow, I am in a ranty mood today, aren't I?

Back to the story. The ring. Yes, the ring! Not since Lord of the Ring have I thought of a piece of jewellery being so significant. But it was, and ours is. Even more so. Those hobbits are such drama queens.

I must apologise for overstepping here and not, at the time of my writing, realising the significance of Rob's ring. I promise to self-flagellate later. If I were to re-write, it would go something like this...

'Squinting as the sun glinted off something in her lap, Fanny looked down to see the small, delicate band of her mother's ring circling her middle finger and smiled, knowing that her mother was always with her and everything would work out, just as she always said it would'.

And now that our wonderful readers have that in their minds, the ring – Rob's ring – is still a secret. Does that save my ass?

I look forward to reading about your 18th century London. When I think of the city at that time in history, I think of it as dirty and smelly. The kind where chamber pots were emptied, via an open window, onto the streets below with little warning. I imagine the stench that would linger throughout the day and into the night when the night soil men would clean the mess up. I imagine the deadly labyrinth of streets and alleys, lined with hovels and shacks soon to become permanent residents for the poor, whilst the rich built their houses and filled their courts. While the class divide grew stronger, all walked the streets amid the filth of decaying animals left to rot, and all breathed deep into their lungs the sooted, coal-stained air and fog. But these are the obvious, well documented examples. I'm sure your research will discover something different and titillating.

I have yet to visit London. But I am told, these days, it is a beautiful city filled with a delightful cacophony of modern life. I'm not one for crowds though. Perhaps I can ask the locals to take a sick day when I visit?

I look forward to reading about Fanny trading sex for money. I wonder

what tricks she may have up her…skirts.
Debbie.

Debbie,
Well, here's the next instalment and no-one has done anything remotely sexy. I'm not sure why not, but I suppose you have to pause for breath sometimes.
Anyway, the big news is – Ta-Da! – in the late 18th century London was the sex capital of the world. I was vaguely aware that prostitution was common and visible but, wow! The scale of it! I found a book called The Secret History of Georgian London: How the Wages of Sin Shaped the Capital *and it's all about how the sex trade was one of the biggest businesses. Even bigger than brewing. There is a contemporary estimate that about 40% of London women were either in the business or had been at some point. OK, a great deal of it must have been pretty cheap and basic, but there were all sorts of brothels, including gay ones.*
Thank God for Google. Each time I write a sentence, a new trap door opens. Were there taxis then? Yes, they were called hackney carriages and were basically unregulated. Would you drink a cup of tea at home? No, you would actually have a dish *of tea – like a cup but shallower and possibly without a handle.*
I have not tried to put common people's speech down phonetically. I could try, but it makes for difficult reading. On the other hand, a lot of slang was used around London. Some of it was so far from conventional English you would not understand the criminal classes at all, unless they wanted you to. They had their own language, known as Thieves' Cant. If there is a word or two you don't follow, please look it up. And by the way, have you ever met a tosheroon?
I have introduced a new character with potential – a young man well versed in the back streets of London. I have called him Art with a nod to Dickens and The Artful Dodger. He will be handy helping the girls around town.
What I would like to suggest is that Fanny is persuaded to work as a bookkeeper and welcomer in a very classy brothel. The Madam is a woman with all the right connections who finds a suitable Lord to support her and, eventually and not too soon in the book, take her off

to the Hellfire Club.

If you like the idea of the classy brothel, would you mind calling the Madam Rosie Palm, after Terry Pratchett's famous madam? He's my favourite author at the moment and I have all his Discworld books on my Kindle.

Anyway, do write back and tell me what you think, what needs more work or whatever. I am looking forward to Fanny being a pampered mistress, with Bridget taking care of her, making sure she eats well and doesn't drink too much, epilating her important bits so her patron is driven wild with desire which he can't satisfy in the normal way because he wants to present her as a virgin at the Hellfire Club.

But we have to get the girls to London first, before we can even think of debauchery.

Regards,

Simon

Chapter Five ~ London is Big - and Busy

Devilled kidneys and questions from the constable ~ thoughts on
Rob Longshot and his todger ~ the Bull and Mouth Inn
~ living in London is expensive ~ visiting Cousin Clarence
~ servants always know all your secrets

Somehow, the road to London seemed smoother now. They swayed along comfortably, Bridget sitting opposite, sleeping with her mouth open. Fanny could not sleep. Recent events ran through her mind again and again. And on top of the pile was a question. Where was Rob Longshot? Was he safe?

The parish constable had guessed his name immediately. Fanny had tried to plead ignorance but that had made no difference. Rob had a local reputation and his name would be in the newspapers.

The inn keeper had sat her down in the empty dining room, far from the door, next to the window where she could look out onto the street. She had badgered Bridget to sit on the other side of the table. If they were travelling alone, Bridget could play the part of companion as well as maid. Why not? Who would know? They had eaten their devilled kidneys, Bridget nervously and Fanny with relish. They were spicy and filling, and took her mind from the door to the kitchen, where maids and cooks kept appearing to peep at the amazing women who had driven a coach right into the stable yard.

And then the parish constable had come, a heavy man with whiskers and a coat with shiny buttons. He stood, cap in hand, and asked if the ladies had been inconvenienced in any way. No, she had said truthfully. No inconvenience had occurred or, at least, none that she was going to share with the constable. No money lost, but she believed Higgins the lawyer had been seriously inconvenienced and may have lost a good deal of money. The constable did not seem disturbed at the news.

The constable had been followed by the inn keeper. If the ladies would see fit, and only at their convenience, of course, would they like to board the coach again? Its late arrival would be causing havoc all down the line, all the way to London. And if the ladies left now, he might venture they would be travelling alone, there being no coach planned for this time of day.

And they were still alone when the coach blew his horn for their second stop. Already they were fifteen miles nearer to London. Soon she would have to stop thinking of Rob Longshot and begin to worry about Cousin Clarence.

She did not like her cousin. There was something fey about him, something unnatural. She should be charitable, she knew. Growing up with her uncle as his father - that would be a burden on any boy. Still, she could not truly take to him. He was a man, she supposed, but she could not imagine taking him as a lover, any more than she could imagine taking the vicar back home and he was a truly unctuous, obnoxious individual. Not like Rob. He had pushed his thing into her. His todger, as Bridget called it. That had felt – nice. Very nice, and she could still feel it inside, if she concentrated...

She shook herself awake. She had been drifting off, thinking about men. Actually thinking about men and their things. What had come over her? Her cousin, wife of the vicar, is this how married women think?

She relaxed, and again the question – where was Rob? What was he doing? He must have taken a lot of money from the lawyer. She wondered what he would do with it. Would he be saving his money for the future? Perhaps he could go to the west of the country where no-one would know him and buy a farm. Although he did not seem like the farmers she knew at home.

What does a man like Rob do? He was not a gentleman, so he must work for his living. She tried to imagine how a retired highwayman might make himself useful to the world. Unless he collected so much money from the likes of Higgins the lawyer that he could afford an estate. Then all he would have to do is collect his rents, as her uncle did. Would he know how to behave?

She could show him. They could have a house together. Bridget could come too, and take care of the babies. They would have to have babies. She wondered how many times you had to do it before you became pregnant. Thinking of the people she had seen married, some of them had babies very quickly. Perhaps they liked doing it very much and worked hard to have a baby. Others took longer. She could think of two couples who did not have children at all. The women must be barren, just as it says in the Bible.

Barren. The word had always seemed harsh and unfair. She supposed it could happen to any woman. Was Miss Hodges barren? She must be. From what Bridget had said, Miss Hodges should be supplying the Priory with a new baby every year but Fanny had seen no evidence. Miss Hodges did not have enough of a figure to conceal a pregnancy under her grey dress. Perhaps for her being barren was a convenience. She could offer herself to Uncle as often as she wished without fear of contracting a problem.

They reached the outskirts of London late in the day. Villages became more frequent, and the intervals between them reduced until the road seemed to be passing through one long village, acrid with the smoke of evening fires. The road was full of people, busy people who gave the coach no more than a glance as it swept by.

Buildings were tall, some several storeys high, and crowded together. Stone buildings, their walls grimed with soot, like nothing Fanny or Bridget had ever seen. And traffic. Carts and wagons were everywhere, plodding into the city laden with sacks, firewood, barrels, and baskets of vegetables. And plodding out of the city, some empty but most carrying stable sweepings.

At last, when it seemed to Fanny that the world could not get any busier, their coach turned into the wide yard of the Bull and Mouth Inn. They would spend the night here, and she would search for Cousin Clarence in the morning.

Fanny stepped out of the coach into the rushing chaos of the stable yard. Up above, she was surrounded by open galleries leading to the inn's accommodation.

"Move along, Ma'am. Ain't no place to stand gawping." A short man wearing a grubby waistcoat in place of his shirt pushed his way past. He was pushing a sack truck laden with a large travelling chest, and its wheels would have run over her toes.

Bridget stepped down behind her. "Run along and find us a room, Bridget. Not an expensive one, mind. A small one, and we'll share. I shall wait here with our bags."

The man in the waistcoat had re-appeared. "Where to, Ma'am? I'll call you a carriage." He spoke quickly, clipping his words in a strange accent.

"No, thank you. We'll be staying here. I'm waiting for my maid."

"What luggage, then?"

The man had hardly got their two bags down to the ground when a stout woman in apron and mob cap appeared, leading Bridget. "Miss Howarth? Welcome to the Bull and Mouth, dearie. I'm Mrs Bones, but you may call me Sally. Now, those your bags? Bring'em up, Wally. They're in number 17.

"I've got just the room for you, m'dear. Nice bed, all the linen fresh washed, and there's a truckle bed for Bridget. Window too, though it don't close proper. It's the damp, you know, makes the doors and windows stick something terrible. I shall get Wally to look at it tomorrow." She was speaking over her shoulder as she climbed the stairs to the first gallery and turned to climb again to the second. She spoke so quickly and with the accent of London that Fanny struggled to catch her words.

"It's a nice room. Small, 'tis true, but you'll like it all the same. Quiet too, 'cos the taproom's way over there. Bridget says you don't want no private room to take your dinner; is that right, Miss? Very good, then you come down to the parlour when you're ready and cook'll make you some supper. We've got good beef – I always buy the best – and the oysters are as fresh as you could wish for."

Mrs Bones unlocked a door and passed the key to Bridget. The room was small, the bed taking up nearly half the space. At its foot stood a small table with a jug and basin. The sticking window allowed some smoky evening light into the room, and a sconce over the bed head held an unlit candle.

Mrs Bones could not stop talking for long. "Do you set your bags right, and come down to the parlour, m'dear. I'll tell cook you're on your way. And don't give Wally more than a penny – that's twice as much as he needs anyway," she said as she left.

Bridget pushed the door closed. It occurred to Fanny that Bridget had done well. The room was small and surely not one of the best in the inn, but it suited a young lady unsure of her income. "Well, thank you, Bridget. We will be very cosy here. Did she tell you how much it costs?"

"Surely, Miss. It's three shillings each night, but Mrs Bones says if we're going to stay longer to be sure and tell her because that might go to two shillings."

Three shillings a night. That means a guinea would stretch to a week, if they did not eat anything. That sounded frightening, but Cousin Clarence would accommodate them and she supposed she could ask him for pin money. And Bridget could work in his house. She might even be better rewarded in the big city than she was at the Priory.

Next morning, after breakfasting on eggs and black pudding with a dish of tea, Fanny followed Bridget to find Mrs Bones. Fanny was puzzled. How did Bridget, who had arrived with her only last evening, already know so much about the inn? She stopped confidently at a door and told Fanny to wait. Within minutes, Mrs Bones appeared, wiping her wet arms on her apron.

"A carriage for Holborn, dearie? I shall get you one shortly. Now then, this is your first time in town, I can tell, for you do stick out like a pair of sore thumbs. I can see you getting into trouble as soon as you step outside. I'll get you a blackguard boy to keep an eye on you, that's what I'll do. I'll look for Art, he's got the making of a rum-cove if ever I saw one. He don't look much, but he's as sharp as they come. He'll stop you getting your pocket cut, at least. And I knows he's safe, 'cos he won't get any supper if he lets you down. You bide here, and I'll see if I can find him."

So they would have a bodyguard out on the streets of London. Was that necessary? Bridget soothed her. "I think it's the right thing to do, Miss. I was in Liverpool and, I can tell you, a lady by herself, she's fair game for any pickpocket." Fanny shrugged. She did not want to appear at Cousin Clarence's house with a wild boy in tow, but better a guide now than tears later.

Mrs Bones returned with a short boy, made smaller by his over-sized coat. Perhaps he planned to grow into it and had rolled up the sleeves until he did. His tall hat spoke of better times. His face looked grubby and his curious dark eyes were taking the measure of Fanny. "This here is Art, Miss. He don't look much, but he's willing. He'll keep an eye on you while you're in town."

"Six pence a day," said the boy.

"Don't give him more than tuppence, Miss, or I'll find another boy and Art can go back to toshing for a living. Hear that, Art? Tuppence, and none of your lip neither."

The boy scowled half-heartedly at Mrs Bones. "Got a carriage then?"

"William is waiting outside. I told him to take care of you, Miss, and bring you back here when you're done. Don't you pay him nothing – I'll do that for you."

This morning, the streets were far busier. As well as the carts and wagons, people everywhere were hurrying on business. Mostly servants, she guessed, for they all carried baskets on their arms or sacks over their shoulders. There were other hackney carriages like her own, pushing their way through the traffic, and occasionally she saw a closed coach with fine horses and a crest on the door. The girls were fascinated by the elegant buildings, and the sight of so very many people all at once.

The carriage pulled up at a house and Fanny supposed they had reached Holborn already. She heard William talk to the boy.

"Hey nipper, get down there and open the door for the ladies."

"What? Can't they do it themselves?"

"Get down there or you'll feel the back of my hand."

Bridget had reached for the door, but Fanny waved her back as Art pulled it open. She stepped out and smiled at the boy. "Thank you, Art. You're a real gentleman."

Surprise filled his face for an instant, until he whipped off his hat and bowed extravagantly. He was still holding the door as Fanny climbed the stone steps and pulled at the iron fist beside the door. Inside, she heard a bell ring.

A footman in livery and a bobbed wig opened the door. He stood stiffly and waited for Fanny to introduce herself. "I have come to see my cousin Clarence. Please tell him Miss Francisca Howarth is here."

The servant looked at her for a moment and said, "I will see if Master Clarence is in, Miss Howarth. Perhaps you would like to wait in the sitting room? I shall take your servant to the kitchen."

He led her to a room that was severely elegant, filled with light from a large curtained window looking out onto the street. A round table had been set before it, and delicate chairs with striped cushions. Fanny sat to wait.

She had never seen a room like this, so perfectly presented and presumably unused. There were paintings on the wall, a mirror over the fireplace, and an urn in the Grecian style stood in a corner. Nothing human caught her eye. No sign of occupants. She thought back to the living room in the Priory, where something always disturbed order. A ball of thread and crotchet hooks, an embroidery frame, a collection of smoking pipes in a bowl on the mantelpiece. Here there was nothing. Even the chairs looked perfectly new and unused.

She was standing absorbed in the view of the street when there was a tap at the door and the footman re-appeared. "Master Clarence, Miss." Duty done, he stood aside to let his master enter.

Clarence was looking well. He wore a long Indian smoking jacket in red silk, with black velvet cuffs and collars. It looked shocking, but Fanny supposed it must be fashionable in London. She ran to him and, seizing his shoulders, kissed him on both cheeks.

"Clarence, you look wonderful. And such an elegant house. I had no idea you were such a great man in London."

He reeled back from her attack. "Er, not my house. My patron, you know. Lord Harmsworth. I handle his business, and so I stay here. It's perfectly fine."

"Isn't it? I've never seen such furniture. And that footman is as proud as you can imagine. He made me feel quite small."

"Ah, yes. We are a little formal here. May I offer you a dish of tea? Do sit down." He pulled on a wide silk strap beside the fireplace, and came to sit opposite her.

"So, it is a surprise to see you. How is the Priory? How is Father? It must be, oh, two years since I was last there."

Fanny smiled. "Yes, but the Priory never changes. And your father too. As vigorous as ever, and always up to something or other. I am so taken with London. So many people. I'm sure there are all sorts of things to see. I want to go to St Pauls – I've heard it's a treasure of modern architecture. And the river, of course. And St James."

"Where are you staying?" Clarence asked abruptly.

"Oh, the Bull and Mouth. Isn't that a strange name? It's quite comfortable, but very busy. And noisy, when you step outside."

"Of course, of course. Quite unsuitable for a young lady on her own. You should look for lodgings with a respectable family. How long are you planning to stay?"

There it was. How long was she planning to stay? Who knew? She did not see herself as a London lady – that would be out of the question with the money she had, and she would starve rather than ask her uncle for more. She wanted Clarence to invite her to stay here, in this strangely formal house, but he did not seem to understand. She would have to explain.

"Clarence, I'm afraid I've run away from the Priory. Your father, well, he had plans…"

Now she had Clarence's attention. "Oh no, not you too. The old bastard wanted to take you too, is that right?"

She looked at the table in confusion. She had not realised there was such bad blood between father and son. Speaking quietly but with a vehemence that etched every word, Clarence said, "I'm not going back, you know. Never. I'll die in the gutter first. The things he did – he does – no, that's over. Never again. I've got my life here, Lord Harmsworth cares for me. There is nothing Father can do to me here."

A tap at the door and it swung open. A maid carried in a tray with a tea service. They stopped talking as she served the tea and left.

"Clarence, I think I can guess what you are talking about. I have left him too and now I am desperate for somewhere to stay. Like here."

Clarence reacted as if she had spilled her tea on him. "No! Absolutely not. Completely impossible. My Lord would never allow it. I might be able to help a little, but you can't stay here. He won't even like that you have visited when the butler tells him. Wait here; I'll come back shortly."

He hurried from the room and left Fanny tea in hand. Where was he going? Why so urgently? She sipped her tea and waited. If he was going to help her find suitable lodgings, that would not be so bad. Staying with her own family would have been better, but she had never got on well with Clarence when he was a boy. Perhaps he could find her a family with children she could help educate. Or an old lady who needed help.

She was still adjusting her ambitions when the footman returned. "Your carriage is waiting, Miss."

She stood, confused. "But Master Clarence..."

"Master Clarence sends his apologies but he has been called away on urgent business."

She allowed the footman to usher her out. Bridget and Art were waiting at the open door of the carriage. As she mounted, the footman said, "Mr Clarence has left a package with your maid, Miss." He stepped back to let Art close the door and William shook the horse back to life.

Fanny sat in a daze. What had Clarence done to her? Why had he done it? She was aware of Bridget leaning from the window and telling William to take the long way home. Why did she do that?

"Where is the package, Bridget?"

"There was this letter, Miss."

She unfolded it and read:

Dear Fanny,

I am so sorry I am unable to help you, but my patron is very jealous of my time and would be most upset if I engaged myself to arrange accommodation for you. It is most fortunate that you came when he is out, for I feel sure he would have refused you entry. Please try and understand that I would have been delighted to have been of more service, but there we are. The most I can do is make a small gift, and I must beg you not to contact me again. His Lordship does not take disobedience lightly.

Your loving cousin,
Clarence

She was on her own. Just her and Bridget. Before she could mope, she asked, "He said a package, Bridget."

Bridget lowered her voice. "It's in my shift, Miss. He said it was money, fifteen guineas and it feels as if it might be. I didn't want anyone to know."

"What? Money? We must return it immediately. How dare he? And how dare you? It's not your place. Turn the carriage around!"

Bridget shrank from her. "Please, Miss, listen to me. We need to eat. I can earn some money, I'm sure. Maybe working at the inn, but it won't amount to much when we're paying rent. We'll need money to eat. Please don't be proud. Take the money and, when we've got our feet on the ground, we can come back and stuff that fifteen guineas up – give that snooty footman the money for his master.

"Don't be upset, Miss. I'll take care we don't starve, one way or another."

Bridget looked at her face and laid a hand on her arm. "Don't cry, Miss. It will turn out well enough, I'm sure. You can count on me, and I'll lay that Mrs Bones is not a bad sort either. Cheer up, and we'll find something to keep body and soul together.

"And let me tell you something I heard below stairs. Your cousin, he's a real Miss Molly. It's true – every night he gets all figged up in a gown and a lady's wig. He paints his eyes, puts on rouge and waits for His Lordship to come home. That's right, he's His Lordship's bit of squeeze. The cook brings them supper and a bottle of port, and they lock the door and get up to all sorts of things.

"That's why he didn't want us to stay, you see. He didn't want you looking at him in his gown."

"But they're both men…"

"Well, yes, but it takes all sorts, doesn't it? Some men just prefer other men, but a lady like you wouldn't hear about those things. His Lordship goes around London all day raising his hat to the fine ladies, but when he's at home and the door's locked, he can do what he really likes. Looks as if Cousin Clarence likes it just as well, and they fairly wear each other out."

"How do they know?"

"I'm sorry, Miss?"

"I mean, the servants, how do they know what goes on? You said they lock the door."

Bridget chuckled. "Oh, you can't hide anything from your servants, Miss. Everything gets around. If they want to play husband and wife at night, you can be sure that's all the staff will be talking about over breakfast. If you ever want to know what goes on in your house, ask the servants."

"Husband and wife? But how do they do that? I mean, they're both men… they can't –"

Bridget blushed and mumbled, "Everyone's got at least one hole, Miss."

Fanny sat in stunned silence at the pictures forming in her mind. She had heard of Sodom and Gomorrah, of course, but had never understood exactly which sins were involved. And Clarence was playing the girl. Well, he'd never be much of one. You wouldn't catch Rob Longshot falling for him.

Simon,

You…you…you man! How could you! Just the mention of that "E" word makes my blood run cold. Epilate. Oh. My. God. Have you ever used one? Have you ever had your tiny, defenceless, deep-rooted hairs ripped from your skin? I bet my life that you haven't. All men should have their balls kissed clean by the modern-day-in-home-recommended-torture-device that is an epilator, or its waxy cousin, and then maybe our somewhat male-dominated-societal-governance would change because there is no way men would be willing to do that to themselves because that was what us women 'prefer'.

Why does her pussy have to be bare? Was it even fashionable in those days? I must admit I haven't researched it prior to my rant, but come on, I can't even begin to imagine how scary it would be having a cut throat razor down there. What if she sneezes? It would be a blood bath. Maybe they used candle wax for that kind of thing? Hell, I can't even let candle wax drip onto my fingers because it hurts.

What is it you blokes find attractive about a hairless body? Do you fantasise about ground-moles? They have no hair. Or maybe those uglier than ugly hairless cats? The ones with names like the Ukrainian Levkoy, Donskoy, Peterbald or Sphynx. If Fanny ever needs an alias can we call her The Donskoy?

How about if Fanny gets epilated, so do you? You could do it publically and raise money for charity. Imagine all the women that would cheer you on from the sidelines. We could even shield your todger with one of those cones from the vet. You may even make the news. Ooooh, sounds like a plan. I'd even fly up to sell the tickets.

Ok, let's take the focus away from your groin and women cheering its beautifying torture.

Well, my recuperation took much longer than anticipated and is still ongoing. My desire to write during this time was one of absolute delusion. I've watched more TV in the past three months than I have in the past three years. No joke. I am now on board with a large portion of the world waiting on good 'ole George for another instalment of Game of Thrones. Damn writers, always so slow. I watched so much Netflix that there is nothing else of interest on it. Although, I must admit, not being able to write during this time was possibly a blessing in disguise. Our heroine may have razed towns on her way to London in consolidation with my days of post-surgery misery. I have begun to read The Secret History of Georgian London: How the Wages of Sin Shaped the Capital. *What sad times a lot of women had faced. It's interesting how not a lot has changed in the few centuries that have passed. Sex workers are still prevalent. Still come in all shapes, sizes, fetishes and costs. And they are still doing it to put food on the table and keep a roof over their heads.*

I really enjoyed how William Hogarth's The Harlot's Progress, *was explained. As with all artwork, for me, it falls into a category of whether I either like it or not. It's that simple. I don't have the mindset to look and understand the art within the art, or the picture within the picture, as is the case here. All those little tell-tale signs were fascinating, and very sad. For this woman, or in this case, many women within the one, it reflects the unseen influences that countless others can have on an individual's downfall.*

I loved Fanny not handing over the reins as she and Bridget drove through Whealdon. You can easily imagine how scandalous it would have been to the townsfolk seeing the two women on top of the carriage. Gossip like that always finds its way back. I like her show of strength of character. And Bridget's too. I think our girls are going to need it.

Art is an interesting introduction. The scales of my imagination are yet to decide if he is good or bad. Time will tell.

As soon as I read about Cousin Clarence images of Nathan Lane's, Albert Goldman from The Birdcage came to mind. He would be a right royal Miss Molly. But what an annoying, lily-livered chap Clarence is. I feel like saying, "Seriously man. Grow a set...or stop taping them down," or however they did it back then. Can we throw him in the Thames?

That's all for now. I have actually found this reply mentally exhausting. How annoying. I look forward to your reply.

Debb

Dear Debbie,

I am so glad you are coming back to life again, but that's not going to mean I cut you any slack when it comes to the important things in life. You know, sometimes women really annoy me on the subject of hair. I heard a lady just last week talking to two friends about her hair style. She was celebrating thirty years of having close-cropped hair. Easy to wash, easy to dry, she never needed a hair brush. She thought she looked just fine, and she did – if you picture a coconut on a stick.

So you run straight into a wall. A woman is entitled to keep her hair any way she wants – that's an absolute right. But... are we talking about rights here? Every morning I get up and shave my face. That's right – every morning. Why do I spend all that time and effort when I could grow a beard? Because my lady prefers that I do. A beard can be trimmed easily once every couple of weeks or I could grow a beard a pigeon could nest in – but I don't. I care about what she thinks.

I have a pile of light blue cambric work shirts – very comfortable and convenient, never need ironing and look presentable. She doesn't like me wearing them into town, I might whinge a bit but I wear something less uniform instead. That's the way relationships go.

Women have a more difficult situation to cope with. The world seems to accept men who are clean, reasonably groomed and wearing presentable clothes – but it asks far more of women. Women are expected to be attractive as well, with a bigger wardrobe, make-up and uncomfortable shoes. There is an unspoken pressure to dress as the world expects, although their partners are permitted to make suggestions as well. Unless a woman is like the coconut lady, the world generally wins out and skirts are far longer than her partner would prefer.

But what about hairy legs and armpits? Personally, I don't like the look of hairy legs in stockings and most women agree. Only the most rabid hippies go around with bushes under their arms, and that's fine too. Then we come to the hidden hair...

Of course, men generally prefer smooth and hairless pussies. Why wouldn't they? A pussy is such a wonderfully beautiful thing, why would anyone want to hide it under a jungle of hair? I can't help feeling that most female protests – including yours, my dear – are mere hypocrisy. Sure, tending your pussy means devoting some of the same attention you give to your face. That means work, so excuses are inevitable.

The first is an attack. Men like naked pussies because they like little girls. What rubbish! Most men only recognise little girls as having future potential. They don't see a twelve year old girl as sexual – yet. Why would they want to mess around with a young teenager who doesn't know anything about sex and relationships? Much better to concentrate on a partner who knows how things fit together.

And besides; does anyone really think that removing a little hair will magically transform a mature 20-year old woman into a little girl? It would take much more than that.

Then all the excuses about how difficult hair removal is, especially as some of it is so hard to get to. You are right about shaving. It is primitive and while it might give a smooth finish for a few hours, the aftermath is savagely abrasive and men don't want to put their sensitive bits anywhere near it. So forget shaving, but you could think about creams. If your skin tolerates them, they work very effectively and regrowth is much slower. And also softer, which is nice. Plus most creams inhibit future growth so habitual use results in very much less hair if you ever stop.

I don't favour waxing. Not because the results are not nice and smooth, but because you need at least 3 weeks of growth before the wax can grab the hairs – meaning that for two weeks in three, you are not looking or feeling your best. Fanny would probably be exposed to sugaring (using a sugar paste instead of wax), but the Rolls Royce job would have been plucking -- something that would keep her and Bridget busy for hours at a time.

We have not mentioned modern permanent methods. You can already buy home-use lasers that will leave you silky smooth after several repeats. Or you can go to a specialist parlour for a finish worthy of a film star.

70

So excuses about difficulty are just that – excuses. What other reasons are there for hanging on to your bush? Absolutely the coldest, most damaging response is, "But no-one sees it, so why bother?" Really? You might do something about it if people could see it, but because the only person who does is the one who truly cares about your pussy and would like to lavish attention on it for hours, you don't care? Oh come on..! You will give it a trim to wear your bikini or visit the gynaecologist, but not for your lover? And think of the practical benefits. Easier to clean, yes, but I mean the important ones. Oral sex is easier and less abrasive to your lover's lips, so he will do it for longer. And when he comes into close contact, there will be no unwanted friction. Just lovely smooth, soft, slippery, sliding back and forth and all over. Oh dear, time for a coffee break and cool down...

Back again. Let me tell you about one of the finest things a woman with a smooth pussy can do for a man: you can lay him on his back and slide along his cock as it lies on his tummy. That's a very fine feeling, and visually exciting. Try that with a hairy pussy, and your fun won't last long. Try it with one of those Hitler Moustache pubic trims and it will finish even faster, because each stroke ends with a sharp attack of bristles in just the wrong place.

But that's not the finest thing I was talking about. For that you need to lie on your sides, face to face. The man does not have to do any more than that, although he is welcome to cuddle, stroke your hair and whisper his delight. You grab his cock and press it against you as you slide your clit back and forth over the head. Of course, this feels wonderful for both of you, but for him the idea of having a sex-crazed woman using his cock to get herself off piles delight upon ecstasy. Nothing quite like it, and totally impossible with hair.

Still, that's just me and I know you won't give my feelings too much weight. So I went looking for something more authoritative and, luckily, I happen to know Sir Francis Dashwood's man of business. I asked if he could obtain an opinion from the great man, and this is how he replied:

Sir Francis is much against there being a surplus of hair in this area. He opines that, when he desires to taste a sweet cunny, he should not be obliged to search through a forest of wild and boisterous hair in order to find it. Furthermore, this hair is coarser than that on a lady's head and consequently somewhat abrasive. Sir Francis has observed some soreness of his lips and cheeks after as little as half of an hour's enjoyment of his favourite *hors d'oeuvre.*

Sir Francis has in the past been much inconvenienced by such hair, finding that when exploring those areas with his pego, allowing it rein to venture here and there wherever it will, and enjoying the soft and lubricious nature of those parts, contact with such a bristly mop can have unfortunate results. On occasion, his considerable enjoyment has been abruptly and prematurely terminated by the unaccustomed friction bringing on an unplanned crisis, halting the exchange of pleasure for some considerable time.

Finally, Sir Francis wishes to lay stress on the appearance of a carefully cherished cunny. It is his convinced opinion that nothing in the mind of man compares to the prettiness of a delicately displayed, naked cunny. The sight of its rosy pink lips and honeyed entrance touch the very essence of his soul, and he wishes that their owners will love and care for them as much as he does himself.

That comes from the man who was invited to share the bed of the Empress of Russia herself, and is widely renowned for his devotion to Venus. You have to listen to someone like that.

Regards,
Simon

Dear Simon,
Settle down man! Take a deep breath. I am not sure if I should call you Chatty Cathy or Ranty Raelene. Definitely leaning towards the latter though. I hope you did not twist a delicate ankle climbing down off your soapbox.

I have to say your long winded, and somewhat draconian, hair removal argument is very insightful, especially coming from a man. Did you snuggle up on the couch with Mel Gibson and a blankey and watch What women want? *For research purposes of course. Or do you have a more personal experience with all those hair removal products? Perhaps Sir Francis' man of business has been whispering a little too much in your ear?*

Your readiness to meet your lady's needs show just how evolved you are. It also shows signs of a smart man. Happy wife, happy life and all that. But you are correct, the scales definitely tip in favour of what is, or rather, what is not, asked of a man. Appearance is so simple for you lot. Perhaps we should bring back the periwig to spice things up? I must admit there have been a few times in my life where I have longed to be the coconut lady you described, especially in the winter months, when my hair takes hours to dry naturally, but I just cannot bring myself to go the short-back-and-sides style. My ears are a little too pointy. Many years ago I did have my hair cut off to my shoulders. I cried. I am still scarred to this day.

I have to say that I am more of a low-maintenance woman than not. Probably just like our Fanny. Boy, is she in for a surprise. My hair is naturally wavy so I learned to embrace the 'just got out of bed look' years ago. Oh, if I had a dollar for every time I was asked as a child if I had brushed my hair. For me, make-up is just confusing and expensive and, if it stays on my face, it is a miracle. And the whole 'contouring' movement. OMFG. What a scam! Have you ever seen a how-to example? It should be classed as a special effect for how drastically it can alter the structure of a face. It reminds me of an African war mask until it is blended in. If you dare google 'How to contour', you will see just what I mean. My make-up generally consists of BB cream and lip gloss. Enough to blur the paleness and blotchy-redness together. Simple as that.

Oh, and don't go knocking the hairy legs and stockings. The mohair look is very warm in the winter months and a style I have sported many times. And who looks that closely anyway?

I do agree with something very strongly though...the whole men-who-prefer-bare-pussies-prefer-girls argument. I have to say this short-sighted, ignorant comparison just annoys the fuck out of me. I have probably said this before, but I'll say it again, what if all those do-gooders focused their abundance of energy on the non-consensual acts that happen, rather than the consensual, imagine the difference they could make. I'm sure, Sir Francis would agree with me.

Anyway, I have one simple word to solve the 'hair or not to hair' saga in an instant. Obsidian. Ladies and gentlemen, the deal is done. This time.

Now onto what to do next with our heroine. Her current financial situation is one that will require attention in the near future. How does Fanny go about making a living enough for her and Bridget? The easiest way would be as a whore, bare pussy included. An upper class one at that. Could the friendly innkeeper at the Bull and Mouth be a bawd in disguise? I won't accept our girl becoming another edition of The Harlot's Progress. *I am a sucker for happy endings after all. Perhaps she can become a governess or a bookkeeper?*

What are your thoughts?

Debbie.

Debbie,

I agree. Fanny is a lady, an educated lady, and should not end up as a drunken and diseased whore. Then, as now, the sharp city folk used to keep an eye out for lost girls coming in from the countryside. They could be trapped into a brothel and mostly that did not end well. I am sure the innkeeper at the Bull and Mouth would know the right people...

I had thought Fanny could spend a little time free but friendless until, perhaps, she catches Bridget turning tricks to keep their finances going. Then she could ask the innkeeper for help and get steered to Rosie Palm's house in Mayfair. This was a developing area and becoming genteel, and the gentlemen who visit Rosie are definitely upper class. Fanny could take a position there welcoming the gentlemen downstairs, serving drinks and engaging them in conversation.

Of course, Rosie Palm has other ambitions for her. She offers Fanny to a kindly older gentleman, friend of Sir Francis, who genuinely wants to help Fanny. He also wants to present her at Medmenham as a virgin, novice nun, so he does not make love to her. He does inspect her very closely and prepare her to be offered up to the very sophisticated members of the Hellfire Club. Clothes, make-up, deportment…

I added Art so we could use his knowledge of London life. As he does a little pick-pocketing himself, he might save Fanny's money from a cutpurse? He would know all about the Covent Garden coffee houses. He might even introduce Fanny to one of the loose women – that might be both interesting and exciting.

While you are doing all the creative things, would you like to explain why – in general – women hate prostitutes so very much? It seems to be a visceral thing and I don't understand it at all. The hatred seems very strong and deep seated, enough to make a young lady live in penury hairdressing or manicuring when she could earn her weekly salary in an hour or two one evening at the pub. Strange.

Through it all, Fanny is thinking about her highwayman. Asking after him, but not actually expecting to find him…

Does that help with the plot mapping? You're in charge,

Simon

My dear Simon,

You, my friend, are an ever inspirational genius to help me get back on track. Your suggestions have stimulated the stubborn, and often wayward, creative juices flowing in my mind. I've gone old-school with my research, borrowing an eclectic pile of books from the library. I'm too photosensitive for a screen at the moment. This section is being typed behind the welcomed dullness of sunglasses. What an inside-fashion icon I am. Friends and family always find it amusing when they find me watching TV with sunglasses on.

The more I delve into our selected time period, the more I discover that change is more of a 21st century accomplishment, and even then it's at snail's pace for anything but technology. One of the books that have tickled my imagination is Loathsome London *by Terry Deary, it forms part of the wonderful Horrible Histories series of books and (children's) television programs.*

In this particular edition it gives two accounts of London, and whilst both were written around 1190, I can't help but think that they also reflect life in London during the 1700's. The first was written by a monk named Richard...

> "I warn you! You will find all the evil of the world in that city. Do not go to the dances, do not mix with the wicked women, do not play dice, do not go to the theatre or the pub. It is full of actors, fools, villains, drug-sellers, fortune-tellers, tricksters, robbers. Magicians and common beggars. If you want to keep away from evil, then stay away from this city."

The other account is written by a priest named William FitzStephen who, as further research has discovered, was quite an important man, for a priest. He wrote...

> "Of all the great cities in the world this is the most famous. It is far greater than all the others. It has fine weather, good Christian people, strong walls, fine women and excellent men. They enjoy good sport. Their houses have beautiful gardens full of trees. Outside the city are pleasant meadows with streams of clear water. There are forests with stags, boars and wild bulls for hunting."

Obviously neither of these accounts are verbatim of the original writings. The author is wonderful in his ability to bring history into mainstream and capture the interest and understanding of his audiences.

To me, these accounts reflect the atypical positions of the have and have-nots. I was unable to find any further information on Richard, but as a monk, I assume he would have led a very basic life of servitude. William FitzStephen on the other hand, led a life of importance. He was the right-hand man to Thomas Beckett, the murdered Archbishop of Canterbury. My English neighbour also assures me that the "weather is never fine," in the mother country.

It seems to me that over a very long period of time - centuries - London was a depraved pit of humanity fuelled by the fat purses of the rich and their desire and greed for what they wanted and the unwilling destitution of the lower class that had no other option than to serve the rich in order to survive. I know we are going to lead Fanny down into the dirty depths of prostitution, however, we need to gently nudge her naivety away a little beforehand and

I have a few things in mind to do that. Things that she had not heard whispered among the servants in her closeted existence back in Langston Priory become reality. My imagination is tickled by the 'collections of curiosities' as featured in coffee shops or gardens and the fantastical stories and rumour they created. Also the 'Cock Lane Ghost', and similar stories could also be an eye-opener for our girl.

I'm also thinking about Fanny's shock and disgust at her first encounter with a prostitute and think that Art may have something to do with it. Good or bad, who knows? Still not sure about this lad.

By the way, did you know that, globally, the 2ⁿᵈ of June marks International Whore's Day? Sex workers from around the world gather together, under their red umbrellas, to quash the stigma and raise awareness of the plight of sex workers. This particular date was not chosen by chance. It does in fact recognise a day in 1975 when over a hundred French sex workers occupied a church in the city of Lyon.

These women were protesting the reprisal of the police and the actions that led to sex workers having to carry out their work in secret, resulting in further violence against them. Due to the lack of intervention by the government, two women were murdered.

After eight days of chanting their songs...

"When we occupy the churches,
You are scandalised,
Religious bigots!
You who threatened us with hell,
We have come to eat at your table,
At Saint Nizier."

...and voicing their demand for better treatment and to end the stigma, police intervened and cleared out the church. All was not lost, or forgotten, as this event marked the beginning of obtaining rights for sex workers globally.

I do wonder how much it has really changed though. After all, in the amount of time between Fanny and the French protest, some 200 years, conditions were still appalling. Especially as even now in 2017, 42 years after that protest at Saint Nizier church, we are still hearing the same stigma-attached stories told and sex workers are still being violated. At the end of the day if you remove the glorified aspect of prostitution that stems from Hollywood type stories, we are left with women, and men, earning a living by having sex with people who want to have sex with them. What is the big deal?

As for your request for me to explain why women hate prostitutes so very

*much, this is something that fascinates me. And you are right, it is such a
visceral thing. It's not something that is class specific, and, yes, I use 'class',
because they still exist. They're just labelled differently these days. I
honestly think the hatred stems from fear. A double-edged, primal fear. One
that evolution has failed to eradicate.*

*Firstly, we intuitively know that if a woman's life falls apart and she find
herself without money and has no other way of earning it, if she becomes
homeless and unable to feed her children, there exists an option for her to
earn income that requires very little skill. She can sell her body. Sex is an act
that can be carried out discreetly and quickly with very little preparation. It
is not necessarily something that she has to enjoy for her customer to be
satisfied. After all, from the dawn of time sex has been used as barter to
sustain the very basic of human needs, namely food and shelter.*

*Secondly, I think the age-old, green-eyed monster that is jealousy, adds fuel
to the fear. You know that whole, "What can she do for you that I can't, or
what does she have that I don't?" rationale. I have seen this in action, the
scenario being a male friend with a new girlfriend after an amicable divorce
and it was downright ugly. I know more than a few women who think of sex
workers as dirty. The lowest of the low, and people who deserve the violence
that they often receive. These women have an unsubstantiated phobia of
'whores'. A word I hate, by the way. It's almost as if a greater proportion of
females have an inherent sense of insecurity and jealousy. And no, I'm not
gender bashing, I know men can be like that as well. But my life experience
so far has shown the scales tilting toward the 'fairer' sex. I do wonder if this
is something we are born with and is made worse by the conditioning of
society and social media.*

*What do you think? Give me a man's point of view. I look forward to reading
your thoughts. I, in the meantime, will start penning Fanny's next chapter.
Debbie.*

*P.S. Oh, by the way, I discovered the reason behind why I leave two spaces
after I end a sentence. It comes from learning to type in school. Apparently
this was the norm and we have my teacher, a very stalwart lady by the name
of Mrs Beven, to blame.*

Debbie,
*You are teasing again. I am hungry for the next stage of the story. By the
way, I suggest you might tolerate Art for the moment. He may well be useful
in the future when Fanny might be living a closeted life and in need of
someone to do things for her – like find stagecoach tickets or a suitable boat
for America. And perhaps you will come to love him anyway. Charles*

Dickens did.

I am sure I have seen tinted overlays for your computer screen. But perhaps you prefer to look like a dissolute jazz musician…

Interesting comments on London. It is a wonderful city with a history I understand because I was raised in UK. I'm afraid I don't have any experience of the working ladies there, if only because they are apparently so horribly expensive. I understand there are some extremely glamorous escorts in the West End who attend their patrons while dripping in diamonds. I guess, at the other end, there are more-or-less amateurs, in the pubs where ordinary people live, who turn a trick or two to pay the rent. The Government still has its head up its Puritanical backside when it comes to legalising prostitution. That's really stupid because sex for money will <u>always</u> exist, so it is better for society if it is organised. Anyway, London is so big and so diverse you can find whatever you fancy. Good or bad, it's just a matter of looking. And paying, of course; nothing is free there.

Personally, I feel prostitution makes life more interesting. Certainly made my life more interesting when I was a young man without ties, travelling and working in SE Asia. Ah – happy times!

As for London weather, your friend is partly right. It is NEVER as good as it is up here in tropical Queensland. On the other hand, on a fine day, it can certainly bear comparison with Van Diemen's Land. Hot summer days, when shop girls and secretaries take their boyfriends to the park for a quick cuddle on the grass. That sight gives the day a happy feel.

Your excuse for leaving two spaces between sentences does not hold water. I, too, learned typing on a clunky old upright. I forced myself to touch-type at a respectable speed until I recognised I could type far faster than I could think, so speed was not important. Unless I was going to spend long periods typing out some-one else's thoughts, and that was not part of my career plan. I spent my working life being just too junior to be assigned a secretary. If I had started work five years earlier, it would have been secretaries all the way. As it was, I had to learn word processing and so did not become fossilised into using two spaces between sentences. Not that you are fossilised, of course. I will have to think of another word…

Regards,
Simon

My Dear Secretary,

Can I call you that? It has a nice ring to it, don't you think?

I also type much faster than I think. I do that with talking sometimes as well, but don't we all? What fun is life if you can't blurt out what (generally) everyone is thinking but too afraid, or too well heeled, to say? You have to admit it is enjoyable making people squirm.

I must confess Fanny was not talking to me this time around. I started to write this next chapter three times and each time it just fell flat. Finally, I thought about how our girl was coping with being in a new city and I wondered how the class divide and stress of her financial situation was impacting on her. She has been so stalwart so far.

My research has taken me down many 17th century pathways. Some very much in the shady parts of town. How I wish I had a time machine to experience it all at first hand. Safely. And then come back to my normal life because…well…I am not stupid. I like modern life. But history does have a tendency to draw me in. The motherland more so than other places, possibly because that is where my heritage lies, by way of Ireland, Scotland and England. I have the trifector!

I do love that in our chosen period of time some of the cities were still in their infancies and houses, shops and workshops mingled with the greenery of fields. I read somewhere that after the great fires of 1666, the aristocracy moved to the outer country areas of London, beyond the slums, and began to develop these areas into what they are today. I cannot even imagine how the poorer locals felt when buildings such as those in Grosvenor Square started to take shape. It certainly must have set tongues wagging.

One of my favourite discoveries was the coffee houses. Just the thought of them now conjures up images of tobacco filled rooms, bitter coffee, newspapers and a clientele that gathered together even though their stations in life made for vastly different opinions and experiences. The coffee houses were a place to share and debate all aspects of life in a genteel environment. Not at all like the franchise coffee shop I walked into today. Nope, no voices passionately discussing the current state of the world could be heard at all. It really is a shame.

These days there are so few places where one can discuss opinions without someone getting their nose out of joint. Do you agree? Since when did it become a 'badge of honour' to be offended?

There was a recent article about one of Australia's singers starring in a new film clip. In it she was the passenger in an old car and therefore only wearing a lap belt, not seen on camera, and therefore deemed to not be wearing one at all. All of a sudden there is huge outrage because this woman is a 'role-model' and should be behaving as such. The clip was pulled from air. Since when was it the responsibility of a famous person to educate someone else's child? What happened to the "In the olden days…", talks I used to receive and now pass onto my children? Surely this situation could have been explained away by saying, 'Cars in those days didn't have the seatbelts we have today'. But of course not! People just become offended and blame others. Where the hell did common sense go?

Anyways, talking about the olden days…can you imagine what it was like to walk into an establishment and be stared at as if you did not belong? I think you might be able to. I think it is something we all have experienced at least once in life. Whilst coffee houses of the day generally admitted all men who could afford the 1 penny coffee as an entry fee, when it finally came time for women to be allowed entry, things were different. Perhaps if they had not protested so loudly in 1674 that coffee was responsible for the low birth rate by making their men sterile, going against the long held belief that coffee had medicinal benefits, they would have had an easier time of it.

Coffee in London has a fascinating history of how it came to be as we know it today. It is a story full of theft, and skulduggery and I love it! According to Professor Peaberry of the gocoffeego website, in 1710 those wonderful French started wrapping ground coffee in linen before steeping to take away the gritty grinds. Bravo! I say. There is nothing worse than grit between one's teeth.

In 1713/14, the Mayor of Amsterdam gifted King Louis XIV of France a young coffee sapling. The King had it planted in the walled protection of the Botanical Gardens in Paris where it was frequently admired by himself and his court.

In 1715, with over half a million residents, London was becoming one of the largest cities in Western Europe. At this time people had already had a liking for coffee and there were over 2000 coffee houses to choose from.

In 1723, the King's much admired and protected tree was full grown and thriving. A French Naval Officer, Gabriel Mathieu de Clieu, who was on leave from Martinique, requested a clipping. A request that was denied. It turns out he was a very patient Frenchman, and when the time was right, and after thoroughly enjoying the full benefits of court, the waning moon provided the perfect night for him to scale the high walls of the garden and steal a cutting from the hothouse. That night he made a quick getaway back to the French colony of Martinique in the West Indies.

During the journey, Gabriel kept the cutting below deck in a glass cabinet, only bringing it out to bask in the sunshine. It wasn't all smooth sailing though. One of the crewmen, who apparently spoke with a Dutch accent, fought Gabriel for the plant, only to end up in shackles for his efforts. A few days later Pirates attacked and it took the ship's crew a whole day to fend them off. As if that was not enough drama, the ship almost sunk in a storm and the glass cabinet that housed the coffee plant was shattered. Gabriel continued to nourish his weakened sapling with what little fresh water he had. Fortunately, they made it to Martinique safely.

After almost two years, the first harvest was ready and Gabriel distributed it amongst the island's doctors and intellectuals. Three years later coffee plantations spread to the sister islands of St. Dominique and Guadeloupe. The coffee harvest became so large in the Caribbean that King Louis XIV forgave Gabriel for his thievery, and even made him Governor of Antilles.

Over the next 50 years, from that one little sapling, there would be 19 million coffee trees grown in Martinique alone, and it was the stock from which plantations in the Caribbean, South and Central America originated.

In 1727, the handsome Brazilian, Colonel Francisco de Melo Palheta, was sent to arbitrate a compromise in a border dispute between Brazil, French Guiana and Dutch Guiana. However, his mission was simply a scam. The Brazilian Government had decided that it wanted to grow coffee and when Francisco asked for a plant the French Government denied his request. The Colonel was a crafty man and had arrived with a backup plan. After several discreet liaisons with the Governor's wife, she gifted him a farewell bouquet sprinkled with fertile coffee seedlings. Those early seedlings grew into the largest coffee empire known today. Who says sex doesn't pay!

In 1730, Sir Nicolas Lawes, the former English Governor of Jamaica, transported the first coffee plant to Jamaica. Cultivation first started in the foothills of St Andrews and quickly moved its way into the fertile Blue Mountains. Today it is favoured for its mild taste and lack of bitterness. Sounds like my ideal cup of coffee.

In 1757, the British East Trading Company gave up the coffee trade to the dominant Dutch and French. Soon after, tea became very popular, surpassing ale, gin and coffee. And so began the history of tea and afternoon/high tea.

Can you imagine a life today without coffee and tea? How awful would that be? What would we waste our money on? Even now I need to go and refill my cup. I'm sure there is a slow leak in it somewhere or perhaps a wayward fairy stealing her next hit of caffeine. There she sits, watching patiently with her tiny straw in hand, waiting for me to leave the room.

I do hope you enjoy this little insight into how Fanny is feeling, and the little twist at the end. I look forward to reading what you do with it.

Debb.

Chapter Six ~ Alone in London

A broken dish ~ visiting a new coffee house in Mayfair
~ a reservation for Rosie Palm ~ coffee and lace
~ Rob Longshot will hang ~ Art returns a treasure

"It's just a dish, Bridget!"

Fanny stared at her maid, wondering what had happened to her. Had living in a large city somehow made her daft? Why such a panic from a dish of tea falling onto the rug?

"But, Miss…" Bridget started, twisting her hands in her skirts. She knew too well that Mrs Bones would certainly care that a dish had been broken, and that a large amount of Miss Fanny's extra strong tea now stained the rug.

"I truly don't understand what the fuss is all about, girl! It's just an old dish, not very stylish either, and well, the rug has seen better days anyhow. One of the maids will clean it up in no time."

Fanny watched her maid as she sighed, and her shoulders relaxed. Why so much fuss over such a small mess she would never understand.

"Yes, Miss. I'll see Mrs Bones right away." Bridget quietly backed out of the room and headed for the kitchens.

"This whole place has seen better days," Fanny mused, hands on hips, as she looked around the small parlour situated in the front of the Bull and Mouth Inn. Tiresome. It was the first word that had come to mind when she had been shown into the room after requesting a private area to dine in last Sunday.

Eating in the public area had been fine for the first couple of weeks, but then the locals started to intrude on her space. Poor manners, the lot of them. How dare they ask questions of her! She was a lady after all. What concern of it was theirs how she came to drive a coach or why she was unchaperoned or why she was staying in this end of town in a cheap room? On and on the questions were asked.

Oh, they were never asked of her directly. At least they had a little respect for her. They were spoken just out of earshot, fast mumbled sentences that Fanny was never quick enough to catch. A word or two was all she understood. It's as if these people had never been taught the King's English. She was not stupid though. Her schooling, however brief it may have been, allowed her to put one and one together and know exactly what they were gossiping about. Even Bridget had played innocent when asked what people were saying. "They're just curious, is all, Miss," she had said.

A muffled commotion caught Fanny's attention and she turned as Mrs Bones skirts brushed hurriedly through the doorway.

"Ahh, Miss. Your girl Bridget dropped a dish of tea, then. Well, I dare say that don't signify too much. Are you alright, dear?"

These past few weeks Fanny had learned not to focus on every word that Mrs Bones spoke. If she did, the sentence would be completed well before the words processed in her mind. It was much easier to focus on the one or two words she understood clearly, rather than try to decipher what amounted to ramblings of an old woman.

"Why, yes, I am, Mrs Bones. I was just telling my maid that there was no real harm done. A broken dish and a stain. All in a day's work for an inn, I would think."

Quietness hung in the cool air of the parlour as Mrs Bones gathered her thoughts. She had dealt with ladies before and their inability to see things as they really are. This one was no different. No, not at all. "Yes, dearie, all in a day's work here at my little inn. I'll have one of my girls fix it right up."

Fanny nodded agreement. Bridget could surely learn a thing or two from someone as practical and efficient as Mrs Bones. There was never any point in crying over spilt milk, or tea, as was the case here.

"Now, perhaps some sunshine is what you need today. I've heard there's a new coffee shop that just opened and allows ladies in. Has the best tea in all of London, they're saying. It even has one of those cabinets full of mysterious things from around the world. There's even a shank bone from one of those gyants." Mrs Bones paused for a few more seconds for the idea to take root before adding, "It's down in that newer part of town everyone is talking about. Big fancy houses and the like. Archi'ture like nothing I've ever seen before. Safe there too. William will be back in the hour and I'll send him up." Mrs Bones turned and walked away without waiting for a reply. Excitement overtook Fanny. She could feel the boredom lifting already. It would be fun to explore further.

"Umm, Miss Fanny? I don't think this is a good idea. You see…"

"Oh, Bridget," she cut in angrily, tired of the silliness. "What has come over you? Where is your sense of adventure? It will be fun to explore something new and exciting. Just you see."

Fanny stared out from the open shutter of the carriage as they passed through the busy streets of Mayfair. Never had she seen such a sight! It all looked so new. Wide streets cramped with horses and carts carrying all manner of things. Some loaded to the brim with building materials, others with produce from the nearby markets.

Weary men, women and children littered the streets. Many covered in a sooty coating that matched perfectly with the partially completed terrace houses they had just passed. Everywhere she looked something was happening.

A breeze flickered around her and Bridget, filling the small confines of the carriage with dust. The warmth of the late morning sun heated the smells of the busy street. Reaching for her handkerchief to cover her nose, she quickly decided that it offered little protection against the combined stench of factories, smoke and horses. It was a small price to pay for exploring a new city though, something she had very little opportunity to do back at the priory. There she had always felt so closed in and had spent an "unladylike" amount of time outside.

The carriage slowed its approach as they waited for the road ahead to clear. Small knots of excitement twisted her stomach as the long forgotten memory ghosted her mind and quickly disappeared. When they arrived, the street-level coffee house was a narrow redbrick and white timbered building that reached high above ground. Situated on the corner of the main road and a dirty alley, the shopfront was just wide enough for a large double door and a window to the left of it.

Standing out on the footpath, Fanny tilted her head to take in the full height of the building. Adorning each of the three levels above the coffee shop were several large arched windows, trimmed in white, with tall pillars of pale coloured stone in between. A blackened, ornate balustrade ran the whole width of each balcony, and was topped with boxes of red and blue flowers.

Fanny marvelled at the decorative stonework and wondered what style it was fashioned in. She thought Italian in the modern style, although she was not certain. Perhaps it was the Baroque style her mother had spoken of but had never seen. The door opened and with it came the familiar smell of tobacco and coffee. The memory tugged at her a little more and was quickly brushed aside by Fanny's eagerness to experience her first coffee house as an adult.

Standing just inside the doorway, she gazed around the long room. Several trestle tables, designed to encourage men to freely discuss the important news of the day, took up a large portion of the room. A handful of smaller tables were scattered towards the right-hand side and the back of the shop.

As Fanny walked further into the room the smell of vegetable soup, steaming over the large hearth that was positioned half-way along the left wall, gave the space a welcoming feel. White walls made the room feel airy and were decorated with framed paintings of landscapes and portraits. In one corner there was an odd collection of paintings, drawings and writings haphazardly stuck to the walls. The joins in the bare timber floors, that ran the depth of the building, made the space feel much longer than it actually was. She noted, disappointingly, that there was no curiosity cabinet, something she must remember to tell Mrs Bones.

Taking a few more steps towards the centre of the room, Fanny, feeling a sharp bump at her hip, suddenly found herself falling towards one of the smaller tables. It was only due to her quick reaction, and a lot of luck, that she did not end up face down on the floor, tangled in her skirts. Thankfully, her pivot allowed her to land firmly on her backside.

She coughed at the small cloud of dust that surrounded her as she thumped down on the floorboards. Glancing down at the sea of pale yellow surrounding her, Fanny was relieved to see her skirts still covered her legs completely.

"Do be careful, child!" An angry voice scalded.

Fanny looked up from her position on the floor to see disdain flaming in an older woman's eyes. What right did she have to be angry? After all, it was her clumsiness that had put Fanny on the floor. Not the other way around.

A few men from the trestle-table rushed to help Fanny to her feet, elbowing Bridget aside. The husk of a strong, feminine voice raised above the noise.

"Do be careful, men. That's not a sack you're lifting."

All at once the hands reaching for her slowed and gentled, lifting Fanny to her feet with delicate ease. After thanking her saviours, who surprisingly appeared to be men from all walks of life, Fanny searched for the owner of the voice that had put a halt to the rushed paws that had grabbed at her.

As the men walked away Bridget moved in close, unshed tears in her eyes. It seems she too was given an earful from the old goat that had knocked Fanny down. "Miss Fanny, are you well? That old woman was terribly rude to you."

"Yes, Bridget, I am well. Nothing that a steaming dish of tea and a chair can't repair."

As Bridget scurried away, Fanny looked about the room and moved towards an empty table by the large window at the front of the shop.

"'Scuse, Miss. That there table is taken."

Raising her head to meet the eyes of the man in front of her, Fanny found it interesting how he shuffled slightly from foot to foot as he spoke. His stiff white shirt and apron doing nothing to hide his unease.

"Taken? How can an empty table be taken?"

"One of our clients, Miss. She uses it at the same time every day. And now is that time."

"Can't she simply take another table? There are several spare." Waving her hand around to indicate the half dozen small, and very empty, tables towards the back of the room, Fanny noticed a woman walking towards her.

"It's alright, George. I'll use another table for today. This one is for Miss..?" With a raised eyebrow she looked directly at Fanny, waiting for an answer.

"Howarth. Miss Francisca Howarth. Please call me Fanny."

With a dismissing nod to George the woman smiled, "Well, Fanny. It's always nice to meet a new friend, and such a pretty one as well."

Fanny looked over the woman before her. She was pleasant looking, if not a little old. Probably not too much older than Mrs Bones but well past her prime. The rich cobalt blue of her gown favoured her eyes. Once she would have been a very handsome woman. Perhaps a hard life had tired her face early? Her smile was wide and displayed an almost full set of slightly yellowing teeth. They were large and sturdy, reminding Fanny of an old nag. If you looked close enough you would certainly notice the single tooth missing from the upper left side of her mouth.

"Why, thank you, Mrs..?"

"Never mind that, dear. You can just call me Rosie."

Fanny nodded to the woman and took one of the seats that allowed her to look directly out of dusty window to watch what was happening on the busy street. At least Mrs Bones had been correct about the architecture. One mansion in particular was blinding white with large pillars that lined up across its front. Although only four-storeys high, its windows seem to stretch on forever towards the private parkland at the end of the road.

The street was still crowded with people and carriages coming and going. Porters from the nearby markets were delivering produce to the numerous shops along the road. From her position Fanny could see a pork butcher, an ale house, a dressmaker and a baker. There also seem to be businesses on the second level above some of the shops but there were no signs in the windows to indicate what they were selling.

Fields of green were still mingled with shops and buildings in varying degrees of completion. She wondered if Mayfair would become as overcrowded as London. Fanny hoped not. She liked the open spaces. They reminded her of home.

The scent of strong, bitter coffee reminded Fanny of the distant memory from childhood. It seemed like only a few years past that her mother had taken Fanny for her first, and only, visit to a coffee house. She could remember how excited her Mama had been after voicing her initial annoyance in the carriage, "Why it has taken this long for women to be allowed in I'll never know!"

Another memory from that day was how the men had quietened as soon as they had walked into the coffee house. Some viewed them with interest, others were downright annoyed at their presence. Her mother didn't seem to notice at all. Head held high, she quietly took a seat, ignoring all those around her.

Fascinated by the publications scattered about the table top, Fanny passed over *The Spectator* and *The Tatler* before reaching for a sale bulletin displaying the newest fashions from France. It seemed that the popular dark coloured fabrics were giving way to much lighter and brighter styles. Lace was also becoming very popular again.

Lace.

Fanny could remember how much she hated the delicate fabric and how easily it would catch on the twigs and leaves when she would play in the woods behind the priory. As a child she had hated fashion. She did not understand why things had to change, especially her dresses. Fanny could still hear her mother's sage words echo in her mind. "No one likes change, but it has to happen, otherwise we stay in the same place doing the same thing." On that day, many years ago, she had spent the whole afternoon with her mother, talking excitedly about anything and nothing as only a ten year old girl, drinking her first coffee, could do.

The memory faded as Bridget returned followed by the server with her tray. A commotion on the street drew Fanny's attention. A small group of porters had gathered, Art and William amongst them. In the centre of the commotion was goat lady. Perhaps someone had knocked her down Fanny hoped uncharitably. Losing interest quickly, she returned her attention to the tray before her.

A surprising sense of melancholy descended upon her. She could ask Bridget to share her table but knew that this was not the place for a lady to be seen dining with her maid. Twisting her mother's ring upon her finger gave her a measure of comfort and settled the lonely unease in her mind. "Everything will work out," she whispered quietly to herself. Her mama's often spoken words had always brought her comfort, not today though. Being responsible for not only herself, but Bridget as well, was tiring and affecting her good mood.

An hour had passed before her tray was finally empty. She could never abide the waste of food and had made herself finish every last piece. With a nod across the room to Bridget to settle the bill, Fanny stood and smoothed out her skirts before making her way to the door. As she stepped onto the street, Art was there waiting for her.

"Miss, I have something for you. I found…" Art's anxious voice was drowned out by the boisterous excitement that had suddenly gripped a group of people on the street.

A man nearby ran up to the group, waving a broadsheet high above his head. "I tell ye it was him. Seen it with me own eyes. Ain't no missing that jagged scar on his face. He's going to hang. Rob Longshot is going to hang!"

Fanny's gasp was loud enough to draw Bridget's attention to her. "It's alright, Miss. He won't get near us again. They'll hang him for stealing the King's mail for sure. You just wait and see."

She stared at Bridget, speechless, thankful that she had misunderstood her concern for fear. Oh, she knew that if he was ever caught, they would hang him. Surely that lawyer, Higgins, would want him to pay for what he stole. If it were anyone else she would not care, but now she did. How could she not?

With a nod of agreement, she allowed Art to assist her into the carriage. "Miss, as I was saying before, I found something. The old woman had it. I didn't take none of it neither, I swear." He pleaded.

Fanny stared at the small boy in front of her. He really could do with some clothes his own size. A nervous fear was bright in his eyes and she had absolutely no idea what he was rambling on about. It was not until he shook the coins in front of her that she realised he held her purse.

Shocked fingers grabbed at her waist, feeling the now empty space of where she had securely tied her purse this morning. It was gone! She snatched it from Art and carefully inspected the special knot that Fearnley had taught her as a child. It was still as she had tied it, keeping her money and Rob's ring safe. Perhaps the long, bumpy ride had loosened the pouch from its waist-chain on her skirts.

With a shaky sigh she thanked Art for his honesty and felt her heart soften seeing his small chest billow with pride. She really must make more of an effort with the boy.

Resting her head against the worn inside of the carriage, Fanny sighed deeply. What had started out as a pleasant excursion had left her feeling the full weight of her predicament. She dare not think what would have happened if she had lost her purse. Although she had been smart enough to keep half her money hidden away deep in her trunk, she could not afford to lose even a penny. They had been in London for almost a month and soon she would need to find a way to earn money. She could not call on Cousin Clarence again. He would not like that at all.

They passed a scruffy child standing on the corner of the street shouting out the headlines of the newspapers he was selling. Closing her eyes, Fanny lowered her head and prayed as she had never prayed before. She prayed for herself, for Bridget and yes, for Rob Longshot.

Debbie,
I am sitting upstairs in our Polish family's home and have some time alone with the computer. We always come to England and Poland, every year, because my mother and Jana's are both frail old ladies we must visit while

they are still with us. Frustrating, of course, because neither of them get out of the house much, which leaves us trapped indoors.

Outside, they are having what they call their Golden Polish Autumn which, for once, is happening as it should with clear skies and warm sun, and apple and plum trees full of fruit. I wish I could get out more, but there it is.

There is so much history here... I look out of my window over fields that were the crucial turning point of the Battle of Tannenberg in 1914. A great conflict between the Russian and German armies in the opening days of the Great War that shook everyone's confidence in their plans and predictions of how the war would go. This part of Poland used to be the border lands between Russia and Prussia. Poland did not exist then, but Polish people and culture did. I suppose many of the dead soldiers on both sides were ethnically Polish. Unfortunately, when Poland was moved north and west by the WWII settlement, the Communists erased any local history that was non-Polish so my brother-in-law has no idea about Tannenberg, and no interest in the part his village played in those great events. Mmmh.

I have had time to slowly re-read our story right from the beginning and I am impressed. It is really interesting and not like any other sexy romance I recall reading. That's good, and we're about a third of the way through already. Isn't it terrible how authors use word count as a way of keeping score?

Anyway, I like the coffee shop, although I would have liked a little more description of the other customers. Mostly male, I suppose, but doing things like arguing politics, sharing the newspapers, doing business. And smoking, of course. They couldn't think without a clay pipe to suck on. I don't suppose there would be many ladies at that time of day, and unaccompanied ones like Fanny and Rosie would be even rarer. I want to meet Rosie again – perhaps she will tell us something of a working girl's life. In fact, it's probably time for Fanny to realise that a) her money won't last forever, and b) working for someone like Rosie will be her only way to survive. What do you think? Is it time for Fanny to dip a toe into the world of high class prostitution, starting out as a non-participating helper in Rosie Palm's classy bordello? Or should we add to the encounter with Rosie and have them sit together and talk? Then Rosie could discreetly contact Mrs Bones and make an offer? Whatever – I believe it is time for things to get sexy again.

Regards,
Simon

Hi Simon,
How I envy the Polish Golden Autumn that you describe. It must be truly

beautiful. And to be surrounded by all that history makes me truly, truly envious. Spring has finally sprung here and that means windy days and if it's a southerly blowing straight from Antarctica, it's damn cold. Otherwise we have a few days of warmth and then a few days of rain and so on.

That time of the year has finally come where we have turned the clocks forward one hour for daylight savings. Something unheard of in your neck of the woods I bet. The longer days for me mean the late afternoon sun shining into my living areas. Something that I lose for about five months over the cooler seasons.

As for word counting, sometimes I think it the bane of a writer's existence. I remember a conversation with a very successful writer and she said that all of her books had to be 55 000 words by decree of the publisher. I can remember thinking, what if she had more to write and it was all relevant? How does she decide what to leave out? Although on the other hand, I remember last year hanging out for the next edition of a particular series I was reading and then thinking that there seemed to be words in it for the sake of having a large word count. It was really off-putting and unenjoyable. I guess it's all about balance.

Back to our coffee shop. Isn't it so like me not to describe the obvious – the men in the room – yet I'll describe a set of teeth that most people wouldn't even notice. Is that my female brain at work?

Yes, we need to get sexy again! How we do that is all up to you of course. I do think a meeting between Fanny and Rosie would work. Perhaps Mrs Bones may have a hand in it in the fashion of procuress Elizabeth Needham from The Harlot's Progress?

I would also like to read about a working girl's life. I don't believe that it would be a very nice existence. What were the sexual diseases of the day? Just the thought of a 'French letter' makes me squirm.

The ball's in your court or should that be 'the whore's in your bordello'?
Debb.

Debb,

At last, I have managed to sit down and <u>write</u>. No excuse; these things just happen. For goodness sake, I'm retired and so ought to have all the time in the world, but we have things going on in town.

One of the first things the sturdy Victorians did when they arrived in Cooktown around 1880 was build a railway line in towards the goldfields, around 200 km away. It never got there because the gold ran out by the end of the decade, leaving us with a railway as far as the very small town of Laura. It soldiered on as a local line in an era of few roads and bridges, *hauling people and freight from the port. In the early 1930's, they stopped using steam engines and simply ran a kerosene powered railbus. That stopped running in 1961, the rails were ripped up for scrap, and everything just faded into the bush.*

I think it is criminal to let the history go, so we are pushing for a historical railway park over the old service area. I have been poking away at the Shire, cutting bush, begging materials, laying paths, all the things needed to get the job done without the support of the bureaucrats. We're making good progress. A Phase 1 park this year, and by the end of 2018 we hope to have a properly maintained site with pathways, signs, perhaps even a covered display.

So that's my excuse; now, back to work.

We have a problem. Fanny is well brought up and educated, with all the manners and prejudices of her class. Sure, she has an itch for a highwayman with a gold earring, but that's normal behaviour – don't most girls have a soft spot for bad boys? It doesn't mean she has gone to the Devil, or even put her prettily booted foot on the first step of the slippery slope. Far from it.

But that is exactly what we need her to do. We want her to experience everything, to become a mature, sexy woman who understands society and her place in it. I don't think I could bear to write about a proper English miss, on her way to becoming a dried up maiden aunt. She is not a TSTL (Too Stupid To Live) heroine, but a proper woman who can stand up for herself and is not ready to be pushed around by any privileged male. I think Rob Longshot will have his hands full when she catches up with him.

So how do we manage to give her some modern attitudes and experiences? I'm sure you're right – Sir Francis Dashwood is the man for the job. He got up to all sorts of fun but the best thing about him is that he was not a hypocrite. He thought sex was a great gift to be celebrated, not enjoyed in a hole-in-the-corner way as the Victorians did later on. Well-off men would use lower class women (and very young girls) for their pleasure, and still stand up in church on Sunday as pillars of society.

Sir Francis had been around the block (several times, I believe) and he knew that the best female lovers are the ones who really think about what they are doing, and want to enjoy it at least as much as their partners. Of course, he wanted female members of the Hellfire Club. He wanted wives and sisters to don their habits, and leave their modesties at the door. Yes, there were never enough free-thinking women to go around (that hasn't changed, even now) and the ranks of the sisters were supplemented with courtesans. But they were select courtesans, ones who really enjoyed their profession, and that makes all the difference.

So how is Fanny going to join their ranks? How are we going to say to her, "Miss Howarth, we want you to come with us this weekend, into the caves of Medmenham and, dressed only in a veil, spread yourself over that altar and let the lucky High Priest have his way with you. And afterwards we'll have a big banquet, get drunk, and you can't imagine how much fun you and the other girls are going to have".

That might be a bit much all at once. We will have to get there step by step, so here goes...

Regards,

Simon

Chapter Seven ~ Joining the Club

*Thoughts on bacon and the Cardinal of Naples
~ Mrs Bones sits down ~ selling kisses does not suffice
~ Mrs Palm's club for gentlemen ~ a beautiful and
comfortable place ~ the attraction of spotted dick
~ Fanny serves her first drinks*

Fanny breakfasted alone, at the small table under the window. Mrs Bones always kept it for her, even in the busy times. Surprising, when Fanny thought about it. So many people passing through the inn every day, and Mrs Bones still had time for her. She wondered why.

From her chair, she could look out onto the street. People everywhere, hardly a square yard of pavement free of hurrying feet. The street was busy too, with carts and coaches and humble market barrows pushed by their owners. Would she ever tire of the spectacle? London had so much to offer. Here she sat, bacon, eggs and fine white bread in front of her, a copy of *The Gentleman's Magazine* on the table. She could look out at the biggest city in the world, or she could study a scholarly account of the eruption of Mount Vesuvius compiled for the Cardinal of Naples. Langston Priory could provide the bacon and eggs (and better than these, she added proudly) but it could never match the excitement of London.

The latch clicked open and Mrs Bones peeped around the door. "Er – if you have a moment, Miss…"

"Come in, Mrs Bones. What can I do for you?"

"Miss, it's just that, I've been talking to Bridget." She faltered, and a shiver ran up Fanny's spine. This was going to be about money.

"Yes, Mrs Bones. I hope everything is well? She has paid our fees, I hope?"

"Oh, yes, Miss. No problem there. She's a good girl, that one. As hard a worker as I ever did see. She'd work all hours if I let her…"

"Bridget? Working for you?"

"That's right, Miss. Oh. I can see she didn't tell you about that…"

"Working for you? I had no idea. Why is she doing that?"

"Ah well, Miss. Now you've put your finger on it. Now, you know me, Miss. I talk as I find, and I've been wanting a chat about things. Do you mind if I sit down?"

Her request surprised Fanny, but she must have agreed because Mrs Bones took the other chair. She set her plump elbows on the table and spoke as an equal. "It can't go on, you see. I don't poke my nose in where it's not wanted. I don't see what I don't need to see, and if Bridget's selling kisses on the side, well, that's natural, I say. I know the two of you is short of the hard stuff. That's why I go easy when it comes to taking your money, but it can't go on forever. Young Bridget can't work hard enough, not that you'd want her to.

"So it's like this, Miss. I've got a friend with her own business. She's a good woman, an old friend, but she ain't so smooth, you know. Didn't have much in the way of schooling. Proper manners don't come natural to her, no more than to me to tell the truth, though she's worked hard to hide it. Anyway, she needs help. She needs a real lady to sweet talk her customers. Make them feel at home. Someone who can read proper, like you and that magazine there, someone who can talk to gentlemen about more than the weather.

"What do you say? Shall I talk to her for you? I'd say she runs the best house in town at the moment, elegant as you could wish for. Wouldn't let the likes of me through the doors, 'cept maybe through the kitchen. I'd say it's just what the two of you need. It'd be free board and lodging for the both of you, and pin money too. Shall I send around to make a time?"

Fanny shook her head and hoped she had not been sitting with her mouth open. Of course Bridget had been paying their charges, but she had no idea she had been using her own money as well. And selling kisses? Bridget? What did that mean?

"I can see you're thinking about it, Miss. Believe me, I'd jump at the chance if I were you. You can't do much in this wicked old world without money and, forgive me saying, you don't have enough of it. A lady like you needs a home and a place in society. I'll send Art around to see Mrs Palm, shall I?"

Fanny found her tongue. "What sort of business is it?"

"It's a club for gentlemen, my dear. Real gentlemen, I mean. Lords and the like. Rosie gives them a place to meet each other, a comfortable place, like home. Well, better than home, I reckon, because there's no wife and no kids. No-one to tell the old boys what to do and when. She says you can see the weight of it all drop from their shoulders as they come in.

"I won't spin you a line; there's girls too for when the old boys are feeling their oats, but mostly it's just sitting and talking with their friends. She says she wishes they'd do more of that because she swears she makes more money from the brandy than the girls. Your job would be to make them comfortable, keep the brandy and cigars moving. Make sure no-one is sitting with an empty glass. Make sure no-one falls asleep in front of the fire, because they don't spend money while they're sleeping."

What had Bridget been doing? The thought that she had been working for Mrs Bones along with taking care of Fanny, that rankled. Bridget did not deserve that. She was a servant, and her mistress should be taking care of her, not sending her out to sell kisses to pay the rent. The thought was shaming, and she would have to make things up to Bridget.

But they needed money; Mrs Bones was right about that. Clarence might be good for a little more but that would not last. It would just be delaying things. She could write to her uncle but – she resolved that would be the last thing she would do. What else could a lady in her position do to gain a living? She could not take a governess position with a family here in the city because what could she teach? She had no useful experience of life. And she would just be a governess, no more. It would not be possible, anyway. She knew no-one in the city, and any respectable family would require a reference at minimum before taking on a stranger. She could not bear the thought of a future employer writing an enquiry to her uncle.

She would do as Mrs Bones suggested. She was sure no-one at Langston would think it a respectable position, but free board and lodging – that counted for a lot. Talking to old gentlemen could be an acceptable occupation, in the right circumstances. And if there were girls around, she was sure she would not be obliged to mix with them. And besides, who would know? No-one from Langston, that was certain. Her uncle never came to London so he would never know. And I don't care if he did, she added to herself. He would be shamed, and that would be her revenge.

She smiled when she thought how readily she was turning her back on her old life. Only weeks ago... She didn't need to worry about anything back then. Until her uncle had betrayed her.

Mrs Palm's club for gentlemen looked impressive, a grand new building in Charles St, off Berkeley Square. The steps up to the front door were wide and the stone was still sharp and little worn. There was a bell-pull beside the door and Fanny heard the bell ring deep inside. She waited.

After several long minutes with no result, she pulled again. Twice this time, just to be sure. She heard the tap of hurrying feet and the door being unbolted. It opened to show a maid, caught in the middle of her work. Her hair was bound up in a cloth, and her rolled up sleeves and red hands showed she had been scrubbing. She stared for a moment, assessing her visitor, and Bridget standing with Art on the street. She smiled, and spoke without deference.

"I'm sorry, Miss. Mr Rutham's normally here by now, but he's not and we're all at sixes and sevens. Are you wanting to see Mrs Palm?"

"Yes, if it is convenient."

"Please come in, Miss, and I will see if she's in." She waved at the basement steps leading downwards beside the front door. "And if your people would like to go on down, I shall run around and let them in too."

Fanny stepped into the hall and almost gasped out loud. The room glittered. A marble staircase wound up on one side, with a richly carved banister. In fact, there were marble carvings everywhere. Ornate pilasters with fruit laden capitals lined the walls on both sides. A bas relief faced her, Artemis the Goddess, charmingly naked and caught at the instant of loosing an arrow. A mad goldsmith had been set free to gild every detail he could reach, including some interesting points of the Goddess.

Dominating all else and demanding attention, a life-sized statue of a woman carrying a pitcher of water on her head. She stood on a low plinth with her back to the front door, one arm raised and her weight on one leg, knowing every visitor would be staring as she swayed her hips step by step. She had only the very thinnest of covering from the waist down.

The maid clicked her tongue in frustration. "Look at that, Miss. The gentlemen can't keep their dirty paws off her and I have to scrub the poor dear's bum every day to keep the greasy marks off. I shall have to ask Mr Rutham to give everyone gloves. And they only have to wait a minute or two before they can be patting the real thing. Much more fun."

She showed Fanny to a small doorway below the stairs. "This is Mrs Palm's office, Ma'am. Perhaps you could wait here while I find her. Shall I take your coat?"

The office was small, and cozy. There were no shelves full of ledgers, and no high desk for a clerk to stand at. Instead, a small padded chair and a sofa gave a homely air, and a silver kettle on a spirit lamp stand hinted more at comfort than work. Fanny chose the sofa. What sort of person was Mrs Palm, she wondered. Her club was certainly very grand, far richer than anything Fanny had seen before, but judging by the maid who had opened the door, she treated her servants with great familiarity. Which was not a bad thing, she reminded herself. Servants were people after all, and a twinge of conscience reminded her of Bridget's help with their funds.

An elegant oil painting hung over the fireplace, a chubby Cupid bothering a reclining Venus. The brightness of her nude torso and the startling blue of the robe she lay on filled the little room with light. Venus looked radiant and commanding, even though she was lying alone in the forest and her clothes were failing to conceal her charms. Fanny supposed the painting was art – indeed, it drew her eye again and again – but did it hang there for purely artistic reasons? She could imagine the gentlemen members finding this Venus uplifting, and she envied her. It must be pleasant to have so many admirers, but if the way to gain them involved displaying herself wearing scarcely a stitch of clothing, Fanny would disqualify herself immediately.

"You like my painting, then?" Mrs Palm was standing at the door. Rosie from the coffee house. "Beautiful, isn't she? I bought her from the artist. Such a gentleman, he was, my Giuseppe. We sat for hours because I had to chaperone the model. Well, I didn't really – she could take care of herself – I just didn't want them playing around when he should have been working. I needn't have worried, he had eyes only for me. He'd paint all morning, then oysters and toast for lunch, and we'd take a siesta. Wonderful times, and he left such a wonderful picture to remember them by.

"Well, Miss Howarth. We meet again." She held out her hand.

She was the woman from the coffee shop, the one with the blue dress. Fanny jumped up and shook her hand, surprised, and Mrs Palm waved her back to the sofa. "So, my dear – may I call you Fanny? Good. Mrs Bones has been telling me about you. An educated young lady escaping from her uncle. That's sad. At least, sad for you but it might be a great help for me. What did Mrs Bones tell you about us?"

Fanny was examining her hostess. She seemed to have risen recently and wore only a loose linen dressing gown, tied at the waist, over a lace night gown. Her black hair was gathered under a simple mob cap and she wore no make-up. Mrs Palm smiled. "We work late, my dear, and we get up late too. The top floor is as quiet as a cemetery until lunch time. Now, what did Mrs Bones say?"

"I'm sorry. She said you have a gentleman's club here."

"That's right, a gentleman's club. Not, and I want you to be quite clear about this, a fancy bordello, far less a common knocking shop. We are a club, and we entertain guests. Select guests, to be sure, who pay their way. The gentlemen run the club, you know. They decide who gets in, and that suits us very well.

"Would you like to see? Come along. There's no-one up and about yet, apart from the maids." She led Fanny out into the hall and past the statue of the water carrier, who looked just as enticing from the front as she had from behind.

"It's all very beautiful…"

"Yes. I enjoy beautiful things, and so do the gentlemen. Of course, it's all beautiful girls for them. I'd like to see a few beautiful boys as well, but some of the members get very tongue-tied at the sight of a nice male bum. As if everyone doesn't know just how they spent their school days. Here we are…"

She waved Fanny through into a grand room with a high ceiling, almost a hall. The decoration was in an ornate modern Baroque style, and the goldsmith had been busy here too. On one side were shelves of bottles, and serving tables for the staff. The other was dominated by a large fireplace surrounded by comfortable chairs, large enough and comfortable enough to accommodate portly gentlemen. Or perhaps ordinary gentlemen with intimate companions. Beyond them were tables and chairs, suitable for drinking coffee or playing cards. A pianoforte stood in the far corner, beside a miniature dance floor and a low stage. Mrs Palm and her girls must offer more formal entertainments as well.

"It's very impressive," said Fanny.

"Yes, and so it should be. Impressive, but when it's full of people dancing and enjoying themselves, it's exciting as well. This is for fun, but we have a dining room over there, next to the library."

"You have a library?"

"Of course. We want the gentlemen to feel comfortable here, and then they will come back day after day. I'm afraid some of them spend more time sleeping under their newspapers than reading them. They can do things here they are not allowed to do at home, like eat spotted dick pudding after dinner. And drink as much port as they like, of course."

So this is what a house of ill repute looks like, thought Fanny. It's so elegant, not what I'd imagined at all. I thought it would be all rough drunken women, not a library and spotted dick pudding.

"Er, Mrs Palm, what exactly do you want me to do here?"

"Oh, not much. Make the gentlemen happy and comfortable mostly. The girls take care of them, sit on their laps and take them upstairs but that doesn't take too long. I need someone to talk to them afterwards about, oh, I don't know, Parliament, the news, literature. Whatever they are interested in. And make sure their brandy glass is topped up, of course.

"That's in the evening. During the day, I want you to keep up with the books. Make sure yesterday's charges are entered up, and send out the bills at the end of the month. Do you think you could manage that?"

Of course she could manage. She used to help with the books back at Langston and keeping track of the gentlemen's brandy should be much easier than that. "Do they pay their bills?"

"Oh yes. Without fail. If anyone is late, no more spotted dick and the club president will be having a word in his ear. What do you think? Do you want to give it a try?"

"Um - I don't have to sit on anyone's lap, do I?"

"Not unless you want to. And you won't be taking anyone upstairs either. The girls do that and I'm sure they do it much better than you could. Not that you couldn't learn, you understand, but I need you to do the things they can't."

She did not need to think about the offer. She needed a home, and she needed money.

"I'd like to try, but I've got a maid to take care of. Bridget."

"I heard. Is she any good?"

"Yes. She works very hard, and I'm fond of her."

"Good. She can take care of you, and then I'll find her plenty to do afterwards. I pay well, you know. You'll have a room, and clothes for the evening, and half a guinea a week. And I expect some of the gentlemen will leave you a tip now and again. It all helps. As for Bridget, we'll see what she can do and I'll pay her what she's worth. Do you want to see your room?"

She had been trying to read but the view from her window distracted her. She liked her new room. She had a wardrobe, and a table with a mirror. The large bed was comfortable, and the counterpane matched the curtains. She supposed this room was in the better part of the house; the girls lived and worked in rooms above the main room, reached by a separate stairway.

Bridget would be sharing an attic room with two other maids. Fanny would have to visit her soon, to see that she had all she needed.

Mrs Palm came at four o'clock. "Are you ready? Let's have a look at you... Ah – well. Not quite what we need. Never mind, it won't do too much harm if you look like a country girl on your first night. Yes, that's what we'll do. You can look like a governess to start with, and we'll push you downhill a step at a time.

"We'll have to visit the dress maker tomorrow, but I'll see what we have around the house that you can borrow. The girls must have something, and I've got a chemise that doesn't fit any more. At least it doesn't button up to your chin. No point dressing up as if you were going to church. The gentlemen like to look down your front. It cheers them up. Mind you, it cheers them up even more if they think your chemise is coming off soon. They're all the same. Show them a bit of bosom and you can do anything with them.

"So, come along. Let's get you started."

Mrs Palm led her down the main staircase. Fanny might try to make an entrance, but Mrs Palm would dazzle anyone watching. No grey skirt and white blouse for her. She wore a royal blue gown over a sparkling white lace petticoat. She was tightly corseted and her bosom blossomed from the frills of her chemise, ripe and tempting for any lecherous old man. Black curls cascaded from a tiny hat; they must be a wig, Fanny guessed jealously. She swept down the stairs and Fanny followed in her shadow.

There were no members in the main room, only two maids tidying and dusting the shelves of bottles. They were dressed in black with white pinafores, and each had a starched white cap pinned to the top of their head. But these were not normal maids. They wore their hair

101

long, running down their backs in loose ponytails. And their uniforms were short – far too short. Surely they could not do much work in skirts that short...

"Sally and Gwen," said Mrs Palm in introduction. "And this is Miss Howarth, but as she's here to help us, we can all call her Fanny, can't we?"

"Er, yes." She was uncertain. Did that mean Bridget would also be calling her by her Christian name? She winced mentally, and accepted her fate. After all, she would be working in a club for gentlemen. She was no longer respectable and she must change her ways to suit.

As she shook hands, she asked, "Um – what do we have to do?"

The three of them looked at Mrs Palm who nodded approval.

"We have to give the gentlemen their drinks, Miss, I mean, Fanny." said Gwen. "We take the glasses from here, and pour the wine or whatever -"

"And?" demanded Mrs Palm.

"Um – and write it in the book. And then we put the glass on a tray, even if there's only one glass, and carry it over to the gentleman. It's easy, really, once you remember all the gentlemen's names, but we can help you with that."

"Fanny might help you when things get busy, but she's really here to chat with the gentlemen. She's going to make them happy, and make sure their glasses are never empty for long, which will make me happy too. Isn't that nice? And she'll keep an eye on the book as well, because tomorrow she's going to enter everything into the members' accounts. So it will be her pulling your hair if she can't read your scribbles. Be told!

"I'm going to run along, Fanny. Get them to show you which bottle is which, because I don't want you selling brandy at the price of claret. They'll take care of you."

Fanny took a deep breath and asked, "Right, what do you want me to do? How can I help?"

Their first guests caught Fanny by surprise. Suddenly there were male voices in the hallway and two well-dressed men came in. Nodding to the girls without stopping their conversation, they went straight to the seats by the fire.

"They'll have port," whispered Sally. She took a bottle from the shelf and carefully filled two glasses. "Then we write it down, one for Lord Cardwell, one for Sir Alfred. See? And that's it. Do you want to carry it over for them?"

Fanny took the tray over to the men, realising on the way she had not asked which one was the lord. Would it matter? Would he mind if he was not served first?

They did not seem to notice, but they did notice her. "Are you new, young lady?"

"Yes, Sir. And here you are, the first two glasses I've ever served."

The men seemed to be taking an interest in her. "Not a London girl, I believe?"

"No, Sir, I'm a country girl. From Suffolk."

"Well, you don't talk like a country girl. What's Rosie doing hiring a lady to serve drinks? You're not dressed for it."

"I also take care of the books, Sir. I dare say I will amend my dress as we go along."

"Oh dear, forgive me, Miss – what's your name? I had no intention of commenting, none at all. Most impolite of me."

"You may call me Fanny, Sir. And I shall follow your advice. This is not the dress for such a fine place."

To her surprise, she was trembling as she walked back to the others. They were staring at her. "Oooh, you talk just like they do," said Gwen. "I expect you went to a proper school, didn't you?"

"No, I had a governess-" and she realised she had said too much.

Sally pounced on her admission. "A governess? Bridget said you was quality. What are you doing here?"

"Never you mind," said Gwen. "Bridget said it was private. You leave her alone."

Fanny had to say something. Whatever she admitted to would probably be better than what the girls could imagine and share with their friends downstairs. "Oh, it wasn't anything much. I was just fed up with the country, so I came to London. Life's better here."

Sally agreed. "Yes. You're right, as long as you've a decent mistress, and there's not many as good as Rosie."

Debb,

You know what? I think I will stop here and let you introduce the working girls and paint a picture of distinguished gentlemen having fun with half-naked nymphs sitting on their laps. I had a similar situation in my The

Prince and the Nun *and found I had to forget about what the girls did with their clients and just concentrate on conversations between them. They're all simply people having fun and we want the club to be a fun, friendly place. Another reason for stopping now was I did not know exactly how to dress Sally and Gwen. They are (I think) trainees waiting for a chance to move to the upper floor, so I wanted them to tease the men, and be teased in return. They are already dressed in very short skirts, so having one of them sitting on your lap (my lap, anyway) would be a lot of fun. I had also imagined that, under their pinafores, they have a dramatic décolletage. Why? Because later in the evening when the party heats up, they can lose their pinafores and easily put their boobs on display.*

But that's terrible! Well, not really. Men do love boobs to distraction. They are so beautiful and such wonderful playthings, so the more men see of them, the happier they are. I sense that modern women would criticise this behaviour and I have two answers. Firstly, we are talking about the 18th century when men were nowhere near as sensitive and caring (or possibly hen-pecked) as they are today. And secondly, that's the way we are. It's universal and any story that pretends otherwise might be politically correct, but it will not be real. But I shall leave these matters in your hands. All four of them, in the case of Sally and Gwen.

I have been imagining Fanny will meet, in passing, Sir Francis. But another man needs to take her under his wing. A friendly older man who cares for Fanny and her sharp intelligence. Perhaps he could have dinner (and Spotted Dick) with her in a drawing room near her bedroom. He doesn't try to make love – perhaps he is past it? He does enjoy the finer things in life – perhaps they bring back memories – so he (I) would like to see Bridget serving the dinner, dressed in her new serving girl uniform, without the pinafore, of course.

The man (Lord Who?) will have to prepare Fanny to play a starring role at the Hellfire Club. It's a funny thing, but being on stage permits shy women to dress in ways, and do things, that they would never contemplate in real life. That might be a way in. Also the man could assure her that she can always stop if she feels uncomfortable – which might be fine over dinner in London but would be very different when you are spreadeagled over the altar under Medmenham Abbey.

So I think that's your task, to make us comfortable with the club, and cosset and care for Fanny until she is ready to experience the Hellfire Club (I'm sure Bridget and Lord Who? will help you...)

Simon

Hi Simon,

Well, that was fun. I want to visit your gentlemen's club, if to do nothing more than visit the library and today is the perfect day to do just that. You see, the weather and whether it be hot or cold, is the topic of the past week down this way. First. we had a week long heatwave with horrid 30+ days and a southern right whale frolicking in the bay (that was pretty special), and now we have torrential rain with 40mm of snow through the highlands. Hello, Mother Nature! It is summer time and that means no-snow time.

I learnt a poem when I was in grade three, and the second verse has stuck in my brain ever since, about this amazing country of ours, however, I'm not sure when Dorothea MacKellar was writing My Country *she thought to include Tasmania in her observations. Perhaps it was because the first draft was written in England that she forgot about my wee island altogether. She was certainly right about Australia being "A wilful, lavish land."*

This inclement weather makes my mind restless though, unless I have a log fire to curl up in front of, which sadly I don't. So, it's a day for wonderings. You'll have to excuse my prolific use of the word below, it's going to happen a lot!

Here goes…

Do you ever wonder if a writer's work should reflect the social conscience of the day? Even as fluid as that can be.

I don't, because I think a person's mindset changes often. I know mine does. It's not that I'm fickle and go with the flow, I don't tend to follow the social conscience or trends. I do like to be aware of them though. The opinions I have expressed whilst writing reflect me at the time of writing, will they be the same once published? Who can say? Generally, my opinions change the more educated or aware I become on a certain matter.

But given the whole #metoo movement and the growing number of 'rich and powerful' men whose offensive behaviour is being exposed, and by proxy, putting all men under the microscope, I wonder if you, as a male author, adjust the way you would normally write to conform with the current mood. Do you now consciously write so as not to offend? Has it become harder for a man to write about sex and a woman's sexuality?

I don't believe there's ever been a time in history where human behaviour, particularly male behaviour, has been so publicly scrutinised on a global scale. I also wonder if it is fair. Not all males are offensive, yet it seems only too easy for them to be all herded together into the one pig sty!

And it's not just the male authors who are affected.

A few years ago I attended a seminar in which a female author spoke of her need to rewrite a scene because she was unsure of how it would be accepted.

Initially the author wrote a scene in which a man grabbed a woman by the arm in a heated argument, spun her around and then kissed her. She was willing, so was he. Argument ends and they both have sex. Win. Win. For me there was no problem but the author rewrote the physical contact of him grabbing her arm, in case it was viewed as abuse. Perhaps the key is understanding what a character's normal is and conveying that to the readers. Consent is everything after all.

I was recently watching a well-known UK talk show on which American Adam Sandler repeatedly touches the thigh of Claire Foy, clearly making her uncomfortable to the point where she halts his hand with her own and then subconsciously feels the top half of her clothing presumably to ensure it's in place. He seemed oblivious to her discomfort and there was an awkward laughter from those around. See for yourself here; https://youtu.be/5zbiwNxX1wc

You know, I will never understand a (semi?) stranger touching another person in this way. I don't believe they had met beforehand. Whilst I can be all hugs and kisses and touchy-feely with people I know, there is no way in hell I would touch an unfamiliar person in the same way as Adam did Claire. Whilst the incident above appeared quite innocent, to date there is no record of Adam Sandler ever being a sexual fiend/predator etc., and criticism of the incident saw it being labelled and accepted as a "friendly gesture." I wonder if it made him more personally aware of the big issue facing his industry at the moment.

Is this how predatory behaviour starts, though? Just a quick fondle here and there to see what one can get away with? Is it in those first few seconds a predatory person gauges how another reacts to them and then that dictates how much he/she can victimise that person? Possibly.

Sadly, and unfortunately, I think the whole 'Weinstein movement' will be all but forgotten in two years' time. I personally hope not, but if history shows us anything, it's that people will just get on with their lives after the rich and powerful have laid a pathway of misery for them to tread upon. What other choice do they have?

By the way, did you know that the #metoo movement is now over 10 years old? A chap on twitter advised me of this and that it initially started as a response to a campus rape in America. I wonder if it has assisted in the decline of assaults. Something to research.

I do wonder how much of this whole sordid situation has made the average person on the street stop and think about how their own behaviour may be perceived. Both male and female. I already know of men who are wary of how their friendliness might be conveyed. And then there's the age-old story of women being friendly only to be labelled a dick-tease because she smiles and is polite. I get that we all dress up to attract the prince/princess, but sometimes we attract the toad/toadette instead. Do we naturally reject the attention of someone we consciously find unsuitable and then deem them creepy? Are our wants and needs in a mate dictated by the social conscience? Who knows?

And does that mean we are a society of people who are categorised as either attractive/suitable, creeps or dick-teases? If beauty really is in the eye of the beholder, then we are all screwed because we are all ugly sometimes. It seems to be a no-win situation. Three cheers for human behaviour. Not!

Do you find that even when you have a strong female character who is confident and wants to explore her sexuality, she still gets labelled a slut or a whore? Mostly by women. I remember discussing Five Delights *with an acquaintance once and she wanted to know the history of abuse the female character had suffered. Now you may remember from the story this was not the case at all. However, my acquaintance refused to believe there was no horrid backstory of abuse because for her mind, a female exploring her sexuality had to be a male driven thing. Yeah, no.*

Whilst we can never control the way a person interprets information or a story, I think the onus is on us as writers to convey clearly what a character's normal is, especially in a storyline that may challenge readers. In the case of the male character grabbing the arm of the female, kissing her passionately before having fantastic make-up sex, why not? That's their normal. There was no mention of violence, just a heated argument (and we've all had them), that ended the moment he kissed her.

We all have our own level of 'normal' in every aspect of our lives. It's not the same as the next person simply because we are not the same people.

Having said all that, yet, here we are writing a story set in a time where the rich and powerful took advantage of all those around them. Oh, I'm sure there were some good apples amongst the bad. Or were they just nicer in their approach to get what they wanted? Did girls like Sally and Gwen enjoy their work?

Now whilst you ponder my wonder, I shall consider how to get Fanny out of that nanny frock.

Debb.

P.S. I have taken the liberty of numbering our pages. There was an incident the other day with a coffee in one hand and this manuscript in the other, and bumble-footed feet, and the fact that coffee will never be sacrificed, and pages fluttering to the ground can look quite pretty in their freefall.

Debb,

Interesting. I have never had power over women in an office, and if I had, I hope I would have encouraged rather than groped them. I am pleased the logjam seems to have broken at last and hope women will feel free to protest instantly in future. The only way to get harassment under control is for the groper to face consequences.

I hope you are not one of those people who dislikes cats or is allergic to them; I'm not sure I'd forgive you. When a normal person (like me!) is near a cat, we naturally want to stroke it. Men easily relapse into that feeling when they are comfortable with an attractive and friendly woman. Of course, we keep our hands in our pockets to avoid being scratched, but the feeling is there just the same.

The reason for my apparent diffidence with Sally, Gwen and the ones to come is that we are writing for an audience that includes male and female, and I would like to appeal to both. That's why I ask you – someone who specialises in being female – whether the average reader will put aside their personal history and enjoy the picture of Sally and Gwen enjoying serving port to randy old men with, and here's the touchy part, their boobs on display.

I am not worried about the morals of the time, even the morals of today. I am bothered that you, as the personification of everything modern and female, will be repelled by how much I enjoy the idea. I wouldn't force Sally and Gwen to pander to my voyeurism, but I'd certainly encourage them with large tips and a present at Christmas time. You see, I do love boobs and I think you'll find I'm not alone in that. Nice to see, even better to play with, boobs are just so female. I'm not even picky about size or shape or colour – they're all wonderful. So if you can write Sally and Gwen feeling pleased to be admired, that is just great!

Being happy, that's the whole point. I get the impression that Mrs Palm's girls are smarter than most, and well cared for. They are not faced with the choice of sex or destitution, as many of the street girls would have been. If they play their cards right, they may end up being kept by a rich lover. Or even getting married – it did happen. They work with a will, and the gentlemen appreciate them. We want a happy club!

So, looking forward to your imaginings of our Gentlemen's Club with its happy, compliant waitresses.

Regards,
Simon
P.S. Am I allowed to pat their bums too?

Hi Simon,

Honey, you can pat as many bums as you want, and boobs too, if they'll let you, and I think our girls will. Actually, I know they will. Gwen, Sally and the other girls at the club are smart. They are exactly where they want to be. And who wouldn't? It sounds like a great place to be.

I enjoyed the enchanting story that is The Prince and the Nun. *What would have been, and possibly still is, a horrible practice in the days of war, was written in such a way it allowed me to suspend all knowledge of reality and float along in the relative comfort of the story. I have read up to chapter 36 before I had to put it down to write my next piece here. I'm looking forward to seeing what becomes of the* Prince and the Nun. *I'm thinking happy ever after but you just never know.*

I have forwarded our timeline by many weeks. This allowed for Fanny to experience her new role long enough for me to take her further down the path of naughtiness. I did and it was fun. Although I did find I had to be more conscious of the time period in which our story is set. I had written about dimming the lights and then wondered when dimmer switches were invented before remembering that electricity did not exist in London until the late 1800s, even though a chap by the name of Humphry Davy did invent an arc lamp in 1806, but the light was blinding and the power required could not be sustained beyond a few minutes.

So how to dim a room full of candles? Well that's quite easy, you snuff the majority of them out of course and place a dimming screen in front of the fire. I have no idea if a 'dimming screen' was ever a thing, my imagination conjured up a large black, solid screen with just enough holes in it to allow light through. Works for me.

And then there were the furnishings. What style of back would the dining room chairs have? Wow, so many to choose from. I went with Anthemion because the style reminded me of a peacock expanding his feathers to attract a mate. A bit like some of the gentleman of the club.

I do believe our girl Fanny is thriving in her new environment. Even the discovery of hair removal didn't traumatise her too much.

See for yourself.

Debb

Chapter Eight ~ A Decadent Life

*The new Fanny ~ Gwen and Sally, new friends
~ Bridget the hot wax torturer ~ a secret pleasure
~ a very special night at the club ~ shocking behaviour
in high society ~ a virginal forest imp*

Fanny stood in front of the mirror intently studying the changes in her body. It had now been four weeks since she had taken the position of hostess at the gentlemen's club. The late morning sunlight filtered through her windows, warming her back as she gazed at herself in the mirror and the thin shift that she was wearing. She smiled. The past weeks had created a change in her, and all for the better. The rich foods from the kitchen had transformed her girlish body into that of a woman, with a womanly figure. "A plump peach," one of the Lords had remarked yesterday as he pinched her bottom.

Her skin did indeed have a flush to it and her smile was almost a permanent fixture upon her face now. She looked down to where her shift gaped at her breasts and, encouraged by her new found confidence, she threw it off, freely allowing it to pool at her feet, and stood proudly naked.

Cupping her breasts with both hands, she liked feeling the weighty fullness of them. Another welcomed change. Ruby coloured nipples came to life and she began to squeeze the buds between her finger and thumb, enjoying the subtle pain she caused. Closing her eyes, she focused on the other fingers as they stroked across the soft underside of her breasts and mused about her new life.

Initially, it had taken her a while to settle into the odd hours that the household kept. She certainly was not used to late nights and sleeping-in until noon-time. At first she tried to continue to rise early, only to find herself falling asleep on the ledgers mid-morning. It wasn't until Rosie had pointed out the errors Fanny had been making that she decided to embrace the schedule of the house. Bookwork was now done in the mid-afternoon, or at night if she had a quiet period in the club. Which wasn't very often.

Her hands fell to the soft, roundness of her belly and then splayed out over the narrowness of her waist before coming to rest on the lush flair of her hips. Contented eyes tracked from head to toe and back again, stopping to inspect each new change of her body.

Her friendship with Gwen and Sally had been most welcome. Never in her life had Fanny expected to meet two women who discussed their bodies so freely. They laughed as they shocked Fanny with stories about the club members, and if she were honest, she really enjoyed discovering how they managed to manoeuvre the men as if they were small boys.

Surprisingly, Gwen and Sally enjoyed their life at the club. They were smart too, knowing exactly how to get the best from each member. "It's about keeping their secrets and giving them what their wives won't," Gwen had confided with a wink.

The men of the club were as varied as a field of wild flowers in the spring. Some just wanted conversation and Fanny spent many evenings talking until her jaw hurt. Others wanted a pretty girl to sit on their lap whilst they discussed business amongst their friends. The more adventurous ones were quick to let their needs be known and even quicker to go upstairs with their favourite girl.

Sally had told her about an older gentleman who had quite the reputation amongst his peers as being a man with an insatiable lust for women. She soon discovered that all he wanted was for her to dine with him, and his male lover who always discreetly made his way into the room through a side door. Once she had understood, Sally would leave the men alone together without anyone being the wiser. It was a lesson for Fanny that things were not always what they seemed.

Fanny's gaze lowered to the newly acquired nakedness between her legs. The redness had gone a few days ago and now she was left with baby-smooth skin. She closed her eyes and remembered grabbing hold of the small cushion that Bridget had left beside her, placing it firmly over her face. Bridget was right, it did muffle her scream.

"Oh, whose idea was this?" She had grumbled to herself knowing that it was hers. She couldn't blame anyone else for her curiosity.

Her body had tensed as she felt Bridget firmly placing her hand on her thigh, holding her down. Her maid muttering about not moving was no help at all. Fanny held her breath and as soon as she felt the candle wax start to lift, she screamed for the fourth time in as many minutes. Tears spilled from the side of her eyes. The pain alone was the sole reason Fanny was certain none of the society ladies she knew would ever do this.

Listening to Bridget's calming instructions, Fanny bent both her legs, bringing her heels close to her bottom and parted her knees as wide as she could. Cool air soothed the partly hairless skin.

'Now, Miss, this part, 'tis delicate. I need you to hold still as I put the wax in there."

Fanny felt Bridget part her lips and carefully apply the warm wax to the most intimate part of her body. Her heart raced and sweat beaded on her forehead as she squeezed her eyes shut.

"Tis the hardest part, Miss. All those little hairs hiding away in there. If ye move, the hair is missed, we have to do it again, and you don't want that," Bridget scowled politely.

Sally's encouragement from the day before echoed in Fanny's mind, "The men like it smooth. They've got their own whiskers, don't need us girls having 'em too. Don't mind the pain, you get used to it, and it's all forgotten for the next time."

Now Fanny wouldn't describe herself as a delicate woman, she was far too practical for that. Her childhood had been spent outdoors, climbing trees, and helping with chores in the yard - much to her uncle's disdain. As such an active child she had had more than her fair share of grazed knees and the occasional bloodied nose, so she believed she had good tolerance of pain. But this pain was something she had never experienced before, or cared to again.

"Stop moving, Miss!" Bridget scolded.

Fanny covered her face once again, ignoring the sick feeling in her stomach. As she felt Bridget's nimble fingers test the edge of the wax, she screamed into the cushion. Bridget was right, the inner part of her lips hurt more than the rest.

"All done, Miss," Bridget advised as quick fingers searched for wayward hairs. The damp cloth she placed on Fanny cooled her skin and her tensed leg muscle began to relax from clenching against the pain.

"Have you done this, Bridget?" Fanny asked suddenly, curious about her maid's efficiency.

"Yes, Miss, back when we first arrived, I overheard the maids talking. It hurt really badly the first time, I almost passed out."

Fanny sat up, staring at her maid. Why would someone do this more than once? "First time, Bridget? What do you mean the first time? How many times does it have to be done?"

"It depends on the hair, Miss. Some girls' hair grows really fast, some slow."

"And you?"

"Three times, Miss. Each time the hair is less, as is the pain. The cool cloths work just fine and one of the girls gave me some balm to stop the rash. I have some for you after your bath. Come along, Miss." Bridget had moved Fanny into the tub with the efficient ease that only a long-serving maid could have.

Fanny looked into the mirror once again. Sally had convinced her that the gentlemen liked all the girls that way, but at the time she wasn't sure. She almost fainted at the small spots of blood she had seen when sneaking a look. It wasn't until Fanny lingered in the cool bath afterward did she feel much needed relief and the pain soon eased.

And now as she stood unabashedly studying herself in the mirror, that memory was all but forgotten. Fanny's awareness of her body had become an ever present companion in her mind. Especially when her undergarments would rub against her skin. Her body felt alive.

She slid her hands 'down there', or as Gwen liked to call it, her pussy. Her fingertips glided over her outer lips, enjoying the soft, fullness of them. Since being at the house she had explored her body in front of the mirror many times and enjoyed learning how she liked to be touched.

Positioning herself sitting-up on the edge of the bed, Fanny spread her legs wide and looked at herself in the large, standing mirror. It was an unusual sight for her to be hairless. The smooth, plump lips between her thighs were almost translucent and with the sunlight shining brightly on her, she could make out the faint scar on her hip from falling out of a tree as a child. She did like her body hairless though. What had started as need for cleanliness, leading her to remove her leg and underarm hair, turned into a deep curiosity as she continued to discover her womanly needs.

Her fingers tracked back and forth over her closed lips creating a ticklish sensation along her moist seam, and making her breath quicken. She cupped her hand over the pale mound, filling it completely, and then rocked gently against the heel of her palm, raising her hips to increase the pressure. She really liked this and spent time testing the rocking speed and height of her hips so she could learn how to achieve the best pressure.

Dampness seeped through the slit of her now swollen lips and she used her finger to dip inside. The moisture glistened in the sunlight, and not for the first time did she taste herself. She tasted of a warm musk. Savoury and sweet just like cook's apple pie.

Parting her lips with her other hand, Fanny watched herself stroke the length of her pussy. Somehow watching herself made her even more excited. She paused occasionally to gently bob her finger inside her body, gathering the wetness, before sliding it up to that little nub that made her jolt whenever she touched it.

An illicit thrill ran through her body. It was like her own little secret, yet it wasn't a secret at all. From her many conversations she had had since coming to work at Miss Rosie's, she knew all the girls had their own secret spot.

Raising her hand to her mouth she flicked the tip of her finger repeatedly with her tongue, before taking in its full length, wondering how a cock would feel inside her mouth. Her knuckles rested on her chin as she pushed down upon her tongue, breathing through her nose, resisting the gag reflex at the back of her throat.

"Better to practise than be sick in a Lords' lap," Sally had said, laughing hard at the astonished gasp Fanny had almost choked upon.

"But why would you do that?" Fanny's eyes were the size of a dish. She had seen and heard many things in the farmyard but never that.

"Lots of reasons," Sally began, without humour this time. With her slender pointing finger pressing against the fingers on her other hand she counted out the reasons, "The men like it. It's quick and clean. No chance of a babe this way. The ladies like it too."

"What!" Fanny stammered, causing the humour to dance in Sally's eyes once again.

"Aye, you'll see. Next time you give yourself some special attention, imagine it is a tongue. Don't matter if it's a lady or man, the result is the same. Although the ladies' lips are far softer."

With Sally's shocking admission fresh in her mind, Fanny lifted her legs, resting her feet on the ornate side-hinges of the mirror. She moistened the tip of her finger, this time pushing it all the way inside of her body before sliding it slowly along her slit, and up to her nub.

Resting her other hand on the top of her mound, she spread her plump outer lips wide with two fingers. The dark pink of her inner lips shined with her arousal. With slow movements, Fanny circled the tender flesh around her nub, careful not to touch it. Around and around she moved this way and that, avoiding a rhythm that would bring about her release quicker than she wanted.

Her breath quickened, blowing down over her chest as she watched her nipples harden between her thighs through the reflection in the mirror. They stood proud, high above the fullness of her breasts, as if they had been suckled by the invisible lover in her mind. Normally a dusky colour, they were now a deep pink as they gorged on the arousal of her body. Tiny buds tightened her areolae, making them small and hard and aching for her release.

Raising her finger, Fanny paused just above the nub of her clit. Closing her eyes, she imagined the tip of a tongue and began to flick back and forth over the sensitive flesh with the tip of her nail, gently at first, and then harder and harder until wicked splinters of desire made her nub ache. Using the mirror for support, she arched her back, welcoming the onslaught. A frustrated groan fell from her lips as the pleasure turned to pain and she became more tender than aroused.

Her whole body started to ache as the wetness between her thighs heated. Needing something more, Fanny, lowered her shaking legs and stood in front of the mirror, slipping her fingers into her body. She bent forward onto the glass, watching her breasts as they swayed heavily back and forth. Her nipples were the hardest they had ever been. Another sigh fell from her as she rocked against the finger circling her nub and the other two that were deep inside of her.

As her panting fogged the mirror, she began to feel a sensation she had only briefly felt the night in the carriage with Rob, but this was so much more. Her body was heavy and tense. The faster she moved her fingers, the tighter her pussy clenched, and the harder her breasts rocked, slapping her nipples against the mirror. Whimpers filled the room and suddenly she didn't care if anyone overheard her. She needed this to happen. As her hips sped to a quick rhythm, she leaned into the large mirror, not even caring if it fell over. The cold against her nipples made her gasp and she bucked desperately against her fingers, thrusting hard until she reached her peak and tumbled over the edge amidst her loud, ecstatic whimpers.

Exhausted from her release, Fanny lowered her shaking body to the rug, curling into a sated ball of ever-increasing womanhood and closed her eyes.

Bang. Bang. Bang.

"Wake up, Fanny! Tonight is the night!" A muffled voice yelled from the other side of her bedroom door.

Fanny startled awake from her position on the floor. How long had she been asleep? She quickly grabbed her robe and made her way to the door. Standing on the other side were Sally and Gwen, both had their hair piled high on top of their heads, elaborately styled with ringlets and already dressed for tonight's event. Gwen was wearing a robe made of red silk with an oriental bird pattern decorating the lapels and the cuffs of the open sleeves. It was belted loosely at the waist and Fanny could tell easily that Gwen was naked underneath. Her mask was made from white feathers that flared around the side of her face. Sally's outfit was a little more demure, but not by much.

"Do you like me apron, Fanny? I sewed it myself just for tonight."

Fanny smiled as Sally turned round. Where there should have been a bow tied neatly at the small of her back was a very large double bow that covered up her pert bottom. The bib of the apron had enough material to cover her large breasts completely and the skirt fell to just above her knees. All around the edges were rows of stitched flowers that must have taken months to complete. She wore a matching headpiece with the same delicate flowers on it.

"Yes, Sally. I like it very much. You have wonderful skill with the needle. You both look very handsome."

"Why aren't you ready? Guests will start to arrive soon," Sally asked urgently.

Fanny checked her window as they walked into her room looking for an indication as to how late in the day it was. The sun was now low in the sky. "Tell me again what to expect."

Gwen smile was wide and Fanny could not help but smile too. "Tonight is all about the wives of the club members. There are many…"

"Last time we had about twenty wives," Sally interrupted thoughtfully, resting her head against the pillows.

"Yes," Gwen agreed. "There's many who like to behave as the men do. They come to the club and drink and discuss the latest gossip, but it's all a secret, you see. Their friends in society would never speak to them again if they knew what they did, especially on nights like tonight."

"What is so different about tonight?" Fanny asked, surely drinking at their husband's club couldn't be all that scandalous?

"Why, tonight is the best night of all," Sally begun, rubbing her hands together with glee. "Tonight they come dressed in the barest of clothing, wearing elaborate masks, some even make special trips to France for something to wear! Oh, they might look all prim and proper when they arrive but once their cloaks come off, it's a feast for the eyes. And they don't mind you looking. When they're here like this, they are nice as cooks's pie."

"Last time, one even asked me to go with her husband while she watched." Gwen interrupted, nodding to herself.

"You should see the look on your face, Fanny. The shock!" Sally smiled as Gwen began to giggle uncontrollably. "Make no mistake, some of these ladies of society, your ladies, like to have the same fun the men have. Some even share lovers. Just you wait and see."

Fanny's brows raised in disbelief at the amused women in front of her. When would she stop being shocked by what they told her? Sure, she had heard many stories since she had been in London, many from her time at the Bull and Mouth, but she thought they were just that, stories. Now she knew different.

"Why should the men get to have all the fun?" Gwen interrupted her thoughts, speaking exactly what Fanny was now thinking.

"They shouldn't. Not at all," she agreed passionately.

Fanny walked into the club room, surprised by the changes that had been made for the masquerade party tonight. The brown velvet winged chairs that once sat in a formal fashion were now grouped intimately in twos and threes around the room. In the far corner a small space had been cleared for the musicians. On the right-hand side of the room there were two rows of Chippendale dining chairs with red leather seats. They lined the wall with a small table placed in between every two, and a matching chaise divided the rows.

Sally looked up from her perch on old Lord William's lap and winked. The bib of her apron had been untied and her breasts hung freely, making it all too easy for the Lord to lick up the whisky that he had poured over her nipples. As he suckled, Sally laughed loudly and tipped her head back, resting it on the shoulder of the club member behind her. This allowed time for the Lord, who moved spritely for a man of his age, to tip whisky over her throat before lapping it up with long strokes of his tongue. Still laughing, Sally sat up and looked down at the wet stains upon the apron she had spent many hours sewing, feigning annoyance as she gently swatted Lord William's hands away.

A quick whisper in her ear and Sally was soon standing in front of him, she turned, slowly untying the bows at her back and exposing her plump bottom for all to see. Lord Williams, now sitting on the very edge of his seat, motioned with his fingers for her to turn around. With the subtleness of a dancer and holding her apron as a screen, Sally swayed her hips slowly as she turned several times, knowing it was exactly what the Lord liked. She had been his favourite club girl since arriving three years ago. His hand grabbed her wrist, halting her in front of him, her breasts level with his eyes as he reached to slide the apron's skirt down her thighs. Sally loosened her grip, enjoying the look of longing that passed on Lord Williams' face as her sex was revealed. With deft fingers he parted her lips, smiling proudly at their moistness, and slid a finger into the warmth, feeling for her nub.

Fanny was sure she could hear her own heart thumping in the quietness of the room. Everyone in the club was captivated by what Sally and her Lord were doing. With a nod from Lord Williams', two other members walked to Sally's side, each taking hold of one arm to support her as her foot was lifted and placed on his thigh, opening her legs wide for him. As he stared up into Sally's eyes, his mouth cocked to one side in a half smile. The Lord moved his hand faster between Sally's thighs, a short while later her head lolled to the side and Fanny could hear her whimper her final release.

Murmurs of approval uttered around the club as she watched Sally climb back onto Lord William's lap, contentment brightening her face. Smiling freely, she accepted a glass of whiskey and made eye contact with Fanny, raising her glass in a silent toast.

As Fanny continued to search the room, she noticed a stylish modern bed had been moved into the club. It had been placed strategically near one of the fires so that the flames would illuminate the goings-on around the games that would be played. The four dark posts were draped in a sheer fabric that might close the sides of the bed, allowing a small measure of privacy should anyone want it. After hearing all the stories about the last party the club had had, Fanny felt for sure that the curtains were for decoration only. She was fast learning that seeing and hearing lovers in the act was all part of the excitement. The first time Fanny had overheard one of the girls having sex she was shocked. All too soon that shock turned into arousal, making Fanny moist. Oh, how far she had come from her days at the priory!

As she looked further around the room, she saw a few members with their wives. Sally was right about the way they would be dressed. Gwen was preparing drinks at the serving table, a few of the other girls were walking around serving elaborate finger sized food that cook had created especially for tonight. And although it was early, she guessed that one or two members were being served privately in the back rooms.

"Well, here she is. Thought we'd have to come and find you."

Rosie smiled as she walked towards Fanny. How delightful she looked tonight. Her greying hair was arranged in tight, shoulder-length curls covered by a black and gold, ornate tricorne hat. She wore a matching riding jacket that flared at her hips. Her gold brocade and black velvet style would normally be masculine, but Miss Rosie kept her outfit feminine by leaving the top buttons open, exposing her large breasts bursting from the red lace of her silk shift. The red of the lace matched perfectly with the colour on her smiling lips.

Two gold buttons cinched the jacket favourably across the softness of her stomach and opened again over her hips, showing the remainder of her shift that barely covered her sex. Lush thighs were covered in sheer hose and were held in place by black suspenders that disappeared under her shift. Small booted heels accentuated her stoutness and an ornate red and gold eye mask rested on the bar in front of her. It was styled in a similar fashion to eye glasses, with arms that tucked behind the ears, making it easy for her to de-mask. The narrowness of the mask would highlight the paleness of Miss Rosie's blue eyes, while the elongated roundness would give her eyes a feline shape. Fanny had never seen her look more beautiful.

"Are you feeling unwell, my dear?" Rosie continued, with the arch of one brow. "Nervous perhaps?"

"Oh, no, Miss. I am well and only a little nervous."

"Well. That's to be expected, child. Now turn around and let me see you in that dress."

Fanny twirled with enough speed to allow her skirt to billow gently. The dress had been a gift from Rosie. It was white and made her glow in the dimly lit room. And although it covered Fanny from shoulders to toes, there was certainly nothing demure about the style of the dress.

The bodice was made of fine Italian lace and lifted her breasts overly high. Wide strips of lace capped her shoulders and made way for the plunging curve of the back, exposing her skin almost to her bottom. Around her waist, the lace flared out in petals resting upon the white silk skirt. The fullness of the skirt was eased by the long slit up the front that flowed open when Fanny walked, allowing anyone to peek at her legs.

Her half-face mask was silver with small pearls circling her eyes. Her hair had been set in curls and left to hang freely, allowing for the mask to be tied neatly at the back of her head with velvet ties. Fanny felt sexy and confident all the way down to her bare toes.

"Well, don't you look just like a virginal, forest imp? Spritely and full of life. You'll be very popular tonight indeed. I even have a very special club member for you to meet."

Fanny glowed under the praise from Rosie and walked proudly as she carried trays of glasses to the members. How strange it was that other peoples' kind words had come to mean so much to her.

Laughter drew her attention to a small group of people sharing a joke. The whole room had a relaxed, jovial feel to it tonight. The members' easy smiles nestled amongst the warmth from the fires and the heavy cigar smoke that drifted high in the ceiling. As she looked about the club, she saw that quite a few of the members and their wives had now arrived. There were a few mistresses as well. They were easy to spot as they were usually much younger than the member they accompanied and were often introduced as a niece or cousin. Costumes and masks of every colour and style livened up the room. To her delight, she noticed all of the women wore far less clothing than usual; their voluptuous bodies were covered in lingerie that had a distinctively French or Italian feel to it. A lot of the men were partially naked too. It was such a feast for the eyes.

One woman wore white stockings tied at the thigh with a pink ribbon and matching white and pink striped silk corset cut so low it exposed the top of her nipples to everyone. With her dark hair piled high on her head, a black lace mask and a single string of pearls at her throat and a cunny that was clearly bare, she captured the

120

attention of everyone in the room.

Her husband, Lord Something-Something – Fanny had served him when they first arrived but she couldn't remember his name - stood at her side, bare chest puffed out, proud as a peacock. His face was now covered in a scary, bird-like mask and he wore his black breeches with the laces untied to expose the hair low on his abdomen.

The snuffing of many candles and the dimming screen placed in front of one of the fires indicated that a few hours had now passed with Fanny busy serving drinks. The near darkness of the room was the unspoken signal that the fun could begin. It wasn't too long before Fanny heard the sounds of passion coming from a darkened corner beside the stage. As she turned her attention towards the noise, she had to squint against the darkness and could barely make out the shape of a person's bottom.

From the corner of her eye, she could see a candle passing through the room and coming to rest on a shelf behind the naked lovers in the corner. Fanny's eyes widened as she watched the woman, straddled upon her lover's thighs, raise her breasts for him to feast upon, which he did with great delight. Mesmerised, Fanny watched as the woman reached out to grab the wings of the chair, using it as leverage to make her hips rise and fall against the man she was riding.

"She's a beauty, isn't she?"

Startled, Fanny turned towards the man who had spoken. His voice had been so husky and warm it sent a shiver down her spine.

"My wife, she's beautiful, isn't she?" He asked, unable to take his eyes from the lovers in the corner.

"Oh, yes," Fanny agreed. It was the same woman she had noticed earlier tonight, only now the pink bows of her garters were untied and hanging at her ankles. The husband had also unmasked and Fanny thought he was beautiful too.

"Her name is Ella. She would like you. I will introduce you later tonight."

"I would like that, Sir." Fanny smiled, watching as the man turned his brief gaze back to the lovers.

Fanny couldn't help but watch either. Sweat glistened down the woman's back as she circled her hips against the man. His hand reached up, fisting her hair, pulling her head back as far as it would go. The other wrapped around her waist, pinning her down onto his cock. As he thrust up into her, he bit at her breast. A whine of pain fell from her lips and she scratched her nails down his arms, causing blood to seep but not fall.

Fanny let out a small gasp as pain etched across the woman's face but she couldn't look away.

"Don't worry. She likes it rough." The understanding on her husband's face was enough to reassure Fanny.

A small crowd had gathered now, men and women, all engrossed in the lovers ever-increasing sounds of sex. Their orgasm echoed noisily throughout the quietened room. Watching as the husband walked over and kissed his wife's mouth, Fanny realised their performance had made her pussy soaking wet.

"That was something, wasn't it?" Gwen said admiringly as she waited for their glasses to be refilled. "Ella is his third wife. The other two old bats died shortly after he married them. Bad hearts, both of them, it's said. Didn't do him any harm though, fattened his coffers up nicely. Ella's much younger than they were and can keep up with her husband's demands and, my girl, is he demanding," she said with a knowing wink.

"It was a right surprise when Sally told me about their dinners upstairs with his discreet lover. Did you know they share the lover?" Gwen said, as Fanny's mouth hung open in shock.

"Who? Ella and her husband?" Fanny whispered loudly.

"Sure do. Whose lap do you think Ella was riding before? The lover's! Rumour has it that she used to be a working girl in Paris and has a taste for the forbidden. Just like her husband."

Feeling the port run over her fingers, Fanny cursed, another enlightening habit she had picked up since being here. Every day she was learning something new about people and their behaviours that were kept hidden behind securely closed doors. She wondered if the lord's fellow members of parliament had any clue what he did privately.

"And what about you, Gwen? Do you like the forbidden?"

The smile that lit up Gwen's face promised Fanny the telling of a good story or two, but they were interrupted by Sally asking her to meet Miss Rosie in the dining room upstairs. Fanny licked her fingers clean, screwing her face up in distaste, handed the drinks to Gwen and rushed off.

A little breathless when she reached the top of the stairs, Fanny took a moment to check her appearance and fix her hair in her room, which was located not too far from the small dining room. The warmth of the night left her dress clinging to the dampness on her skin. The moisture gave her face a dewy look and the hurried walk up the stairs heightened the pink of her cheeks. Smoothing her hair down, she replaced her mask and made her way to the dining room, knocking quietly before entering.

"Ah, Fanny, dear. I have some people I would like you to meet. Lord Beaconsfield, Sir Francis Dashwood, may I introduce Miss Francisca Howarth?"

Fanny could feel her cheeks flame under the intense gaze of the two fully dressed men in front of her. A small eternity passed before one of them spoke. Francis Dashwood was a handsome man. Tall and very elegant looking with a dark brown wig. He took her hand to his mouth and slowly kissed her knuckles. It was more of a caress than a kiss but Fanny didn't mind at all.

She found him terribly handsome. The humour dancing at the back of his eyes told her that he would be a lot of fun. A disposition she soon discovered that most club members freely displayed when the mood took them.

"Francisca, why, you are a beautiful sight all dressed in white."

"Oh, please call me Fanny."

"Fanny, it is."

Blushing under the intensity of his gaze, Fanny turned her attention to the older, shorter gentleman and smiled kindly. Placing her free hand in his, he too brought it to his lips, although unlike Sir Francis, Lord Beaconsfield released her soon after.

"Why, you, Miss Howarth, are a truly beautiful sight for these old eyes. If I was to go blind tomorrow, your face would be the one that I would remember for always."

"You are too kind, my Lord," Fanny said with a slight curtsey and a tip of her head, joining in the playful fun of the moment. Too many compliments often left Fanny speechless and she looked towards Rosie for support.

"Now, now, gentleman. Let the poor girl go. She's not going to run away anytime soon."

Whereas Lord Beaconsfield had already released her hand with a friendly pat, Sir Francis once again brought her fingers to his lips, winking salaciously before letting Fanny go. Gwen had told Fanny that men get a look, a "come and let me have my way with you," look, she had said. And that their "mouths hitch into a crooked smile that'll make your heart beat faster and your thighs wet," and that Fanny would know it when she saw it. Well, Fanny was really sure she had just seen *the look* on Sir Francis' face.

"Fanny, dear. Sir Francis is here to invite us to a gathering. He is one of the oldest and most distinguished members of the club, and several times a year we all attend his party in High Wycombe. We spend the days and nights eating his fine food and frolicking with other guests. All of the girls will be going." Rosie said, watching Fanny closely for her response.

"I would be honoured if you can join us, Fanny. It will be the last gathering for the year and I believe I have a very important role for you to play."

Fanny beamed under Sir Francis' charming invitation. It had been a long time since she had been to a gathering and certainly never as an adult without a chaperone. At all of the balls her uncle had given, she had been a child and was treated accordingly.

"Thank you for your kind invitation, Sir Francis. I would be delighted to attend and help you with whatever role you have in mind for me."

'There you are, Sir Francis. It's all settled," Rosie exclaimed with a sharp, single clap of her hands.

"Splendid. I look forward to having you, Fanny. For now, I will leave you in the capable hands of Lord Beaconsfield. He will teach you all you need to know for now."

With a curt nod of his head, Francis and Rosie left the room, closing the door on their way out. Suddenly, Fanny became aware that she was alone with Lord Beaconsfield. The girls had discussed Fanny taking a lover many times and it was decided that when Fanny wanted to, she could, and not before.

"Don't look so worried, child. I am way too old for whatever is running through that young mind of yours at this minute. All I ask is that you join me for dinner," Lord Beaconsfield smiled as he stepped aside, allowing Fanny to see the small dining table in the far corner that had been hidden by his body.

"Of course, my lord," Fanny said, her embarrassment making it difficult to make eye contact for the time being. As Lord Beaconsfield escorted her to her seat, Fanny breathed a sigh of relief and was happy to see Bridget make her way into the room with their plates of food.

Debb,

Well, that was fun, and I don't have to feel guilty about making Fanny do things that will make readers think I'm just a crazy man who doesn't understand what women feel. I will have to read it again more carefully to get everything clear in my head. Particularly Grace – where did she come from? Did I invent her or is she one of yours?

Also, don't think you are going to get away with Anthemion for the style of the chairs. That was not popular until after the Napoleonic Wars – some 40 or 50 years after our period. I suggest you look at Thomas Chippendale who achieved the remarkable feat of becoming a master cabinet maker and a gentleman at the same time. He was also an author and so deserves your attention. He died in 1779 and would have been at the height of his powers in our period. If you don't like him, there is a less well defined style named Georgian for the first three King Georges. A term you can't use, of course, because we are in Georgian times and they didn't get that name until later. So I substituted 'modern'.

I see Rob Longshot has faded from the scene. Wasn't he in prison? Or had you arranged for him to escape already? I had better put a passing reference to him in the next chapter because we will need him later.

I'm not so sure about using Lord Wharton as Fanny's mentor either. The real Lord Wharton was a bit of a ratbag anyway, and he lost £120,000 he didn't have in the South Sea Bubble. He ended up broke and squalid – not much fun at all and so I have edited his name out of your chapter above. How about using Lord Beaconsfield as her mentor instead? We're safe enough with him as the title did not exist until Queen Victoria created it for Disraeli a century later. And the town of Beaconsfield is only 18 km away from Medmenham and the Hellfire Club.

Right, I shall sit down and start writing. I think I ought to get at least as far as Fanny's initiation into the Club,
Simon

Hello Simon,

How pedantic you are! Can't a girl just choose the style of a chair because it's what she likes to look at? Like we do with our lovers? You have to admit it has a far more ornate back than the Chippendale style. And yes, I did check him out along with the fiddle, ladder, bent wood and stick styles of chair-back designs. Do we really need to be that accurate? Can we not just enjoy the ride, or seat?

Grace is neither of ours, she was meant to be Gwen. But we could just leave her in, ta-da, new character. No, I have already gone back and re-named her. This is a side effect from writing post-migraine, my brain is fogged for days. I am finding that co-writing makes it challenging for me to keep track of the characters. Do you? Generally they live snug in my mind and develop there nicely. With this story I found I needed to rummage through the house, searching hopefully for some long forgotten index cards left over from a child's schooling, and write our characters up as if they were Grandma's secret family recipes. I also discovered an app that does the same thing, but, for me, there is something freeing in physically writing. It opens up the mind.

I politely brushed over Rob whilst Fanny was enjoying her body. I think you're right and I put him behind bars. Perhaps he fell into a ditch of hot tar, taking Art along with him? Just kidding. I'm sure he's lurking in some tavern having sex with the wenches and leaving them unfulfilled.

Now onto Hellfire!

Debb.

Chapter Nine ~ Spiced Beef and Syllabub

Shopping in Cheapside ~ the sins of Mrs Winthrop
~ reflections on sex ~ Miss Hodges' flagpole ~ the best
the India Company can provide ~ Mrs Bailey's Tea Shop
~ news of Rob Longshot ~ a revealing dinner

Fanny and Bridget made their way down Cheapside with Art as their guardian. They did not see him often now, but word sent to the Bull and Mouth was usually enough to have him knocking at the door. He approved of Fanny's new clothes. When he had first seen them, he had been shocked into silence – for a moment, at least. Then he swept off his hat and ushered them to the cab with a deep bow. He said she looked flash, a real sharp, a proper lady. He made her giggle, something she was sure a flash lady would not do. Since then, he seemed to have made an effort to tidy himself up, or perhaps that was Mrs Bones insisting that he at least washed his face before leading his charges around town.

It was good to leave Mrs Palm's for a morning, especially a clear October morning like this. Under a sun giving the last of its summer warmth, a fresh south-westerly carried away smoke from numberless chimneys and gave the jaded old town something to smile about. The girls paid no attention. Lord Beaconsfield was coming to dinner in only three days' time, and he had been discussing Fanny's clothes with Mrs Palm. Fanny did not know what they had decided, but she had been dispatched to buy five yards of the finest white cambric.

"Why white?" she asked half to herself. "I'm sure white's not a good colour for me. And why cambric? It's not an exciting fabric, after all. It's very plain. It's not as if I'm ready for a shroud yet."

"You'll look just fine, Miss," Said Bridget. "I'm sure Mrs Palm will be wanting you at your best, and she's got an eye for dressing the girls so they turn heads."

"She's got an eye for dressing the girls to turn male heads. Half the time men go around with their tongues hanging out. I suppose we should be grateful it's only their tongues, the way she lays out everything the girls have got to show. I hope she's not going to do that to me."

Bridget smiled. "I'm sure you've got more to show off than most of us, Miss, but no. Mrs Palm wants you to be all lady-like. Butter wouldn't melt in your mouth. Or anywhere else."

"Bridget! I don't mind a little respectability, although – some of the ladies the other night… I didn't know what to think or where to look. They were just doing it, right there, with everyone watching. I never thought to see something like that. Did you?"

"No, I never did, Miss. But, Miss, you know, ladies – real ladies, I mean - sometimes they just don't care. They don't care if their maids see them or not. You remember Mrs Winthrop? She didn't care. She was famous for it, because the all her girls gossip, of course. She never wore a stitch in her room, if it was warm enough. When she was getting ready in the morning, she'd just wear a thin gown, near transparent it was, with a little pink bow at the neck. No buttons, nothing, to hold it together. Unless she wrapped it around her, it just fell open and there she was. She used to have her girls take care of her too. Wax her cunny until it was as smooth as a baby's bottom. Then they'd have to rub olive oil into it and all over. And if Mr Winthrop was away, she'd make them keep rubbing until she spent. Really! They said they didn't mind because she'd have a terrible hunger on her by then and spending didn't take long. And Mrs Winthrop was as sweet as an angel afterwards."

"But that's terrible. Those poor girls – making them do something like that!"

Bridget chuckled. "I do your hair, Miss, and don't mind at all. You're certainly looking as sweet as an angel yourself now."

"Ah – but you're different. You're not just a maid. You're – um…"

"A companion? Thank you, Miss. I know you'll care for me, and I shall care for you. I'll even make you spend next time, if that's your fancy."

"Oh no. That'd be wrong. I can't believe Mrs Winthrop makes her girls do it."

"Like I said, Miss, real ladies sometimes just don't care. One time they were just finishing off with the wax when Mr Winthrop walked in, and she didn't say nothing. Just 'Hello, George. Let them finish and I've got a job for you.' Then she pulled him over and as they were rubbing in the olive oil, she was untying his breeches and pulling his thing out. As soon as they were done with the oil, she just stuck it in and sent the girls off for some warm water and a flannel.

"The girls were both hot and creamy by then, but there was nothing they could do. They came back with the warm water as quick as they could, and Mr Winthrop was still going at her. They said it was a sight to see, sliding in and out, and Mrs Winthrop shouting at him to do it faster. They stayed until the end and gave them both a quick wipe afterwards. They said it was good fun, and Mr Winthrop pinched their cheeks and gave them a crown each. They said they hurried off to the linen closet and diddled each other as hard as they could."

Fanny carried on along the pavement deep in thought. How could a lady behave so brazenly? She knew Mrs Winthrop. She saw her in church every Sunday, and one Christmas had even been carolling to her home. It was hard to imagine her enjoying her husband's services. One just did not think about normal people doing it, especially people she had looked up to when a child. She knew how babies were made, of course. You could not be around the home farm and the stables without understanding the general principles, but thinking of adults that way...

And she had never understood the pleasure of it. Horses did not seem to enjoy themselves, but when she thought back to Ladies' Night at the Club... There was no question about what the gentlemen and ladies were doing. They were enjoying themselves to exhaustion and did not care who saw them. In fact, in her own confusion she recognised that watching and being watched might add to the pleasure of it all.

Her uncle – did he behave like that? Bridget said he had taken all the maids downstairs. And Miss Hodges, of course.

"I suppose Miss Hodges likes sex too," she said out loud.

"Oh yes, Miss. She's a great one for climbing the pink flagpole. So I heard, anyway. She has your uncle lying on the table, and a girl to help her climb up and sit on his thing. They told me she rides him like trotting a horse, until he can't take no more."

"But the girls don't do that."

"No, Miss. I believe she doesn't like to share. The girls get fingered and played with, but she's the only one he spends in."

"I can't believe she lets anyone watch, even the maids."

"Oh, she gets to play the queen in front of them, and gets her cunny serviced too."

"I can't imagine doing it with an audience. Well, truly, I'm not sure I can imagine doing it at all, but having people watch me – here we are. Number 16." She looked over her shoulder to smile at Art, and climbed the stairs to the glass-paned door. It opened as they reached it and an old footman waved them into a long hall. The room was full of light, dappling down from a glass above. Counters ran the length of each sides, and behind them hung draped lengths of rich, colourful fabrics, new from the Indies. Large rolls lay on a shelf above. The girls stood in wonder, until a severe lady in a long black dress came to them. Fanny dug in her purse for Mrs Palm's letter and held it out. "For Mr Millard", she said.

The woman looked at the letter, then at Fanny, and walked off with her nose in the air. "Oh dear," said Fanny. "I think I've just been promoted to work on the top floor."

"Never you mind, Miss. What does she know? And I'm sure you'd never find our gentlemen taking an interest in a dried up old stick like her."

A middle-aged man hurried towards them. He wore a long apron over his breeches and had a measuring tape hung around his neck. "White cambric for Mrs Palm, ladies? Let's see what we can do for you…" He lifted down a roll of white fabric. "It's not like Mrs Palm to be asking for plain cambric. She's a great one for pretty chintz, and silks from India, as lovely as the day is long. But here we are – cambric. Five yards. We like Mrs Palm here at Millards. Fine lady, and always pays her bills too, which is more than some of her betters do." He was running the fabric out together with his tape measure, then produced a large pair of shears from below the counter. As he cut confidently, he asked "Is there anything else you ladies want? Ribbons for your hair? Lace from Ghent? Fine stuff, but I always say Honiton lace is as good and cheaper too. Shall I show you?"

Fanny hesitated. She wanted to look, of course, but – Mrs Palm was in charge of her clothing and she would decide. "No, Sir, although you are very kind. I'm sure Mrs Palm will send us back if she needs any trimmings." They watched as the man folded the cambric and wrapped it in brown paper. "Your cloths are very fine, Sir. So beautiful, and such colours."

"The best that the India Company can provide, Miss, the very best. We have silks fine enough for a queen, believe me."

"I believe I will have to marry a prince and let him dress me."

"He'd be a very lucky man, Miss, if you don't mind me saying so. Now, here you are. Please come back soon."

Art was sitting on the steps outside. He stood up, dusted his bum and asked, "Where to now, Miss?"

Fanny gave him a winning smile. "I think we would like some tea, Art. Do you know where we could find some?"

"Well, North's Coffee House is just round the corner in King St, but you wouldn't like that, Miss. It'd be all smoke and book-reading gents, not to mention the gin. Why don't you come along to Mrs Bailey's Tea Shop in Foster Lane? It's not far, and it'd be more your dish of tea, so to speak. Will I put your parcel in the cab, Miss?"

Mrs Bailey served her tea in a pleasantly bright room crowded with small tables and chairs. Today, she was not busy and Fanny and Bridget were ushered to a window seat. Bridget sat down without hesitation; the freedom of Mrs Palm's establishment had rubbed off on her and she no longer behaved as Fanny's servant. Or perhaps Fanny's standing in society had taken a tumble, she reflected, and Bridget felt more equal.

"Did you ever go to school, Bridget?"

"My mum sent me, Miss. For more than two years. I learned my tables, and my letters too. Although, honestly, I'm not much of a hand at writing. No call for it, really."

"Would you like to learn more? You could help me at my books."

"Perhaps I should try, Miss, but I'd never be able to do all that addition and subtraction you do. Not in a hundred years."

"I'll help you. You never know when something like that will be useful. Ah – tea. And scones."

The maid set out their tea, with scones and strawberry jam. Bridget looked at them suspiciously. "They look more like bread than proper scones."

"Yes. It's the city way of baking, I'm sure. They use baking powder. The jam looks nice but – no cream. Not like home. I suppose cream is not worth having if it's not fresh. Never mind. Perhaps we will have cream when we go to the country to see Sir Francis. What do the rest of the girls say about that?"

Bridget chewed her scone while she thought. "I believe they think we're very lucky, Miss. They say it's mostly ladies who go although sometimes a couple of the girls upstairs go along to make up the numbers."

"What do they do, exactly?"

"Honestly, I don't know. All I hear is just talk. I know Sir Francis and his friends have a sort of club at his country home, and there's a cave. Apparently, they all dress up as monks and nuns, and they have dinner."

"What? In the cave?"

"I think so, Miss. But why they need to be dressed up so, I can't imagine. I can't see Sir Francis and those ladies being very holy, can you? Lady Montagu is always there."

"Do I know her?"

"I expect you'd recognise her, Miss. She was the one accommodating two gentlemen at once at the Ladies' Night."

"Ah. Flexible then, but not holy. Who else will I know?"

"I did ask Gwen and she said most of gentlemen might go, except the old ones, of course. All the ladies you met the other night and a few more. Wives and sisters, mostly, but some gentlemen bring actresses. Even their mistresses. Apparently, the party is usually not very big. About a dozen gentlemen, the ladies, and they make up the numbers with the girls from upstairs if they have to."

Fanny tried to imagine the party, a group of randy gentlemen and wild ladies, sitting down to dinner in a cave. It did not seem reasonable, especially as she looked out on the street outside, full of people going about their ordinary lives. Art was sitting on some steps opposite, enjoying the autumn sun.

A thought struck her. "If they're having dinner in a cave and it's anything like Ladies' Night, won't they be cold? Caves are cold and damp."

"Um – you're right, Miss. Even if they were dressed up, they'd feel cold. And if they're playing around half naked…"

"I'm going to ask Mrs Palm as soon as we get back. We might have to take woolly drawers."

Bridget avoided her eye and said, "I don't think Sir Francis holds with drawers for ladies, Miss. Gwen says she heard him say they're the work of Satan himself. He said they should be avoided above all things. Said they are unnatural."

"Mmh. I'll definitely speak with Mrs Palm when we get back. I'm not freezing to death in a cave. Not for Sir Francis or anyone else."

As they left the tea house, Art stopped them. "You know Rob Longshot, Miss? You was asking about him."

A cold wave gripped her. She had not thought about him for weeks, and now Art was going to tell her how he had died. Strung up on the gallows for everyone to watch.

"He's gone, Miss. Last night sometime. They came for him this morning, and he weren't there. Gone. Clean as a whistle, good luck to him."

"What? He escaped? That's not possible."

Art smiled. "Ah, Miss, that depends on how much of that yellow tin you've got. That stuff can open any door. Anyways, he's gone and good luck to him. They'll be singing songs about him, I tell you true. If they'd managed to just string him up, we wouldn't have heard no more of him."

Gold. Fanny supposed Rob might have a fair amount of it, if he hadn't wasted it all on gin and women. He must have taken an appreciable amount from Higgins the lawyer, and goodness knows how many other coaches he had robbed. Oh, well. As Art said, good luck to him. As the cab rumbled home, she felt her purse. Rob's ring was still there, tucked into a corner. Rob. He had been so gentle with her. She had expected worse, much worse. His heavy pistol and his bulky riding cloak had frightened her and it was only when he talked that her heart slowed a little. And then he had rubbed her feet – how did he know? And he had gone from rubbing, to caressing, to pushing his way into her. She squeezed her legs together and wondered if she would ever see him again.

Mrs Palm was sitting alone in her office under the stairs. Fanny handed over her parcel and asked, "Rosie, what's going to happen? I mean, to me, when I go to Sir Francis's house."

Mrs Palm frowned. She seemed reluctant to talk. "Well, you see, it's All Hallows soon. Sir Francis and his friends, they like to dress up and celebrate. You know, have a bit of a party. Eat too much, drink too much, make some mischief. You'll enjoy it."

"Are you coming?"

"No. Not this time. Someone has to stay here and mind the club. But Lord Beaconsfield will take care of you. He's an old friend and you can trust him. He's coming to dinner on Thursday, isn't he? What are you going to give him? He likes a soup of mushrooms and cream, and roast beef, but see the cook early. And you'll need our best claret – he's very particular about his wine.

"How are you getting on with him?"

"He's a nice old man. Like a kind old uncle, really. I like him. And he's very wise about London and the government."

"Have you sat on his lap yet?"

"No. He doesn't seem to want that sort of thing. I wouldn't mind, though. He seems very gentle."

Mrs Palm chuckled. "Perhaps he's slowed down a bit. He used to be a rare one for going hunting in the forest, but that's changed. I hear he doesn't like much of a forest down there anyway. Are you taking care of yourself? It'd be a shame to upset him and besides, there was nothing like him once you'd got him all fired up. He's had me walking bandy legged before now, believe me."

That did not fit with the Lord Beaconsfield that Fanny knew. The idea of the grandfatherly old man enjoying Rosie Palm was too strange to be real. "Rosie, what exactly does he want me for? Will I be doing the same sort of job at Sir Francis' party as I do here?"

"No more questions. You can ask him yourself on Thursday, and I have to get your dress done before then, because he will surely want to see it. And Bridget too, although I'm sure I have something for her already. Run along now."

Time had dragged until Thursday. Fanny had seen the cook and, to please Bridget, had asked for Irish spiced beef. And Bridget had rejected spotted dick for pudding. "Cook is going to make you a syllabub. They make it on sack wine from Spain down here – not like home at all. Cook had never heard of making it on beer – you should have seen her face!"

"Very well, Miss Slyboots, how are you going to serve dinner? And where? My room's not big enough and I don't want Lord Beaconsfield to see my bed anyway."

"Mrs Palm says we can have her sitting room, Miss. The room at the end. It's only a few doors away from yours and right next to the stairs, so the food won't have a chance to get cold. Cook will have her girls bring up the dishes to a corner table, and I shall serve."

"I think you're looking forward to it."

"Oh yes. I like Lord Beaconsfield, and I think dinner is going to be fun."

Fun. Yes, Fanny thought, it probably will be fun with a nice old man like Lord Beaconsfield. But her new clothes would not be ready. She would have to dress as she did to work downstairs. And Bridget too, she supposed. Not that Bridget seemed to mind. She was blessed with pretty breasts and seemed to like showing them off when the members made her remove her pinafore. It shocked Fanny to think that only a few weeks ago she would never have imagined mixing with girls who displayed themselves for male delight. And she would never have tolerated a servant who showed her breasts, no matter how pretty they were. But now – now it really did not seem so important. She had yet to display her own, although the members were quick to peep down her blouse as she served their drinks. And that included Lord Beaconsfield.

"Bridget, have you heard any more about what we'll be doing with Sir Francis?"

"No, Miss. To tell you the truth, I think the girls have been told not to tell us. I do know I'm meant to be dressing up as a nun, and Mrs Palm has a lot of nun's habits here. Perhaps we all dress up as nuns. Except you, of course, because you have a special dress and it'll be white."

"All she would tell me is that we dress up and have a party. We'll have to get it out of Lord Beaconsfield."

On Thursday, Fanny waited in her room for her dinner appointment. She felt nervous. Mrs Palm had told her to dress for bed but wear a dressing gown on top. But she had insisted on jewellery and rouge as well, and Bridget had arranged her hair. Where was Bridget? Making last minute preparations for their dinner perhaps? She opened her door to look along the corridor. Mrs Palm was hurrying towards her.

"Why are you still there? Get along with you. You should be waiting to welcome him. I think I saw his carriage pulling up."

They hurried to the sitting room. Bridget and the girls had done well. The table stood in the bay window, curtains drawn against the autumn dusk. The cutlery glittered invitingly in the candlelight, and a low fire warmed the room.

"That's good,' said Mrs Palm, "Now, what are you wearing? Let's have a look at you…" She brushed a stray hair back and looked carefully at Fanny's face. She pinched her cheek, "Very well. You look exactly like an innocent cousin from the country, all fresh faced, cream and strawberries. His lordship will like that. Now stand there, and I'll go and find him."

Fanny waited, standing alone and wondering what the evening would bring. Why had dinner turned into such an occasion? There was a noise in the corridor, and Bridget opened the door for Lord Beaconsfield.

He smiled. "Good evening, my dear. You are looking delightful. Truly delightful." He took her hand to kiss and turned her so candlelight shone on her face. "I shall ask Mr Gainsborough to come and paint your portrait. Shall we sit down?"

They settled Lord Beaconsfield in an armchair by the fire, with a small circular table for his glass of Madeira. Fanny sat opposite but did not risk wine so early in the evening. She had a task that needed sharp wits.

"My Lord..." but he cut her off.

"Please, my dear, don't be so formal. Not when we're *en famille* like this. Why don't you call me Uncle Harry? Rosie does. She's always called me that."

"Ah – I might – it would be difficult. But please, Uncle Harry, tell me what we're going to do with Sir Francis. Everyone is avoiding our questions."

He chuckled and said, "Yes. We told them to keep you in the dark."

Fanny waited but Lord Beaconsfield did no more than grin at her. "They've told Bridget she'll be dressing as a nun. Is that right? And what am I going to wear? Mrs Palm sent me to buy white cambric."

"I suppose I'll have to tell you something, or the pair of you will burst from curiosity. Have you heard of the Hellfire Club? No? Ah, well. It goes like this. Sir Francis has an abbey. Not a working one, of course. They'd hardly let him in, the old sinner. It used to be an abbey until King Henry dissolved it. Now, it's just a country house. Comfortable, not very grand at all. Just cosy.

"Anyway, you've met Sir Francis. He's a rare man. A great talent, and he's always been a disciple of Venus. And Bacchus too, come to that. A great mind, but he has trouble keeping his breeches on. He must have furgled an army of women in his time, and he's still hungry for more. The Empress of Russia let him into her bed, so they say.

"Still, that's not the point. The thing is, we used to dine together, a whole club of us. We'd invite some fellow with an interesting tale to tell, a politician perhaps. Or a general if we could find one more intelligent than his horse, and who didn't look as if he had a broomstick up his, er, coat. We've had the odd bishop too – some of them are very odd. We had the Bishop of Antrim once, and he told us he overheard a labourer digging a ditch on his estate telling his friend *A spade or a bible would last His Grace a long time.* Just told us straight out and made a joke of it.

"I'm wandering again, aren't I? The thing is, we used to enjoy those dinners. Really enjoy them. Good food, brilliant men talking to us, enough wine to re-float the Armada. And girls? Once word had got around, we had a coterie of girls to bring our food, bring our wine, sit on our laps. Those were good times. We called ourselves The Hellfire Club because that's where we pretended to be bound. We had officers, and every dinner was presided over by the Grand Master – that was Sir Francis – or someone else if he was not present.

"But there was talk. For all that we were secret about our friends and follies, wives and sisters began to ask questions – you know how it is. There's nothing so destructive of a man's pleasure than a good woman. Her jewellery box might be firmly locked but she'll be spitting like a vixen if she hears he's been opening another lady's."

"But not Lady Montagu?"

"No, God bless her. I wish there were more like her. Most women get married and start to shrivel before your eyes. Anyway, what with the noise about us, Sir Francis decided to move our society to his abbey at Medmenham. The best thing that could have happened to us. No prodnoses are welcome there, you can be sure. Of course, the house is fine enough. Not too grand, but you'll have a dinner to remember. What really makes the abbey special is the cave underneath it. But I'm not going to tell you about that. You must wait until you get there."

"Oh! You're so mean. Someone told Bridget about a cave. That will be exciting, I suppose, but the only caves I have visited are cold. We'll have to wear woolly drawers or we'll catch our deaths."

"Drawers? I urge you to do no such thing. If Sir Francis finds you with drawers, you'll be over his knee in no time, and he won't hold back. That's if you're lucky. If he thinks you did it out of malice, you'll be over the table and everyone will have a whack at you. You'll have a bum like a big red apple.

"Now, I'm hungry. Shall we dine? But first, you are to be the Queen of our ceremonies at the abbey, and you will not only leave your drawers behind, you will lose your gown too. Yes – of course. Don't look at me like that, my dear. You will be playing the part of

Diana, goddess of the woodlands. Now, I want you to make your old uncle proud and not behave like a simpering miss. Can you do that?"

Fanny supposed she could but…

"Very good. Can you sit in front of everyone, dressed just in the glory God gave you? Yes, that's more difficult, don't you think? So tonight, we will have a rehearsal. I want you to go to your room and come back wearing nothing. Not a stitch between your shoes and your earrings. Can you do that for me?"

Debb,
A little help here, please. The perverted old lord wants to sit at the dinner table with Fanny completely naked. Is that a good thing? Well, I mean, is that a good thing for our readers? It works very well for me and it is something I would like to encourage, especially up here in Cooktown where the climate is warm enough.
Bridget is going to sit on Beaconsfield's lap and they will wait for Fanny to re-appear, fighting her embarrassment and trying to behave as if nude is normal. Fanny will not have any sexual fun – that will wait for Medmenham. Bridget will not have any either, although I'm sure she will show off her charming breasts as she sits on Beaconsfield's lap and might even give him a quick squeeze through his breeches.
If I am on the right track, I suggest I take the girls right on as far as the statue of Venus pulling a thorn from her foot which was just outside the entrance to the Medmenham caves.
What do you think?
Simon

My dear Simon,
Only a man from Cairns would have a person sit naked at a table. Folks like myself from Tasmania, and indeed London, would be quick to think of how cold the weather was going to turn. Hence the current weather situation in Tasmania, cold mornings without frost (so far), but with a deft coolness to the breeze that would have a Queenslander, such as yourself, arrested for refusing to get off the plane.
I have no problem with our girl sitting naked at the table – as long as the fire is roaring. And Lord Beaconsfield keeps his hands to himself. For me, it seems a bit of a stretch putting Fanny onto his lap, but we have to get her ready to dive headfirst into the lusty pleasures of the skin somehow. I look forward to reading how you do this. The cad has obviously been behaving himself in Fanny's presence. Rosie seems to know a completely different

man.

It threw me for a minute reading the name Beaconsfield and not Wharton. I then reread over your justification for the name change. I knew of Wharton's hard luck story but it was the link to the previous Hellfire Club that attracted me to him. Speaking of Beaconsfield...

Did you know we have a township of Beaconsfield down here? Ironically, the name taken by Disraeli when he was created Lord Beaconsfield in 1879 by Queen Victoria. It was a reward for his work as Prime Minister of the United Kingdom. You might have heard of it from the 2006 mine collapse that garnered worldwide attention and put our current leader of the opposition, Bill Shorten, deep into the media spotlight as a union representative.

The town itself would have to be a favourite of mine. Initially called Brandy Creek, due to the colour of the water. Full of tannins, I assume. Its European history began with exploration around 1804, followed by limestone mining that led to the discovery of gold in 1847. Underground mining began in 1879 but by 1914 the gold mine shut down due to frequent flooding. It re-opened in 1999 and at this time an ore treatment plant was also built.

On Anzac Day in 2006, a small earthquake caused a rock fall in the gold mine, causing the death of one man and trapping two other men for a couple of weeks. 14 workers also escaped. It made headlines around the world. The Foo Fighters even released a ballad in tribute to those effected. The gold mine was closed in 2012. The town now features the Beaconsfield Mine and Heritage centre as its main tourist attraction and displays over 10,000 pieces in its collection.

I have fond childhood memories of visiting the bakery there. Back when I was a northerner. I've been a Southerner for about 30 years now. Yes, the whole north/south divide is still strong down here. Never discuss where the football/cricket/concerts are being held! I'm pretty sure the border lies around Oatlands, in the Midlands, somewhere. It all depends on the perspective of the locals. I still manage to cross it several times a year.

Oh, I noticed your choice of dessert too. Syllabub. Just the thought of cream/milk, sugar and spices all mixing with ale, or in our case, sack wine, and set aside for a couple of hours so that a curd formed on the top makes my stomach churn. Give me trifle any day!

Now it's time for you to work your magic and get Fanny comfortably onto Lord Beaconsfield's lap. I await with eagerness.

D.

Debb,

I remember the Beaconsfield (TAS) tragedy now. I had forgotten.

I have never eaten syllabub although it keeps popping up in stories of the 18th/early 19th century. I am sure it is not as stomach churning as you imagine, but there's only one way to find out... I will let you know. Right now I am pickling some beef to make Irish Spiced Beef but that takes about a week so I may have to come back and describe the dinner again. We should by now have had some cep (porcini) mushrooms in our garden, but it has been too wet so far this year. Jana makes wonderful soup from them – she calls them prawdziwki and it only takes half an hour between picking them and sitting down to eat soup that puts all other mushroom soups into the shade. Certainly Lord Beaconsfield could have eaten them in the countryside, but in London? I don't know. I'll stick to regular field mushrooms. Possibly with boiled chestnuts – yum!

Back to Fanny and dining naked. This could be a challenge.

Regards,

Simon.

Chapter Ten ~ To the Gates of Hell

The importance of clothes ~ a peep at Hell Fire ~ syllabub
or boobies ~ on Uncle Harry's lap ~ by coach to Medmenham
~ an early breakfast ~ a secret Valley ~ Venus bars the way

I can't do this, thought Fanny, alone in her room. It's not natural. He'll be looking at me. And I'm not like Lady Montagu. She thought about that. Lady Montagu would have no hesitation taking off her clothes in front of friends. On Lady's Night at the club, she even made love in public. To two gentlemen at once. She seemed to be enjoying herself and obviously did not give a damn who was watching. In fact, she might have been enjoying herself all the more just because she had an audience.

Well, Fanny was certainly not going to be doing that, no matter what Sir Francis wanted. And, come to think of it, Lord Beaconsfield would never put her in that position. Would he? But he did want her to take her clothes off, and that was not normal. At least, it was not normal at home. Except it was not normal at home until she had found out that her uncle had a club of his own in the cellars and amused himself by poking any woman he could get hold of. Including Bridget. And sour faced Miss Hodges whose cunny was so hungry that she was jealous of all other women and apparently rode her uncle like a horse.

Fanny was still standing by her bed. She shook her head and started to untie her dressing gown. Lord Beaconsfield would take care of her, and if he wanted to see her eat her dinner naked, she would do that out of kindness to him.

She looked at herself in the mirror but the single candle showed little. Never mind; Lord Beaconsfield would have to be satisfied with what she was. There was nothing else to offer. She stopped with her hand on the door latch. How would she get back to the others? Anyone in the corridor would see her. She cautiously pulled the door open and peeped out. A maid was disappearing down the stairs. She waited a moment, took a deep breath and dashed for Mrs Palm's sitting room.

She burst into the room and closed the door behind her. Bridget was sitting on Lord Beaconsfield's lap. Her pinafore had disappeared and her breasts were on display. Lord Beaconsfield was absently caressing one of them. They were staring at her. The fire crackled in the silence.

"Bravo, my dear. You look wonderful," said Lord Beaconsfield still playing with Bridget's breast. "You look even more beautiful than I had expected. Please excuse my not getting up. Although – you'll have to get up, my dear, and order our dinner. I'm hungry. I'm sure we all are. Let's sit at the table."

Bridget stood up and pulled the front of her dress together. "I have only to ring twice, and the girls will bring the soup." She went to the bell pull beside the fireplace.

"They will see me!" said Fanny, her fragile composure lost.

"Stand up straight, my dear. There's nothing they haven't seen in the mirror, and I'm sure you're prettier than they are. Don't you think so, Bridget?"

"Oh yes, Sir. Much prettier. I'm sure she's more beautiful than any of the girls on the top floor as well."

"There you are, Fanny. Stand up and look them in the eye. Now, may Bridget eat with us? I'm sure she deserves it. Can you find another chair, Bridget? I'd sit you on my lap again but I intend to use both hands for my dinner. I'm half starved.

"Now, Fanny, you sit there with your back to the fire and I shall sit here and admire you."

Fanny felt her cheeks blush. "Stop it! You're embarrassing me."

"You have nothing to be embarrassed about. Keep your chin up and soon you will feel perfectly comfortable."

There was a tap at the door and Bridget came back, carrying a chair and followed by Gwen and Sally bringing bowls and a tureen in the Chinese style. Bridget sent them back for another spoon and Gwen returned quickly. She set the spoon in front of Bridget and gave Fanny a big wink. "I expect that'll be all for the moment, Miss? Just give us two rings when you're ready and we'll be up with the beef. Enjoy your meal, Sir."

The soup was good and Bridget served Lord Beaconsfield a second helping. The spiced beef was rich and tasty, far grander than anything they had eaten at home. Together with the glass of claret that Lord Beaconsfield insisted they take to accompany it, Fanny felt her cheeks glowing. Bridget was smiling and talkative. She suspected she was also enjoying herself too much but she had questions to ask.

"Um – Uncle Harry. Please tell us what Sir Francis has in store for us. We're frightened."

Uncle Harry smiled and raised his glass to her. "Well now; you understand I can't tell you everything, don't you? We never talk about the Hellfire Club to outsiders. And once you are initiated as members, well, you'll know everything anyway."

"Oh, that's not fair! We want to know what you're going to do to us. Will it hurt?"

"Hurt? Of course not. And it won't be me anyway. Certainly I'll be there to take care of you but Sir Francis is the Grand Master, although you must never tell anyone that. Really, I'm talking too much already. Don't ever tell anyone I told you, will you?"

"But what's going to happen? Will the Devil be there?"

"Not unless you bring him yourself. It's the night of All Hallows and we call it by its old name – Samhain. There might be some strange spirits around, but none as strange as us. We'll stand you both on the table and have you drink a glass of wine with us. And then you're members and you can ask all questions you want."

Is that all, Fanny asked herself? Just standing on a table with a glass of wine? Except – "What will we be wearing?"

"You are too suspicious, my dear. Bridget will be wearing a nun's habit, and you will be dressed as the Bride of Winter. You will look wonderful. Have some more wine…

"You know, I think that was the finest beef I've eaten in years. The cook must have magic in her fingers. What's for pudding?"

"Syllabub, Uncle Harry."

"Oh, my dears, you are too kind to an old man. Do you think it might be ready now?"

Bridget giggled and went to the bell pull. She's a little drunk, thought Fanny. But then – I'm a little drunk too. I like Lord Beaconsfield, and he's letting us call him Uncle Harry. I wish my real uncle was like him.

And I'm going to play the Bride of Winter. Well, I suppose winter's not far away. I wonder who will play the bridegroom. Not Uncle Harry, I'm sure. Sir Francis? He's nice enough but too old. I want a handsome young man. Well, not too young. He has to have some character, some experience of life. Like Rob Longshot. Why did I think of him? He wouldn't fit in with all the fine folk. He'd probably try to rob them all. I wonder where he is now.

A tap at the door announced the syllabub. The girls collected their dinner plates and Bridget set out their glasses of syllabub piled on sack wine. Each confection was crowned with a ring of thin apple slices. They looked delightful, but Fanny worried at the prospect of more wine.

As Bridget returned to her seat, Lord Beaconsfield said to her, "My dear, I believe I will need some assistance with this wonderful delicacy. Do come and sit on my knee and we will fight it together."

Bridget giggled again and hurried to climb into his lap. She pushed open the front of her dress as if it were the most natural thing in the world.

"Wonderful," said Lord Beaconsfield. "Now I don't know if I should start feasting on the syllabub, or these beautiful round boobies. Perhaps I will have a little of each, turn and turn about." He lowered his head to lick at the nearest nipple as Bridget held him close.

That's terrible, thought Fanny. She must be really drunk. She'd never behave like that normally. I must speak to her later. And then came the realisation that Fanny herself was sitting at the table dressed only in her shoes. If Uncle Harry asked her to sit on his other knee, she would have even less protection. And, to be honest with herself, she would have even less hesitation.

The syllabub tasted rich and creamy, with all the excitement of lemon and sweet wine to set it off. Bridget was feeding Lord Beaconsfield small spoonfuls. He had wrapped one arm right around her to reach her breast and was squeezing and teasing her nipple. With a start she realised his other hand was out of sight, presumably under Bridget's skirt.

Bridget blushed as she was distracted from her spooning. "Stop it, Uncle, or I shall spill it all over you. And Miss Fanny is watching."

"Oh, that doesn't matter." He smiled across the table at Fanny. "You don't mind, do you, my dear? I'm just giving her a little reward for her efforts." Bridget stopped his speaking with a heaped spoon of syllabub.

Did Fanny mind? She supposed not. Not here, not in Mrs Palm's house. And not with Uncle Harry, whom she really liked. From the glow in her face, Bridget welcomed his attention too.

"No, I don't mind. And she's worked so hard on our dinner she deserves a special reward."

Bridget had stopped feeding Lord Beaconsfield and had closed her eyes. Fanny could not see what was happening beneath the table but Lord Beaconsfield's arm and shoulder were moving rapidly. She watched as Bridget slowly raised her face, eyes still closed. She grimaced for an instant and her expression grew strained and fixed. She opened her mouth soundlessly, and her head began to nod. "Ah... Ah..." and she was writhing in Lord Beaconsfield's lap, pushing his arm away and curling up against him. "Stop – stop – oh no, stop!" She lay with her head on his chest, trembling.

He let her rest there and smiled knowingly to Fanny. When he judged her ready, he lifted her face and kissed her gently on the lips. "Sweet. Very sweet. Don't you think so, Fanny?"

Yes. It had been sweet, and watching Bridget had excited her.

"I know what we shall do," said Lord Beaconsfield. "Let's move the table and drag the sofa in front of the fire. Then we can all enjoy it."

They lounged on the sofa, Lord Beaconsfield in the centre with his arms about the girls' shoulders. Fanny felt cosy. Uncle Harry smelt masculine, and felt big and strong. His hand moved down to her waist and he gently stroked her hip. With a start, she remembered she was naked. Naked and cuddling up to a man on the sofa. Uncle Harry had been right. Once she had become used to wearing no clothes, they really did not matter.

She glimpsed a movement on Uncle Harry's lap. Bridget had loosened the panel of his breeches and slipped her hand inside.

Fanny smiled to herself. Why not? She tried to catch Bridget's eye, but she was too busy. Fanny felt completely relaxed, contented. The warmth of Uncle Harry and the glow of the fire on her feet and legs were soporific. She no longer felt the sharp hunger for sex that had come over her when she realised Uncle Harry was playing with Bridget's cunny. She had eaten well, she had enjoyed watching Bridget, she wanted nothing more. It was as if Bridget's excitement and ecstasy had been enough for all of them.

A gentle snore came from above her head. Uncle Harry had fallen asleep. They laid him on the sofa. Bridget brought the blanket from her bed upstairs, while Fanny unlaced his shoes. They snuffed the candle and crept away to Fanny's bed. The weather was too cold for Bridget to sleep in her attic room without a blanket.

They left London far too early in the morning of a grey day, planning to reach Medmenham in one day. Mrs Palm had arranged a carriage for them; Fanny, Bridget and four of the other girls. Gwen and Sally had tossed a coin to see who would go and Gwen was with them, in a normal coat and dress. It was the first time Fanny had seen her without her revealing club uniform.

The six of them had space enough in the carriage and, as the early start had left them tired, most of them quickly fell asleep, curled up against each other. Fanny did not. She had slept badly, continually waking to ask herself what would happen at Medmenham. She still had little idea of what was in store. At least she now knew what they would be wearing. In the trunks stored on the carriage roof were nuns' habits for the girls, and something that looked very similar all in white for her. Bridget and Mrs Palm had brought them to Fanny's room and the girls had tried them on.

Bridget had looked perfect, as long as you did not catch her eye and start her giggling. The habit might suggest chastity, but her smile contradicted it. Fanny could not help a feeling that the world would be a happier place if all nuns had smiles like Bridget's.

Her own costume, she was less in love with. Her white cambric had been turned into a long, simple gown which fitted her shoulders and her height, but had no shape at all. It fastened at the neck with a hook inside on her right shoulder and a plain wooden button on her left. The overlap at the front fell from the top to the floor and there were no more hooks or buttons. The gown was held together at the waist by a length of soft linen rope. The rope and the overlap meant she could stand, walk, even raise her arms without displaying her underclothes to the world. Not that she would be allowed any underclothes; Mrs Palm had been very insistent about that. She had also pointed out that Fanny had only to undo the hook and button, untie the rope, and with no more than a shrug of her shoulders, the gown would be piled at her ankles, leaving her as naked as a statue. Mrs Palm did not say when or how that might happen.

The world was passing by outside. Already they had left the smoke and bustle of London behind them, and she could see villages, busy places with workshops and potteries, surrounded by wide expanses of market gardens. The vegetable patch for the whole crowded city. Autumn was in the air but there was still plenty to do. She could see men digging the ground for next year's crops. They were pruning and clearing, throwing the waste onto smoky fires. Some crops remained unharvested, lines of cauliflowers and Brussel sprouts standing like soldiers, and wild patches of parsnips, all waiting for the first frost. Some gardens had earth clamps, hiding potatoes, turnips and cabbages for winter. Suddenly she missed home. In London, she had been living a modern life, out of touch with the land. For the first year since she could remember, she had not picked any apples. And Christmas was coming; she could not imagine how city people celebrated it.

"Please, Miss, can we stop for a minute?" One of the girls Fanny did not know.

"Er – stop?"

"Yes, Miss. I have to piss. Really soon."

"Certainly, lean out and tell the driver."

She unhooked the window and let it slide down. Holding her hat on, she leant out and shouted, "Mr Driver, please could we stop? We have to piss."

Fanny did not hear what the driver said but the girl shouted again. "You'd like that, wouldn't you? Shall I tell Miss Fanny? She wants to go too." She wriggled back inside and pulled up the window. "The sauce of the man. He told me he couldn't stop. He wanted me to stick my bum out of the window and go that way."

The carriage rolled to a halt beside a chestnut coppice and everyone took the opportunity. The dead leaves under Fanny's boots felt homely after the hard cobbles of London's streets, and she took her time to enjoy the trees.

It was not until they were rolling again that Fanny wondered why she was suddenly Miss Fanny to the other girls, and why they had asked her permission to stop. They had been with Mrs Palm longer than she had but somehow they treated her differently. Perhaps even bordellos respected gentry.

They stopped twice to change horses but did not break their journey until they reached The Black Horse in Windsor. As they climbed down into the stable yard, the coachman sought her out. "Do you have your dinner here, Miss, but we shall have to move on just as soon as we can. We still have a fair way to the Abbey, and the days are drawing in. I'll ask the cook to hurry things along for you."

They sat alone in the dining room, six girls on a journey. None of them were shrinking violets, and Bridget chattered as if she had known them since childhood. How were they different from the girls at home? That was it, she supposed, they did not shrink. No-one lowered her eyes to the table and waited to be served when their food came. They took an interest, jumped up to help the serving girls, passed the mugs of small beer around, chattering all the time. They did not shut up until they addressed their steak pie and potatoes.

When the plates were empty Fanny hurried them out, greasy and contented, to the waiting coach and they were on their way again. With full tummies, the girls fell asleep. Fanny did not. She had things to think about.

They were woken by a gong banged persistently. She had slept badly, although the bed she had shared with Bridget had been comfortable enough. Sir Francis cared for his guests, even the lowly ones like Fanny. They had a pleasant room in West Wycombe, with a window looking over the lake. Still, it was far too early for anyone used to Mrs Palm's club and she had to pull the covers off the other girl's beds. They all draggled down to breakfast, bleary eyed and discontented.

The breakfast room was empty of guests. If other guests had been staying the night, they were either still asleep or eating in their rooms. Two elderly maids served breakfast from chafing dishes on a side table. Bacon, sausage, kidneys, lamb chops, it was difficult to choose. They settled at one end of the long table, reached for the bread and began to eat.

Fanny finished her chops and wondered if she had room to try the local cheese. Bridget did not hesitate. After eating her way through sausage, kidneys and bacon, she had a hunk of bread in one hand and cheese in the other. "Miss, do you know what we have to do now?"

Fanny did not, but one of the girls said, "I've been here before, Miss. Nothing much happens until afternoon time when we help the ladies to dress. And get dressed ourselves."

That would be sensible, Fanny thought. Her dress was hanging behind her door, with Bridget's black habit. "Has everyone got their evening clothes ready? We have to look well; Mrs Palm is counting on us." The girls nodded. They would be ready when called.

"What shall we do now, Miss?" asked Gwen.

Fanny did not know, but she did want to stretch her legs. "I think we'll take a walk. The park looks very beautiful."

"We could go to the caves," said the girl who had been here before. "Tain't far, and I believe I remember the way."

With a blustery autumn wind on their backs, they followed a narrow road around the village. The cottages looked strange to Fanny with their flint walls and thatch far thicker than she was used to. Behind their hurdle fences, the front gardens had been dug over and waited for the winter frosts to crumble the soil. She wished it was summer when the gardens would be rich and full of life, but now their distant quiet suited the weather.

The road was climbing a little, ready to take them up to the parish church on the hill above, but they came to a tall stone wall with an arched gateway large enough to admit a carriage. They stood looking at the forbidding wooden doors, wondering if they should knock, when the narrow wicket door opened and a short, grey-haired man peered out. He was holding his hat in his hand. "Good morning, my ladies. Are you looking to come in?"

The door closed behind them and they found themselves in a secret garden. Beyond the hard standing for carriages, paths led into a wild tangle of trees and bushes, turning this way and that, with the view always blocked. Fanny looked back. The entrance had already disappeared.

The path opened onto a miniature park in a valley bottom, with leafless trees scattered over carefully cropped grass. On either side, chalk hillsides sheltered the little paradise and Fanny no longer felt the wind. Someone with an artist's eye had laid out flower beds, statues of fauns and naked maidens, and shaded stone benches. In summer, Fanny could imagine ladies and gentlemen walking in the gardens, out of sight of the villagers and the cares of the world. Even in autumn the sight made Fanny's heart lift.

In the distance, at the head of the little valley, an arched stone entrance had been built into the hill and double doors stood open. A pony and trap stood waiting. This must be the way into the caves.

As the girls watched, two maids came out and took a heavy basket from the trap. They carried it between them into the darkness.

"So – here we are," said Fanny. "I wonder if we can go in and look. Come on, Bridget, let's get closer."

The path they were following curved along the bottom of the hill slope towards the entrance until it was blocked by a life-sized marble statue. Bridget drew a breath. "I've heard of this one, Miss. She's

Venus, taking a thorn from her foot."

She was beautiful enough to be Venus, and she had certainly bent over to do something to her foot. She wore a ribbon in her hair, and nothing else. She was facing towards the cave entrance, and presenting her plump female bum to any visitor. It was impossible not to reach out and touch her.

There were words engraved on her lower back. *Hic locus est, partes ubi se via findit in ambas: Hac iter Elysium nobis.*

"What does it mean, Miss?"

Fanny struggled with her schoolgirl Latin. "Um – *in this place.* Then *the way divides in two. Take your road to Heaven.* What is she saying?"

Bridget was blushing. "I think she's telling the gentlemen they can, oh Miss! You know, she's saying they can stick it in where they please."

Fanny felt her cheeks redden as she thought about the choice.

"Fanny Howarth. Just who I wanted to see. I was going to send the trap for you, but you've come to my doorstep."

Debb,
There you are, I've brought you all the way from London, ready for the Hellfire Club Samhain celebrations. And the ritual sacrifice of the (allegedly) virginal Fanny to the Father Superior of the Order. You are going to have fun. I am imagining nude Fanny, lying on a stone altar (with a blanket cover or she will freeze to death), her legs held up by two nuns and surrounded by all the members of the order. The Grand Master standing on the ground and working away inside her – should he come there or do you want the visual of him coming on her tummy? You decide!
And you will have to decide about the Order of Service, and when the big event happens, and what they have for dinner etc. etc. Have fun.
The last sentence of my contribution was intended to be from Lady Mary Montagu Wortley who was a very worthy person, but also active in the Hellfire Club. I like that idea; worthy women who can also let their hair down on occasion and do really, really sexy things. If that is how you choose to portray her, I will be interested to hear her thoughts on why it is sometimes desirable for a well-educated lady to service two cocks at once and go to bed exhausted.
Do you think Cousin Clarence should appear in his nun's habit? That might be fun – for everyone.
Anyway, that's close to 60,000 words of our story, and we are still in

England. I suppose Fanny will return to London for a while, before deciding to cross the Atlantic in search of Rob Longshot. But let's see what an exciting dinner you are going to conjure up before we worry about that.
On Saturday, I have to pontificate at a writer's breakfast in a local restaurant. After breakfast, the festival moves down the street with authors who are getting paid for attending! *Well, bugger them. I bet I end up having to pay for my own breakfast, and they get paid for just turning up?*
Looking forward to your next section,
Simon

Geeze, Buddy boy, there's nothing like dumping a girl at the altar like a wayward groom fleeing his shotgun bride!
You whisper sweet-nothings in my ear about the English countryside and then dump me at the gates of Hell – pun intended. After your words describing secret gardens and winding paths and cotters cottages, I was looking forward to hearing you describe the hell fire caves. But, did you? No! You dumped me at the door, barefoot and very pregnant. At least the doors were open, small mercy there, and a very welcoming Venus to entice all those who dare to enter.
I am so grateful you let me in on who the disembodied voice belonged to. I was racking my brain for a suitable body. I assumed it was going to be male. I have not heard of the Lady Mary that you mention, but shall find her.
So where do I go from here? Straight into researching the caves and the delicious and risqué sex play of the day, that's where. I have never been into a cave lined with chalk. Have you? I'm trying to discover what the atmosphere would have been like. Chalk is absorbent, England is wet and cold. Does this mean the underground caves were a damp, smelly place to be? I don't know. With the help of modern technology I have been able to 'view' the caves via some online footage. But nothing compares with actually being there and feeling the caves in person.
Another thing I have been researching is early forms of contraception/disease avoidance. Did you know birth control, in its various forms, has been practised for hundreds of years, possibly thousands? The history boffins can't quite agree on the timeline. Early inceptions of condom-like products have been made from animal intestines/bladders, leather, linen (soaked in a chemical solution to prevent disease), and animal horns. A horn upon a horn one might say.
In was interesting to discover, but not surprising, that from around the 1600's onwards some 'educated' men voiced their disapproval of condom use. One even asked for them to be deemed illegal, where another deemed

them to be immoral. You men are funny creatures.

Speaking of men, let me introduce you to Thomas Rowlandson, an English artist and caricaturist who lived from 1757-1827. You may already know of him. He was a man of great talent that was evident in his boyhood, his characters are described as robust and bawdy. His observations of social life are often gentle and full of humour.

It was Rowlandson's erotic work that caught my eye. Women with big bosoms and bottoms, and men with erect, naked cocks are captured in the daily aspects of life, where it appears, there is always someone having sex. His erotic imagery is delightful and all seem to be having a jolly good time. The titles given to this art are interesting though. Some with names that include Connoisseurs, Fishing, Meditation among the Tombs, and The Astronomer, politely betray the type of art one may expect to see. Others, such as, Flirtation Class, The Observers, and The Sanctified Sinner, give an insight as to what will be discovered.

One observation that stood out for me, and destroyed what little romanticism I had left of carriage travel, is Sympathy, or A Family On A Journey Laying The Dust, which clearly shows the need for all passengers to toilet themselves at once. This piece of work hangs in The Met, and can be seen here -

https://www.metmuseum.org/art/collection/search/736328. *I'm sure Fanny and Bridget would avail themselves of the nearest bush.*

Whilst at the time, Rowlandson's highly explicit erotic works were produced only for private clientele. They later were published in a collection titled The Forbidden Erotica of Thomas Rowlandson 1756-1827, in 1970. And here is a sexy tid-bit, his work must have been appreciated far and wide because in 2017, Jaipur in India, released stamps commemorating six erotic images. A quick google of 'Jaipur Thomas Rowlandson stamps' should show you a photo.

Alas, I must leave descent into another of history's rabbit-holes and find my mojo. I had made a good start on my next chapter then scrapped it completely. Fanny is a bit quiet in my mind at the moment so I need to do something to awaken her again, namely reading some erotica. Read as you write, isn't that what they say?

Bring on the sex!

Debb.

Debb,

Chalk? There I can help you, being a geologist by education and inclination. Chalk is simply a soft limestone composed of the hard bits of microfossils. It

152

is around 600m thick in southern England, but in Poland it is perhaps double that (and much harder). Being a pure limestone, it is very permeable. There are hardly any streams in chalk country – all the rain soaks away. The caves were (I believe) originally tunnelled for the limestone but there are others, much older, dating back to the Stone Age. They were tunnelled using antlers as picks and the miners were looking for flint – the best flint in England comes from the chalk.

So, as caves go, the Hellfire ones are pretty dry, with white walls and no visible water drips. Pleasant places to be as long as you have a fireplace with a flue to the outside.

I'm sure I remember Pepys or Boswell referring to having a prostitute 'in armour' – meaning wearing a condom. Presumably made from sheep's intestine and perhaps tied behind the balls to stop it falling off. Amazing what you will put up with in the name of sex.

All the best,

Simon

Oh Simon,

Tied behind the balls? Oh my, that sounds like a strangulation hazard, which is fine if that's your thing, wink, wink, nudge, nudge.

I have always been interested in geology and it is something I shall study one day. I like the idea of being able to look at a cliff face and identify and understand why it is the way it is. I have a basic understanding about the layering of sediment being passage/events in time, but that's about it. I always like to know how things work or why they are the way they are.

What a wonderful character our Lady Mary turned out to be. I get the feeling she has many stories to tell about herself. Bridget seems to have picked herself up a man. My, our girls sure are getting what they want. He's a good Welsh lad and she is a smitten kitten. Cousin Clarence hasn't made an appearance. Maybe that's something you would like to do? As for Rob Longshot, what do you think I did with him?

It's a little interesting that I wrote this piece and then reread over your (above) vision for the altar scene and in some ways, they are similar. We definitely share a vision of what it would be like to be a member of the Hell Fire Club.

I did say "Bring on the sex" and that I did. It's always the easiest part to write, don't you think? Fanny enjoyed herself and that's what is most important.

Hope you enjoy!

Chapter Eleven ~ Nuns and Monks

Meeting Lady Mary ~ across the River Styx ~ an altar
of marble ~ brothers andsisters all ~ a surprising sacrifice

Fanny started at the sudden appearance of a woman. Heat stained her cheeks even more now knowing that their conversation had been overheard.

"Why, my dear, your enthusiasm is delightful. I wasn't sure how you were going to go about all of this when Francis told me about you."

Fanny stared at the beautiful woman standing in the grand, arched entrance to the caves. Statuesque, with hair the colour of a dark sunrise. Her bright green dress was tailored exquisitely to display her breasts with just a ruby hint of nipple peaking above the white lace edging.

The woman's husky laugh brought Fanny's attention back to her face. Painted white with powder, she looked ethereal. Angelic even. Golden hazel eyes peered down upon Fanny. Blood red lips pouted perfectly, defining her deep cupid's bow. With a tilt of her head she gathered her plump lower lip between her teeth at one side.

Her hair had been coifed tightly under the front of her matching green silk hat. An abundance of auburn curls gathered in a net, billowing artfully at the nape of her long, slender neck. Eyes danced with amusement above her pert nose, and a quirk of a smile shaped her lips, enhancing the high cheekbones of an aristocrat.

"Like what you see, dear?" Humour livened her face and her too-wide smile made Fanny blush as she felt the woman appreciating her just as closely.

Feeling the weight of another woman's appraisal, Fanny was suddenly unsettled with nervousness, causing her voice to quiver a little as she spoke. "Good morning. I am Francisca Howarth. How do you do?"

Bridget, sensing the subtle change in her mistress, moved closer to Fanny, their shoulders almost touching as she took up position just behind her.

"My, such formality is a sin in our little part of Hell…"

Fanny gasped behind her gloved hand. Apparently, just the mention of *hell* had shocked the child still within her, a child who had spent many years sitting ramrod straight in the front pew, setting the example for the common folk, listening to the endless sermons she had to endure. And this woman knew it, too.

"My dear, you can take the girl out of the country but never the country out of the girl. And that is all part of the allure of Fanny Howarth. You do still have that wholesome look about you," she nodded delicately to herself. "It's good to see Old London Town hasn't aged you, as it does most. I can see now why he chose you."

Fanny's smile returned and the warmth from the other woman's appraisal surrounded her like a warm bath on a winter's night. She turned her head towards Bridget who smiled brightly, obviously happy with the praise her mistress had just received.

"Do come along, there is no time for snooping. It will ruin the surprise."

Fanny and Bridget's shoulders slumped. They had hoped to see inside the caves they had been hearing so much about. Surely it would be helpful for them to know their way around before tomorrow night.

Spurred on by the sudden crestfallen look on her young charge's face, the woman changed her mind.

"Fanny, my name is Lady Mary and I am here to ensure you have a wonderful time. Now, why don't we start with a tour of the cave? They're a bit dead at this time of day, but once they come alive, it's like being in a world that Venus herself would truly enjoy. Follow me."

Fanny stared wide-eyed as they walked into the caves. Although poorly lit at this hour, she could see how magnificent the entry was. The high ceiling arched at the top, pale grey walls surrounded her and led the way down a long, darkened passage.

The air had a slightly stale smell, possibly because, as she had overheard someone mentioning at dinner, the caves had not been used for a matter of months. There was also the coolness of a gentle breeze flowing towards them from the passageway. Anticipation fluttered away in Fanny's stomach. It made her feel ill and excited at the same time.

"This way, girls, and lift your skirts, there's still some wetness underfoot," Lady Mary advised, the rasp of her voice echoing in the vastness. Lifting one of the two lit torches from the wall, she walked towards the blackness of the passage.

Grabbing fistfuls of her skirts, Fanny followed obediently, staring at the walls surrounding her, wanting so much to reach out and touch them but too afraid to dampen the hem of her dress so early in the day. As the light passed over the walls she could see etchings carved into the soft limestone. She hoped she would have a chance to explore them before she made her way back to the city.

"My dear Sir Francis arranged for the local men to carve out the caves as a means of providing income for the local families in these hard times. The chalk was used for the road that you arrived on. The families of the area are proud people and were very happy to have employment."

Fanny and Bridget nodded, both remembering their conversation about how few holes the road had on it in the final five mile approach to the town, and up to Sir Francis's estate. It had been the smoothest part of their trip after departing from the George and Dragon, and the even swaying of the carriage had made them sleepy.

"You may notice the design of the caves is very unusual. It was inspired by the architecture of the Ottoman Empire that Francis discovered on his grand tour. It seems boys will always be boys and will make their fantasies come to life wherever they may be," Lady Mary said with a knowing wink.

As they continued to walk, Bridget pointed out several masonic symbols deeply etched into the wall. There were names too. A few Fanny even found familiar. Many of them from the grandest of families.

"Here we have the steward's chamber," Lady Mary indicated, stopping at the arched doorway recessed into the wall. "If you ever get lost, find your way here and Mr Whitehead will make sure you get to where you are going. He is a jovial fellow who keeps things running smoothly here at the caves and is always willing to help a Lady with whatever she needs."

Fanny poked her head into the small cave, waiting for her eyes to adjust to the low light. Ledgers lined the high shelves on the wall in an orderly manner. Although there were many, they were bound in only red or green leather. Green to the left, red to the right. Light from a single candle flickered on the desk next to a thick, black book whose title Fanny could not read. A large chalice that was placed in between a pair of ornate candelabras, sat on a low shelf just above the desk. The glow from the candle made it shine and its jewels twinkle. Several monks' robes hung on the wall just inside the doorway. On

156

the opposite side, were several nun's habits and wimples. The paleness of the cloth was luminescent in the dark.

As Fanny stepped back into the passageway, she noticed that a faint ray of sun light beamed all the way down to the door of Mr Whitehead's cave and made a mental note that this was the way to exit, should she ever be lost.

Making their way further into the labyrinth, Lady Mary pointed out several other spaces such as the Triangle, Lord Sandwich's Circle and an old miners' cave, from which the sound of muffled voices came.

Further along, in the banquet hall, Fanny found a long serving table and several curtained alcoves lining the wall.

"For the shy ones, Miss Fanny," Bridget whispered, which was pointless because even a whisper echoed down here, much to Bridget's annoyance.

"Now for the exciting part!" With her smile beaming in the semi-darkness, Lady Mary walked towards the sound of running water.

"A river!" Bridget exclaimed, surprise evident in her gasp.

"The River Styx to be exact. Once you pass here there is no turning back. Some say it's a crossing from Heaven into Hell. Or as I like to say...from a saint into a sinner. Either way, once you pay the ferryman, you will never be the same."

All three stepped into the small boat, the ferryman declining his fee with a brisk wave of his hand. They sailed a small way into the subterranean level of the caves. The fast running water added a cool moisture to the air, leaving Fanny feeling chilled. It was quiet, really quiet. All that could be heard was the flick of water each time the oar breached the water.

Fanny looked behind into the darkness and her heart thumped in her chest. Not from fear, but from excitement. She had heard whispers from Miss Rosie's girls of what happened in the inner temple and was eager to discover them for herself.

The boat stopped with a gentle thump against a wooden platform. A single torch lit the few steps at the water's edge.

"'Ere ye go, ladies. If I'm not here when ye're done, pull on that bell there and I'll come back for ye. Same as if I need ye, I'll ring the bell." The stout, well-dressed ferryman, with long grey hair, smiled a toothless grin and tipped his hat before steadying the boat for them to alight.

Fanny spied the shiny bell glowing in the flickering light. A braided black, leather rope hung from its tongue. It moved gently in the breeze coming from further downstream.

A few short steps and they were at the entrance of a vast cavern. It was much bigger than the entrance or the hall. Their single light domed willowy shadows on the walls. Both Fanny and Bridget watched as Lady Mary walked to the very centre of the room, pointing upwards.

"Did you know in this very spot, three hundred feet high above us, is Saint Lawrence's church? That's our little joke with God. Yours too, now." With humour thick in her voice, she winked and smiled salaciously.

Fanny eyed Bridget, who was smiling widely with a glint of mischievousness sparkling in her eyes, she laughed when Bridget winked at her too. Oh, if only the villagers knew what happened beneath their feet.

Fanny ran her hand along a wall as she moved further into the room, feeling her way through *hell*. How wicked she felt. The excitement she had experienced on the boat had now settled low in her tummy, causing an ache of awareness between her thighs, and her skin to heat. The altar in front of her gleamed in the low light and at times it sparkled. Walking over to it, she climbed the few steps that raised it a few feet higher above the ground, and used both her hands to touch, no caress, the length of the table. A lover's touch – warm and gentle with an urgency she could not explain.

"Magnificent, isn't it?"

Fanny turned to Lady Mary, noticing the dream-like look upon her face. She too, was touching the stone.

"Francis had this carved from his choice of the finest Italian marble. He personally oversaw the work and chaperoned its journey home. He was gone for almost the year. This altar is the sole reason that the passageways are wider than you would expect them to be. He always had this plan…"

Fanny and Bridget stood quietly while Lady Mary told her stories, appearing entranced as the fond memories washed over her. She spoke of them with pride.

"I was the first to be sacrificed at this altar. I remember it as if it were yesterday. I felt as if I had been reborn into a world where I was meant to be. Not just be a part of. Not just another woman to be flouted by her husband. I felt like myself. My dear Francis, he taught me that and so much more. All women should feel such things."

Lady Mary sighed contentedly as she turned to Fanny, kindness brightening her eyes. "Tomorrow will be your night to be reborn, Fanny. You will never be the same again, just you wait and see."

Before Fanny could ask any questions, the dull gong of the bell summoned them back to the boat.

Fanny laid down upon the altar and closed her eyes, noting the stark coolness of the stone under her arms and the warmth of the fur under the rest of her body. The softness contrasting against the gentle roughness of the stone. Each time she fidgeted, it grazed her skin and a skimming pain ran along her arms, tapping the edges of her soul to wake it up.

How did she get here, she mused, and smiled in the darkness.

How? Why? She no longer cared. She liked the adventure of sexual self-discovery she had been undertaking these past months. She had long forgotten to care or ask why people frowned upon sex. The more she discovered, the more she realised that sex was akin to being alive.

It had often made her question her religious habits and what it meant to be a Lady, but not anymore. At the very least, she had concluded, that some forms of religious teaching were only to control, not enlighten, its followers. Surely, if God thought sex was a form of sin, of evil, would he have made it so pleasurable?

Taking a deep breath, Fanny relaxed, feeling her surroundings to her very core. Glimpsing through the darkness near her, she stared into the abyss above her head. Squinting up into the high void, she now knew that above ground at this exact point was the priory. She giggled, naughtiness on her mind, wondering if the abbot knew what happened just a short distance under his feet.

Smoke from the candles that lit up part of the vast space, wafted into the vented peak of the vault. Quiet voices echoed around the room and mingled in with the warmth and glow of the fires, adding a surreal layer to the atmosphere. Thankfully, the smoke from the fires was drawn to the outside of the caves, leaving the air clean.

Fanny could feel the presence of a few people nearby. Their closeness, and their seeing her laid out as she was, livened her body. She liked to be watched. She knew that Bridget would not be too far away. Always close by, watching over her mistress. Smiling inwardly, not for the first time Fanny acknowledged how dear a friend Bridget had become. It no longer mattered that Fanny was the Lady and Bridget was her maid. No, not at all. What mattered in all aspects in life, she had discovered, was the love and friendship that was created by like-minded people. The kind of people who accepted you for who you were, and you them. That new found realisation warmed the very heart of her. A warmth she had only ever found in the arms of her mother, never amongst the often cold-hearted people of fashion.

These past two days at the mansion had been spent meeting such people. They were all accepting. Dinner times were full of frivolity, people talking and laughing, touching and caressing each other and having sex, which they did often.

Her education had been furthered by the discovery of a shelf of phalluses, some crafted in glass or stone, but mostly wooden.

Last night, it had been a real eye-opener to watch a man being pleasured by three women. They had tied him naked and facedown to a large tapestry frame, his legs and arms tied to the sturdy woodwork. All three then used their mouths, hands and a smoothed, wooden phallus, to pleasure him to the point he was incoherent. His resulting stupor bought about a round of applause and boisterous jeering from the men, and some women, of the room.

Fanny had also met many new people. One, they called Brother Ben, spoke with an accent she couldn't quite place. He was a short, rotund man with a high bald crown, who at times seemed too serious, but was very well liked by all. He had an affection for expensive cigars and carried a cane everywhere he went. He was important enough to have his own alcove in the caves.

It was at dinner last night that Fanny had discovered what a French letter was, and it surprised her to learn it had nothing to do with writing in French at all! Later that evening, one of the ladies showed Fanny her husband's. Encased in a wooden box, it was a fine piece of sheep intestine that was used by a man to cover his swollen member before inserting it into a woman, or man. Instructions were written inside the lid on how to take care of it so that it could be used again and again. Whilst the Lady confessed it could be a bit uncomfortable, especially if it hadn't maintained its softness, it was used to stop sickness and babies.

Fanny blinked her memory away and stared towards one side of the room at the most unusual statues she had ever seen. Positioned a short space apart, were two identical statues made from luminescent, white marble and carved to feature a woman from head to thighs, her hands holding her bountiful breasts.

"I can see you are mesmerised by our beautiful *Fontana delle Tette*, or as us English like to say, the fountain of tits." Sir Francis smiled.

Fanny's eyes glazed as she stared at the fountains. She felt she had drunk a few too many drinks, even though she followed the instructions not to drink this afternoon. She was drunk on the lusty atmosphere that she had felt from the very first time she had entered the caves.

Sir Francis continued, "We can thank our Venetian friends for the inspiration. Although mine are carved in the likeness of an English maiden, because they are beyond compare, like you, Fanny. The Venetian tradition is to have red and white wine to flow from each of the nipples at the same time. However, I do not like the taste when it mixes into the bowl. That is why one of our maidens gifts red wine from both her beautiful breasts, and the other, white."

He chuckled at the surprise on Fanny's face. The image of a woman's breast providing anything but milk for her babe should be distasteful at least, but here, amongst these people, it seemed so normal that something so pure could be so enticing. As if to prove her thoughts, she watched as a man knelt before one of the maidens, his monks robe flowing about him as he opened his mouth to take his fill of red wine straight from the right breast, and then the left. Once full, a few tiny drops were wiped cheerfully away on his sleeve and he walked away laughing.

"And what of you, Fanny? Will you dare to drink from another's bosom?" Sir Francis asked, raising her hand to his lips and kissing it. The deep sparkle in his eyes held Fanny's before he walked away with a knowing smile.

A quiet bell echoed from within and then the gentle rumble of staffs striking the floor began, sending a tingle of anticipation flowing through Fanny, gathering at the sweet spot between her thighs. When Lady Mary had told of what to expect tonight, she mentioned that the beginning of the ceremony would begin with everyone gathering in front of the altar. The men would be dressed in monks' robes with the cowls covering their bent heads, raising and lowering their staffs in unison. The women, dressed as nun's, passive at their side, casting their eyes to the floor.

As candles were extinguished around the room, the area behind Fanny had been lit up like a summer's day. The heat radiated towards her, causing small beads of sweat to cling to her dress. She looked out towards the people gathered in front of her but all she could see were the silhouettes of robes and habits. The rumble of the staffs fastened into a loud thumping, keeping in time with her heartbeat.

Silence descended swiftly and, from the corner of her eye, Fanny caught sight of the Grand Master as he entered the Inner Temple, his red cape billowing behind him as the members cleared the way. She watched as the horns atop of his red, half-face mask floated above their heads as he passed along the aisle they had made for him. Sir Francis was taller than most, and tonight he took on the look of the devil himself.

Extra candles had been lit around the altar, and in her stark white shift, she must have appeared to glow to the rest of the room. Warmth flushed over her as Fanny felt Sir Francis take up his position, standing behind her head. Two sharp strikes with his staff upon a stone brought everyone to attention, lifting their heads, their hungry eyes descending on Fanny. Closing her eyes, she breathed slowly, stemming the excitement she could feel running through her veins.

"Brothers and sisters, welcome to the final meeting of the year before the winter buries our sanctuary deep in its cold-hearted embrace." Sir Francis began, enjoying the excited anticipation that filled the room and seemed heavy enough to dull the echoes of his booming voice. The altar room felt far more intimate that it had that afternoon.

"Tonight, we embrace the devil on this All Hallows Eve. May wickedness and wantonness find you wherever you may lay, here and forever."

A sudden and deafening gratitude erupted and staffs thumping the ground startled Fanny into opening her eyes. Sir Francis was looking down on her, smiling reassuringly. He then raised his hands, motioning for silence once again. Expectant eyes of the crowd stared up at him, all eager for the night to begin.

Nervously, Fanny closed her eyes and fought to steady herself.

He held them silent for a while, forever the showman, building the tension in the room, feeding the sexual anticipation boiling in every member there. He looked around. Some of his monks in the front row were already aroused, if their tented robes were anything to go by.

Fanny opened her eyes again as a hand cupped her face and roughened thumb stroked over her cheek. Eyes she never thought she would see again stared down upon her. His mouth descended fast and she offered herself up to him wantonly. Moisture pooled between her legs as she felt strong hands part her thighs, holding her open wide.

As the kiss ended, Fanny felt a hand slip between her legs, testing her moisture, "She is ready for you, my son. Seldom have I felt such arousal from a kiss," Sir Francis exclaimed loudly.

More hands lifted her feet, holding them high into the air, and with one swift movement, she was dragged down the table until her bum was at the edge. Fanny's long hair splayed out behind her.

She smiled, her body feeling the heat against her thighs as she looked at the man holding her legs against his shoulders. He was staring down at her cunny, open and freely offered. His robe had been pushed back over his shoulders exposing his lean, naked body beneath "Are you ready, Miss Fanny?"

His voice shocked her. She recognised it but with lust overflowing in her veins, she nodded eagerly. She knew him and she was ready for anything he might do to her. He took her mouth again so hard that her lips bruised. His deft fingers reached for the opening of her shift, ripping it open to expose the wanton body beneath. The sudden chill sent goose pimples over her skin, yet they smoothed easily away as he took her breasts in his warm hands.

"Your breasts are bigger," he mumbled, taking each tightened nipple in to his mouth. He suckled like a man dying of thirst, the grip harder than Fanny could ever manage with her own fingers. Feeling him pull at her nipples with his teeth was all Fanny needed to release the built-up pressure and spill her wetness down the slit of her pussy. Her soft whimper echoed in the chamber for all to hear.

Taking her mouth in his as she panted her lust, he bruised her mouth once again before leaning down to whisper in her ear, "Tonight will be for them, every other night will be for us."

Fanny gasped for breath and watched as his head moved lower, his kisses trailing their way across her body. He raised his head and looked deep into her eyes, "Your hips are wider too, my love. This pleases me. You are even more beautiful than I remember."

He walked back to the end of the altar and stood between her open legs. Staring again at her sex, "This is new also," he smiled and kneaded his palm into the hairless mound. With his fingers trailing over her wet slit, Fanny raised her hips against the people holding her legs tight.

A hushed laughter filled the air. "She is eager for you, brother!" Someone from the back of the room shouted.

"That she is, and she shall have me soon enough." The last word was said with a wink, and he leaned into Fanny, smelling her sex, trailing the tip of his nose along her slit, moaning with appreciation.

Fanny's head lolled to the side, lusty eyes looking out over the crowd. She had forgotten they were there, and now it was as if she could feel every heart in the room thumping in time with hers. She could see many faces she knew. Bridget smiled brightly at her. Fanny had never seen her friend look more beautiful.

Fanny could feel her hips rise as she rocked against the slow tongue licking the wetness from her swollen lips. His arms wrapped around her parted thighs, holding her tightly against his face. His beard grazed against her skin, the sweet roughness something she would never forget. Her fingers dug into the fur at her waist, clenched so tightly her hands tingled.

She began to whimper and squirmed against the people still holding her legs open wide, her release building inside her. Suddenly he stopped, standing upright between her legs. Leaning over her, he smiled dreamily before taking her mouth softly in his. The essence of her sex glistened on his lips. Fanny drank her taste from his mouth, fisting his hair in her hands, holding him to her with a desperation and passion she had never experienced before.

His cock entered her with one smooth stroke. His strong fingers grabbed her hips, his thumbs digging into her flesh at the side of her mound. She knew she would wear his touch for days to come. His heat filled her more than she had been filled before.

Sliding slowly in and out of her, he made sure that Fanny's pleasure was equal to his own. Her moans filled the room and the crowd around her started to strike their staffs against the ground. The higher she climbed to her release, the faster the staffs pounded on the floor, the harder he impaled her.

He laid down upon her, his hands holding hers tightly above her head. Her legs were spread wide, still being held by disembodied hands she could feel holding tight at her knees and ankles. His panting fell upon her face as he watched Fanny's climax building, her faced distorting with pleasure.

"Open your eyes!" he commanded, satisfied as she did so immediately.

Fanny began to squirm, and the pitch of her moans rose above the noisy room. She felt his weight shift as he raised himself up on his arms and stared intensely down at her. He nodded to someone at the side and suddenly the mouths of two monks were suckling her nipples, and a set of hands holding her arms high above her head.

Arousal wailed from her mouth and the painful pleasure gathered deep inside her was desperate for release. As his thrusts became fast and deep, she dug her nails into the hands above her, and arched into the hot mouths that feasted upon her breasts. Her whole body burned with a shaking need, her moans matched each of his grunts as he thrust hard against her. The sound of his thighs slapping noisily against her bottom filled the room. The hands holding Fanny tightened as her whole body was now shaking from his powerful thrusts, suddenly she screamed out her release, startling the now silent watchers.

Staring at the woman underneath him, he watched her come all over his cock for the very first time and grunted his release soon after. The crowd erupted into applause.

Debb,
Very interesting, of course. I think I will take it to bed and read it very carefully.
Now, you're not going to get away with 'Dearie' in Lady Mary's mouth. I realise you are a proud product of Van Diemen's land and so do not naturally take to the English class system, but dearie is very lower class. I never use it myself (of course) and prefer 'my dear' or perhaps 'dear'. But you are right, Lady Mary was a wonderful character and nice to have around. How much female energy has been wasted over the years in sweeping sex under the carpet and maintaining a 'proper' front. Lady Mary

165

showed a woman could be powerful, intellectual and sexy as well.

I confess to a little disappointment because Fanny did not get more respect from her audience. I'm sure all the men would have liked a little feel of such a beautiful and ripe woman, and I suspect the nuns would have played with her too. At least, they would in my male imagination; I always wonder what female readers think about women touching women and suspect it is a step too far for many of them. There is nothing that gives a man quite as much pleasure as the chance to play with a woman. Giving a woman an orgasm must be the finest thing in the world, and I recommend the experience to anyone – especially other women, who need the experience to complete their education.

And I did not see Rob Longshot appearing – congratulations on a great idea. I wasn't so sure about him saying he would keep Fanny for himself, because he is a rat-bag at heart. If Fanny is to pursue him to the end of the book and ultimately dump him in favour of maintaining her independence, he should be a little more equivocal perhaps?

Cousin Clarence; I don't want to forget about him (her). He will give us a chance to comment a little on M/M relationships. And a little M/M sex as well – modern women do seem to be fascinated by men having sex with men. Me, I'm just fascinated by sex, of any variety, with exceptions for children or uninvited pain.

Right now I am sitting in an isolated cottage in Devon and, as there is no internet or mobile signal, I will have to drive into town and find a wi-fi link to send this email. A real pain, but once I start writing the next section it will take a while before I can email again. We are flying off to Frankfurt Oder next week (that's not the big Frankfurt but a much smaller place on the Polish border). We will be renting electric bikes because both Jana and I are suffering from wobbly knees at the moment and will need the help. Jana's brother, sister-in-law and nephew are meeting us, and we will cycle up the Oder and Neisse Rivers into the edge of the Czech Republic. Should be five days of pleasant country and old towns. Plus good food and beer, of course.
Regards,
Simon

Chapter Twelve ~ In Lincoln's Inn

The sights of London ~ the glories of Lincoln's Inn
~ Lady Mary and some special friends ~ meeting Clarita
and remembering home ~ the convenience of split gowns
~ a rewarding homage to Sappho ~ the club and
members approve ~ a visitor from the future

November had laid its hand on London. Nights had drawn in, evenings slipping slowly into smoky, misty night. Sunshine was no more than a distant memory, with daylight seeping slowly through choking coal fumes as the servants in every house lit their morning fires and began the day. Winter lay in wait, already glazing the cobbles with ice and giving the carters and cab drivers red noses and cold hands.

Fanny was enjoying her life at the Club. She had duties, and friends who filled most of her time. Some were colleagues like Gwen and Sally but increasingly, the members themselves had become friends. She enjoyed their company and their simple pleasures. Inside the Club there were no sour wives to criticise, and the members could seat a lively girl on their knee, a girl who understood just how the sight of her pretty breasts was appreciated. That made a respectable husband feel a very fine fellow indeed.

The members did not see Fanny's breasts, of course. Except for the ones who had attended her special night in the caves at High Wycombe. And Lord Beaconsfield. She always had kind feelings for him and he did enjoy dining with her and Bridget when they were dressed in next to nothing. He had not yet laid a finger on Fanny but he loved playing with Bridget - and she enjoyed his attentions. He had not taken her fully, but he always sat her on his lap after dinner, with her arm about his neck, and his hand out of sight between her thighs. He would play and diddle her for half an hour at a time, making Fanny feel hot and more than a little envious.

And Bridget would show her gratitude by kneeling at his feet and playing sweet music on his pink oboe. That was especially disturbing. Lord Beaconsfield's sighs and Bridget's sucking noises made Fanny crave sex herself, and she wished for Rob Longshot with his magic cock.

She still did not know how Rob Longshot had appeared at the

Hellfire Club. He knew Sir Francis, that was certain. And knew him well enough to take over his deflowering duty at the ceremony. Fanny was not sure how she felt about that. She had expected Sir Francis, or one of the senior gentlemen, and instead she found Rob Longshot in her cunny again. And again without her invitation. It was hard to know how she should feel, but she certainly wanted to discuss the situation with him.

After the ceremony, she had tried to catch him, but she was carried away in a crowd of people congratulating her, and showering her with compliments and sly invitations. She had eventually been hustled away by Lady Mary who insisted that one cock was enough for her first evening. But even Lady Mary was unable to keep everyone completely at bay and she found herself caressed, fondled and even kissed in all sorts of places by all sorts of people.

Next day, the girls left early to return to London, while Sir Francis was presumably still tucked up in bed with a fortunate lady. No-one knew anything of the mysterious stranger who had initiated her, and they were not curious. The important thing was that Fanny had been a glorious bride and welcomed into the Hellfire sisterhood with the appropriate instrument. Next time she attended a celebration, she would be expected to wear the same black habit the other sisters wore. Or at least, she would start off wearing it. Most of the sisters had lost their outer clothes by the time Fanny left and she found Hellfire sisters wore the finest and most stimulating lingerie under their habits.

Fanny did not rise for early mornings. Mrs Palm's Club went to bed late and rose as late as they could manage, and Fanny had no reason to leave her bed before the house had warmed up. Back at Langston, rising at nine would have been inexcusable, but she was a city lady now. Experience had let her organise her work and she usually had her ledgers in order by mid-day. That left the afternoon to her, with the freedom to wander in London, to see the sights of the great city. Dressed in her ordinary clothes, with Bridget at her side and trailed by Art, she had visited Westminster Abbey and Sir Christopher Wren's new cathedral on Ludgate. She had seen the home of parliament in Westminster Palace and was able to walk in the courtyard of the Tower.

Most of all, she enjoyed the curiosities in Sir Hans Sloane's British

Museum, the perfect place to shelter from wind and rain, and view curiosities from all the countries and ages of the world. The museum was always worth visiting, although Bridget did not like it. She did cheer up when Fanny persuaded Lord Beaconsfield to escort them to a grand exhibition of paintings by members of the Society of Artists in an auction house in Charing Cross.

The greatest occasion the girls attended came as a surprise. Lord Beaconsfield appeared one afternoon, and sent them to their rooms to dress modestly. He showed them to his carriage, and took them to the church of St Martin in the Fields for a performance of Mr Handel's *Messiah*. It was a wonderful experience and Fanny returned home with the music still ringing in her ears.

The year was coming to an end and members were visiting the club less often. Perhaps there were so many other events to attend, or perhaps the miserable weather kept people at home. Fanny and the girls were grateful. Some of them could go to bed early each night.

And then there were the invitations. Not to members' homes – that would be taking a liberty with the honour of their wives and daughters – but usually to the theatre or to a quartet. Fanny and Bridget were taken to hear *A Winter's Tale* performed by Mr Garrick and his company in Drury Lane. It seemed London always had something grand to offer, entertainments that would never be seen anywhere near home. And in Lord Beaconsfield they had the ideal teacher to accompany them.

Then an invitation arrived, from a member who rarely came to the Club – Lord Harmsworth. It came with a note from Lady Mary saying *Do come. Ld. Harmsworth's entertainments are always interesting and I am sure you will make an impression. I will come to Mrs Palm's and act as your maiden aunt and warden.* That sounded interesting already, especially from Lady Mary. The invitation, written on heavy card, simply requested the pleasure of Miss Francisca Howarth's company for a dinner and entertainments in Lincoln's Inn Hall. She took it down to Mrs Palm immediately.

Lady Mary seemed happy to see her and sat Fanny next to her in the carriage. "You're radiant, my girl. Are you looking forward to the evening?"

"Oh yes, my lady. May I know what we will be doing?"

"Fanny dear, if you call me 'my lady' in private once again, I shall... Well, I don't know what I'll do, but I'll make sure you don't like it. Mary will do. And perhaps Ma'am in public.

"And I don't know what we'll be doing. The boys usually have something interesting arranged, probably a grand ball. They do like dressing up their little friends as real women and no-one is allowed to spoil the illusion. So be careful, understand?"

"I'm sorry, um, Mary. I'm afraid I don't."

"They're all mollies. You know, bum boys, although I don't call them that to their faces. Not that there's anything wrong with a nice round bum, or having it plugged. I'll swear I have more fun that way than doing it properly. Anyway, the boys bring their little friends and parade them up and down for everyone to admire. Some of them are not bad looking. You'd never tell at first glance, and then you see the big hands. And something about their jaw line, too. And of course, once they've got their shirts off, there's nothing to see. But we'll have fun, you'll see."

Mollies. And Lord Harmsworth. Did that mean she would see Cousin Clarence again? What would he think of her now, keeping company with a proper Lady? Even if Lady Mary had the worst reputation in London. But what she was meant to be doing at such an occasion? She asked Lady Mary.

"Oh, nothing much. Just talk to the girls and congratulate them. Be polite, I suppose. I think the men like to see their little friends out in society, and this is the only way they can do it."

"There'll probably be dancing, and I hope you've dined because there will be nothing to fill your stomach. Just little French canapés. Elegant, of course, and the wine is always the best, but I'm damned if I can play the Grand Mistress if they only feed me scraps of toast and smoked herring. Never mind. I look on it as a duty really. All those mollies shut up at home and never acknowledged. All very well when they're young and pretty, but they've got no future. Nowhere to go when their master throws them out, or dies. I've heard some are kept on as personal servants which must be hard when their master takes on some fresh young boy in their place."

She glanced at Fanny, "You don't mind mollies?"

"Oh no. I've a cousin who's a little that way... Actually, thinking about it, before I came to Mrs Palm's, I probably would have looked down my nose at them, but now – now it doesn't seem to matter so much."

170

"That's right. None of my business what people do to have fun. And the ones I meet are interesting gentlemen, for the most part. The English are strange people. All church and honour and respecting the sanctity of their wives, and in private they're up to having their bare arse whipped by charming boys dressed in no more than a satin ribbon around their cocks. People would throw stones at them in the street if they knew what goes on when the curtains are closed. But next day they're in the House of Lords, or being the Right Honourable This or That in Parliament."

"Do they really enjoy being whipped? I should imagine it hurts terribly."

Lady Mary gave her an enquiring look. "You really haven't tried it, have you? Don't blush. It only makes you prettier, and gives me the urge to turn the carriage around and take you home to play with. Another time. My secretary shall find a time for me to hold a short class on the real world."

The carriage pulled into a secluded courtyard and a footman led them into the dark palace of Lincoln's Inn. The doors to the Great Hall stood open. One footman whispered to another, and they were announced. "Lady Mary and her protégé Miss Fanny," shouted to the footman, and everyone in the bright and crowded hall turned to stare.

Only 'Lady Mary', Fanny thought. Well, perhaps that makes sense. I don't suppose anyone here wants their full name shouted out loud. And I have been promoted to protégé. That is kind of Lady Mary, but I wonder what I have to pay for the privilege.

Lady Mary led her into the Great Hall, a large room with hundreds of candles doing little to dispel the darkness of its high walls and ceiling. In the island of light and colour at the room's centre, their hosts and the girls were talking loudly, their animated faces reflecting the champagne they were drinking. Lady Mary dived into the crowd and reached Lord Harmsworth, a tall, clean-shaven man with a glass in one hand, and the other behind his lady – Cousin Clarence.

"Well, Billy," said Lady Mary, "I see you're still doing yourself proud. I don't think I've seen so much champagne in one place since Versailles. And such a pretty companion - are you going to introduce me?"

Lord Harmsworth was examining Fanny. "Indeed, my dear, and I see you're not stinting yourself with such a fine young lady on your arm. May I introduce Clarita, my niece? Shake their hands, dear. And be very careful of Lady Mary. She has been known to lead young girls seriously astray."

Clarence offered his hand diffidently and Fanny thought she saw a plea in the eyes. She took the hand and said, "Good evening, Clarita. I must congratulate Lord Harmsworth for having such a gorgeous niece."

Lord Harmsworth beamed and pulled her in to kiss both cheeks. "Miss Howarth. I had heard of you from Mrs Palm. She praises your talents as a manager of business, but I see she could have said more. Much more. Clarita, my dear, take Fanny to meet some of the other girls. I have business with Lady Mary."

"Thank you, Fanny," said Clarence as he led her away. "He doesn't know about us and I'm too shy to tell him. I suppose you think I look silly."

Do I, she asked herself. She stopped and took his arm to pull him around. "No," she said. "Not silly. Actually, I believe you look more interesting than I do. I could never carry that rouge, and your gown… Your gown is wonderful. Lord Harmsworth obviously has taste when it comes to fabrics. And I'm sure the making of it was not cheap."

Clarence smiled demurely. "I'm glad you like it. I never gave a thought to women's clothes before I came to London but now… You can buy anything here, you know, and my lord does like the finest in everything. My Lord buys me so many under clothes. I'd be happy to lend you some, you know. Only, please don't visit." They were pushing through the crowd and Clarita was chattering over her shoulder as if no-one else existed. "I hate it when he has ladies come to visit. He really can't help himself, but he has to lift every skirt he can. I don't mind too much when he lets us play together, but sometimes the ladies are too shy. Then I have to sit upstairs by myself while he's doing them in the drawing room." She stopped and pulled Fanny close. "I feel so bad when that happens. I can't give him what they give him. He says he prefers me to any cunny in London, but that doesn't stop him, you know. And if you visit, he'll be after yours, I'm certain."

Fanny patted her on the shoulder. "Don't worry about that. He'll have to talk to Mrs Palm first and she takes care of me. And besides, Lord Beaconsfield is my friend. He visits me in the Club, and he's my guardian angel."

"Oh. You're as bad as me, then?"

"Bad? Um – I'll have to think before answering that. Are you bad? Am I bad, come to that? I'm sure Uncle would say yes, and everyone back at the Priory. Even Miss Hodges, and she's far worse than us."

Clarita looked at her for a second, and steered her to a cushioned pew against the wall. As they sat down, a servant brought a tray of champagne glasses. Clarita passed her one "Do be careful, Fanny. Just sip – this can be dangerous if you're not used to it.

"You know, I think about the Priory most days. Stupid, aren't I? There's nothing there for me, and there never was, if I'm honest." Clarita stared at her glass, watching the bubbles rise. "I never loved my father. I don't suppose you did either. In truth, he's not a man you could love. I don't hate him, you know. I never did. Not even when I ran away and had to walk most of the way to London. I suppose you only have one father, even if he's so blind.

"But Miss Hodges... she was the worst. The worst person to ever have charge of a household. She used to whip me. Really. She'd help my father tie me down over a table and she'd whip my bare bum. Not too hard, you know, just hard enough to make my bum red and hot. And every now and then, she'd stop to – to pull my thing. She'd make it as hard as she could, and show my father. They'd laugh and say what a fine young man I was growing into, and she'd whip me some more.

"Usually, she would go and rest over the other side of the table and my father would stick it into her, and fuck her hard and fast. Just enough to make them both drunk with it, then he'd stop and she'd come round the table and whip me some more, and pull my thing again. She always knew when to stop. I'd be near tears wanting to come, but she'd be off enjoying my father hammering away at her. And when they had finished, she'd throw me my night-shirt and let me find my own way back to my room.

"All the servants knew. They used to be kind to me afterwards, give me extra breakfast, or smile for me. They used to spend time over that table too, you know. If they were late, or dropped something, they'd be called down and whipped, like it or not. I don't know if they minded too much because they'd never talk to me about it. But I minded." Clarita was still staring at her glass, her mind miles and years away.

Fanny did not know how to lighten her mood. Clarita had seemed happy with Lord Harmsworth, but it seemed things were not so simple. "How did you find Lord Harmsworth?"

"Ha! He found me. I was tired of walking and spent a little on a ride into the city and a room at the coaching inn, the Bull and Mouth where you were staying. There was a woman there – Mrs Bones - who knew what to look for and she sent a message. My Lord's man of business came to see me next day at breakfast, and said he might have a position for a bright young man with some schooling.

"That did not turn out as I had expected. The position was under Lord Harmsworth, as I'm sure you understand. The funny thing is, I liked it." Clarita looked at Fanny defiantly, searching for a sign of disapproval. "You know, my father and Miss Hodges may have given me just the education I needed. Perhaps I should write and thank them.

"Oh, look. They're going to dance. Come on." A violin struck up a tune on the far side of the room. Clarita clapped her hands and said, "Allemande. Come on, Fanny, let's dance. You be the man. I've been learning this from one of My Lord's friends and it really is the finest thing."

Clarita had shed her pensive mood and she threw herself into the dancing, bright eyed and smiling. Easy for her, not so much for Fanny who struggled to dance as a man would. She knew she was clumsy. She was thinking about her feet, and no good ever came from that. She was glad when Lord Harmsworth appeared beside her and she could hand off Clarita to him.

She stepped out of the crowd and looked back at the dancers with their animated faces and hands wandering without licence. Not in the best of taste, and it would never serve at all for a ball full of mothers and daughters, but perhaps 'nieces' were expected to enjoy themselves freely. She looked back to Clarita and found her trying to dance with only one hand. The other had burrowed deep into Lord Harmsworth's breeches and she seemed to have all his attention.

Where was Lady Mary? Had she found a niece to play with and a quiet chamber to indulge her fancies? No, there she was, sitting on someone's lap, in the centre of a small crowd. Between the bodies, Fanny could see her stockings. How could that be? She hurried over and pushed her way into the ring of spectators.

Fanny had not realised that Lady Mary's gown and petticoats all opened at the front. No-one would notice when she was standing; Fanny certainly had not seen anything unusual as they had walked into the Hall. The overlap at the front of her gown suggested nothing. Now she had spread herself in the lap of a handsome gentleman. One leg reached down to the floor, but she had hooked the other over the arm of the chair. And then she had thrown decency from the window by laying open her gown and petticoats to either side, displaying herself naked from the waist down. Her stockinged legs, so long and feminine. She looked beautiful, commanding and arrogant, and her admirers had eyes only for her and her beautiful cunny. Even here in this room, the men could not resist and - to a man - were fumbling in their breeches or their neighbour's. The man Lady Mary had chosen to sit on had reached up under her thigh and was slowly diddling her cunny. He seemed to have three fingers inside her, and was rubbing her clit with his thumb. She was lost in her pleasure and her admirers did not interest her at all.

Until her eye caught Fanny. "Come here, my love," she ordered. "I'm sure you can do better." She pushed the man's hand away and gestured for Fanny to kneel between her legs. Her order was clear, and Fanny did not think to disobey. Later, she would ask herself why not, but now she placed a hand on either side of Lady Mary's naked cunny, and stared. It was beautiful. Already moist and swollen, Lady Mary's indecent pose had opened her crinkled lips. With her two thumbs, Fanny opened her further, until she could look into Lady Mary's depth.

"Lick me..." whispered Lady Mary, trying to spread her legs further. Fanny leaned in and gently touched her tongue to the little pink bud. Lady Mary sighed, and Fanny began to flick her tongue over the sweet spot. Lady Mary shuddered and quickly held Fanny's head away from her sensitive places. "Slowly," she said, "Gently..." and pulled her close again. Fanny licked and explored, enjoying Lady Mary's sighs. It felt good to make Lady Mary suffer, to hear her, and feel her moving beneath Fanny's tongue. She enjoyed tormenting Lady Mary's swollen bud until she had to push Fanny away, just out of reach, and hold her still while her pleasure subsided and she could pull Fanny close again.

All around her, the audience was silent and unmoving. Fanny paid them no attention, and neither did Lady Mary as she was drawn up and up by Fanny's insistent tongue and the two fingers in her tunnel. She reached her final crisis with her legs trapping Fanny's head, as Fanny was trapping and crushing her clitty, holding rock still as the waves of pleasure swept through her lover.

They applauded. Really, they applauded. Fanny was back in reality with a jolt and the men around her were applauding. Lady Mary was smiling at her, enjoying her confusion. She slipped her arm through Fanny's and said, "Find us some champagne, dear, and somewhere to sit. A girl can only take so much fun without refreshment."

Lady Mary did not leave her alone. As they sat sipping champagne, her arm was still threaded through Fanny's, and she was smiling contentedly. Like a cat that had found the cream, thought Fanny and smiled back happily. "That really was most pleasant, my dear. Rosie Palm has been training you, and she did not tell me. What else has she been teaching you?"

"Nothing. Honestly. Actually, I've never done – um, what I did to you before."

"Really?" Lady Mary pulled her around so she could look straight into Fanny's eyes. "Never? I find that hard to believe. But you've had it done to you, and you're a good student."

"Only at Medmenham. Did I do it correctly?"

"Correctly? What? My dear, that was the summit of correctness. Rosie has told me you're a lady of great talent but I thought she was talking only of her ledgers. Obviously, there is more to you. I shall have to take you in hand. Many a good woman has been squandered for want of a practical education. I believe I have found you just in time. But of course; Sir Francis found you first.

"Who was that man who took you in the caves? He looked quite a dish, with a good strong back and legs. I tried to ask Sir Francis, but he brushed me off."

"I don't know, Mary. But I'd like to meet him again. I wonder if Sir Francis would tell me where he came from. I wouldn't mind spending a little more time with that man. Whoever he is."

Lady Mary chuckled. "I'm not sure I'd let him anywhere near you. Not after your performance this evening. Are you sure you've never tried that before? You were quite delightful."

The colour rose in Fanny's cheeks and to divert Lady Mary she asked, "But why did you do it, Mary? I mean, they're all, well, mollies, aren't they? I wouldn't think they'd be interested in women."

"My dear, every man is interested in all classes of sex, no matter how he normally enjoys himself. Show them two women pleasuring each other, and their pricks will stand up in an instant. And if they are ladies like us, that's a sight rarely seen in public. You know, a lot of these gentlemen are my friends and it's only a kindness to help their entertainment go with a swing. I think we did that, don't you? We'll be the talk of the town tomorrow, you mark my words."

Fanny's hand went to her mouth. Oh no – not that. She had no wish to be famous at all, and certainly not for that. She looked at the crowded floor with its chattering people, grand men of the kingdom with boys aspiring to be women beside them. She did not belong. She might fit into the Club with her friends, and Lord Beaconsfield always there as a kindly uncle, but she did not fit into this edgy hidden world of powerful men hiding their secrets. How did they live in two worlds, honourable gentlemen in daylight and despised mollies in the dark? She wanted to go home.

She rode back to the club alone in Lady Mary's carriage. She had been sent back because Sir Francis had appeared in the crowd and Lady Mary wanted his attention for herself. She had tensed like a hunting dog and Sir Francis's secret would certainly be discovered. No man would be able to resist Lady Mary for long.

Fanny was glad to be back in the friendly warmth of the Club. The main room was so much lighter than the Grand Hall, and her friends were so much more comfortable to be with. And Lord Beaconsfield was there, sitting in an armchair by the fire. She poured a glass of port for him and, without asking his leave, placed herself on his lap.

He was twinkling, just as the best sort of uncle should. "I'm charmed, my dear Fanny, but why have you suddenly decided to make an old man so happy? I thought you had been invited to an entertainment by Lord Harmsworth. But you have returned early – wasn't to your taste, eh?"

Fanny did not meet his eye. "Perhaps, but I was with Lady Mary. She sent me home because she had business with Sir Francis."

"Business best done alone?"

"Oh, nothing like that. I don't think Lady Mary would care at all if that sort of business was private or not. She was trying to prise some information out of him."

"Ah. Well, I hope Sir Francis is prepared to have his soul laid bare. I have never met such a persistent woman as Lady Mary when it comes to winkling out the truth. Especially if she is digging for something embarrassing.

"Tell me – did you enjoy your visit to High Wycombe? The caves are very interesting, aren't they?"

Lord Beaconsfield had taken the conversation exactly where Fanny felt most uncomfortable and, to make things worse, she saw Mrs Palm hurrying towards them.

"Good evening, My Lord, did you know you have a veritable Aphrodite sitting on your lap?"

"I'm sure she comes as close as a human can to Elysian beauty, Mrs Palm, but it would be unlucky to say more. Aphrodite does not take competition lightly."

"I did not mean that, Sir. Has she told you what she has been up to in Lincoln's Inn?"

Fanny buried her burning face against Lord Beaconsfield's neck and whispered "Oh no..."

"Lady Mary decided to put on one of her little exhibitions, and guess who joined in. In front of all the best mollies in London! One of the member's drivers told the kitchen, and now everyone knows."

Lord Beaconsfield pulled Fanny back so he could see her face. "Well? What did you do? Who have you been playing with? How many?"

Fanny was near tears. "Lady Mary, Sir. She wanted me to...I'm sorry, My Lord" There was nothing else she could say.

"Hmm. Jump up now." He levered himself out of his armchair and taking Fanny by the elbow, led her to the dais at the end of the room. There were not many members present, only two tables of whist players, and several more gentlemen chatting over their port. They all turned to stare at her, standing with her head down and hoping to disappear into the ground.

"Fellow members, pray give me a moment." Lord Beaconsfield's public voice was rich and strong, and his speaking in the House of Lords was respected and listened to. "I have some surprising news. You all know our Miss Fanny?"

Yes, yes, agreed the members. Fine girl. Clever too. Quite the lady.

"Well, I have grave news. This evening, at Lincoln's Inn and in front of some of our more gracious colleagues..." He was cut off by laughter from the members who knew exactly which colleagues he was referring to. "I said, in front of some of our more gracious colleagues and their little friends, our Miss Fanny was led astray by Lady Mary."

Unfortunately, the members knew Lady Mary very well and cheered loudly. One voice called, "Exactly where did Lady Mary lead her, Harry?"

"I understand Fanny was led in a generally Sapphic direction." More cheers and Lord Beaconsfield asked her, "Is that right, my dear? You played with Lady Mary alone?"

"Did she enjoy it?" they shouted.

Lord Beaconsfield bent his head to listen but she could not bring herself to say anything.

"I understand Lady Mary did indeed enjoy herself, and Miss Fanny has been overcome with the emotion brought on by the happy event. Now, gentlemen, raise your glasses. I give you the prettiest clerk and fairest lady in London!"

Everyone drank and, amid the clapping, started to sing *For she's a jolly good fellow*. As she suffered on the dais, Fanny could see Sally, Gwen and Mrs Palm clapping too.

Lady Mary came to the club the following afternoon and took Fanny from her books. They sat at a card table in the main room and waited for their coffee. Lady Mary Looked very elegant in a modern russet riding habit and redingote, and Fanny wondered if this gown and petticoats were also designed to fall open at the front when required. Lady Mary seemed relaxed, as if nothing special had happened between them the previous night. Perhaps it hadn't, for her. Fanny felt less sure of herself.

She had not yet decided whether she had enjoyed pleasuring Lady Mary because making someone happy is always pleasant, or whether she had enjoyed it because it was naughty. Because it had raised a satyric wantonness deep inside her. In the quiet of her bed last night, she had relived the experience and remembered everything. The warmth of Lady Mary's thigh against her cheek, the divine slipperiness of her cunny, her taste, the passionate grip of her fingers in Fanny's hair as she fended her off to rest for a moment, and then pulled her back to her task again. Fanny took a wicked pride in the effect of her tongue on Lady Mary, but she also knew that she had only been saved from utter depravity because none of her audience had come to take her. That was a worrying thought, that she could so lose control of herself. Her cunny had been begging for attention. Attention from anyone, and she would not have argued.

The vote of approval she had received in the Club afterwards had helped. She was not an outcast and even took some perverse pride in her friends' applause. They would no longer see her as a prim Miss but a lady who understood the ways of men and women.

Lady Mary had no doubts about her. "I was right, my dear. You're the talk of the town. At least, the male part of the town because no-one tells respectable ladies about things like that. Anyway, they wouldn't know what the words mean. And I hear you were honoured in the Club too. That's nice. It's always good to be appreciated. And respected, of course."

"I don't think anyone will be respecting me for what I did with you."

"Oh, they will. Oh yes, the gentlemen admire that sort of thing. They always live in hope that, if you've done it once, you'll do it again when they are present. Don't contradict them. It's better to leave them with some hope."

Fanny waited for Lady Mary to give her some news, and in the end she had to ask.

"Ah, yes. Your young man. I had to work hard to get the story out of Sir Francis, so now you have a debt to pay me. As soon as I think of a suitable way for you to pay it.

"You were right. The man *is* Sir Francis' son, by the daughter of one of his gamekeepers. Sir Francis cares for him and his mother, of course. He says the boy was such an engaging young scamp, he took an interest in him. His name is Robert Bowyer, by the way. He grew up wild – even Sir Francis couldn't keep him at school – and took to the road when he was old enough.

"Apparently he tried a little of this and that, but ended up robbing mail coaches, which is an invitation to a short life. Just recently, Sir Francis bought him out of the condemned cell, on condition that he goes to the Americas. Sir Francis thinks he is ready to sail, but there are no ships at this time of year. He had come by High Wycombe to say farewell to his mother and Sir Francis, and when he heard you were to be initiated, kicked up quite a fuss to take Sir Francis' place. Sir Francis is a soft old thing, but he must be very fond of young Robert to pass up the chance of having you."

Lady Mary was examining her, and Fanny could not meet her

eyes. "You've met him before, haven't you? Sir Francis felt sure, but he couldn't guess where or when, and Robert refused to say. Why do I think he was returning to familiar pastures that night? Come on – tell me, Fanny. You know I can keep a secret."

Fanny could not satisfy her curiosity. As they sipped their coffee, she was thinking. Rob Longshot *was* Sir Francis' son. He had escaped from the gallows with Sir Francis' help and was on his way to freedom in America. Still only on his way, because no ship would set sail into winter storms. When spring came, as the primroses bloomed, Rob would be sailing. Leaving England forever.

Deb,

Well, there you are. Fanny has learned more about Rob Longshot, who will shortly be setting sail for America. If that's where you want him to go. I believe it is a good place because many of our readers will be American and it's nice to give them something a little familiar. Please give me your opinion.

For purely selfish male reasons, I particularly want Fanny and Bridget to sail to America in search of him. I'm imagining them first taking a coach to Bristol and finding a ship heading for Charleston. I would like them to pick up a black girl, an ex-slave, because – remember I am male and I appreciate fine things – when they inevitably get taken by pirates, I want the pirate captain to take a fancy to them. I am picturing the three girls, in the warmth of a fine Caribbean afternoon, the coconut palms waving over the lagoon where the ship is moored. The pirate captain has bent the three girls over the ship's rail, with their skirts thrown up over their backs. He and the ship's mate are admiring the picture of three shapely female bums - just as I will.

It's a wonderful thing being a writer, isn't it? It would cost me a great deal to persuade just one lady to put on a display like that for me. Jana can be quite resistant sometimes. But I can always write the things I fantasise over. Having three obliging ladies putting on a display all at once… it makes all this writing worthwhile.

Talking of ladies, how did you feel about Fanny pleasuring Lady Mary? I understand that our readers will be happy enough to read about male sex, but might resist woman on woman sex. Or am I just being prejudiced?

I don't think women really understand the pleasure men take in their pussies. They can't believe how beautiful men find them, or how they are driven to kiss and lick and suck. How can I convince them of the pleasure a man gets from feeling them come and come again just from a little licking and kissing? It really is a wonderful experience but – naughty girl that you are – I'm sure that something in your chequered past has taught you exactly what I am talking about.

So, please give me your opinions. I can always adjust things to suit you,
Regards,
Simon

Hello Simon,
Merry Christmas, Happy New Year and Happy Valentine's Day my friend.

What a few short, busy months it has been. I have packed up my life in Australia and now live in the islands to the north of the continent. What a change it has been for this Tassie girl.

My new home is a place as beautiful as it is poor. Seeing children and adults scrounging through rubbish bins for their daily needs is something I'll never get used to! I've known poor before, but this is something entirely different.

We arrived and settled into our compound-living a bit over a month ago. It is very interesting to say the least. Not quite four solid walls but a secure housing area and the fast realisation that I cannot walk around freely, outside of the compound, as I did at home. I really felt the restrictions/confinement of a country where sexual harassment (and domestic violence) is common, on day three and poor David came home to me saying "I'm done with this place." It didn't take me long at all and I really don't take well to being confined. To be fair I was sick, and irrational, sensitive and overwhelmed. It's just that here there is such an environment of machismo that one doesn't experience coming from Australia and it's very unnerving.

Just last week I went to a 'safe area' and unfortunately happened to be the only white female at the restaurant at lunchtime. Two local guys closed in on me at different times. The first walked about 80 meters down the beach towards me, raising the hood of his jumper so it was low over his forehead and stood under a tree about 10 meters away, watching me. The second actually stopped his motorbike, walked onto the beach, circled me twice, before taking up position a few meters behind me. When I turned and told him to go away, he just smiled, and his disappointment was obvious when I walked away a short time later. Both were ogling, winking, smiling, head nodding (the whole shebang). It would be funny if not so serious. I lost my nerve after 20 minutes of this and went and waited for my lunch under the portico of the restaurant. I did manage to take both their photos, although pointless because they didn't commit any crime, and being a creep is not illegal.

Thankfully, unlike some of the other women, I've yet to come across a man masturbating in his car, or whilst standing on the footpath who quickly pretends that he is rubbing his tummy instead (yeah, no dude, we all know that movement) or being followed way too close by a guy on a scooter wanting sex. Generally, the shopping and market areas are safe, but my new norm is taking a lot of getting used to. These events happen to a lot of women here, even the locals.

An 'event' doesn't happen every time I go out yet there is always an awareness that something could. The authorities are starting to crack down on it, along with more understanding and better education, but let's face it, even in Australia, sexual harassment and domestic violence are still prevalent.

The house we have been given is lovely though, and full of natural light. It is also very large for two people and has four bedrooms and three bathroom/ensuites. All the walls are drab beige in colour and all the furniture is a dark wood, so palette wise, it's a good starting point. We have all the mod-cons, although there are some things that aren't quite right, like the placement of light switches and Australian power points that'll take a three-pin but not a two-pin plug. Little things like that that make you scratch your head and wonder why.

Workmen come and go at all hours during the day to do work in our small walled courtyard. There is no schedule as such and at least once a week I come home to find my pool closed for maintenance. Yes, I have a pool! First time ever. Its blue, small and kidney shaped and on a warm day it's like having an outside bath. It is such a wonderful relief from the heat. I feel very spoiled and it is definitely one of the upsides, along with the small café, gym and lap pool in the compound, of living where we do.

Another thing I have never had in a house before are air conditioning units. Us people in the far south use them as heaters that have a reverse-cycle air conditioning function. I'm more of a wood heater girl, anyway. In this house there are six units. 6! And every single one of them has either iced up, leaked or needed to be re-gassed. I get the feeling this is very normal.

I have acclimatised well to the heat and don't need to use them as much. Initially, the coldness would trigger my typical response to 'wintery conditions' and I had tonsillitis on and off for the first few weeks. It was annoyingly ridiculous.

What I do find interesting, now that I have acclimatised, is that it can be a 40° day, the pool water is about 30° and as soon as the breeze gets up, I get goose bumps, shiver and start coughing. I think my brain needs a complete climate overhaul.

I have realised that the wonderful heat makes my injury feel better and therefore I am more active (something I desperately need to be). However, activity causes more pain, so I continue to be in this vicious cycle of chronic pain even in a warm environment. This hinders being able to focus on writing and learning a new language. I know it's only been five weeks since I arrived, but it is so damn frustrating. Did I ever mention I wasn't a patient person?

Fogging for mosquitos happens several times a week, especially when rain is due, and it is often a mad dash to the line to get the clothes in. Apparently, the chemicals are safe, but I'd rather not have them on my clothes. The fogging starts with the sudden and intrusive sound of a loud motor and then vapouring the whole area into a white cloud – which I assume is why it is referred to as 'fogging'. The overbearing noise and diminished view make it seem apocalyptic, if only for ten minutes.

Previously, my life in Australia had become somewhat of a secluded existence with contact reduced to a few friends and family – an unfortunate side effect of life for someone with chronic pain/injury is that it can be very isolating. Here it is a village full of wonderful and varied people. I hadn't realised how much I had missed that until now.

It was to this wonderful, (complete) village of people that I, via email, announced that it was my birthday soon and I would be going away and unable to attend another birthday party. I place the blame on replying to an email late at night (which I know I should never do) and the fact I have to use a Samsung phone whilst I am here, and by proxy, I also blame the telco's of Australia for not getting on board with the e-sim technology of my beloved iPhone.

You see, the default reply on a Samsung email is 'reply to all', on an iPhone you must select that. My brain did not compute this and the next day was spent with new friends, and almost-strangers, wishing me happy birthday and one or two cheeky friends pointing out that I didn't have to reply to everyone. We all need friends like that, don't we?

We have inherited many household pets; assorted sized geckos with their wonderful, cheeky laughter, the odd crane spider (a.k.a. daddy long legs), gnats with their triangle shaped wings who can be found lurking en masse in toilet pans, and cockroaches the size of mice! Well…maybe not quite that big but they are huge and come with babies stuck to their legs. Eeek!

Oh, and FYI, I have concluded that if geckos were the reason for the annihilation of mankind, I would still find them adorable.

Weather wise we are still in the 'wet', which isn't as wet as I thought it *would be, although I have been told it is a particularly wet season this year. The countryside is lush here now and the red soil of the steep hillsides are covered in deep green foliage. Roadways wash away under the pressure of the enormous volumes of water that have been channelled by engineers into what seems to be too-small waterways to the ocean. At intersections with roads leading into the hills, there is always a large amount of rock and mud wash that comes off the hills and flows onto the main road, causing blockages.*

The stone that is here seems mainly to be shale and quartz with a very poor topsoil, around the greater city area anyway. In the hills the soil is apparently much better, and this is where the local fresh produce mainly comes from. I pick up my first veggie box this afternoon grown by the farmers in the hills and I am so looking forward to it. A friend gave me her zucchini from such a box the other day and of course we discussed how you choose the size of a zucchini…be you hungry or horny and for the record…I made a wonderful zucchini slice with it.

I find the food here is very simple and does not contain the additives that we have back home. More often than not, there is no salt and pepper on a restaurant table because the food does not need to be seasoned. The downside to that, no…it's an upside, is that I can no longer stomach a lot of the processed food imported from Australia because of how salty it is. The bacon I use here is from Canada or Portugal and as soon as I open the bag, I can smell that beautiful smoked scent that we no longer get in our supermarket bacon back home, and it is so flavoursome.

I discovered quickly that having domestic staff is a way to help the economy here and I have (finally) taken on a woman to clean two mornings a week. The pressure to have a cleaner is very real, although not a requirement. For many local women, it's the only way to earn income and as they have usually worked for previous families who have left, there is this environment of automatically taking on the cleaner of the family who previously lived in the house. Not that I did.

It did take me 3 weeks to 'cave in'. As there are only two of us, we don't make much mess at all. I do have to stop myself from cleaning too much and have slowly adapted the mantra of 'leave it for the cleaner', which sounds incredibly pompous but is necessary, otherwise I would be paying her to do nothing.

I must admit that I do like coming home to find the massive amount of floor tiles that we have, are shiny clean and smelling of oranges (from the cleaning product). We are halfway through our 1-month trial and my cleaner does a wonderful job, is very efficient and even washes my car. My early stages of learning the local language make for some confusing and humorous conversations. Thankfully, my cleaner understands English enough for us to get by.

I have been keeping an eye on all those terrible bushfires in Tassie and found it amusing that they also had snow in the highlands the other day, whilst the fires are still burning. That is so Tasmanian. There are approximately 23 different fires still going and the authorities talk of alpine regions completely burnt through that will never recover. It is very sad to watch on TV.

And what of the heavy rains up your way? That tropical cyclone was relentless. The news report on the unreliable satellite TV here also stated there are fires in the West, Victoria and New South Wales. What a summer Australia is having in 2019!

Now, back to our story...

I have picked it up several times and have been unsuccessful at adding anything to it. I put this down to my new surroundings, the repeated repairmen interruptions and how social my life has become in my wonderful, new village. Add to that, every time it rains the internet goes out and with download/upload speed normally sitting at around 1MB, the connection is slower than islander time. Anyone who has been to a tropical island will understand 'islander time', things happen when they happen.

I frustratingly asked my pc the other day if the speed could get any slower, and guess what, within a minute it proved that it could, and the modem shone its little orange no-internet-connection error light brightly. One should never talk to computers.

I am so easily distracted that I am making brownies every week. For anyone. I've discovered mixing a jar of maraschino cherries and a little syrup to the batter makes them heavenly, and we are all getting plump! I'm sure distraction is a writer's superpower. What do you end up doing to avoid writing?

Right now, we are getting one of those wonderful afternoon downpours that cools off everything and makes the surroundings appear clean. I'm sure you know the kind of rain I am talking about. Hopefully, it won't knock the internet out and I can send this off soon.

This weekend we are heading to a little B & B to spend the weekend for my birthday. Might as well tell one more person. There is no internet or tv – how wonderful – and I am taking our story with plans on adding to it whilst listening to the waves crash onto the shore. Something I do really miss from home.

Off I go birthday-ing and Fanny-ing.
Debb.

Debb,
At last an email from the travelling neo-colonialist (with added servants). You must be having a great time with a new culture, new climate, new colours. Just make sure the gin and tonic does not get to you. Even though I have finally settled in Cooktown and will not be living anywhere else, I admit to some jealousy.

But your new experiences are not what our book is all about. As you say, now back to our story – except you go on to complain about tradies, and condescend to mention your download speeds are so terrible they reach what Telstra gives us in Cooktown. Plus a quick break for making brownies, before heading off for an exotic weekend break.

I need work, dear author, and to start with I still do not have your opinion on the F/F scene between Fanny and Lady Mary. Do I have to re-write it to accommodate the sensitivities of female readers or not? I don't think I should (remember our readers' poor husbands who will definitely appreciate it), but you be the judge of that. I react positively to the picture, no matter what sex the participants are but I guess some people don't.

Have you thought about how we are going to get Fanny out of London and off on her travels (if that is what you think we should do)? Do you think Fanny's uncle and Miss Hodges would fit in here? I think it would be fun to give Miss Hodges over to Sally, Gwen and the rest – she deserves it. I dare say Rosie Palm could manage a male servant or two as well. Or perhaps a visiting chimney sweep... Just imagine his strong hands, engrained with dirty black soot, gripping her smooth white hips as he takes advantage of her being tied over a table, and Miss Hodges forgetting herself enough to ask for more.

Ah – what a delightful sight. Do you think there is something wrong with me?

Looking forward to your next piece,
Simon.

Debb,
You won't know me because I have travelled here from the future... As you will read later on, I really need to introduce a new sub-plot and we agreed (yes, you will agree with me in the future) that I should come back and sow some seeds. So here goes...
Simon

As Fanny was finishing the books for yesterday, Mrs Palm watched her curiously from the doorway. Fanny concentrated on her work, not looking up until she finally tapped her pen clear and dipped it into the water bottle for cleaning.

"Oh – you gave me a start."

"I always like to see someone head down and working hard. How are we doing?"

"Very well, Ma'am. I'd say very well indeed. The manager of the bank must be very pleased to see you when you visit."

"Oh yes. I remember him looking down his long nose at me when I started. Ha! That changed soon enough, once word got around. Then he was angling for an invitation to the club, but that could not happen. Two of the bank partners are members and they certainly don't want to see their employed staff here. But he can't help himself. He'd have his hands under my gown in no time at all, if I gave him half a chance.

"Tell me – do you remember Mrs Bones?"

"From the Bull and Mouth? She's a nice lady. She didn't know me from Eve but she took care of us. It's true; she did what she could and then introduced me to you. I ought to visit her, really. Just to say thank you."

"So you should, my girl. Always care for your friends. You never know when you'll need them. Or they'll need you, come to that. It amounts to the same in the end.

"She sent me a note this morning. Someone has been asking after you. A country lady, Mrs Bones said, but well-spoken. Didn't tell her anything, but Mrs Bones was quick enough to send young Art after her when she left. She'll send him around if he finds anything. Do you have any idea who she might be?"

Fanny lied. "No. None at all. I don't have any lady relatives. No-one at all. Just Clarence."

"And an uncle. I believe you mentioned an uncle when we first met."

"Well, yes. But I've run away from him. And so has Clarence. Neither of us wish to meet him again. He's a hard man, and violent too. And he'll never drag us back, no matter what he does."

Debb,

188

So there you are – seeds sown. I'd better rush back to the future before I shoot my own grandfather and disappear at both ends. Or make love to my own grandmother and have two of me… is that how it works?
Simon

Hello my impatient friend,
I love it when you crack the whip!
Lady Mary is certainly a woman who knows how to take what she wants. I think you were sensitive enough, although I don't believe our female readers need you to be. As for me, I can close my eyes and imagine what it would be like to peer through the revered hall, air thickened with frivolity and cigar smoke, over the shoulders of partially naked men, to watch Lady Mary with her legs open wide as Fanny lapped the sweetness from her plump lips. I imagine the subtle whimpers Fanny made as she tasted another cunny for the first time, initially hesitant, then devouring another woman's taste with hunger. I also imagine the heightened arousal of Mary, feeling between her thighs the body of the innocent-looking Fanny, the tip of her tongue flicking Mary's clit and the thirsty wet sound of fast fingers plunging deep inside her, echoing for all to hear.
What a stunning collection of buildings Lincoln's Inn is. And the hall! Wow. When I first thought to research it, I was expecting to find a fancy travellers inn for the well-to-do. Not the playground of barristers. I'm sure lots of unspoken fun has been had there since the 1400s.
As for Clarita…isn't she gorgeous! What beautiful vulnerability she has, too.
I would love to see Miss Hodges handed over to the girls from the club. I'm sure they could make her purr like a kitten. Fanny's uncle too! Although I think he should get a taste of his own medicine, dosed to the eyeballs by none other than Miss Rosie.
I shall leave Miss Hodges in your hands. I'm sure you know what to do with a wild woman. As for the uncle, I have some wonderful ideas of what to do with him, I do like a man begging on his knees, but not just yet.
Debb.

Debb,

Yes, Lincoln's Inn is certainly a wonderful place – an island of ancient tranquillity in the centre of London. So many distinguished men have worked in chambers there or nearby, and then gone on to be great politicians in Parliament.

But there is a well-known joke about the place that I think you would appreciate. The Inns of Court were busy places, especially as the barristers were mostly not able to commute and spent most of their time in residence. They were all men, well off and, after work, they sought good dinners, fine wine and… amusement. Of course, there were ladies of a certain class who were ready to provide the amusement and the story concerns one of them.
She was well known and much admired for her skills. So much so that people used to say that if she had as much law in her head as she had taken in her tail, she would make the wisest judge in all England.
I felt you would enjoy that thought,

Simon

Chapter Thirteen ~ Ending and Beginning

Christmas is coming - and so is Bridget ~ an ending
~ a letter from Lord Compton
~ a pleasant surprise

Light snow had fallen in the weeks leading up to Christmas. How happy Fanny was. Bridget too. Her Mr Evans paid regular visits and Fanny was a little envious to see their love blossom.

Christmas was always the time she missed her mother most. Oh, what fun she had made of it. The whole house had been joyous and Mother's laughter, often echoing in the halls, had been infectious. This year was different though. This year, surrounded by new friends, Fanny did not feel the heaviness of her mother's loss.

The club had been festively decorated, and the few members left at this time of the year, enjoyed it immensely. Most of the girls had returned to their family homes to visit loved ones. Those who remained spent quiet nights warmed by the fire, sharing mulled wine and tarts and singing carols.

"Fanny, this letter just came for you," Gwen announced, flapping the letter in her hand. She was covered in fresh snowflakes after braving her daily walk.

Fanny held the thick card in her hands, there was no indication of a sender, apart from a very distinctive floral scent that she couldn't quite place. Untying the ribbon, neat words from a mysterious hand told how much someone missed her and longed to see her in the New Year, stared up at her. She furrowed her brow.

"Who is it from, Fanny?" Gwen asked quickly, noting the confusion in her friend's face.

"Why, I am not sure. There is no seal, nor signature."

"I bet it is from one of those new Lords' that have been guests of the club these past weeks. They've sure been pleased with you."

"Hush now, Gwen," Fanny jokingly snapped, feeling her cheeks reddening. "They have been no such thing. I serve them drinks, and maybe sit on a lap or two. That is all."

"Aye, that's all it needs to be," Gwen smiled and winked, turning to leave the room.

Fanny unfolded the note, Gwen was right, there had been a few new potential members introduced to the club. All had been well-mannered, and Fanny hadn't favoured one over the other. Of all the members of the club, Uncle Harry was her favourite. The cheeky devil made her laugh and there were countless times she had been jealous of the pleasure that Bridget enjoyed at his hands. Uncle Harry had been absent for the past few weeks, an unusually heavy snowfall bringing him illness and Fanny and Bridget were only too pleased to welcome him when he came back.

It had only been last night; Fanny had entered the private dining room to find Bridget slowly undressing in front of the fire. One by one, she removed pieces of clothing, draping them on and around Uncle Harry. For a few moments, Fanny watched quietly from the corner near the door as Bridget turned slowly, enjoying the collective audience. Standing side on, Bridget arched like a cat as she reached to pick up a single hose from the floor that had fallen from the lounge. Fanny's eyes traced the top of her head down to the bold curve of her spine and over the lushness of her fleshy bottom and down her legs.

With her large breasts swaying gently, Bridget moved to face Uncle Harry, placing her hands on his knees, parting them, her eyes never leaving his. She leaned into him, kissing his neck and straddled him widely. Fanny, feeling the itchy tingle of arousal along her spine, eagerly joined them on the lounge.

Bridget, mastering the man before her, bounced her breasts freely in his face and he took each nipple into his mouth. She held his shoulders tight, thrusting her hips up and down, jiggling her breasts as fast as she could, yelping with excited pain every time he caught her nipples with his teeth.

Fanny could tell by the look of pleasure reddening her friend's body, Uncle Harry's fingers were somewhere deep inside Bridget. Their lusty moans filling the room, made her damp between her thighs and she quickly knelt beside them. Reaching for the bib of her apron, she freed her breasts, aligning them with Uncle Harry's mouth and reached into his pants, fisting his hardened cock tightly. Empowered by the instant upward jolt she felt in her hand, Fanny began to stroke him hard, matching the rise and fall of Bridget's hips. Welcoming his wet lips on her harden nipples, Fanny's head fell back, her eyes squeezed tight, finding it hard to focus as someone's fingers made their way into her cunny.

The sounds of wetness and stuttered moans filled the room above the crackling of the fire and Bridget found her release shortly after.

Fanny gritted her teeth, holding out until Uncle Harry spilled his seed all over her fist before bucking through her release, collapsing onto the panting bodies beneath her.

Thoroughly satiated, Fanny and Bridget had seen Harry back down to the club rooms and retired to Fanny's room for the night.

"Miss Fanny, wake up!" Bridget pleaded, tears streaming down her face as she raced into the bedroom.

Fanny sat up, taking in the pre-dawn light through her window. "Calm down, Bridget, and tell me what the problem is."

"He's dead. Uncle Harry died in his sleep; they're saying." Bridget sobbed, throwing herself into Fanny's arms.

Speechless, Fanny held her tight, so many questions racing through her mind. She knew the girls would not be able to attend the funeral. Not even Miss Rosie. Only respectable friends would be permitted, and that did not include Uncle Harry's friends who worked at the club. Her heart was heavy, and she closed her eyes and let her tears fall.

A month later and the winter weather was dreary and wet, and a sombre mood had wrapped itself around not only the club, but the house, too. Members who had left town for the holidays had returned to pay their respects to Lord Beaconsfield's family. Harry's funeral, held privately at the family estate, had been by invitation only, which, even by the strangeness the ton often exhibited, was unusual indeed. Fanny had thought that perhaps the Christmas timing of Harry's death had made arrangement difficult.

Today, the club was full of members who had made their way to the club for a collective goodbye to their dear friend. Fanny enjoyed hearing many stories that his lifelong friends were only too happy to share as they gathered around the fire in the main room. She watched from the bar as easy laughter of boyhood escapades settled into long moments of quietness as they stared into the flames, a brandy nestled in their palms.

"It is with great sadness that we are gathered here today to farewell our brother. Harry was a man unlike many of the ton...sedate in his later years," Sir Francis began with a wry smile. "His early years were spent wilder than the boars that we used to hunt in his sprawling woods. I will never forget the time he startled a sow suckling her babes; She was fiercer than any nursemaid could be. With a belly full of ale making Harry believe he was quicker and smarter than the sow, he decided to grab one of the fat-bellied piglets who had wondered a short distance from its mother. Now, I have no idea what he planned on doing with that piglet, and I don't suppose he thought it through either, because as soon as the piglet started to squeal, Harry froze, and immediately realising his mistake, he dropped it."

"The sow let out a guttural war-cry and leapt up, her nursing piglets tumbling in all directions. She lurched at Harry with such ferocious speed that he screamed! Then, as pale as a ghost, he ran towards me, hollering for us to get up the old oak tree. I don't know if you have ever climbed a tree when deep in your cups, but I do not recommend it." The room filled with laughter and Sir Francis continued.

"Now, with Harry, being on the shorter side, he needed a boost to reach the lowest branch and by the time I was pulling myself over, I had not only the sow biting at my feet, but two boars the size of small horses – perhaps that is the ale still talking."

"The noisy ruckus scared off our horses all the way back to the barn. It was almost nightfall when the search party found us high in the tree, all because an angry sow wanted to settle the score with a drunken Lord. We never did venture into that part of the woods again but to this day, it is known as angry sow corner."

Amid the laughter of the room, Sir Francis raised his glass, "To Harry, never was there a better friend."

Next morning, Fanny was working on her books when she was called to attend Miss Rosie in the main room. She was sitting at a card table under the window with a man, a well dressed man in a sombre grey coat. He looked distinguished and although his temples were touched with grey he was young enough to have a full head of dark hair. He stood to greet her.

"Fanny, I expect you know Lord Compton?"

"Certainly. Good morning, Sir. Can I fetch you some refreshment? Tea, perhaps? Or coffee?"

"Sit down, Fanny. The coffee is on its way and Lord Compton wants all your attention. He has news for you."

He smiled happily. "Yes, Fanny. And I rarely have such news to pass on. You know Beaconsfield has passed on… well, he has mentioned you in his will. I am acting as executor and I'm here to tell you he has left you £10,000 and you now have your independence. What do you say to that?"

What could she say? £10,000! An extravagant sum of money... She would be safe for life.

"Your mouth's open," said Rosie.

She snapped it shut. "That's... that's ridiculous. What will I do with that much money?"

"That's for you to decide," said Lord Compton, "But I'd counsel you to keep it somewhere safe while you make up your mind. I don't want to intrude, but do you have other funds in care somewhere?"

"No, Sir. I'm afraid I came to Mrs Palm with scarcely a guinea to my name. And my uncle will not spare a bent penny, I'm sure."

"Very well. Once probate is granted – that will take a fortnight or more – I will arrange for a deposit at Hoares in Fleet Street in your name. Forgive my asking, but are you able to accept the money in your own name, or must I contact a relative?"

"Oh no! Please don't. I only have my uncle and I know that he will take it from me. He is my guardian after all. Can't it just stay in the bank until I'm old enough?"

"Ah. I'm sorry about that. But don't worry. I'm executor of Harry's will and I'll arrange for the money to be held in trust and I expect your uncle will never hear of it. I'll arrange for an allowance, if that suits you, so you can support yourself in the meantime. Let's wait for the probate and I will accompany you to the bank.

"By the way, Harry included a note that you should continue to care for your maid Bridget. I'm sure that won't be a problem, will it?"

Hello Simon,
Death in the 1800s was an interesting affair. I had initially written to have Harry's service at Westminster, but given the traditions of the day, that would have been very unlikely. And his friends returning to the city after retiring to the country for the festive season I think would have been difficult as well, especially given what the winter weather could be like.
So, Harry would most likely have been displayed in the front parlour of his home. The custom of the day was that family would have sat with him during the day, and close friends by night to ward off evil spirits. Speaking of customs; did you know a wake comes from a three-day period in which the

deceased would be supervised to ensure they would not wake-up? Also, did you know that when funeral homes came of use, the parlour became known as the living-room because the dead were no longer displayed?

If I had access to a library, I could regale you with far more information about death in the 1800s. Frustratingly, so much of my internet searches lead to American customs or academic papers – which I am sure are a wealth of thoroughly researched information, but there is nothing like an armful of historical books and pictures to liven one's curiosity.

You'll read that Harry has willed Fanny a tidy sum. I'm not too sure about wills of the day, perhaps you can enlighten us all about them?

Debb.

Debb,

Now we have changed our penniless book keeper into an heiress in her own right, I suppose it is time to let her begin throwing her weight around a little. Let her grow into something of a leader, because she will need all her self-confidence before she starts out on the next stage of her journey.

Help! I am missing a bit. Fanny is already an heiress and Uncle Harry scarcely cold in his grave. I'm sure there used to be an account of Fanny getting a letter from Uncle Harry's executor... Definitely there is a bit missing. I will go and search for it.

I can't find it! I've gone back through the saved versions but it's not there. I have had to write Fanny's £10,000 in Uncle Harry's will and put it in the right place...

And we still have Miss Hodges to deal with. She could make a delightful contribution to the club – you know all those upper class Poms went to expensive schools and were flogged regularly. The senior boys were allowed to have youngsters as their servants, and discipline them with the cane when they had been naughty. Or perhaps when the senior wanted to indulge himself.

I had thought of introducing Annie Hodges here, but that seemed a little abrupt and so I'm going to jump into my time machine and take a quick excursion into the past and give her a small introduction there. I feel apprehensive. I'm told the past is a foreign country and that they do things differently there... I do hope I don't have any problems.

Well, that wasn't so bad. I just sowed my seeds and returned. I could say it took no time at all, but that wouldn't make any sense, would it? It felt both quick and easy, and the great thing is that no-one will notice, because for them it has already happened. So let's get on and tend the seedlings,

Simon

Chapter Fourteen ~ A Surprise from Home
*A visitor from home ~ being hard on your servants ~ tied up
and polished ~ punishment at the Priory ~ the benefits of goose fat ~ a new
member of staff ~ Lady Mary's warningand a hot posset
~ Art's warning ~ safety in Grosvenor Square*

"So – how's Miss Money-bags this morning? I'll call for coffee –
come along and take a break."

Rosie was disturbing her at her books again, but she welcomed the
break. She cleaned her pens, made a note of the last figure in pencil
and followed Rosie into the main room. It was good to change from
her office desk to the open and airy space of the main room. As she
settled at their card table, she could see Rosie had news.

"I have a name for you, Fanny. What would you say if I told you
Anne Hodges is coming to visit?"

Anne? For a moment, she was confused and then she understood.
Miss Hodges. It had to be Miss Hodges, who apparently had a
Christian name Fanny had never known. "Um – a slim woman?
About thirty or thirty-five years old, with red hair?" she asked. "The
housekeeper at home was Miss Hodges. Oh dear. If she's looking for
me, my uncle can't be far away."

Rosie smiled grimly. "That sounds like her. She was here
yesterday, asking for a position."

"A position doing what? She's not – she's not a very nice person,
Ma'am. She used to whip the servants."

Rosie snorted. "You country people! They say you are tough on
your servants. We have to be softer here because servants in the city
can easily run away."

"Oh no, it wasn't just that. It wasn't normal. She used to order the
girls down to the cellar and tie them up. Then she and my uncle
would whip them. On their bare backsides."

"And worse, I dare say."

"Oh yes. Much worse. She's horrible. Sometimes my uncle used to
tie her over the table as well, to whip her and, er, use her. And the
worst thing is, she loved it. You could see it in her face."

Rosie's smile grew wider. "And I'm guessing she had you tied
over the table too, am I right?"

Fanny felt her cheeks redden but she could not share that story,
even with Rosie. It made no difference. Rosie guessed, and carried

on. "And your uncle. Did he use you too?"

"Oh no. That's why I ran away. He was going to town and he said he would – take me when he came back. He touched me, and watched Miss Hodges whipping me."

Rosie stirred her coffee and thought. "Now that puts some colour into the picture. A lady who enjoys having her bum polished, and she's looking for a position. What can she hope for here that your uncle doesn't give her? Or is she just looking for you and the position is neither here nor there? I'd better put Art on to finding your uncle. And in the meantime, we shall see how much Anne Hodges really wants her position. Something tells me there's more to her than she's letting on.

"Oh well, I dare say I shall find out. She'll be here at two o'clock. Make sure you're in your room out of sight. I'll call you if things get interesting."

Rosie could not be found when Fanny finally gave up waiting and went down to the club. Bridget had not seen her, and neither had Gwen or the new girl Susan. The curtains had been drawn over the tall windows in the main room, to keep out the smoke and frost of the winter evening. One table of members sat quietly playing whist, and two old men were stretched out in chairs by the fire. One of them was sleeping under his newspaper. Fanny made a round of the lamps to trim their wicks, and went back to the serving table. She sat for a moment, looking over the room that had become home for her. It looked comfortable, welcoming, a place she could meet the members and gossip about their lives in business or parliament, or even about their families. She felt they were her friends, not simply men who should be served and cosseted.

She caught herself looking at the door. It had been more than a month, but she still expected Uncle Harry to push the doors open. He would never do that again and the sadness of it clutched at her throat.

He had been the best of them. Friendly and caring, loved and respected, because he was Uncle Harry. His memory would always stay with her. And she thought of the money he had left her. She had never worried about money when she was back at home, but once she had reached London... That had been a cold and desperate time with her want of money colouring every moment. She had even begged for money from Cousin Clarence, until Mrs Palm had taken her in, given her a place and a new family of friends. The fear of poverty had not totally left her, but she had lived on in spite of its shadow in the background.

Now that had gone. She was an heiress. Mrs Palm had hinted at marriage, and that might be possible. Eventually. Not now, if only because the members were *old*, far too old, and she never met any other men. She did not feel the need for a man in her life. Tucked up in bed, she sometimes dreamed of Rob Longshot, but no other man troubled her. Just the sadness of Uncle Harry's departure.

She shook her head. Moping would not help, and she began to pull the port bottles from their rack and dust behind them.

"Mrs Palm wants you." Sally had come up behind her. "She's in the bakery. She says you're to come in quietly and not say anything."

"Why not?"

Sally smiled. "Curious! Curiosity killed the cat, you know." Fanny would learn nothing, so she left Sally to finish dusting the bottles and went off to the room that served the club as bakery and brewery.

As she hurried along the corridor she heard a voice calling out, a woman's voice. "No, no! No more, Mistress, please. No more…" The cry was cut off by a loud slap followed by sobs, uncontrollable sobbing.

"Enough of that." Now she could recognise Rosie Palm's voice. "Enough. You just wait until I get my pencil and paper, and you can tell me the whole sorry story again."

Through the open doorway to the bakery, Fanny could see a woman bent over the work table. She had been stripped down to her shift and stockings, and her dress was hanging from a rail along with the brewing pans and tools. She had been tied at the ankle to the legs of the table and Fanny guessed that, out of sight, her wrists were tied too. Her hair, auburn red, lay disordered over her shoulders, and her face was hidden in a black blindfold, tied in a firm knot behind her head. Her bum glowed dark pink from her spanking and Fanny winced in sympathy. Between the woman's thighs, her cunny peeped pink and wet through dark curls. She was crying quietly.

Rosie smiled as Fanny came in, and held a finger to her lips. She was holding a slipper and she rested it on the woman's back. "Now my girl, my secretary's here and we're going to get to the bottom of this. First, what's your name?"

"Annie, Mistress, Annie Hodges." It was Miss Hodges' voice

whispering. Fanny was shocked. She could not imagine Miss Hodges tied naked over a London table, but there she was.

Rosie gestured for her to sit down and write in a notebook beside Miss Hodges. "You write this down, and we'll make a fair copy for her to sign later. Now, Annie, where do you come from?"

"Langston, Mistress, Langston Priory."

"And what do you do there?"

"I'm the housekeeper, Mistress."

"I see. And who's your master?"

"Mr William Howarth, Mistress."

Rosie patted Annie's bum with the slipper and she shivered. "Now, let's get down to business. How many servants did you have under you?"

"Eleven, Mistress. Including the cook, Mistress."

"Eleven. And did you punish them when needed it?"

"We took them downstairs, Mistress. The master had a special room for – for things like that."

"I see. You had a special room for punishing the maids. So what did you do to them?"

"It would depend, Mistress. Sometimes the master had different fancies, but mostly he wanted them tied over the table and whipped."

"Tied up as you are now?"

"Yes, Mistress."

"And whipped. But I haven't used a whip on you, have I?"

"No, Mistress."

"I've been kind to you, haven't I? Kinder than you were to those poor girls, is that true?"

"Yes, Mistress."

"And next, Miss Anne Hodges, what did you and your master do to the poor girls after you had whipped them?" Rosie looked at Fanny and winked. "I hope you're writing all this down. Annie will be signing it in a minute. So Annie, what did you do to the girls – no, wait a minute. How were you dressed while this was happening?"

"The master liked me to, um, undress."

"So, let me paint a picture. A helpless girl tied across the table, with her skirts over her shoulders I'm sure. And you running around in just your shoes and stockings, I suppose. You must have been cold down there in the cellar."

"I always had the fire lit an hour before, Mistress. To keep the cold away."

"I suppose all the whipping would have kept you warm anyway. Did you use the whip, or your master?"

"Both of us, Mistress."

"Did your master use the whip on you too?"

"Yes, Mistress. Sometimes. He said it was good for me."

Rosie rolled her eyes and gave a little whack with the slipper. "And was it good for you? Did you like it?"

"I liked it a bit, Mistress. It made me feel warm."

"I'm sure it did. And then what happened? I'm sure your master wasn't content with simply whipping the girls."

"He, um, took them, Mistress."

"Right there in the cellar, with you watching. He doesn't sound like much of a gentleman. Did he have you too?"

"Yes, Mistress."

"And you liked it, didn't you?"

"Yes, Mistress."

"Yes, Mistress – I'll lay you were howling with pleasure. Whipped and fucked, that's what you wanted, wasn't it? That's what little Annie loves. A hard cock shoved up her. Would you like one now?"

Miss Hodges did not want to answer but another whack of the slipper opened her mouth. "Yes please, Mistress. Oh God…"

"Well, you're not getting one. You're in no state for the gentlemen just now, and the porter's gone home. You'll just have to please yourself when we're done. I'll ask cook to lend you a rolling pin.

"Now, did anyone else live in the house. Your master, you, and the servants - was there anyone else?"

"There was Master Clarence, Mistress. He was the master's son."

"And where was he when you were punishing the girls and letting your master fuck you over the table? Did he come down and have his fun with you too?"

"No, Mistress. Master Clarence was a weak boy. His father was very disappointed in him and we used to whip him too, to make him stronger and more like a man."

"Honestly? Whip him to make him more of a man? I doubt that would work. How has he turned out?"

"I don't know, Mistress. He ran away a couple of years ago and the master has not heard from him since."

"Wise boy. I'd run away too. Was anyone else living in the

house?"

"Yes, Mistress. Miss Fanny. She was the Master's niece."

Rosie's smile was back again and Fanny smiled in return. Now she might find out what devilry her uncle had been up to. Rosie again put a finger over her lips, and cupped a hand around her ear. Yes, Fanny would be listening very carefully.

"So, young Annie. Tell us about Miss Fanny. Did she know about the room downstairs?"

"Oh, no, Mistress. We kept it all from her. Her room was a long way from the cellar and she couldn't hear anything. And besides, the master wanted to marry her off as a virgin so he wasn't going to lay a finger on her."

"Marry her off? Who to?"

"I'm not sure, Mistress. There was an old man, Mr Sinclair. He seemed to be keen on Fanny. And there was Mr Darnley – he was younger and I think he had more money."

Fanny was shocked. Mr Sinclair? He was nice enough, she supposed, but so *old*. How could her uncle even think of forcing her to marry him? And as for Darnley, just the memory of him turned her stomach. Thank God she had run away when she did.

"So Miss Fanny never found the cellar? She was never punished?"

"There was once, Mistress. Right before she ran away. We took her down and punished her a little. Not much. Not like the girls. And the master didn't have her. He wanted to show her off as she was. He didn't want to sell her as damaged goods."

Just a little? Just a little? Fanny could remember very well just how her bum felt the morning after they had spanked her. And 'damaged goods'? She bristled at the thought.

"I see. So Miss Fanny was married off?"

"No, Mistress. She ran off next day, along with her maid. We didn't see her again."

"Disappeared? You didn't hear any more of her?"

"No, Mistress. We did hear tell that her coach had been robbed. The other passengers and the coachman ran away, and Miss Fanny drove the coach herself, all the way to Whealdon. But we've heard nothing of her since. Er, Mistress, Mrs Bones at the Bull and Mouth said you may have some information about her."

"I may do. But first, exactly what are you doing in London? Your master sent you to find Miss Fanny?"

202

"He brought me, Misstress. I've been asking after her, but no-one cares. Not in London. There's so many folk here. But you can help me, Mistress?"

"And if I do? You'll make trouble for Miss Fanny and just rush off back home. That's no help to me. It's not as if her uncle will pay me anything."

"He might, Mistress. He really wants to find her."

"To marry her off to some old man?"

"I think it's changed, Mistress. Even if he catches her, she'll have no reputation left. I can't imagine a gentleman taking a woman like that to wife. I think her uncle wants her for money. It's something to do with her mother's will."

"Oh-ho! Now we're getting somewhere. There's a will and money involved. He's more interested in money than cunny. Why am I not surprised?"

"Mistress, I heard him say something about catching Fanny before she turns twenty-one."

Time stopped for Fanny. She stared at the pale, scrubbed wood of the table, with Annie stretched over it. Her hair was spread to one side, and her face pressed against the tabletop. Annie longer sobbed but appeared tired. Her blind eyes saw nothing. She did not know she had opened the yawning sadness of Fanny's mother and hurt Fanny again.

What was she saying? She had always understood her mother had nothing when she died. Her uncle had told her so himself. She lived on his charity, and by his rules. She wanted to know more, but Rosie had her finger across her lips again. She left the room for a moment, and returned with a jar from the kitchen.

"Here; goose fat. Rub it over her bum while I get some more answers out of her."

Fanny dipped two fingers into the fat and began to spread it over Annie's abused skin.

"There," said Rosie. "Does that feel better?"

"Yes, Mistress."

"Good. But keep talking. What do you want from me, Annie? Why did you come and see me."

"Mrs Bones sent me, Mistress. She said you might help me to a place."

"But that's not why Mr Howarth brought you to London, is it?

Where are you staying, Annie?"

"Shoreditch, Mistress. Mr Howarth took a room for me. Over Mrs Jollet, the pie maker."

"And Mr Howarth? Are you keeping him warm at night?"

"Oh no, Mistress. He never takes anyone to bed with him. He's staying somewhere near the Temple. I don't know exactly where."

"The Old Cock Tavern in Fleet St. That's where you find him every morning, when you tell him what you've been up to. And whether you've found your Miss Fanny. You see, I've been checking on you, Annie. I want to know if you're all you say you are. Do you want a position, or are you just weaselling your way in here because your master sent you?" Rosie gave her a whack with the slipper, and Annie screamed in surprise. "That's for telling me pork pies, Annie. Don't do it again."

Rosie bent and began to free Annie's ankles. "Now, my girl, you've told me a lot but I doubt you told me everything. What do you want from me?"

"Please, Mistress, could you take me in?" Miss Hodges sounded small and uncertain. "I'm a good worker, honestly I am, and I'd love to work in a house like this."

"I dare say you would. But what about your Miss Fanny? I haven't told you anything about her."

"Oh, Mistress, if you take me in, I don't care about her at all. Only if I can't stay, I'd have to keep looking."

"Mmh. Well now, I suppose it's no harm to tell you. I did hear of a woman like her, a few months back, a proper lady but working in Butler's gentleman's club on Strand Lane. Just gossip, you understand. Can't say if it's true or just moonshine.

"Now, I'll think about giving you a place. You can work under our clerk – she's the one who organises all the cleaning and laundry. Do well there, and we'll see if we can't get some special duties for you. We have a few gentlemen who enjoyed being tied down just as you do.

"But if you're staying here, don't you go to Butlers. Oh no. Butlers is by way of being competition to me. So you can have a position here, or you can serve your master. Not both. Pay up your lodgings and be here at midday tomorrow."

Rosie waved Fanny out of the room and pointed towards the front room. She left silently as Rosie said, "Now, young Annie, I hope you've got a nice warm bum. You'll have to take it home alone, I'm afraid. Get dressed and I'll have a cab take you home."

The club was busy, and Fanny busied herself carrying drinks to the card players and chatting with the members gathered around the fire. Rosie did not come for some time, and when she did, she was dragged off to play whist before Fanny could question her.

Fanny's news shocked Bridget at breakfast next morning. "What, Miss? Miss Hodges is here?"

"Don't burn the toast! She wants to work at the club, and I think Mrs Palm will give her a position." She smiled at Bridget's confusion. "Can't you imagine her sitting on a member's lap with her bubbies on display?"

Bridget stood with her mouth open and the toast cooling on her fork. The idea was unthinkable.

"Toast, Bridget, or the butter won't melt."

She hurried to slide the toast onto Fanny's plate, and set another piece of bread on the fork. "But she's too old," she said.

Fanny felt smug. "Oh, I don't know. She's no older than Mrs Palm and the members like *her*. She's never short of company. And besides, Miss Hodges looks a lot younger with her hair down. And we don't call her Miss Hodges any more. She's just Annie now. That will be fun, won't it?" She concentrated on spreading butter on her toast, and waited for Bridget to bubble over.

"Annie? I can't call her that!"

"Why not? If she comes back today, she'll be starting at the bottom, doing the laundry and so on. You'll be more important than her, and that'll put her nose out of joint. And besides, Mrs Palm has already had her tied over the bakery table and given her a good spanking. She was very sore, believe me. I rubbed goose fat into her bum before she went home last night. Careful, now you're burning the toast. Come and sit down. Eat your breakfast."

Bridget sat down, thinking. "You've seen her, Miss? What did she say?"

"She didn't say much at all. She was blindfolded and didn't know I was there. Then Mrs Palm asked her questions so I could hear the answers. You wouldn't have recognised her. Honestly, she sounded quite, well, nice. Not a dragon at all. She wants to come here even if she has to start at the bottom and work up."

Bridget chewed her toast slowly. "I don't understand how she found us."

"You remember Mrs Bones? She told her to contact Mrs Palm when she was asking questions about us. And my uncle is in London too. She been reporting back to him every day they've been in town."

"Oh no. The Master... he'll come and take us back. Or take you, at least."

Fanny smiled for her and put her doubts aside. "Don't worry. We have friends now. Mrs Palm, Lady Mary, all the club members. They won't let anything happen to us."

She did not see Bridget again until the afternoon, as she was completing yesterday's entries. A tap at the door, and Bridget ushered in Miss Hodges herself, diffident and looking somehow smaller than she had at home. Fanny carefully finished the entry she was making, wiped her quill and laid it aside. Miss Hodges stood on the other side of the desk, wearing a drab grey dress and a mob cap that had seen better days.

"Well, Annie Hodges. Fancy seeing you in a place like this." She could not stop herself enjoying Annie's downfall. "Why have you come to see me?"

"Mrs Palm sent me, Miss Fanny. She said you will take care of me."

"That's right, Miss," said Bridget, "Mrs Palm wants her to work in the laundry every morning, and come to help you in the afternoons. In the evening she can help in the kitchen. And if she is cheerful and makes friends, she might be able to help serve the gentlemen, but she'll need a new dress for that."

"And you're happy with that, Annie? You are going to stay with us?" She was watching Miss Hodges's face, searching for deviousness.

"Yes, Miss, I'd like to stay."

"Why? Have you fallen out with my uncle? You were housekeeper at the Priory. Here you will be just another girl. At least, until you've shown us you can better yourself. Mrs Palm is fair, but firm. I'm sure you won't enjoy the laundry."

"I don't mind, Miss. Honestly. That's how I started, before I came to your uncle. I always said a bit of hard work never hurt anyone, and now I have a chance to prove it."

"How is my uncle? Is he healthy?"

"He's always healthy, Miss. He brought me here, but you know that, don't you? It was you listening the other night, wasn't it?"

"It may have been. But why did he come? And why did he bring you?"

"I'm not certain, Miss, but it may have something to do with your mother's legacy. He was certainly more upset to lose you than Master Clarence. But I don't know, Miss. Honestly I don't. I do know he's had lawyers looking for you. Perhaps you heard of them? When they didn't find any trace of you, he came down himself. He brought me because he said I could ask at the back doors of the big houses, where he couldn't, of course."

"What have you been doing in London? How long have you been here?"

"It must be three weeks, Miss. Your uncle has had me walking the streets, asking if anyone had seen you. Then he sent me to the Bull and Mouth and I talked to Mrs Bones there. That was a bit of luck."

"What does he know about me? Did you tell him you had found me?"

"But I didn't find you, Miss. Mrs Palm told me you might be at some other place, on The Strand I think it was. But I didn't tell him that. I didn't tell him about Mrs Palm at all. I wanted to leave him.

"London's a wonderful place, isn't it, Miss? All the fine folk and their big houses and pots of money. So busy, day and night, everyone doing what they can to earn a shilling. It's very hard to find a place, if you're down from the country. But you'd know about that, I'm sure."

"Do you know where my uncle is now?"

"No, Miss. I saw him the day before yesterday. Now I expect he's looking for me as well."

Could Miss Hodges be trusted, Fanny asked herself? Perhaps. Time would tell. She picked up her quill again. "Bridget, please take Annie upstairs and give my room a good clean. I believe the wardrobe needs emptying and re-filling. Then Annie can take a sandwich, and go to see what cook wants her doing in the kitchen. I'll see you back here tomorrow at eleven o'clock, Annie. I've some letters to be copied."

Fanny was still wondering about Annie as she worked in the

clubroom that evening. Two naval officers had come in early for pork chops and Madeira punch. They were full of life and wild stories of the Spanish Main. She would have spent more time with them but, having laid a good foundation for later revels, they were off to the theatre followed by a night's gaming at Almack's Club. By then, the clubroom had filled with regular members and the serving girls were trotting back and forth with orders for food and drinks. Fanny joined the girls in caring for the gentlemen with a taste for female company.

Lady Mary found her sitting by the fire and musing while the gentlemen talked politics beside her.

"Good evening, Fanny. I hope you're not leading these gentlemen astray? No, no, do sit down, my dears. This is a gentleman's club and no place for a weak female to disturb you. Although, if you can spare her, I'll take the young lady away to give me some advice."

Fanny smiled as she was led away. "A weak female, my lady?"

"Well, you know how it is. Here, bring some champagne with two glasses, and you can tell me what you and Rosie have been getting up to."

They sat at a quiet table, sipping champagne and with Lady Mary listening intently to the story of Miss Hodges and Fanny's uncle. She sat back and asked, "Have you warned Clarita?"

Fanny was shocked. "How did you know? No, I haven't warned her. I suppose I should."

Lady Mary looked smug. "I keep my ear to the ground. But don't tell him - her. I'll have a quiet word with Lord Harmsworth. Perhaps he'll think it's worth sending a couple of men around to chat with your uncle. Or perhaps Harmsworth can get the Bow Street Runners to scare him off. Where is he staying?"

"Annie says he's staying somewhere in the Temple. I don't think she knows exactly where."

"Right. What's his name? I'll do something about that in the morning. Shall we invite Clarita for tea? Do you want to see her again? And you can bring your Annie along. I'm sure Clarita will enjoy seeing her again.

"But tell me; why is your uncle chasing you? It can't be to marry you off, not after you've been staying with Rosie. You've been completely ruined, my girl. No respectable country gentleman would look at you for a wife. Stuck up prigs. No man worth his salt wants a simpering miss in his bed. He wants someone who knows what she wants, and knows what he wants too. Damn fools.

"But why's he chasing you? I'm beginning to believe there's a good sum of money involved, and Annie's right. You don't know anything about your mother's will?"

"I never thought about it. Mother never said anything to me, of course, and I always thought we were living on Uncle's charity."

Lady Mary raised her glass and watched the bubbles rise. "Money might be a good thing, of course. You can never have too much money, as long as you don't scrabble after it like some of the men at Lloyds. But it can be a bad thing too. You could be at risk of being knocked on the head. Had you thought of that? Unless you've made a will, and as you can't do that until you're twenty-one, your uncle might be tempted to have you disappear. He's your next of kin, after all. He'd inherit everything your mother might have left you."

Fanny lay awake that night, searching for sleep in the turmoil of the day's news. When sleep did come, she found herself fleeing along empty streets. Her uncle was gaining on her, waving his coach whip and threatening to whip her bare arsed along High Holborn.

She woke early and wandered the empty corridors down to the kitchen. Cook looked at her tired face and sat her down at the big table with her back to the stove. She did not wait long before she had a hot posset in her hands, thickened with ground almonds and egg yolks. The business of starting the day went on around her. She soaked up the warmth and friendliness, and the smell of baking bread.

Mrs Palm found her still at the kitchen table, reading through cook's book of secret recipes.

"Well now, Fanny. Just who I was looking for. Come to my office and we'll have some tea."

The office felt cosy, with a small coal fire already lit. Mrs Palm waited for their tea to arrive before starting to talk. "I've been talking to Lady Mary. She thinks you might be in a deal of trouble."

Fanny did not know what to say. The ghost of her uncle had come to Mrs Palm's door.

"You're worried, aren't you?" Mrs Palm reached over to pat her hand. "Don't you fret. I might not be a grand lady, but I have friends. Aye, and Lady Mary has more. We're going to set the dogs on your uncle. Lord Compton will come by later to ask you questions and so on because Lady Mary wants to know about your mother's will. She thinks that's what's behind it all and Lord Compton's a Law Lord. I've got Art keeping an eye on your uncle. He's been asking after Annie mostly, but I dare say he'll get back to asking after you as well.

"How's Annie going, anyway? Is she a worker?"

"I believe so, Rosie. Bridget says she never stops, and that's good. But she's already asking about a better dress so she can serve in the club."

"Good. In fact, that's very good. Lord Compton's fond of having his bum polished – do you think we could trust Annie that far? I normally have to do it myself because the girls we have just now are not trained to it. Call Bridget and have her bring Annie upstairs. Borrow some stays and stockings for her - nice ones, mind.

"I don't know when Lord Compton will come, but she'd better be ready. Use the small dining room upstairs. I'll find some rope and a birch for her. And you'd better be ready too. He'll want to know everything you can remember about your mother, and who your uncle's lawyer might be."

Fanny found Annie upstairs, with Bridget lacing her into black satin stays. She was wearing them over a sleeveless linen shift. The lacy hem of the shift covered her hips, and nothing more. She was looking into a cheval glass, admiring herself until Fanny's arrival embarrassed her.

"Very stylish, Annie! Bridget, where did you find her those stays?"

"Madge lent them, Miss. Miss, you don't have any stockings she could borrow, do you? What she's got are warm, but they ain't elegant."

"Oh, I expect so. Spin around, Annie." She had to admit that Annie looked attractive, far more attractive than she had ever looked in Langston. Bridget had combed her hair out and now it touched her shoulders. Rouge and a single green ribbon added an intriguing depth to her face, and Fanny recognised a pair of her own earrings. For a mature woman, Annie looked slim. The stays emphasised her waist and the feminine curve of her hips. Her bum had recovered from Rosie Palm's attentions; perhaps the goose fat was just what she had needed.

Fanny met Lord Compton in Mrs Palm's office. As a regular

member of the club, she had often served him his favourite Madeira with a saucer of dry biscuits and always stayed for a chat. He liked to tease her for her seriousness in following parliament. He never invited her to sit on his lap, but he did promise to introduce her to Prime Minister Grenville. She liked him, his unpretentious black jacket and breeches, and the diminutive lace jabot he preferred. But he wasn't Uncle Harry.

Tonight, he was serious. His silver pencil skipped over his notebook collecting names and addresses, family connections and likely lawyers her uncle might have used or conspired with. And he wanted to hear all about Higgins, the lawyer who might come from Langport or Whealdon or even further afield,

Eventually his questions slowed and he seemed uncertain until Rosie took pity on him. "No, Ritchie, Fanny's not going to be entertaining you this evening. Or an old hen like me. I've got someone far more interesting for you. A new lady who has come to stay with us – Mistress Anne. You'll like her, I'm sure. I'll go and fetch her."

Lord Compton smiled at Fanny. "Are you enjoying your position here, my dear? Mrs Palm speaks very well of you."

"Yes, Sir. It was a little difficult at first but now I have a proper ledger, I think every shilling is accounted for."

Lord Compton had something on his mind. "You were a very close friend of Harry Beaconsfield's, I believe…"

"He was kind to us, Sir. Just like an uncle. A real uncle, I mean."

"Ah well. Yes, Harry was a kind man. A kind soul, and I miss him dearly. And he was generosity itself to you, I believe. You're a lady of means now. I expect you have young fellows knocking at your door every day."

Fanny felt herself blushing. "I'm sure I don't have time for such things, Sir."

"Perhaps not today, but I daresay that will change one day. I owe Harry a great deal, you know, so I'd like you to come to me if you are ever in need of advice. We'll have this business with your uncle sorted out in no time, I expect. I think I see what he's up to and I can put a stop to it."

"Sir, you didn't ask about my cousin. My uncle's son Clarence."

"A son? I've heard nothing of that. Where is he?"

"He stays with Lord Harmsworth, Sir. Er, one of Lord

Harmsworth's special friends. He ran away from home and my uncle can't bear to hear his name any more." But Mrs Palm and Annie were at the door and she lost Lord Compton's interest immediately. Annie had left Langston far behind and stood now in the shadow of the corridor dressed in the finery of an elegant courtesan. She wore no more than her borrowed stays, buttoned boots and stockings and she had all of Lord Compton's attention.

"Er – Mistress Anne?"

Annie inspected him for a moment and turned to Rosie. "Is this the gentleman, Mrs Palm? I had expected someone with a little more spirit."

"I think you'll have your hands full, Ritchie. Take him upstairs, Anne, and see what you can do with him."

They listened as Annie led her victim towards the stairs. They heard her snap at him "You just want me to go first so you can watch my arse, don't you?" Lord Compton mumbled something and they heard a slap. "What do you mean you don't want to look at my arse? You'll watch it when I tell you, my boy. Aye, and kiss it too if I've a mind."

Fanny still had a smile on her face as she settled to her books next morning. Miss Hodges had become Lady Anne of the Whip; what would her household in Langston think of that idea? And Bridget, had she forgiven the evening she had been tied down and whipped? Perhaps she had. Fanny had been whipped too but that was all so long ago, and so far away. She couldn't find any resentment in her heart because, in truth, Annie had helped steer her to her new life. If she now had to choose between life in London or the quiet of Langston, she suspected she would remain in London, at the centre of things.

Bridget tapped at the door. "Excuse me, Miss, but Art is here. He says it's urgent, Miss."

Sighing over the interruption, she washed her pen and followed Bridget to the kitchen. Art sat by the fire, sipping at a mug of hot milk and honey. He jumped up and removed his hat. "Good morning, Miss. I hope I finds you well?"

"Very well, Art. Very well indeed, but what brings you here?"

Art gave up his attempt at politeness and rushed out, "It's your uncle, Miss. He's gone to Mr Fielding, you know, the magistrate

Fielding with his runners from Bow Street nick. And they're going to come here, Miss."

"Damn that Henry Fielding," said Mrs Palm. "Why didn't he stick to his scribbling and his theatres? He did a deal less harm back then." She had been dragged early from bed and was struggling to pin her hair into place. "Art, do you know just when they'll come?"

"They're getting together in Bow Street at four o'clock, Missus."

"Well, that gives us a little time at least. Damn this hair!"

Fanny manoeuvred her into a kitchen chair and took her comb. "Who's Mr Fielding? Is he bad?" She began to discipline Rosie's hair.

"Bad? No, I suppose not. Then again, he could be a lot better. He used to write plays that would have you falling out of your chair laughing, but the Lord Chancellor put a stop to that and he took to politics instead.

"He used to be fun, all fire and poetry. Long words and ale by the hogshead. But he's a magistrate now. He's broad in the beam and narrow in the mind from all that sitting on the King's Bench. And he's no friend to a working girl, that's certain. Now, where are we going to send you and Bridget?"

"Me?"

"Yes, you. We can't have you mooning around here if your uncle's coming. We might all get taken for kidnapping. Lady Mary will take you in, I'm sure. And Annie had better go along with you. I'm sure Lord Compton would be happy to take her in, but she's got to keep her mystery as far as he's concerned.

"We'll write to Lady Mary immediately. Don't worry, it won't be for long. A couple of nights should be enough. And I want to write to the members – the more of them sitting here this evening playing whist the better. And the girls will have to dress like Sunday school teachers – they won't like that.

"Come on to my office and we'll write that letter. And Art can carry it there."

Lady Mary's house on Grosvenor Square spoke of elegance rather than grandeur. Out here, away from the smoke and soot of the city, its gleaming Purbeck marble shone brightly in the afternoon sun. They climbed the steps and, before they could knock, the polished black door swung open. A tall young footman addressed them with a bow, "Miss Howarth, I believe? Please come in. If you would wait here in the library, I will fetch Mr Canton the butler."

The library was a long room, occupying perhaps half the frontage of the house. Light flooded in through the tall sash windows overlooking the square, shining on plain tables and chairs. This was a room for work, and the furthest table had an untidy spread of books and note papers; someone was taking a break from study.

The wall facing the windows was covered in packed bookshelves. The shelves reached up to the high ceiling, and a moveable ladder hanging from a rail allowed access to the higher books. Fanny promised herself she would ask Lady Mary for permission to explore.

The door opened and Mr Canton pushed in and bowed. "Miss Howarth, a thousand pardons but Lady Mary is not at home. Only last week she set off for Constantinople, but do not worry. Her house is open to her friends and we will certainly accommodate you at Mrs Palm's request. Would you like to follow me to one of the guest rooms?"

Next evening, Fanny sat in the library watching the light drain from the little park at the centre of the square. A maid came to her elbow, bringing a lighted candle, and went on to draw the curtains. She returned to her reading, a curious book of accounts, a record of one merchant's business in settlement of Charles Town in the Americas. How had Lady Mary come by it? And what had possessed her to bind it and keep it on her shelves? Fanny read through the careful entries, reconstructing the life and business they recorded.

James Poyas had made his living supplying the colonists with necessary items from England, wool and linen textiles, iron tools, paper, china and glassware. Even the simplest of manufactured items came from England. And when Mr Poyas's customers were short of real money, he took payment in whatever they produced themselves – wooden shingles, deerskins, indigo, and even rice that he could send back over the Atlantic and sell at a profit.

She pushed the book away and sat pondering the strange life Mr Poyas must have led while he was compiling his records. Charles Town did not sound like a great city if one business could supply so wide a proportion of what was needed. No business in London would sell textiles and iron tools from the same shop. Perhaps it was only a small town – like Whealdon or even Langport. But Whealdon had a mail coach nearly every day. She supposed a ship to Charles Town would take months to arrive and letters from home must be a rare event.

Annie was at her elbow. "Would you like your supper in your room, Miss, or will you be joining us?"

Back home, the question would not have been asked. She would no more have eaten supper with the servants than with the man in the moon. But now, somehow things were different. She had been through some hard times with Bridget, and even Annie was a breath of home. She followed her to a simple dining room near the kitchens and sat on a bench at one end of a long table.

"Lady Mary serves the same food here as they take upstairs," said Bridget. "But it's hotter for us. Not so far to go and no time to cool down."

The steak and oyster pie was excellent, rich and nourishing. Fanny had not realised she could get hungry simply by studying. "Please, Miss," asked Bridget, "Can we go back to the club tomorrow?"

Probably, she thought. If Mrs Palm hasn't sent a message by tomorrow, I will write her a letter and ask Mr Canton to send it. She wanted to go back to her job and her friends.

Mrs Palm came next morning, earlier than she would normally be up and about, and before Fanny could write to her. They took tea in the library.

"You missed all the fun," she said. "Your uncle certainly got his money's worth, what with one thing and another. Fielding marched in with half a dozen of his bruisers and your uncle in tow, but Lord Compton stopped him in the hallway. Made him produce his warrant for entry and search, and that was good. He'd made it out in my name but Lord Compton said that was a nonsense because the club belongs to the members and it holds the lease of the building. He told Fielding to send his men to wait outside, along with your uncle. Then he invited Fielding inside for a chat.

"You should have seen us! All the girls were dressed up like maiden aunts with their hair up and covered. I'd asked several of the members to come in especially, and the girls were serving them coffee and food as polite as you could wish. And some members were playing whist for penny stakes – all quite blameless and proper.

"Lord Compton sat Fielding down and called for coffee. I took it to them myself, and by then Fielding had taken the time to look around and seen just who our members are. Not people to be trifled with, you can be sure of that. Lord Compton asked why Fielding had come and he said he was looking for you. You were believed kidnapped and he had information that you were being held prisoner in the club and being debauched by the members.

"I was surprised he could say such a thing with a straight face and I'm sure I would have scratched his eyes out, but Lord Compton just laughed and told him to look around. Did the members look like kidnappers, he asked? Then he turned to me and said, Mrs Palm, is there any person of that name in the building? Of course, I said no, and he told Fielding, 'You may take Mrs Palm's word for it. I'd vouch for her on any day'. I thought Fielding might see through the question and ask if you had been there or if I knew where you were, but Lord Compton knew his man. He'd lost heart and was happy enough just to finish his coffee and leave.

"I didn't call you back to the club yesterday morning and, sure enough, there's been a couple of rough blades hanging around in the street yesterday and they're back again today. I believe your uncle won't take no for an answer.

"Lord Compton says it will take some time to be sure just what your uncle's after. I went to see him this morning in his chambers, and you owe me a great deal for spoiling my sleep. I can't remember when I last saw eight o'clock of the morning. Anyway, Lord Compton says you need to be out of the way for some time. He says it's best if you're out of sight until you reach twenty-one. Then he can do something public to secure any settlement your mother might have left you, and you'll be safe."

"Twenty-one? No – that's more than a year away. Where can I go? What can I do?"

Rosie put her hand on Fanny's. "Don't worry, love. You've got friends and we'll find a place for you. You have money too, and that's a help, to be sure.

"Lord Compton says he will draw up the papers for you to be made a Ward of Chancery. That means if you have any money, your uncle won't be able to get his hands on it. You'll have the protection of the law then. We just have to hide you away for a little while... What a shame that Lady Mary's away in Turkey. She'd know what to do.

"How about Ireland? We could probably find someone over there. And I'm sure all the club members would give you a home, except their wives would object. There's no family that could take you in?"

Fanny thought hard. No family, except for Cousin Clarence and he lived at the pleasure of of Lord Harmsworth. Uncle Harry would have rescued her. Perhaps Sir Francis Dashwood might help, but she did not know him well enough. She needed to be away from things, away from London, somewhere her uncle would never find her.

"I think," she said cautiously, "I want to go to Charles Town. In the Americas."

Hello Simon,

I think I will interrupt you and put the brakes on there for a bit, I was losing myself in all that has transpired since Uncle Harry's death, and in the world, in general.

It is not as if 2019 was not challenging enough for both of us, we now have a pesky virus whose initial name resembled that of a humourless bottle of beer. At least COVID-19 is a serious sounding name. This time reminds me of a roller-coaster ride I took in Blackpool four years back. Now, I love a good ride, but this one was one of the oldest in the world, made from wood, and I have never been so scared on a ride in my life. With all its creaking and overabundance of movement, it just did not feel safe.

Everyday life has been made out to be that way now. I remember thinking early on that corona was just like the flu that people get every year and many die from. As we now know it is not, and within a space of a few short weeks the world had been brought to its knees. This did not surprise me in the least though. For anyone who travels internationally, we know just what a global society we are. The fact that factories were closing because a single, small part could not be sourced from China, did not surprise me either. Having been involved with manufacturing, I know how reliant the world is on Chinese products. Now the rest of the world does, too.

2020 was going to be a very productive year for me. I had finally settled into life in a foreign country, I no longer suffered from tonsillitis, I had commenced learning the local language, I had chosen what diploma I wished to study for, I had multiple flights booked with the highlight being attending the Calgary Stampede, my new diary had finally arrived and I had colour-coded my plans up until Easter, when we were going to travel in a group to a distant local island for the first time.

Ha! Make plans and God laughs. Isn't that what they say?

Within a space of a few weeks all these plans were redundant, and a couple of weeks after that I was flown back to Australia because as a military spouse, I was deemed non-essential at our posting. I am now displaced in Darwin (I could not stomach another 14 days mandatory isolation if I had headed home to Tasmania), sleeping in strangers' beds in whatever long-term accommodation I can book, until who knows when. Possibly another 6 months I have recently heard.

I am enjoying watching nature heal herself around the world, though. The photos out of Venice, showing the canals running clear are remarkably interesting to see, especially as I was there in December. I have stopped to ponder just how different things may have been if we had travelled just one month later.

Now, back to the story…

My heart is a little heavy with us leaving the mother land, especially as so many of those place names can be found right in my home state. They make me a little home sick. So, farewell to the shared Epping Forest – made famous by highwayman Dick Turpin, the Dovers, Scamanders, Bichenos and Launcestons…the list is almost endless.

Hello to…America? Or was it British America or even British West Indies at that time? I am not sure.

Was North America still part of the colonies then? I have a feeling it was. I remember reading many years ago that although America tried to distance itself from Great Britain at one point in history, the Brits had the titles Americans wanted, and the Americans had the new money that the Brits desperately needed. Hence the merging of many families by marriage.

It was interesting researching the ships of that time and discovering how the nautical terms of port and starboard came to be. Although, from what I have read below, you seem to be a deft hand with the lingo. The approximate distance between the English Channel and coast of America is 3000 nautical miles, or 5556 kilometres. A journey of that distance would have taken between 21-30 days to sail. Those weeks of sailing must have seemed endless back then.

Now that I have caught my breath, I will let you continue…
Debb.

Chapter Fifteen ~ Back on the Road

Leaving London by post chaise ~ the invisible passengers
~ reflections on the pace of modern life
~ breakfast in Marlborough

Fanny peered through the window of the post chaise. There was little to see. Even when the moon broke through the clouds, she had only dark roadside bushes and trees to look at. Beside her in the dark, Bridget and Art were asleep, Art jammed in the corner of the seat against the carriage wall, and Bridget using him as a cushion. They were the closest people she had, almost family, and they had left London at her side without question. Of course, Art would only travel to Bristol, but Bridget had trusted her to find a ship to take them to a new future far from home.

Things happened so quickly that she still felt events had left her behind. Mrs Palm had arranged for their things to be made ready and packed, and she had negotiated the hire of a post chaise. She had called on Lord Compton. He had approved of their plans and sent a clerk to gather Fanny's signature on several papers that would allow him to manage her affairs while she was overseas. Before lunch, Mr Canton the butler had come to inform her that her luggage had arrived and that the chaise was expected shortly. It would come to the mews behind the house, hidden from the street. He had instructed the cook to prepare a basket of food for the journey and hinted mysteriously that arrangements would be made to divert any unwelcome watchers. The subterfuge clearly excited something boyish in the staid and distinguished butler.

Leaving Lady Mary's house was easy. They filed out through the kitchen and there stood the chaise, gleaming yellow with shining brass fittings. Mr Canton stood by the horses talking to the postboy, a middle-aged man with a light blue uniform coat and a low crowned hat. As they stood, they blocked the view so no chance passer-by could look into the mews and spot the three fugitives climbing into the chaise and taking their places on the floor, hidden from view.

Mr Cantor put on a distinguished top hat that he must have borrowed from his master and stepped aboard, carefully not looking at the passengers squeezed uncomfortably into the space about his legs. The postboy and his cad mounted their horses and the chaise began to move. It was a light vehicle, far more responsive than any coach Fanny had travelled in, and gave the impression of skipping down the street.

Mr Cantor did not stay in his seat long, Fanny guessed they had travelled no further than Knightsbridge when he called the postboy to stop. To confuse any curious watcher, he took the basket cook had packed with their lunch to show the postboy, and Fanny heard the instructions for the postboy to deliver the basket to the landlord of the Bear Inn in Guildford. Mr Cantor returned and, opening the door only a little to prevent anyone looking inside, replaced the basket on the seat. He gave Fanny a wink and a big smile. He whispered, "Stay where you are for ten minutes, Miss Howarth, and then you may make yourself comfortable. Good luck."

Complaining, they unfolded themselves from the foot well, sat on the seat and looked around. The view from the chaise was wonderful. Not only could they look out to the side but, unlike a proper carriage, they had windows in front of them. They could look out over the trotting horses and see sights before they swept past them.

They were leaving London and in no time at all they had passed through the villages of Kensington and Hammersmith. It would not be long before the vegetable gardens would peter out and they would be in proper farming country with enclosed fields and occasional woodland. Fanny settled back with her thoughts.

She liked the chaise they were travelling in. If Lady Mary had been at home, she would surely have lent a private carriage for their journey. Instead, Fanny had hired the chaise herself. Mrs Palm had made the arrangements, but Fanny had paid from her own purse. £9 3s 6d! She had never spent so much at once, and she promised herself she never would again. Even when she was buying wine for the club, she had only spent shillings and that was on Mrs Palm's account.

Fanny felt she had stepped into a new world, a busy world where important people hurried to do important things. And everything lay prepared, ready for their call. If a gentleman must be in another town as soon as possible, people leapt to serve him. People, carriages, horses were all waiting for his call, and in this modern world they did not waste time in their beds. Coaches crossed England continually, through wind and weather and at all hours. Even a staid mail coach could roll from London to Exeter in as little as eighteen hours, and Fanny's chaise would travel much faster. But what craziness had the world jolting uncomfortably through the dark night instead of lying comfortably in bed and taking a little longer next day to reach Bristol?

The chaise was swaying on its springs, lulling her to sleep. The grinding of the metal tyres on the road and the clop of the horse's hooves filled the carriage, but she could still make out the murmur of the riders chatting. She wondered where they were. London was already far behind and they must be due for a stop. The horses could not last forever.

When it came, the stop happened very quickly. The horses were changed without conversation and they were soon moving again. She drifted into a doze. There were more stops to change horses and by the time they reached Reading, the light was beginning to fail. As they were changing at The Rising Sun, the postboy came to the door. "We shall be leaving you here, Miss, and Nathaniel will take you on to Marlborough. He's a good man and my cousin. He'll take good care of you." She scarcely had time to thank him before Nathaniel had mounted and the wheels were turning again. They passed on into the night and the roadside trees passed as dark shadows. She did not call a halt until there was some light in the sky. She took to the bushes with Bridget while the men relieved themselves beside the road.

Fanny stretched herself in the cold morning air. Dawn light showed they were running down a long and gentle slope, a valley between rounded, treeless hills. "Do you know where we are, Art?" she asked.

"Not what you'd call exactly, Miss, but they do say that Marlborough's up ahead and that if you wish for breakfast, they say the Castle and Ball is the place to go. Shall I tell them?" Art's stomach was obviously troubling him.

"Yes. Let's all have breakfast. It's a fine day, perhaps we will get by without rain, and we're miles from London." And my uncle, she added silently.

Debb,
So we are well on the road and will reach Bristol tomorrow. I have been amazed at the complexity of travel arrangements back then. We just jump in a car and turn the key, but travelling with horses is much more difficult to

organise. Apparently you would go to a coaching agent to buy tickets for the stagecoach – London to Bristol would take around 10 hours for a fast mail coach and that's about 120 miles of dirt road. You would go to a similar agent if you wanted to book a private trip, say, by riding or in a post chaise. Your ticket would include all the changes of horses every ten miles or so. For scheduled coaches, there would be a team hitched up and waiting. Presumably a team for a post chaise would take a little longer to change. A post chaise needed four horses and two men, the postboy (who could be a man of any age) and his cad or assistant. They would ride the near-side horse of the front and rear pairs of horses. As the rear pair had a pole between them, the rear rider's leg had to be protected from crushing by wearing an iron guard around his lower leg.
A post chaise is a light vehicle capable of travelling fast without tiring the horses. They were normally four wheeled, and the commercial ones for hire would be painted yellow. The drivers wore attractive uniforms, with coats for bad weather. As they did not have a seat for the driver, the view forward was unobstructed and one of the benefits of the chaise was the good view of the passing countryside.
Fanny's journey is smooth and uneventful. No fallen trees or wheel breaking potholes stopped her. No highway men and – most importantly – no lions.
Lions? In England? I will transcribe an account from the British Postal Museum and Archive, 15-20 Phoenix Place, London :-

The BPMA Museum collection consists of a wide range of objects and ephemera including a number of prints and engravings. This small collection of around 200 works is currently being documented and will be added to the online catalogue in the not too distant future.

The prints and engravings are in a number of styles and were produced using a variety of techniques, but all show some aspect of postal history, be it images of Royal Mail coaches unloading at the GPO at St. Martin's le Grand, portraits of Postmasters General, interior scenes of letter sorting offices or motifs of postmen and postmistresses at work. Through this collection one can learn about the workings and development of the British postal service, and the interesting incidents that happened along the way.

One of the more dramatic stories told through the prints and engravings appears in two separate prints *Lioness Attacking the Exeter Mail, At Winterslow Hut near Salisbury, on the Night of Sunday 20th October, 1816* and *The Lioness Attacking the Horse of the Exeter Mail Coach.* Their subject is, as the titles might reveal, an event that took place in 1816 where the 'Quicksilver' Royal Mail coach, on its way from Exeter to London, was attacked by a lioness outside the Pheasant Inn.

A lioness is not what one might expect to see in the English countryside, but not far from the Inn a travelling menagerie had stopped for the night and it was from here the lioness had managed to escape from its keepers. As the coach stopped to deliver the mail bags the lioness attacked the lead horse of the 'Quicksilver', setting its talons in the horse's neck and chest. The two passengers of the coach fled into the Pheasant Inn and locked themselves inside, blocking the door for anyone else, while the mail guard attempted to shoot at the animal with his blunderbuss. A large mastiff dog from the menagerie set on the lioness "with such pluck and fierceness" and grabbed one of its hind legs, which made the lioness release the horse and attack the dog, chasing and finally killing the dog some 40 yards from the coach. During this time the keepers were alerted to the situation and managed to trap the lioness under the straddle of a granary. The menagerie proprietor and his men then crawled in after the lioness, tied her legs and mouth, and then lifted her out and back to her den in the menagerie caravan, while the locals of Winterslow Hut watched on.

This incident became known all over the country, and at a time without telephones, telegraphs or railways it is amazing to find that a mention of the Sunday night attack was made the very next day in the London Courier, and in further publications in the following days. It also became the subject of artistic work, among them paintings by A. Sauerweid and James Pollard, which the prints in the BPMA's collection are based on.

Another noteworthy fact about the incident, and a testimony to the efficiency of the postal service at the time, is that the attack only delayed the mail coach 45 minutes before it obtained a new post horse and continued on its route to London.

There you are. Isn't it amazing what you can come up with to divert yourself from the hard work of getting a good story written… So let's jump back into the chaise and carry on to Bristol.

Simon

Chapter Sixteen ~ Westward Ho!

Mr Burridge ~ Sally is not a slave ~ Bristol Port and
Capt. Smollett ~ a passage for three ~ a nautical cabin
but no sailing ~ pickled cabbage and teeth
~ Hispaniola spreads her wings ~ a friendly face
~farewell to England

They did not reach Bristol until the afternoon. They would be staying with Mr Burridge, Lord Compton's agent in the city, and Fanny carried a letter telling him to arrange their passage on a suitable vessel travelling to the Americas. She must remember to write and thank Lord Compton, as soon as she had an address from which to write.

When they had travelled the final miles into Bristol she found a busy place, a town crowded around its river and confined by the hills beyond. The best buildings of modern limestone shone in the afternoon sun and lacked the sooty coating of London town. A strong breeze from the west swept the air clean of smoke and made breathing a pleasure.

They found Mr Burridge's house in the centre of town, on St Stephen's Street, close behind the church. A four storey building with an elegant façade and an office on the ground floor. The family lived above, and presumably the row of small attic windows were the servants' quarters. Fanny waited in the chaise while her letter was delivered.

The door closed, but soon opened and a short round man hurried out, still buttoning his jacket. He came straight to the chaise. "Miss Howarth? Welcome to Bristol, please come in and I shall call for some tea. Unless you'd prefer coffee? Is it the fashion for ladies to drink coffee in London?" He ushered her upstairs to a drawing room while Art and Bridget took care of the luggage.

The room was lit by two glorious windows facing south. Fanny stood looking out over slate roofs to the fields on the other side of the valley. In the middle distance, a forest of ships' masts marked the quays that Fanny needed.

"Will it be difficult to find me a ship to Charles Town, Mr Burridge?"

"Oh, we have all the ships you could wish for, my dear." He

waved his arm at the masts marking the length of the river. "This is Bristol. Shipping is our town's business, and mostly to the Americas. That's a wonderful place, you know, full of opportunities for a young man to better himself and make his way in the world."

"And a young woman?"

"Young women too. There's no old money over there. No lords and such like, so a man can make his own way. If he has character and energy, there's no telling what he might do. An intelligent girl merely has to get behind a young man like that and her fortune's made."

They were interrupted by the tea, brought by a young brown-skinned woman in a fine gown. Not dressed as a servant, and she looked at Fanny curiously as no servant would.

Mr Burridge introduced her. "Miss Howarth, this is Sally. She works for the family. Sally, Miss Howarth is staying for a little while until we can find her a berth to Charles Town. If you can find the time, perhaps you can show her a little of Bristol tomorrow." Sally smiled and nodded, and left them.

"How unusual, Mr Burridge. I don't believe I've seen anyone quite like that."

"Ah yes. Sally. My late brother brought her back from the island of Jamaica. She looked after his children until they were old enough to have positions of their own. Now she helps around the house and my office. Very clever girl, but she'll never amount to much in England. She says she'll only take a husband who's more of a scholar than she is, but no man of any means is going to take a black to wife."

Sally came to Fanny next morning and took her down to breakfast. Today she was more disposed to talk and told a little of her home in Kings Town, Jamaica. She did not like Bristol. "It's too cold. Always grey and raining. And windy, a cold wind. I want to go back home and see the coconut palms again, with warm and gentle winds. And beaches of white sand and warm seas. Here there's nothing but mud. A muddy river flowing in and out. In and out, but never changing. I hate it."

Her vehemence was shocking. "But Mr Burridge – he seems like a nice man…"

"Oh, he is. There's nothing wrong with the family, and his brother Thomas was a good master too. I'm not a slave, you know. I never was. Mr Thomas gave me a position as governess for his children and gave me an allowance. They say no man is a slave on English soil, but Mr Thomas gave me a letter of manumission just in case. And Mr Burridge signed it as well, and took it along to the Kings Bench to have Lord Justice Baines sign and seal it too. I am NOT a slave."

"But it never occurred to me that you might be."

Sally smiled at her innocence. "I suppose it wouldn't. But Bristol is a different place. There are many respectable men here who have made their fortune buying negroes in Africa and selling them as slaves in the Indies. Christian men who go to church every week and hear about Jesus and his love for his fellow man. Ha! They look at me and think I might be a fine present for their wife. And you can be sure that's not all they're thinking."

They made a fine procession when Sally took them to see the sights of Bristol. Sally at one elbow and Bridget at the other, with Art behind them to guard their purses. The street outside Mr Burridge's house was as narrow and as busy as Cheapside in London but Bristol was small. In no time at all they had reached Broad Quay and the soul of the city. They burst out of the darkness of the street into the bright and busy quayside. It was lined with vessels, each a tangle of ropes, spars and masts, and crowded with men labouring and shouting, loading cargo or hauling barrels and sacks up from the bowels of the ships and onto waiting carts on the quay. The air was rich with exotic smells – spices, coconut oil, pepper, sweet sugar, and over all a waft of rum from the heavy barrels. Much of the cargo travelled only the short distance to the warehouses fronting the quay where different gangs of men were swinging the sacks up and onto precarious platforms high above the street. They stopped and watched how sacks were pulled up to double doors in the platform floors outside each entrance, lifting the doors as they passed through and then resting on the doors once they had fallen closed again. Hands inside the warehouses pulled them in, and sent the hook and pulley back down for the next lift.

The noise and industry shocked Fanny and she was glad when Sally led them off the quay to Broad Street and High Street. There were shops here, familiar ground and quieter. Fanny decided the big difference with London was not simply the size of the place, but the air. The wind was blowing up the river, a fresh salt breeze from the sea, permeating everything. It felt exciting.

They returned home after ten o'clock and immediately Mr Burridge sent for Fanny. He was in his counting house, sitting at a table in a large bay window overlooking the street and talking to a stocky man in a dark blue coat. The gentlemen rose to greet her.

"Miss Howarth, may I introduce Captain Alexander Smollett? He is an old friend, we've worked together for years. He is taking the *Hispaniola* to Charles Town shortly, and has offered to take care of you. And he's shipping general cargo for the settlement – straight there, so there's nothing to worry about."

Fanny shook his hand and agreed to hold herself ready to leave on any day after the coming Sunday. Captain Smollett left without engaging in any small talk.

"A man of few words, Mr Burridge?"

"Yes, indeed. Few words and even fewer smiles, but he has the respect of the port. I've used him time and again, and I hear his men ship with him one voyage after another. That's a sign of a good captain, if his sailors respect him and ship with him again. They won't ship with someone who has a reputation as no sailor, or spends too much time with his brandy bottle. Their lives depend on their captain, and they're very exacting judges of character. You may count on it."

She was called to Mr Burridge next morning. He jumped up to greet her and betrayed his unease by shaking her hand.

"Why, Mr Burridge – what is wrong?"

"Ah, nothing. It's just that I have a favour to beg."

"A favour? Certainly, if I can help at all."

He ushered Fanny to sit at his table and called for tea. "How do you find Bristol, Miss Howarth? Very small, I dare say?"

Fanny did not know how to respond. She had only known London for a short time and could hardly call herself a city dweller. Bristol might be smaller than London but it was still expansive and beautiful compared to her home in the Priory. "I have seen very little of it, Sir, but I'm keen to see more. The quay – I've never seen anywhere like that."

A maid came with their tea and Mr Burridge waited for her to leave before unburdening himself. "It's Sally. I promised my brother I'd care for her, and that is not easy. She has a will of her own, you know. I'd give my right arm to find a gentleman she would accept as a husband but there's no sign of one coming along. And now she's decided she wishes to return home to the West Indies."

He stopped, unable to ask for help.

"I believe you will ask if she might travel with me?"

"Ah – yes. She can't travel by herself, not to those parts. She'd be taken as a slave by the first ne'er-do-well who came across her. I'd be grateful if you could care for her, I really would. She has an allowance of her own, you know. My brother saw to that, and I'll add something of my own. That's only just and fair. She's a part of the family and we will all miss her."

So, there would be three of them sailing the Atlantic, Fanny, Bridget and Sally. That should be fun and she went off to find Bridget and give her the news. Today she planned to walk to Clifton where the views were recommended, and she hoped Sally would join them.

Every day they visited the wharf where the *Hispaniola* was taking on her cargo and supplies. She would have liked to board and inspect her quarters but, without an invitation, they could only stand at the edge of the quay and watch the confusion of rigging and spars. There were always sailors at work, running ropes, splicing, tarring. She could make no sense of the giant spider's web. She supposed the sailors and Captain Smollett understood everything.

Fanny's main concern was packing. What would she need? Sally said good linen could not be found; should she bring linen and rely on local seamstresses to sew it? How about findings such as ribbon and lace? Or buttons? Surely Bristol shops were finer and better supplied than those of Charles Town, so what should she buy? At least she had been able to buy two fine sea-chests for her things and Bridget's clothes. They would at least appear as thoughtful travellers before the sailors.

Papers and money were a worry and Mr Burridge had ordered two oiled cloth wallets they could wear beneath their gowns to keep important things safe. Art would no longer be there to protect them; Fanny had given him two sovereigns to help on his way back to London.

The call came late one afternoon. Their baggage must be on board at first light. They could follow after breakfast, and the *Hispaniola* would catch the morning tide. Fanny and Bridget spent the evening forcing clothes into their chests, and getting ready. They slept badly and were ready for breakfast long before the table was laid.

Fanny's heart was racing as they left their carriage at the quayside. This was the biggest step she had ever taken, across the unstable gangplank with the muddy river below and onto the ship that would be her home for the next months. The deck moved under her feet, and strange smells surrounded her. The three girls were hurried into a low passageway by a barefoot sailor, definitely a seaman because he had both a tarred pigtail and a gold earring. He opened a narrow side door for them to look in. "This'll be your cabin, ladies. Should be the master's by right but he's shifted to make room for ye. Ain't much room, 'tis true, but we'll sling hammocks for two of ye. Milady will take the cot, I'm sure. You'll sleep like a baby there. Captain says you may sit in his cabin for the moment. He'll be in to see you soon enough. Sends his compliments and says you'll oblige him by staying put until he comes."

"Can you tell us when we will sail?"

"We won't be doing much sailing, Milady. Oh no. We're tiding down to Avonmouth and then we may spread our wings a little, God willing. If he ain't, well, we'll surely grow sick of the sight of Avonmouth. It happens, 'specially with the wind against you and tides you wouldn't wish to see. Now, here's the Captain's cabin. Do you sit comfortable and don't touch a thing or he may have you flogged."

Bridget was horrified. "Flogged?"

"Oh yes, my dear. He's the Captain and he can flog who he wishes. Not that we're likely to see you lashed to the ratlines. Not unless you be truly wicked."

Captain Smollett's cabin was a strange room. Low – so low that Fanny's hat could touch the beams of the ceiling – but richly furnished with modern furniture, cushions and curtains. Windows faced them, filling the width of the room. She was looking out on the bows of the next ship tied along the quay. A long comfortable seat below the windows drew the girls and they sat down to take in the rest of the room.

It was sparsely furnished. A gentleman's room, laid out for work. On one side, a chart table with papers, charts and instruments. A small dining table with six chairs filled the centre of the room. Fanny guessed it could seat eight at a pinch, but dinner would be intimate rather than grand. A curtain closed off the other side of the cabin; perhaps Captain Smollett's cot was hidden there.

The girls sat on the bench and waited. "Sally, do you know what happens next?" asked Fanny.

"They'll pull us out into the tide, I suppose, and the river will take us down to Avonmouth. I don't suppose they can put up the sails because the wind's blowing the wrong way."

"But that will take a long time, won't it?"

Sally gave her a knowing smile. "Everything to do with ships takes a long time. Much more than you'd expect. You'll have to learn patience."

"Do you get seasick? I've heard stories…"

"If they were bad, they're probably true. But some people get past it quickly. I just go and lie down when the ship starts moving. I don't feel well, but after a day or two I'm fine. If you're unlucky, you probably want to die. It takes some people that way but it doesn't last forever."

They sat in silence hearing only the shouts and thudding feet of the sailors on the deck above. The ship trembled, and seemed to shake itself free. They knelt on the seat and watched as the ships and houses passed by.

The cabin door opened and Captain Smollett stepped in, ducking his head to avoid a beam. "Good afternoon, ladies. We're under way at last. If you have forgotten anything, it's too late and you'll just have to make do. Have you seen your cabin? Good. You may remain here for the afternoon watch and I will arrange for my steward to serve dinner. You may ask him if there is anything you need. Now, when you hear the bell striking eight for the end of the watch – that's four o'clock on land – please go to your cabin."

The Captain was intimidating but Fanny asked, "May we go on deck, Sir?"

"Not at present. We will shortly drop our tow and tide our way downriver. That's a tricky business and I require clear decks. We will anchor before dusk and I will send the master to guide you on deck. I trust you will soon adapt to life aboard ship. I will invite you to dinner as soon as we clear Flat Holm and you may ask all your questions then. For the present, I am required on deck."

Once the door had closed and the Captain's footsteps had died away, Sally said, "He's not very friendly, is he?"

Fanny thought about that. "No. Not friendly, but he did check on us and ask about our cabin. I suppose being a Captain is a bit like being a king. We're lucky he thought we are worth talking to at all."

They sat and watched the riverbank slide by. Somehow, and Fanny did not understand how, the ship was moving sideways. The Captain was holding it across the river and letting the current carry the ship downstream. Sally did not understand either but she did say she had seen it many times on the Avon.

The door was pushed open and an old sailor came in bearing a tray. "Afternoon, ladies. Here's dinner for three. Do you sit at the table, and I'll set it out." Dinner was three large bowls of vegetable and meat stew, with a hunk of bread. And a saucer of pickled cabbage each. "My name's Adams, ladies. Just come along to the galley and call out if you ever need something. Make the most of dinner because it'll never be this fresh again until we reach Charles Town. You'll be eating hard tack shortly once the bread is all finished, and I wager you'll be sick of salt pork before you see land again. I'll be off and bring your beer to wash it down. Oh, and Captain's orders is that everyone must eat their pickled cabbage, like it or not. You don't eat it, you'll get the scurvy and all your pretty teeth will fall out."

The stew was not bad at all, but Adams' warning sounded ominous. Salt pork and pickled cabbage. It would be a hard life at sea.

As the light faded, there was a tap at the door and a tall young man entered, tall enough that he could only stand with head and shoulders bowed. He had fair curly hair and a sparse beard. He touched his forelock and introduced himself. "James Luxton, master. And I believe you would be Miss Fanny? And this must be Miss Sally and Miss Bridget." Bridget curtsied in return.

His accent was strange. Certainly not like the accents of the country folk back home, but also not like the accents common in Bristol. She would question him when she had the chance.

"The Captain sends that you may come on deck if you wish, and asks me to show you the ropes."

They stepped out of their passageway into the light. The base of a huge mast stood in front of them, draped with hanks of black rope. The mast was bare of sails but the forward mast and the mast behind them each held a sail. The deck at the stern, which made the ceiling of the cabins, was raised and steps led up to it on either side. The ship's wheel was up there and Captain Smollett stood beside the helmsman. He was absorbed with his task, scanning the river downstream and watching the sails.

"This here's the waist of the ship," said Luxton. "When we're at sea, you'll be welcome to come and stand here. That there behind you is the poop deck. Perhaps the Captain will invite you up there in the future. If he does, you must only stand on the leeward side and don't speak unless he speaks to you. That's the side without the wind. T'other's what we call windward 'cos the wind blows from that side."

"Oh dear," said Fanny. "You make the captain sound very severe."

"An' I suppose he is, but that's the way when you're at sea. The Captain is the Captain and he's the law, judge, jury and hangman all in one. Come along – we'll go forrard. What you have to keep an eye for, ladies, is never to get in the way of the sailors. Like those men there; they're tending the jib and when the Captain calls out, they'll haul on that sheet. Letting it out or taking it in, to keep us mid-stream. You don't want to get in their way. We'll go this way."

He led them along the side of the ship opposite the sailors waiting for orders. They climbed up three steps to a small pointed deck. "This here's the bow deck. The men have their quarters down below. It's a fine place to stand and watch the flying fishes when we're in warmer waters but you ladies must remember the men's privies are just down there." They obediently peered over the rail to a small projection that was home to a large spar reaching out beyond the ship. "If you're up in the bows and a sailor comes along, do you step back out of sight and let him get on with his business. Oh look, Miss Fanny. You have tar on your dress already. You've been christened. You'll learn to keep your skirts out of trouble soon enough. I'll find you some rag and turpentine so you may clean it off. But let me take you below. I believe we're losing the tide and we'll be anchoring. You don't want to get in the way."

With all three of them, their cabin was crowded. Fanny's cot was a simple pallet suspended at the head and foot from ceiling beams. There was room for their baggage to be stowed beneath it, and Sally and Bridget were using it as a seat. Fanny had the single chair and rested an elbow on the narrow table that folded down from the wall. Adams had given them a shrouded lamp to hang from the ceiling. It gave just enough light to cast shadows. Reading would be difficult, and sewing impossible.

They all felt tired. "I want to try my hammock, Miss," said Bridget. "I'm sure I'll sleep like a baby."

"You will," said Sally. "I love hammocks. The sea can be as rough as you like and your hammock will still rock you to sleep. You wait until we're out at sea."

They listened to the sailors above. Fanny assumed they were anchoring, and soon enough the noise died away and Adams came to sling their hammocks. Once they had settled down they slept cosily, hardly disturbed by the weighing of the anchor and the resumption of their drift downstream.

Early in the morning, when grey dawn lit their porthole but showed nothing of their surroundings, they felt the ship suddenly heave to one side. They felt movement and heard water gurgling by outside.

"What's happening?" asked Fanny.

"We're sailing," said Sally. "The Captain must have caught a breeze that will allow us to get clear of the river. I want to get up and see."

The cold wind made them wrap their shawls tight around them. The ship was moving through dark muddy water, rippling and rushing along the side. The river mouth on either side showed as no more than dark, uninteresting land and they did not seem to be making much progress. The excitement of the ocean lay in the future. Fanny stared ahead, searching for something, anything, to mark their course but there was only darkness. The cold soon drove them back to their cabin and sleep.

Fanny lay in her cot and stared at the ceiling. The ship was pitching and rolling and the cabin moved around her. Daylight flooded in through the porthole and she was surprised to see a ship's compass set into the roof beam. Mr Luxton could lie in bed and still know his ship's heading. The hanging cot smoothed the rolling but she staggered as she stood up. The others were still sleeping when she ducked under their hammock ropes.

Adams was waiting in the passageway. "The Captain sends his compliments and he's offering you breakfast. I should take it, Miss. He don't invite just anyone. I'll make sure the others get fed, if they ever drag themselves out of their hammocks."

There was the smell of frying in the air as she went to knock on the Captain's door. The Captain was sitting at the table with his back to the door and looking out of the wide window. The ship's wake reached out into the distance, pushed sideways by the current. He had been reading and his book sat beside his breakfast plate.

"Good morning, Miss Fanny. I trust you slept well? Do sit down. Adams will be bringing eggs and bacon. Do you drink coffee?"

"Indeed I do, Sir."

"Capital. We'll make a sailor of you in no time. Tea is all very well but you need coffee or chocolate on deck when the wind's blowing. And your stomach is not protesting the waves?"

Fanny had forgotten about sea-sickness and examined her feelings. "I believe my stomach is coping, Sir. And I slept very well. I was pleasantly surprised, but my cot rocked me like a mother. And now we're at sea."

"More or less. More or less. We're still in brown water, but I dare say we'll leave that behind later today."

Adams brought in her bacon and fried eggs, and for the first time she noticed the raised lip at the edge of the table. That must be to stop plates sliding off when the ship moves, she thought; things are different at sea.

"Captain, may I ask where we are to eat on normal occasions?"

"Oh, Mr Luxton will show you the wardroom. Did you bring any provisions of your own? Adams can take care of them if you wish."

"Mr Burridge did give us a dried ham. He said it would keep well on the voyage."

"Only if it is kept cool and well aired. You had better pass it on to Adams. He will care for it and serve slices as needed. Now, when you have finished your breakfast, shall I take you up to the poop deck? You will have a good view from there."

When he led her up to the poop deck, Luxton was standing next to the helmsman. He touched his hat to her and smiled.

"I shall take the rest of the watch, Mr Luxton. Please inspect our water and check the lashings. We don't want any surprises when the weather turns rough. But first, you may spread topsails. Let us make hay while the sun shines."

Turning to Fanny, he led her to the upper edge of the sloping deck. "Hold to the railing, Miss. You must always keep at least one hand for the ship, or you'll take a tumble. This is what we call the windward side because the wind is coming from that direction. And over there is the leeward side. The ship leans that way. If you or your girls feel the need to vomit, always use the leeward side where it can do no harm.

"That over there – to our right or starboard side – is Wales. And to port, everything there is England. Somerset first, then Devon and finally Cornwall. We'll pass two islands by and by. They are Flatholm and Steepholm. We reckon our voyage begins once we have passed them and are in clear water. Now I'll leave you. Please consider yourself free to use the poop deck when we are not working the ship, but I would be grateful if you stay on the lee rail." He touched his hat and went to stand by the helmsman.

Mr Luxton and a solid block of a man were sending sailors aloft on the main mast, an exercise that required a great deal of shouting. Fanny's heart was in her mouth as the sailors reached a yard and shuffled sideways along it in both directions. They were standing on a single rope, with their arms over the yard, untying ribbons that bound a sail to the yard.

One of the sailors, no more than a boy, looked familiar. As she stared, this boy climbed up to the yard last and so was close to the mast. He was being taught what to do by his neighbour. Her suspicion grew and, as the sail fell, it hardened into certainty. Art. Somehow Art was not walking back to London but had shipped as a sailor on her ship. That brought a smile to her heart and she resolved to speak to Luxton about him as soon as she could. The ship lurched over a little more as the new sail was tightened and began to draw.

They passed between Flatholm and Steepholm late in the afternoon. They were now sailing much nearer to England than Wales and Fanny could make out houses and cottages, even people going about their business. There was a shepherd walking across a field, his black and white sheepdog bounding ahead of him. He made a familiar and comforting picture of England. Suddenly the thought that she was leaving struck deep. This was England, her home. Would she ever see it again?

Debb,

Well, there you are. Fanny is finally on her way to the New World (did they call it that in 1760?) Now it's up to you to get her safely across the Atlantic. We did agree she should meet pirates, didn't we? Of course we did. How could I forget the image of the three girls forced to lean over the ship's rail with their petticoats thrown up over their backs? I'm sure you are far too ladylike to enjoy such a sight yourself but I suspect you are well able to appreciate the fires it will stoke in any man. Ask your own man what he thinks – I'm sure he will agree.

But, as I write this, I realise you will have a major problem with it. But I will leave you to figure out what it is...

All the best,

Simon

Ah, Simon,

You have gone and introduced another character with the name of Sally. Not sure if my wee brain can cope with this. I would have called her Esmerelda. No reason, I just like it.

You and your lust for bare bottoms! It seems as if you have been hoping for this forever. I'll have to see what I can do to satiate you.

I always knew that Fanny's uncle was up to no good. I have had a definite idea in my mind for a while how I am going to deal with the people who do our girl wrong. It's been plotting away in the sinister depths of my mind and keeps simmering all on its own until I realised that it may not be fitting for where you take our story in the final chapters. However, I have a solution, we will both have to write endings and then our readers can choose which they prefer.

I've been finding researching a little difficult to do without having a printer to print out the information, so off to the local stationery store I rode and bought a printer and strapped it to my bike to bring home. It's one more thing I must lug around every time I move, but well worth it.

Bristol is a fascinating place to research, steeped in murky history back as far as you wish.

Did you know that stone tools, hill forts and farmsteads dating back to the Palaeolithic and Iron Age have been discovered in the area? The Romans even had a settlement there named Abona, which included shops, cemeteries and a port.

The murky part of it comes from the slave trades. Known as Brycg Stowe by the Saxons and later changed to Bristol, it was a major Anglo-Saxon trade centre with men, woman and children from Wales and Northern England traded through Bristol to Dublin, where the Viking rulers of the day would sell them to the world.

Some 900 years later, it was still being used as a slave port with some 2000 voyages made by Bristol ships in the late 17th century, this time with people from Africa and Caribbean to America before it was abolished in 1807.

Bristol has such a colourful and very ugly history behind it. It may just be worth a visit one day, when the world starts moving again.

And on to the next part of the story. Including some pirates and, as promised, some bare bottoms.

Enjoy.

Debb,

I know we have been working closely together for a long time now, and I am glad it has been so easy to coordinate our writing... but – wow! You took me completely by surprise with your idea of us both writing separate endings. As if we've been discussing it and made a joint decision... "However, I have a solution, we will both have to write endings and then our readers can choose which they prefer."

Not that I am criticising the idea. I have been mulling it over this morning and – why not? I'm sure I remember from school being forced to read Charles Dickens's **Great Expectations** *and his readers protested bitterly at the sadly negative ending to the first edition. So he went back and wrote a second ending, and published them both. You could choose the one that suited you. So I say – yes. If it's good enough for Dickens, it's good enough for us. We just have to be absolutely clear where the two endings diverge and make sure the readers understand what is happening. As I calculate it at the moment, your ending should be Chapter 19 and mine Chapter 20.*

So you're letting me off the leash. I promise to behave,
 Simon

Hello Simon,

So, Dickens and I cannot be wrong because you have agreed to us writing an ending each! Perfect. It can be my silent nod to all those adventure books with multiple endings I read as a child, already knowing that life offers up multiple pathways.

Debb.

Chapter Seventeen ~ The Hispaniola

On the ocean wave ~ dancing with Sally ~ stormy weather
~ tossed in a barrel ~ unwelcome strangers ~ a sad end
~ in plain sight ~ hope renewed

They had been locked in the cabin by the captain himself, frantically yelling instructions they could hardly hear over the roar of the waves. The storm arrived so unexpectedly that it caught everyone unaware.

Last night the skies had been so clear, the stars shining so brightly that they had not needed a lamp as they walked the deck with Adams. He had been enthralling them with his stories of a life at sea from birth. The story of how he had learned to walk, stumbling his way around a ship, had Fanny holding her breath, when he recalled one sunny afternoon, whilst holding onto railing ropes that were too wide for his chubby little baby hands, ended with him falling headfirst into the shallow waters of an island. He had been quickly scooped up by his laughing mother telling him what a clumsy lad he was. Adams; easy laughter was infectious and soon they were all laughing along with him.

In these past few weeks, their two had become a close-knit three with the addition of Sally. What a refreshing surprise she had been. Dark hair piled high upon her head with colourful wraps keeping it in place. Large lips, that she painted red each morning, smiled often, gracing all those in her presence with the whitest teeth Fanny had ever seen.

She was tall, much taller than Fanny had ever known a woman to be. Her lush bosom was level with Fanny's eyes. Fanny found her neck creaked occasionally when she looked up too quickly into Sally's large brown eyes. Her body was as strong a man's. She had no problem shifting a piece of cargo that had toppled over in front of them upon deck one morning. Her long legs were firm and muscled, and her bottom was so plump she would never need to use panniers under her dresses.

Sally's laughter was joyful and was especially loud when they drank the captain's rum. Three nights after they had set sail, they had danced the night away in honour of the birth of Master Luxton's first-born son, who had arrived in the pre-dawn hours on the morning they left Bristol. Sally swayed in a way that captivated Fanny and all those around them. Shiny beads that glittered like gold and painted seeds shimmered in the candlelight from the belt at her waist, and with every flick of her hips, or stomp of her foot, they rattled.

Her dances were nothing at all like the English ones Fanny had learned. There were no steps to count, no positions to remember, no specific tune was needed. You did not even need a partner! No, all she did was move her body in a way that perfectly matched whatever music was playing.

Feel the music, the beat, Fanny, Sally had said, placing Fanny's hand upon her heart the first night she had danced for them. Day after day, Fanny and Bridget practised. Their stiff English bodies struggled with the fluid movements at first. Fanny's was by far the stiffest and it took much longer for her to feel freedom in her hips and back. Bridget, finding it much easier, surprised Fanny with her graceful movements. They practiced a little each day, but it was always more fun with a drop or two of rum.

Oh, Fanny was now wishing she had not overindulged in all that rum last night. They had been celebrating the birth month of three of the crew and the long evening had been loud and joyous. Her stomach churned as the ship listed badly to port, making her feel sicker than she had ever been.

"Hold on tight, Miss Fanny!" Bridget bellowed above the roar of the storm. She was gripping tightly onto the cabin railing as dishes crashed around them.

Alarmed by the sound of breaking plates, Fanny wished there had been time to dress properly when they were awoken by Sally frantically banging on their door. All they had on were their shifts – no gowns or slippers. At least they were dry though.

"Here comes another!" Sally yelled, feeling the sudden downward swing of the ship.

All three women screamed as they were thrown hard against the locked door. Although dazed, they could feel the bow rising higher and higher out of the water. Stars appeared through the small windows and the ship surrendered a deafening groan as the timber protested loudly from being forced into the sky. They held their breaths, fingers painfully entwined, waiting for the ship to topple at the mercy of the storm. A hard knock to the starboard brought the bow crashing into the ocean once again. Huge waves crested the sides, crashing with full force onto the deck, smashing anything in their way with ease.

As if the storm and thundering darkness were not frightening enough, water began to flow in from the small windows that had shattered when the ship righted itself. Moving precariously up and down, they continued to ride out the storm, sea sickness making them weak.

After an eternity, there was a break in the clouds and the moonlight guided them around the debris in the cabin, allowing them to take up refuge under the solid table that was bolted to the bulkhead. After a while, when the ocean had calmed a little and the wind had lost its relentless howl, Bridget began to cry.

"We'll be ok, Bridget. It's just a storm and we're safe here under this table." Fanny said shaking, silent tears running down her own cheeks as she looked up at the table, desperately wanting it to be much larger than it was. Cradling her maid tightly in her arms, Fanny rocked back and forth, mumbling soothing words the way her mother used to when she was scared as a child. Bridget began to settle.

"It's almost finished now, Bridget," Sally soothed with a click of her tongue. Her perfectly accented English flowed calmly, was laden with her iron-will. "Feel, Bridget. Feel what the ship is telling you. The storm is passing. Feel it." The last spoken almost as a command but Bridget was too far in her fear to heed.

Fanny reached for Sally, her weakened hand gripping a shoulder, feeling her burden lessen as long arms surrounded both her and Bridget. There they sat, wrapped up as tightly as their three storm-battered bodies would allow. Slumped shoulders bore the weight of heavy heads, and Sally began to sing *The Lord is my Shepherd* to a tune unfamiliar to Fanny. Its husky rawness was a quiet whispered plea, loud enough for just them, and so heart wrenching that Fanny closed her eyes and wept.

The day broke its first rays through the jagged glass of the windows and into a cabin in disarray. She stared, confused as to why she was looking through a window first thing in the morning.

She had been warned by many people not to sail so soon, even Rosie had asked her to wait, warning of the spring storms. More had told her that a mild winter made for an even milder spring and what choice did she have? She needed to leave England before her uncle found her.

Bridget's moan brought Fanny's mind back to the present with a start, remembering the storm from last night. She quickly turned to see Bridget and Sally waking from their huddled mess on the floor of the cabin.

Suddenly, her body reminded her of pain. Her bloodied hands were full of small cuts and her fingers blistered from holding onto whatever she could grab during the storm. Her aching muscles felt as if they had been pulled from her bones. Carefully she sat up, avoiding the broken glass and dishes strewn all over the floor.

The sun glittered off a large shard of mirror and she picked it up, shocked when she saw her battered reflection. A small, deep cut upon her right cheek wept a little blood when she touched it. Her lower lip was swollen, and she poked out her tongue to sooth the dried blood.

"We're alive! We're alive, Miss Fanny!" Bridget gasped loudly and burst into tears, her Irish lilt the strongest Fanny had ever heard. Relief and happiness shone brightly in her green eyes.

"Yes, Bridget. We are alive," Fanny mused, wiping away her own tears. "Don't you move. You have a bump the size of a duck's egg on your head."

"Aye, I do feel a wee bit ill, Miss." Nodding her head in agreement as she sat up, Bridget decided to rest against the cupboard and closed her eyes to settle the spinning of the room.

Fanny crawled carefully towards Bridget as Sally sat up, supporting Bridget against her shoulder. She was far livelier than Fanny and Bridget combined.

"What did I say, Bridget?" Sally asked with a gentle nudge, the bruise on her jaw making her strained smiled lopsided. "The storm was passing, is what I said. See, it is long gone."

"Are you well, Fanny?" Sally, not expecting much of a response from Bridget, studied Fanny closely.

Feeling deep brown eyes intently upon her, Fanny tried to smile, stopping before her lip started to crack again. The slightly older woman had become the sister she never had.

"I feel as if I have been tossed around in a barrel all night. All things considered, though, I suppose I am alright. And you?"

"A few small cuts here and there, and a mouth that maybe too sore to talk for day or two, but I am well."

Fanny and Sally assisted Bridget to her feet, holding her tight as she swayed and went as pale as a ghost. The early sun had now filled the cabin and each of them silently observed the damage to the room. How lucky they had been to survive.

A loud commotion outside caught their attention. Fanny could not quite hear what they were yelling but a deft excitement had livened the deck. Edging their way closer to the windows, all three looked down upon the chaos of the ship, or what was left of it. The main yard had fallen to the deck and left an open expanse of sky where ropes and sails used to fill the view. The ship listed slightly to port and there were large breaks in the railings where the yard had landed. The cargo that had been on deck was nowhere to be seen.

A crewman high above in the crow's-nest was waving his arms about wildly. Pointing towards the bow. Seeing other men rush to the front of the ship, the women turned to look out through the broken windows. Squinting their eyes, they could see the blur of a ship on the horizon. Relief energized them.

"We're saved." Bridget gasp, her voice and stance much stronger now.

"That must be why the men are so excited," Fanny mused out loud. From their small window they watched the lively way the crew were scurrying to alert their rescuers. The ships men were foraging to salvage what tools they could find from the mess on the deck.

The women hurriedly dressed, unbolted the door and made their way out onto the landing only to discover the ladder had been dislodged during the storm. The captain yelled from below that they would have to wait in the cabin until another was found. The excitement that took over the ship was contagious, with every uninjured man working to repair the rigging. They would leave hoisting the main yard back into place until they had spread some sail to steady the ship. To keep out of the turmoil, the big old tomcat had found his way into the cabin, heading for the driest sunny spot near the broken windows.

"Look at this wee thing." Bridget muttered, scratching the ears of the raggedy orange ball of fluff that had sought safety in the cabin. He stood up, stretching his spine, scabby chin pointed towards the ceiling. His tail as stiff as a post as his loud purr drew the attention of Fanny and Sally.

"He'll take that all day long, without any shame at all," Sally said. "He belongs to no one the men say, yet everyone belongs to him.

Demanding cad that he is. He followed Adams on ship one day and they have been companions ever since."

"What's his name?" Fanny enquired, keeping her distance as Sally cradled the cat in her arms.

"Do you like animals, Fanny?" Sally asked, noting the stiffness in Fanny's body.

"Animals, yes. Cats, not at all."

"They make her itchy with hives," Bridget offered, nodding.

"Well then, you'd best keep your distance from old Dula then, well, that's what I call him. The crew call him Puss. He has a tongue that would lick the skin off a lion and fur that is dirtier than un-scrubbed decks."

"What does Dula mean?" Bridget asked, enamored by her new furry friend.

"It means king in the place I was born." Sadness crept over Sally's face, as Dula mewled, nudging his nose near her ear.

"My people were attacked by another tribe and they captured many of us to sell to the traders. They were our own kind and they sold us for spices and cloth!" She hissed, tears of anger streaming freely down her face.

"My tribe was small and peaceful, but they still attacked us. We lived in the mountains and were walked for many days across the desert to the port, with little water, some, like my sister, were without strength and perished along the way. I had never seen the ocean before. Never seen a ship."

"The white man bartered for us like pigs at a market. Some of us young girls were placed in a separate cage because we were worth more. I remember girls crying as their new owners dragged them away. Some were beaten into silence. I had no tears or strength left and walked quietly away with the older man who had purchased me. He later gifted me to Mr Burridge's brother. I was one of the lucky ones."

Lost deep within her memory, Sally had failed to notice the small circle Fanny and Bridget had formed with her after Dula had returned to his window seat. Hands linked in solidarity, hearts heavy and cheeks wet with tears. Silently they stood, waiting for her to continue.

"My first master was kind to me. His second wife had been a free black woman and he had loved her dearly until she died. He had educated her and dressed her in fine clothes and never once beat her. I was much younger than she had been, so I spent the next few years being educated and taught the ways of white people. It was then I was old enough and he was able to make me legally his wife, in body and in name. Our wedding was held on his estate, with only a few guests, the priest and servants in attendance. I can remember being nervous, although not as nervous as my husband. He later confided in me that his heart was beating so fast he thought it would give out."

"For three years we had found a way to love each other regardless of the circumstances that had brought us together. Our two sons died as babes and then we could not have anymore. The physician said my husband was too old. He died a short time later. His heart broken. Soon after, I discovered that my husband had previously made arrangements for me to be placed with the Burridge family, for my protection, if anything should happen to him.

Before they could say anything further, a cry went up on deck that sent a shiver down Fanny's back.

"Pirates!"

Fanny felt a chill roll along her spine as soon as the shout went up. Their ship had heaved to while the crew worked on its storm damage. They were helpless. Her heart stuttered when sound of gunfire rose above the panic on deck.

Fanny looked to Bridget who was as white as a ghost, unable to speak. Sally's eyes were as wide as the dishes they took their morning tea in. The ship quieted, so much so that Fanny could hear her heart thumping. The three women cowered in their room. They were not foolish. Everyone knew what pirates did. The broadsheets often reported wild stories of scuttled ships and missing cargo and crews.

It seemed to be a long time had passed before they were summoned on deck. A loud rap at the door startled the three of them into a scream. As the door flew open, Fanny stared into unknown faces of three men sent to retrieve them. Three men for three women seemed a bit much she quickly thought.

All three were darkly tanned and their skin was weathered into deep wrinkles. One smiled, and broken, yellow teeth littered his mouth, as cruelness lit in his eyes. His bare chest was covered in scars, some badly healed and deformed with jagged white skin marking the most recent wounds.

Movement caught Fanny's attention as the smallest of the three pirates elbowed his scarred friend, winking in her direction. He was a rotund little man, with a bald head and filthy clothes. Although he did not seem as threatening as the first man, Fanny knew instinctively that none of them could be trusted.

The third man, quiet, observant and not as rough looking as the other two, speaking with the often-feigned politeness of the English elite, ordered the women to come on deck quietly, lest they be harmed. Fanny almost laughed at the absurdity of his politeness.

He and the fat one stood aside and allowed Fanny, Bridget and Sally to pass, causing them to follow the scariest of the pirates. Holding onto each other's hands, they made their way fearfully into the light.

The sunlight blinded them as they stumbled their way on deck, pushed from behind. Groans alerted them to the carnage on deck as Fanny saw the ship's crew dead or captured, on their knees and tied to each other. Art was nowhere in sight.

Casting her eyes to the poop deck, she could see Captain Smollett, faced bloodied and with a large gash across his chest, on his knees and surrounded by pirates. The women stood quietly, watching in horror as a blade was thrust into his belly, forcing its way through his body.

Not meaning to bring attention to herself, Fanny screamed as Bridget fainted, and Sally bellowed angrily in her native tongue before she was soon silenced by a backhand blow from a dark-skinned man who crossed the deck in order to strike her. The force was enough to knock Sally off her feet, and the man took great pleasure in reprimanding her.

"Enough!" A voice boomed across the whole of the ship, bringing an immediate silence. All eyes stared towards the ghost-like figure. Blood had splattered onto his face when he had withdrawn his sword from the Captain, who now lay dead at his feet.

"Well, what do we have here?" His animal hunger showed in the snarl that crossed his face as he looked over the three women. He was a tall man and the grizzled white hair flowing down his back matched the shade of his plaited beard. His large, hooked nose gave him a hawk-like appearance, and gave Fanny chills.

"Wake up that bitch and let us see how much we can get for them. Strip now!" His angry voice bellowed once again.

Close by, one of the men took great pleasure in dumping a bucket of water all over Bridget, who came to, spluttering, much to the delight of the men. As Fanny and Sally reached down to help Bridget to her feet, a man, larger than Fanny had ever seen, came to stand in front of them. His foul, whiskey tainted breath hung in the air between them.

"Strip now, or I'll do it for you." The menace with which he delivered his threat tightened around Fanny's throat. She did not doubt for an instant that he would.

Fanny stiffened her shoulders and looked directly at Bridget and Sally, nodding a subtle defiance their way, desperately hoping to bolster them with strength that seem to be deserting her. As they had hurriedly dressed after the storm, they did not have as much clothing as they would normally.

As she started to disrobe, Fanny was thankful for the time spent at Miss Rosie's club; her nakedness would not worry her now.

The ship was quiet and tense, all eyes were upon them as they turned to each other to undo their laces, Bridget's proving, difficult because of her wet clothing. Piece by piece, they helped each other remove the layers down to their shifts.

Fanny thought to disobey and remain in her shift but a quick look into the ice-cold eyes of the ringleader bearing down upon them just a short distance away, made her lose all courage. Catcalls and whistles filled the air, and a few words Fanny did not understand, but she could tell by the fear on Bridget's face that she certainly did.

The noise on deck rose to deafening as Sally, who was the last to undress, removed her shift. Vile threats filled the air, they called her slave, many bartering to buy her for their own pleasure or to be shared amongst them. As Fanny and Bridget stood either side of Sally, Fanny sensed the silent tears streaming down her face and reached to hold her shaking hand.

"Line them up, lads!" Their leader yelled to his cheering men.

Fanny stared at him, wondering why a man could hate women so much. She had never witnessed such easy cruelty, not even at the hands of her uncle. He returned her stare and time stood still as soulless eyes made her blood run cold with fear.

Deft hands shoved at her back as she was pushed towards the ship's rail where Bridget and Sally were already bent over, facing towards the sea. The contrast of their skins was surprising.

Bridget, pink and pale, soft and plump, whose short stature meant that her hips were lower than the rail. Hair that had been set free of its tie by the bucket of water, fell about her face. Arms outstretched with her small hands gripping the rails but never going all the way around. Her large breasts were swaying gently with the swell of the sea. Her soft tummy pouted and jiggled along with her bottom. Large handprints marked her skin in red welts. Her shoulders heaved under the weight of tears.

Sally's dark, muscular legs were long and lifted her hips higher than Bridget's. Her bottom was round and firm. Her arms were bent in an arrow shape in front of her, supporting her head as her strong hands gripped at the rail. Handful sized breasts peaked into rosy nipples where beads of moisture gathered before dripping onto the deck. The small of her back glistened in the midday sun as her muscles started to twitch. A man was rubbing his hands all over Sally's buttocks, slapping them hard as if she were a stallion being set free. From the side, Fanny could see her biting her lip as she sobbed quietly.

A harder shove caused Fanny to fall against the rail, cutting her lip further and grazing her breasts against the wood, which caused a cheer of delight from some of the pirates. With shaking arms, she pulled herself up as chants of "taking it like a Lady," filled the deck.

Fanny grabbed the rail tightly with her hands, fear took hold and her whole body began to shake. When her teeth started to chatter, she clenched her jaw so tightly she was sure it would break. She was more scared than she had ever been in her life.

The moment she bent over, the roar from the pirates thundered loudly when they all noticed her hairless mound. Wolf-whistles drowned out the cheers as they started to chant Lady Whore. A heavy, bare foot intruded between her ankles, forcing her legs wider. In that moment, her stomach rebelled and Fanny threw up.

They howled like a pack of hungry wolves, snarling and griping over the best pieces of meat. Sweat made it almost impossible to grip the railing and Fanny's shoulder landed hard against it as she leaned over the side of the ship to empty what little was left in her stomach. She then rested her head on the rail and started to pray.

"Well, well, well… she's shaking with desire for us, lads! Just look at that fine arse wobble." Using his hands, he exaggerated the movements by digging in his fingertips and moving them back and forth, laughing as he squeezed.

Fanny bit back the scream that followed the first slap as it landed on her right side. Oh, how it hurt. Her skin tingled and burned, and began to ache so very badly. She clenched her muscles, hoping to relieve the pain.

"See that, boys, this Lady Whore likes it rough. Not even a single tear!" He yelled, loudly above the raucous cheers, as he grabbed both cheeks in his sea-hardened hands and squeezed again.

"How many, Cap'n?" Someone asked from amongst the crowd and the pirates shouted their chosen numbers.

The leader laughed, enjoying the merriment of his men before quieting them with a raised palm. "Give her another five or so, Jock. We would not want to lessen her price with our fun. This one is special."

Just from the tone of his voice, Fanny knew this Captain did not care at all. She braced herself against the rail for as long as she could. Having Jock's large, calloused hands rub all over her bottom and between her thighs made her wish she had a dagger nearby.

Soon her sobs matched those of Bridget and Sally's. The fifth blow sent Fanny to her knees and then Jock's bruising hand grabbed at her arm, hoisting her viciously back to her feet.

Standing upright and not against the rail, Fanny screamed as the next slap came, and then more until she began to sway, her head light. A sudden silence fell over the deck and everyone stopped as her abuser fell beside her, a short, thick arrow through his head. She stared, confused, the sounds of chaos made her realise that they were under attack…again.

Fanny, Bridget and Sally huddled by the rail, protecting each other as much as possible. Their naked, abused bodies shaking hard as fear gripped them. The noise of men screaming, and weapons clashing was overwhelming and seem to last until the sun was high in the sky.

They cringed and whimpered loudly when a large shadow came over them, blocking out the heat of the day. They held their breaths, too afraid to look. Finally, Fanny slowly opened her eyes to see a darkened hand extend her way.

"My Lady, can I be of assistance?"

My Dear Cute Colonial Friend,
I am chuckling over your interest in the old, old history of England. As

Europe goes, its history is not so rich. The oldest stone tools are on the east coast and dated at 840,000 years ago but – unlike the Mediterranean lands – the ice ages made life in England difficult. Maximum coverage of the ice left the very south of the country uncovered, so the edge of the ice sheet was just south of Bristol at Cheddar (yes, where the cheese comes from). So as the ice came and went, people did decide it was time for a holiday further south for a few thousand years at a time.

Britain wasn't an island when the polar ice caps lowered sea level, so the population was just an extension of the European nomads. During the interglacials, temperatures could get quite warm leaving London with fossils such as lion, hyena, crocodile etc. And after the Paleolithic came the Mesolithic and a rich Neolithic, including the Drew Stenton stone circle just south of Bristol (4-5,000 years old). From then on, England was a fertile and generally rich country so there are HEAPS of historical sites. Who knows what you will find when you dig your garden? You will certainly not be the first person digging that ground.

But the history is fun and Bristol, with its rich history, has always been a gateway to the sea. The lintel stones for Stonehenge were brought up the River Avon on rafts... Bristol is a fun place to visit because it has so many stories squeezed into a narrow valley that means you can walk nearly everywhere. If you base yourself there, you have easy access to Wales, the West Country, the chalk Downs (think of Stone Henge, Thomas Hardy, Bath, the White Horse of Uffington etc.)

Now, enough history. I'm not going to let you get away with Sally's bosom at eye level. I am not tall – 5' 7" and I've probably shrunk a little since then - but if Sally's breasts were really staring me in the face, she would have to be a true Amazon. I suppose I would be allowed to admire them without being thought rude but no, I'd like the lady to shrink to more normal proportions.

And well done with the three naked bottoms over the ship's rail. I just had this mental picture of the three girls exposed for the pirates' delight; a very pleasant image. Pleasant for me, anyway. I can't imagine the girls would enjoy it. But I couldn't describe it without head-hopping. The way we have pitched our story, we can't write anything that Fanny does not see or experience herself – so no picture of three bottoms. But you did arrange for her to describe two, so I must be grateful.

You did not give us enough time! At that season of the year, a ship was likely to cross the Atlantic further south and would avoid the stormy seas in the north. They quite probably sailed via the Azores and further south to catch the trade winds to the Caribbean. I did not get a sense of the slowness of the voyage. I should imagine a typical trip would take a minimum of a month and usually much, much more, so you would have a chance to settle into a routine. Most people get over sea-sickness in very few days, although if you are hit by a storm after a long period of gentle sailing, it can come back.

Anyway, I have only had a quick read so far and will go back and read it more carefully. I am particularly curious about Fanny's saviour – who is he and why is he prepared to help? I hope it is not just because he enjoys the view too. And, being a man, I must know why he is using a bow and not a pistol. I made it a short crossbow as any sort of long bow would be impossible for close fighting, and there were such short bows for use from a horse. But it would still be an antique weapon in 1760. On the other hand, keeping a pistol loaded and primed aboard ship must have been nearly impossible – you would never keep your powder dry – so there would be something to be said for a crossbow.

We have just heard here that we are no longer to be locked up in Cape York under corona virus quarantine. It's time for a party – properly socially distanced, of course. For three months we have only been able to visit the nearest town Cairns if we accepted 14 days of strict quarantine before we could return home. Now we can go to the dentist, the doctor, the bottle shops – luxury! But I shan't go for a while because the Shire has me testing concrete a few mornings each week as they build the most luxurious cycle way. But that will be done in a few days and as soon as Jana has some days off, we're heading for the bright lights...

All the best,
Simon

Well hello there,

Look at you and your wealth of historical knowledge. I wish I could easily recall all of what I learn.

Where to start with this scattered brain of mine. Sally's height. Did you not say that she was of Jamaican descent? I assumed they were a tall people. I could be wrong. I read so much information but forget it just as quickly. I shall check... ok, according to the Gilmore Health News of 2019, the average height of Jamaican women is 1.6m or 5'3" – that is shorter than I am. The whole North American region doesn't tend to lend itself to overly-tall women. So, you can imagine her not with breasts in your face, but with luscious lips that are easily gazed down upon.

As for Fanny and her glorious behind, bare for all to see, I kind of neglected that part of her story, didn't I? I shall go back and slip it in. I was in such a rush to get finished in amongst moving out and the effects of 60+ bed bug that this particular Air BNB has gifted me, that I was a little distracted.

Fanny's saviour could be whoever you choose him to be. Does that work for you? I mentioned a darkened skin, were there any friendly pirates of African descent around at the time? Or could it possibly be our stranger with the obsidian eyes from the start of our book. Perhaps he is a naval officer come to rescue Fanny? So many possibilities. No matter who you make him out to be, I'm sure Art will be there to help her out. Where was he lurking during all the pirate shenanigans? Maybe they knocked him out and threw him down the stairs?

How wonderful it is that some normality has returned to your neck of the woods. I hope you both enjoyed your time in the big smoke!
Debb.

P.S. Oh, and I noticed you have been doing a bit of one space/two spaces between your sentences. Shame, shame, shame.

Chapter Eighteen ~ Dispatched and Matched

Black Ben lights the way ~ Captains Luxton and Beardsley
~ buried at sea ~ Captain Luxton's rule of thumb
~ port and hard tack ~ an invitation to dinner
~ a marriage, a farewell, and landfall

Too frightened to move, Fanny peered back over her shoulder. The man who had spoken to them was now ordering the crew and no longer paying her any attention.

"Get him down below," he ordered, pointing at the late Captain Smollett. "As for Black Ben, I want his head in salt. It's crazy men like him that give letters of marque a bad name, so he's going to be lighting our way from the foremast next time we pull into port."

"Leave the bolt in, Cap'n?" asked one of the crew.

"Certainly. I can spare it. But draw out the brains, if you can find any in Ben's head. And swab that blood up. We can't expect ladies to go paddling through it."

Fanny raised herself on one elbow, curious as to the sort of man who could rule a wild crew such as this. He carried a short cross bow in the crook of his arm, a curious weapon Fanny had only seen in paintings. Unlike the rest of the pirates, he was clean and tidily dressed. His loose linen shirt, dyed pale blue, showed no stains or signs of wear. His dark hair had been drawn back and plaited into a short pigtail finished with a black velvet bow. His breeches were tailored to fit closely and would not have been out of place back in London. But there the man would have worn stockings and buckled shoes; here he was bare legged and bare footed. Here he wore far fewer clothes and his legs and feet were burned brown by the sun, but he walked the deck with all the confidence of a lord. He suddenly became aware of Fanny watching him.

"Where are these girls' clothes? Get them dressed and down in the cabin right now. And don't bloody well stare or it'll be you over the rail with your arse in the air." He strode off to look at the wreckage of the mainmast.

A sailor brought their clothes in a mixed bundle and dropped them at their feet before hurrying away. Fanny untangled her shift and pulled it over her head. "Come on – let's get down to the cabin and get dressed there. Stop snivelling, Bridget. We're safe for the moment."

"But Captain Smollett…"

"I know, but we can't help that. Let's get dressed first and then we'll have a service for him."

Fanny dressed mechanically. Poor Captain Smollett… he had died in front of her, only feet away. She saw the expression on his face; still, grim, expressionless, he had simply closed his eyes and died. They were in his cabin now, disordered by the pirates searching for alcohol and money. Without thinking, the three of them set about tidying, picking up charts from the deck where they had been thrown and refilling the cabinets whose open doors swung gently back and forth with the ship.

Who was the new Captain? Why had he saved them? Who was he that he could kill the old pirate captain and still command the crew?

There was a tap at the door and Bridget opened it for Adams, bearing a tray. "Evening, ladies, I thought you may have worked up an appetite. All cold, I'm afraid. We ain't got the galley fired up yet." The tray offered biscuits along with sliced ham and pickled onions, and a jug of water.

"What has happened, Adams? Poor Captain Smollett… will there be a service for him? We ought to have a service. Was anyone else hurt?"

"Well, Miss, apart from the Captain, we got off pretty light. A couple of cuts and bruises but there's not so many folk have ever met Black Ben and escaped so well. Mr Luxton's taken over so we'll be calling him Captain now. He's busy getting the mainyard back aloft. We'll be rigging like demons for hours yet so you must make do with this for dinner.

"Cap'n Luxton did say he'd be moving back into his old cabin so you may sling your hammocks here, but he'll still be needing his charts so you'll have to share with him. Once you've finished your biscuits, perhaps you'd move your things out of Cap'n Luxton's cabin?"

"Yes, of course, but what just happened? We don't understand – the pirates – where did they go? And who was the man who killed the pirate captain?"

Adams chuckled. "Well, there's a barrel of questions and no

mistake. They wasn't pirates, d'ye see? The *Sweet Rosie* ain't no pirate ship, she's a letter of marque. That means she's free to take Spanish ships but she's to leave Englishmen alone. And Cap'n Beardsley has the *Sweet Rosie*, not Black Ben. I don't know what deal Cap'n Beardsley cooked up with Black Ben, but Ben was no more than First Mate and bound to follow orders. You can call a wolf a dog if you like, but he's still a wolf when it comes down to it.

"Seems that when they saw us, Cap'n Beardsley was over the side in the ship's boat, searching for a top mast hand what'd lost his grip and fallen. Black Ben it was that boarded us, and now he's dead. Good riddance, too. He was as black as they come."

"So Captain Beardsley is a pirate?"

"Bless you, no, Miss. He's a privateer and that's not the same thing at all. Unless you're Spanish, of course. He might look near the same thing to you then. Cap'n Beardsley's a proper gentleman. I expect you'll see him soon enough, once he's done helping us get shipshape. All shipshape and Bristol fashion, that's what we want. Now I shall leave you to your dinner, such as it is. The Captains'll want a bite too, so perhaps you'd clear the table for them. I'll bring the service and glasses in a while."

They had no time to enjoy their new cabin with its wide stern window and hurried to empty the old one. It took moments to bundle up their hammocks and carrying their luggage from one cabin to the next was easy. Fanny and Sally left Bridget to clean up the mess left by the storm. She had begged a broom and shovel from Adams to deal with the broken glass and she would soon be wanting a bucket and swab.

In the main cabin, the girls stripped Captain Smollett's cot and used it to pile their bags and bedding on while they set the rest of the room to rights. Fanny had not understood how neatly the room was arranged, how all the little cabinets were full but not stuffed beyond usefulness, and how everything was secured against the ship's movements. Of course, the pirates had turned order into disorder in only a few seconds. It would take much longer to restore things to their places.

By the time Adams returned with the dinner service in a compartmented tray, the cabin had returned to normal and the two girls were sitting on the long bench below the stern window. It was a glorious place to pass the time, looking out over the ship's wake, a view filled with ocean and towering white clouds. In spite of the storm and their humiliation at the hands of the pirates, Fanny felt a wave of contentment rising through her. Until she thought of Captain Smollett, and then guilt swept over her. How had she forgotten him so quickly? She was sitting in his cabin with his coat and oilskin hanging behind the door and his sea-chest under the chart table, and his memory was already fading? She would never forget his face at his last minute, she was sure of that.

Adams tapped at the door, waited and entered. "We'll be slipping Cap'n Smollett over the side in a minute, if you ladies have a mind to come along. There's a boy to keep him company."

Art! Please don't say the boy is Art. If he had been killed too... "Where's Bridget? She must come too."

Sally held her at the door to tuck stray hair under her bonnet. "Slow down, Fanny. Hurrying is no help and Bridget will come too. Take off your apron. You don't want everyone to know you have been cleaning the house."

Adams shepherded them out into the bright light and up onto the poop deck. Apart from the hand at the wheel, only Captains Beardsley and Luxton stood there and the girls took a place behind them. The crew had gathered in the waist of the ship. All had come straight from their work on the topmast and even the officers showed no sign of Sunday clothing. Captain Smollett lay on the deck, sewn into a sailcloth shroud. A smaller bundle lay beside him and Fanny searched the crew. Thank God, Art was safe. He stood solemnly with his mates, every inch a sailor. He seemed to have grown, even filled out a little. Perhaps the sea suited him, and he was no longer a boy in a disreputable hat. His long hair was tied back; he had not had time to grow a proper pigtail.

Captain Luxton was holding a prayer book behind his back, his thumb marking the right place. This would be his first official act as captain and Fanny wondered what he was feeling. The weight of responsibility, no doubt, for the living and right now for the dead.

"Hats off, lads," shouted the bosun, and the crew shuffled to attention.

Captain Luxton waited a moment and began in his soft West Country voice. "Right, men, we're here to bury Captain Smollett and the boy John Partridge. I shall put their details down in the log so's I can write a proper letter for the Captain's family. If anyone knows where young John came from, come along to the cabin later and I'll give you a letter for his people too, with the time and date and our position. Now, listen up."

He brought out his prayer book. "We've lost two good men today and now we must say goodbye to them. We therefore commit their bodies to the Deep, to be turned into corruption, looking for the resurrection of the body when the sea shall give up her dead, and the life of the world to come, through our Lord Jesus Christ; who at his coming shall change our vile bodies, that it may be like his glorious body, according to the mighty working whereby he is able to subdue all things to himself." The words were familiar but different, tailored for the sea.

The two bodies were dragged to the scuppers and slipped overboard. The railing slammed shut and for a moment Fanny heard only the sound of water rushing along the side. So that was a funeral at sea. So much simpler than on land. A few minutes only, and the deceased people had gone. And gone without a mark, except for a note in the ship's log. No gravestone, nothing for family to visit with flowers. The finality of death at sea, something she had never considered. The three of them went below without exchanging a word.

They began to lay the table for dinner, the same arrangements Captain Smollett had used for them at their first shipboard dinner. Adams bustled in with glasses and a decanter, and took Bridget away with him. "You two ladies will sit here, and Bridget can come along o' me. She can give a hand with the serving. Cook's ready. Everything's at trip and go. Let's hope the Captains is hungry. Cook gets narky if his food's left waiting and drying for want of the gentlemen to eat it."

Adams need not have worried. They heard the captains coming. Captain Beardsley was explaining something about ratlines that Fanny did not understand in the slightest and he was still talking as they walked into the cabin and saw the girls waiting. He stopped in surprise. His confidence slid away and suddenly he was no longer a ship's commander but just an embarrassed man.

What's wrong, thought Fanny? And Captain Luxton looks embarrassed too - ah. I understand. They are thinking of us over the railing and our bums in the air. Well, tough. If we can put up with the memory, so can they. There's better men than them have seen my bum, anyway, but if they say a single word...

"Gentlemen, we have laid places for you both. Shall I pour you some port?"

The embarrassment evaporated and Captain Beardsley took Fanny's hand and bent to kiss it. "Thank you, Miss Howarth. And you too, Miss Sally." He kissed Sally's hand and seemed to dwell over it. "What a pleasant prospect. Yes, please, port for me. And you too, Jim?"

Accustomed over the years to low deck beams, the men bent to avoid them and slipped into their seats. They watched intently as Fanny filled their glasses from the decanter.

"And you, Miss Howarth? You will both be joining us, I hope?" asked Beardsley.

"Simply Fanny, if you please, Sir. We can't stand on formalities in the cabin. I'm sure you have quite enough of that on deck. And, yes, we're hungry too but I don't think we will be taking port with you." She looked at Sally who screwed up her face at the thought. "A bit too rich and too strong for us. I shall ask Adams if he has something more suitable. Excuse me, I'll just go and find him..."

"No need, ladies," said Adams as he pushed open the door with his elbow. "Do you sit down and I shall bring some sherry suitable for ladies. And here are some niblets to soak up your wine." He set a silver saucer of broken ship's biscuit on the table. The men reached for it automatically, took a piece of biscuit and dipped it into their port. Fanny watched in fascination as they carefully chewed their niblets. She had been eating biscuit since fresh bread had run out after the first week of their voyage, but she had never heard of biscuit and port. She wondered what Mrs Palm would make of that idea, or the club members.

Adams returned with two small glasses of sherry and another saucer, this one holding some port wine. "There you are, ladies. You may dip your biscuit too, for it surely won't be tasty without a little soaking first." He was right. The dry biscuit was as hard as stone, but soaked in a little port became quite edible.

"You are bound for Charles Town, I believe," said Beardsley. "Do you have plans for your future there?"

"I don't know yet, Sir. I dare say we will find a place to suit us. Do you know the town well?"

"Fairly well, I'd say. It's my home port. I have friends there – I will give you a letter to them, if you wish. What do you intend to do with yourself? Do you wish to get married and settle down?"

"Oh, Captain, we hardly know each other. It's far too soon to think of that." She was pleased to see a shock come to his face before he realised she was joking.

"Touché, my lady. You have me there. None of my business, I'm sure. You'll find society in Charles Town very dull after London and Bristol. The place is no more than a country town, after all. But every year brings new blood from England and some of them are respectable people. We'll be as proper as Bristol soon, or even London itself.

"We'll be celebrating a century of Charles Town next year, and that will be a party to remember. Our businessmen are as well fed and sleek as any in Bristol. The King has been sending us earls and lords aplenty to teach us how to live and govern ourselves. We have inhabitants from every part of the King's lands, craftsmen, Jews, farmers, merchants. We have banks for those rich enough to need them, and a poor house and hospital for those down on their luck.

"You may belong to the English Church or be a Papist if you prefer. Or even follow the Dissenters – we have many different folk of that kidney. Along with Quakers, of course. And the Africans – they have their own preachers but I don't know much about them."

"You make Charles Town sound very interesting, Captain. I am looking forward to seeing it for myself. I hope we can make friends there. We came away in a hurry and I was not able to arrange any letters of introduction."

Something jumped into Beardsley's mind. "Jim, Jim, here's us sitting and enjoying ourselves and we haven't had any sort of send off for poor Smollett. You do it – you knew him best." He reached for the decanter to fill their glasses.

"Um – I can't believe I'm sitting here, but you're right. So – no, Miss Fanny –," as she started to her feet. "We're at sea and we drinks our toasts sitting down – "

"Because we're usually too drunk to stand!" said Beardsley.

"No! Be serious, Tom. We drink sitting down because there ain't space enough to stand up and drink without choking yourself.

"Ladies, Captain Beardsley. In memory of Captain Smollett who was a gentleman and a fine captain who didn't deserve to die so soon."

They set their glasses down thoughtfully. Fanny broke the silence. "Captain Beardsley, who was that horrible man who killed Captain Smollett?"

"Black Ben, damn his soul. I never should have shipped with him, and I should have put him over the side a good deal earlier."

"But he was your first mate, I believe."

"Yes. No choice of mine, but he came with the *Sweet Rosie* when I took her over. He's no loss to the world. There's a few of the crew – his friends for the most part – who are still stupid enough to be pirates as well, but they're learning it don't pay. I expect they'll be learning a good deal faster now."

A tap at the door and Adams pushed in with Bridget, bearing pease pudding, salt pork and pickled cabbage. And biscuit, of course. Fanny was used to the monotonous fare now, but she still longed for fresh food. Soft bread, fresh meat, cheese – she would sell her soul for a fine juicy apple – but she felt surprisingly hungry and found herself enjoying her meal.

"Captain Beardsley," asked Sally, "Can you tell us when we might reach Charles Town?"

"Not long now. With a little luck and fine weather, you might make landfall in two days. Perhaps three."

"And will you come with us?"

"No, my dear. The *Sweet Rosie* only left port last week and we've got a job to do. Jim, let me invite you to dinner tomorrow, and we shall part company afterwards. All of you, the ladies as well."

After dinner, when Adams and Bridget had cleared the board and the men were nursing the decanter, Captain Beardsley returned to the subject of Fanny's future in Charles Town. "Miss Fanny, when you come to the *Sweet Rosie* tomorrow, I shall write two letters of introduction for you. One is my man of business, Petersen, a reliable fellow. He not only makes a mountain of money out of me, he's also scared that I will kidnap him if doesn't do exactly as he's asked. You can trust him.

"The other will be to Mrs O'Hara. She's mistress of a large cotton plantation. One of the better planters and as welcoming as could be. She'll help you with your domestic arrangements, I'm sure. I don't think I've met a kinder soul. I'm told her slaves worship her, and that's always a good sign. Plenty of those skin-flint planters treat their slaves worse than animals. They think they're the Angel Gabriel in breeches, and if they'd keep their breeches on the world would be a better place.

"Come, Jim, let's take the ladies up on deck. It's a fine evening and it'll put some colour into their cheeks. Miss Sally, please take my arm."

Fanny collected Bridget as they passed Adam's pantry. She knew she did not need a chaperone, but habit dies hard. Sally seemed to have no concern as Captain Beardsley led her onto the poop deck, nodding to the hand at the wheel as he led her straight to the stern. Fanny found herself at the ship's rail with Captain Luxton, watching the sea rush by. The ship was heeling gently and their position leaning against the rail felt safe and comfortable, but her companion was uneasy. He had dropped her hand from his arm as soon as he could and was now saying nothing. Tongue-tied, she supposed.

"Well, Captain Luxton, how do you feel now the ship is your responsibility?"

He brushed his hair back. "I'm not sure how I feel, to be honest, Miss. It's a big thing, being a captain, and I'm not sure I'm ready for it. The Captain went so quick…"

"I'm sure you will be a fine captain. Bridget and I certainly feel safe in your hands. And the owners will be pleased when you return to Bristol."

"To tell the truth, Miss, I never had much in the way of schooling. I can read and write, more or less, and do my sums. Leastways, my additions and subtractions. Divisions is a bit more by chance, as it were, and the owners won't like that. I can keep the log and even write passable letters, but show me a bill of lading and I'm all at sea."

"But I've seen you measuring the sun with the Captain – the old Captain, that is – so you must know your navigation."

"Navigation goes by rule, Miss, and 'tis always the same thing. And I've pricked the chart every day. It comes easy when you're used to it."

"And so does the rest, believe me. I have kept the books for my uncle's estate, and for an establishment in London. If you wish, I could look at your books tomorrow. I don't suppose they're so very different from books on land and you can always help me with what I don't understand."

"That'd be a right blessing, Miss. Very kind, I'm sure." She heard the relief in his voice.

"Miss, I suppose Miss Sally is an educated lady, for all that she's brown?"

"I don't believe her colour has anything to do with it, but yes, she had a position as governess to a rich man's family. She can hold her head up in most of society. Why do you ask?"

"Um, Captain Beardsley seems fair taken with her."

The couple were standing at the ship's rail, deep in conversation. Of course, Captain Beardsley was doing the talking, but he had all Sally's attention. Fanny could see little in the moonlight but their attention for each other shone out. Sally had found a beau for herself! Fanny suppressed a twinge of jealousy and watched Captain Beardsley. He was an attractive man, she decided. He had an air of command that few landsmen could match, and that made his open features and readiness to smile even more interesting. But now she knew enough about men to distrust a handsome face.

"Oh dear, I hope Sally knows what she is doing."

"I'm sure she can take care of herself, Miss. She must have seen a thing or two in her travels. Tom Beardsley may have bitten off more than he can chew."

Fanny lay in her cot, swaying gently with the ship and thinking. Captain Beardsley looked eligible but who really knew? Sailors were notorious for having a wife in every port and God forbid that Sally should fall prey to a man like that. On the other hand, he was clearly a man of means, a gentleman with the respect of others. Did he own *Sweet Rosie* himself, or was he appointed by the owners? Privateer captains took ships belonging to the king's enemies and sold them off with their contents. If Captain Beardsley had no others to share his profits with… She had read of lowly seamen who had returned to England rich beyond all dreams. Captain Beardsley might set himself up with a country estate and drive around in a carriage and four. And he would have the pick of the county ladies and could hardly avoid catching a substantial heiress. Where would that leave Sally?

She rolled onto her back. Beside her, Sally swung in her hammock and she could hear Bridget's steady breathing coming from further away. No sound from Sally so she whispered, "Are you awake?"

"Yes. And you too?"

"I can't sleep. I enjoyed the dinner – did you?"

"It would have been nicer with some fresh vegetables and fruit, but yes, it was an interesting evening."

"What were you and Captain Beardsley talking about? We could see you hanging on his every word."

Sally was silent for a moment. Then, "He was telling me about his ship. He says she's more trouble than a wife and even more expensive to maintain."

"She's his own ship?"

"Oh yes. He said he recently bought her from the old owner who was laid up with yellow fever and not likely to live. The governor signed his letter of marque and now he's off in search of Frenchies and Spaniards."

"Where's he from in England? "

"He mentioned Plymouth but he says he's never going back. He likes the islands too much and he hates the weather in England. He's right about that. I hate it too. He says if a place doesn't have coconut palms, it's too cold for any reasonable human."

"I've never seen a coconut palm. Perhaps in Charles Town."

"Oh no. Too cold in winter. You have to go to the islands for coconuts. I wish I could see them again. There's nothing as soothing as seeing them waving in the sea breeze. I'd feel at home again if I had a coconut palm next to my house. That's all I wish for."

"Perhaps Captain Beardsley could take you back to the islands."

"I wish he would. He's a very interesting gentleman, you know. I never met anyone like him at Mr Burridge's house. But I expect he's married already."

"Probably. And a sailor's not much of a husband anyway. They go off for months or years and who knows if they will come back? Perhaps I'll ask about his family tomorrow at dinner. Now, I'm going to sleep, if I can."

Next day, climbing down the ship's side and into the jolly boat was a challenge. Captain Luxton insisted on a whip tied firmly around her waist and she had tucked her skirts up indecently high to aid climbing, but still the heaving of the ship was frightening. The bobbing of the jolly boat made matters worse, and she was glad to be safely seated and watching Bridget's terrified face as she was lowered with closed eyes into the boat. Sally scampered down the side like a sailor and put them both to shame.

The *Sweet Rosie* had looked nearby but now, from a small boat on the open ocean, she appeared much further away. The two oarsmen were unworried and moved them steadily closer to Captain Beardsley and their dinner. Fanny could see him already standing at the railing and scanning them with his spy-glass. She glanced at Sally, sitting up straight and calm, conscious of the eye investigating her.

The *Sweet Rosie* grew larger and soon they were bumping up against the dark, heavy timbers of her side. Climbing out of the jolly boat was much easier, but Fanny and Bridget were still judged to need a bowline around their waists. Sally did not need one but was shepherded up the ship's side by Captain Luxton.

"Welcome aboard, Jim. And you, Miss Fanny, and lastly, Miss Sally. Welcome to my kingdom."

Captain Beardsley had dressed for the occasion with clean linen and a fine coat. He had shaved with care and his hair was tied back neatly. He could grace the fine rooms of Bristol, except for his lack of shoes. She tried to imagine the members of Mrs Palm's club dressed in fine clothes but barefoot, and smiled. She had not worn shoes and stockings since they had left the cold of England.

Captain Beardsley led them to the stern and they stood watching the *Hispaniola* and the colours the setting sun was painting in their wake. "You have a beautiful home, Captain Luxton," said Fanny.

"Aye. Indeed I do, Miss Fanny. It makes me feel grand. Far grander than I've ever been on land. It's a hard life back there but here – everything's much simpler here."

"And here, you're a man of consequence. No-one to gainsay you."

"But there's always the sea, Miss Fanny. The sea keeps you humble, no matter how puffed up you think you are."

Captain Beardsley came to them, Sally on his arm. "Jim, could you take Miss Sally below? I would like a word with Miss Fanny."

When the others had left, Beardsley seemed to be at a loss, so Fanny helped him. "Well, Captain, what have you and Sally been cooking up?"

"Well, to be honest Miss Fanny, Sally wishes to come with me on *Sweet Rosie*."

"Really? And what does she plan on shipping as? Cook? Cabin boy? She wouldn't make much of a seaman."

"She would be coming as my wife. She wants Jim to marry us, and she wants your blessing."

How strange, Fanny thought. What value does my blessing have?

"I see. And if I do not approve? Would the pair of you elope into the sunset?"

"We hadn't thought of that but, yes, I dare say we would have to manage without your approval. But I beg you would say a kind word to her. She does value you, and she wants someone to write to Burridge in Bristol. She says he would trust you."

"That's as may be, Captain, but what about Sally's future? Can you be trusted to care for her? Do you have the means? The ship is yours, I believe."

"Yes, but a ship's a mixed blessing unless she earns her keep. I do have a place outside Kings Town that will keep us when I leave the sea."

"No slaves, I hope?"

"No. I don't hold with that. If a man can't make a decent living himself, he's no business forcing others to make it for him. I think I can say that Sally will do well with me, and I'm sure I shall do well with her."

There was little to consider. Sally had no-one to care for her and her prospects with Beardsley could only be better. In this world, almost any husband would be better than none. And who was Fanny to say yes or no? "I believe I should speak with Sally…"

Beardsley went below and sent Sally up alone. She appeared looking shy, eyes downcast and hands together.

"Sally, Captain Beardsley has asked to marry you…"

"Yes, and I want to do it. I won't listen to anyone, you know. I've decided myself. I want to marry him." Her face defied Fanny to object.

"You may rest easy as far as I am concerned. You know what is best for you. Now, how would you like me to help you?"

Next morning, Fanny led the bride from the cabin onto the deck of the *Hispaniola*. Of course, the girls had nothing approaching a wedding gown for her but had done their best with two of Fanny's petticoats, a riding jacket and as many ribbons as Sally's stubborn hair would allow. As their little procession emerged into the brilliant sunlight of the deck of the Hispaniola, they faced the crew, all looking tidier and cleaner than normal, and crowding the waist of the ship and ratlines, all staring like the audience at a prize fight. Sally faltered under their gaze, but turned and continued aft to climb up to the poop deck. Here the two captains stood waiting, dressed in their best, including polished shoes. Captain Luxton looked ill at ease, unaccustomed to his finery. He was clutching his prayer book again. Captain Beardsley was wearing a sword and his face looked relaxed above a fine lace jabot. He broke into a smile at Sally's nervous face.

Fanny led Sally to stand on Beardsley's left and stepped back.

Captain Luxton stood to one side, uncertain. Beardsley called him to his station. "Come on, Jim. It's time to do your duty."

It was a marriage unlike any Fanny had seen. The *Hispaniola* had heaved to, and the *Sweet Rosie* stood off a cable's length. Much of her crew had come to see their captain spliced in Holy Matrimony and the service had a larger congregation than Fanny had expected. They stood in respectful silence with the sounds of the sea slapping against the ship's sides and the creaking of the rigging taking the place of organ music. Sally and Captain Beardsley had glanced at each other but now stood looking solemnly forward.

Captain Luxton began in a fine nautical voice that all could hear, and he read well. Shipboard noises, the creaking and singing of the rigging, added to the gravity of the familiar words until, at last, the service wound up to its final declaration *Those whom God hath joined together let no man put asunder,* and the sailors began to cheer.

With his bride on his arm, Captain Beardsley went down to the men to receive their congratulations and to order the broaching of a keg of rum. The men's cups appeared as if by magic; the couple's health would be thoroughly toasted while the wedding breakfast was served in the cabin.

Fanny and Bridget stood at the railing watching the little boat work its way to the *Sweet Rosie.* The figures of Sally and Captain Beardsley, sitting together in the stern, were diminishing as the *Hispaniola* went about and her sails began to draw. When the girls had crossed to the opposite railing, Sally had already climbed aboard her new home. Moments later, the sailors had recovered their jolly boat and the *Sweet Rosie* got under way. The *Hispaniola* heeled with the breeze and headed away on the opposite tack to where Charles Town lay beyond the horizon. Fanny took Bridget below to help her change into everyday clothes and re-pack her chest.

The cabin seemed strangely empty now Sally had left and Fanny found herself wanting company. She had exhausted the ship's books as a mental exercise and was reduced to darning stockings to keep herself busy. As the light failed, she took Bridget up to pace the deck. Captain Luxton offered company, but today she wanted to be alone with her thoughts.

She wondered how Sally was managing her introduction to married life. Would it be a shock? She had surely witnessed closely the working of a married couple, but being a servant, even a respected one, would not prepare her for the role of wife and mistress of her own household. And that thought led to another – what did the future hold for Fanny herself? Of course, she would marry. She was not sure how it would happen, and she could not imagine how she would live in Charles Town. There must be some kind of society she could fit into…

"I'm happy for her, of course," she said to Bridget, "but – it's sad to see Sally go. I liked her. I'd never spoken to a brown person before, but she was nice."

"Yes, and I liked Captain Beardsley too. Quite a gentleman. And he saved us. I wouldn't want to go through that again."

They stood together at the railing, looking out over the endless sea. Suddenly, Fanny wanted to leave, to get off the ship and feel land under her feet again. She wanted to see different people, and eat fresh food. White bread with butter. Fresh fruit; did they have apples in Charles Town? It would be too early in the year, but at least they should have fresh vegetables. And freshly baked bread.

"I wonder what their children will look like," said Bridget.

Fanny thought about that. Sally herself had seemed strange the first time they had met, but that had not lasted. Within a week Sally was just, well, Sally and Fanny had forgotten her colour and the different contours of her face. "I suppose they will look just fine. Children usually do. I suppose they'll be halfway between their mother and father. You don't mind, do you?"

"Mind about Sally? Oh no, Miss. Miss Sally's a perfect lady no matter what colour she is. And Captain Beardsley don't mind, that's certain sure."

Children. Fanny had not thought seriously about children for a long time. She had always assumed marriage would come along and children would naturally follow. That was in the days when her future was normal, when her uncle and the people around her managed her life and she had only to fit in with the way things were.

Well, that had changed. London, Rosie Palm and Uncle Harry had seen to that. She would be making her own way in Charles Town. She wondered what her future would bring.

The girls were fast asleep when the cry came. "Land hoy! Land hoy!" and the deck suddenly echoed to hurrying feet.

They found Captain Luxton already on deck, spyglass under his arm and looking up at the foremast crossing. "What do you see, Jim?" he shouted.

"Flat country, Sir. Can't see nothing of hills. But land for certain."

With a quick "Morning, Miss," he jumped onto the railing and began climbing. From the deck, the girls could see nothing and the cold soon drove them below to dress and take breakfast. Captain Luxton did not appear and they would have to swallow their eagerness until he came.

Debb,

Well, there we are. They have landfall at last and late tomorrow, Fanny, Bridget and presumably Art will be setting foot on the quay at Charleston. What do you want to do there? I must send you some images I found relating to 18th century Charleston.

I believe whatever we do should close the book on Rob Longshot, one way or another. I would like to see him trying for some casual sex and being refused. I had thought of them meeting in the context of an election, with Fanny seeing what a worthless individual he really is and deciding to live her own life instead. And end the book with her stepping out on her own. But what do you feel like? You have to be happy with the plot to write well...

Perhaps once you have decided on the direction to take, I can begin editing, getting rid of typos and flagging places where changes or additions are needed. I know editing will take time for both of us, but at least it's easier and quicker than being creative. At last, the end is in sight and I'm feeling very positive again!

Best regards,
Simon

Hello Simon,

It seems like forever since we set sail and that is on me this time and my un-tasked life. I am so much more efficient when chaos reigns around me and I have too many balls in the air. The life of a spouse in the colonies can be one of boredom and a lack of productiveness if not checked. Sometimes days go by and I have no idea what I did, possibly not a lot at all, but now that has all changed. I have more to do than may be possible in any one day and I love it!

I have been back for about six months and unfortunately, on my little island Covid has finally taken a foothold, a little more than 12 months after the rest of the world. In the first year, we recorded approximately 20 cases – all in quarantine. In the past 2 months, the capital alone has recorded 2000+ cases and 4 deaths due to community transmission that possibly started with an illegal border crossing. There are also multiple clusters in the rest of the country with small amounts of cases.

A hard lockdown had happened approximately 2 months ago and then we were hit with devastating floods, with many thousands displaced, multiple deaths and some people are still missing. This brought about the relaxation of the lockdown laws and so many people taking advantage of this. I have come to realise that there is no one more selfish than some of the ex-pats I have seen in this country. Have I whined about this previously? Is it something many first-worlders do when they move to a 2nd or 3rd world country?

The Covid rule easing was so that the people effected by the floods could access what they required to repair and rebuild their lives, but do not think of this in a western sense. Most people here are dirt poor, and many displaced people are still residing in relief centres, some of which are situated in the open-aired, ground level carparks of high-rise buildings. There is no public housing system for them to fall back on, and assistance varies depending on the area in which they live. Most would have been un-insured and what few possessions they had would have been swept out to sea. And yet they still smile, their brilliant-white rows of straight teeth shining through the wetness and gloom surrounding them. The wonderful people are so resilient. We are now back in a hard lockdown after being freed of it for approximately 3 weeks, although, our parent organisation stipulated that we were to stick to the lockdown requirements, regardless. Latest reports estimate there could be as many as 20,000 undiagnosed Covid cases in the city alone. With approximately 90% of the cases to date being asymptomatic, it is a scary possibility that those figures are correct.

We finally have leave booked and with one fortnightly, reliable flight available, I should finally make it home in June. By that time, it will have been an exceptionally long 16 months since I have seen my family.

Now back to the story…

Pease pudding – I remember this from a childhood nursery rhyme but never understood what it was. The combination of split-yellow peas, liquid and flavourings sounds as appealing as black pudding.

A wedding, what a lovely surprise! I think our simple affair was very fitting. I also think the cat would have stowed away with Sally when she left on the Sweet Rosie.

Thank you for the photos of Charleston, or rather Charles Town as it was then. I look forward to researching this little gem. Did you know there are 22 places in the US with the name Charleston? I had to play 'which Charleston?' for a minute or two whilst beginning my research.

I have had an idea in mind for Rob Longshot's demise since he first appeared. It is a nice little twist that is suitable for a man so unworthy of our Fanny.

Have you left Art in my hands, once again? I do not know what it is with that boy, but I have extraordinarily little interest in this character. I never have. It is a little weird because boys like him would have been everywhere trying to eke out a living. I shall be kind though.

I am looking forward to the editing phase. My mind has bookmarked something in a storyline from a while ago and occasionally it niggles at me, but I cannot find exactly what it is. It is just a sense that I was meant to write something another way. Editing is going to be a great time to go back through all my notes and research and put this one to bed.

Now, as I wait for your reply, I shall find a fitting way to deal with Rob Longshot.

Debb.

Hi Debb,

I don't know why you have taken against Art. That's almost sacrilege, given the special place Dickens wrote for him in our collective memory. But – he's only a side character and now we are drawing things to a close, he is no longer useful. Except perhaps as a courier taking papers back to London and Bristol. Don't forget Fanny is an established lady back there, and likely to become more so if she ever gets her inheritance back from her uncle. So will her stay in America be merely an interlude, or will we leave her there to make her fortune in her own way…?

I think we've known all along that Rob Longshot is too much of a ratbag to settle down in married bliss with Fanny. I just couldn't write that and I bet you can't either. I don't suppose we have to kill him off but he does need to run away. And Fanny will have to learn that good sex is not enough – you need love and romance too.

Well, I wish you would give me some idea of how you're going to end things. And then we can get down to editing. I should imagine we've left loose ends everywhere that will have to be tidied away,

Simon

Hello Simon,
I have finally made it home to Australia for a long awaited family reunion and currently doing time at the famous Howard Springs quarantine centre. I have to say that this place is far more humane than the hotel I was couped up in last April – even prisoners get fresh air. Here we have individual rooms, or 'dongers' as they are known (that's a new word for me), a deck and the ability to move around, in a facemask of course. It is a little weird to have people coming and going at various times during the day and night from our area though. I initially thought we would be housed in plane passenger lots, but I think they house people dependent on risk. Coming from three plus months of lockdown it feels like freedom here. I am now halfway through my stay and am itching to be home – just 6 days and a brain poke (covid test) away.
Boy, I have created a rod for my back, and it is all because of one simple word, obsidian. I had an instinctive pathway in my mind for 'Mr Obsidian' being Rob Longshot and at some stage my characters decided to be two different people, although I have described them in similar ways. So, I have had to back track all because of an eye colour that is a defining moment in this chapter. I cannot even blame this on co-writing as this is all my own doing. Fanny has been having a little fun in this, her final chapter, exploring the best of what the English in the colonies have to offer. And despite my sometimes angst over Rob and Art, I have been kind and found a fitting end to both their stories
Please enjoy,
Debbie.

Chapter Nineteen ~ Debbie's ending and a Happy Landfall

Impressions of Charles Town ~ a mixture of people ~ Art the man
~ A colonial election ~ an invitation ~ Rob's true colours
~ an unexpected visitor ~the truth be told
~a pathway revealed

Fanny looked out over the port in the distance. It had been a few weeks since they had arrived in Charles Town, and she was sure she could still feel her sea legs. She had written to Mr Burridge in Bristol the day after they arrived, advising him of Sally's marriage to the Captain, enclosing a note from Sally herself.

The hustle and bustle of the town was a pleasant surprise and not what she had expected of the colonies. While not an overly large city, it certainly was lively with many ships lined up in the port and there was a restlessness she did not understand.

Although most days had an urgency in the air, yesterday was quiet, with most of the town's people gathering in the square, silently remembering the devastating loss of lives and ships caused by a recent hurricane. A printed notice was handed to Fanny and she read along as the Mayor spoke the words;

"We are here today to remember the devastation of hurricanes, and especially the Great Hurricane of '52, and the many lives it stole from us. Even to this day, some remember it as the hottest summer experienced. The wind howled all through the night and then increased its speed on that September morning, reeking a violent destruction upon all Charlestonians, and for more than 40 miles around. Not only did it fell the grand old Cypress like kindling, blocking up the roads for those who tried to escape, it also blew Johnston right off the map.

"Waves crashed among the town, flooding the streets and came as high as the second story, for those fortunate enough to have one. The towns folk cowered in their upstairs, praying to God to save them, and he listened. For just a few hours later, the wind turned to the southwest, forcing the surge of the sea back upon itself.

"The tempest left our port defenses obliterated, the earth had washed away, and the cannon and ordinance stores in the magazine were damaged or displaced. In the harbour itself, every ship, sloop and vessel were destroyed, their debris found scattered throughout the town and into the woods and swamps.

"Brick buildings, once tall and strong, littered the ground like a puzzle waiting to be solved. Wooden houses and outbuildings never stood a chance, their remnants surged along flooded streets.

"The devastation of this hurricane wiped out almost all the rice paddies, and most of the crops and livestock were destroyed. It would take many years to recover from the food shortage.

"Above all we must remember the lives that were lost. Those poor souls who took shelter in the Pest House, only to drown. The scared orphan children running to escape the roar of the wind who were trapped under the giant trees the fell so easily. And the men of the town, risking their own lives to save others. Brave souls, one and all.

May they rest peacefully in God's kingdom."

Fanny had watched on quietly from the shade of the oak trees near the gateway. Her heart heavy, she stood silently with Bridget, who had tears upon her cheeks. They watched as flowers were placed upon the memorial that had been carved from white stone many years ago. It featured the names of all those lost and missing, over 100 lives, etched into the four sides. A group of three young children laid their own, a piece of Scottish red and green tartan wrapped around their bouquet. Holding hands, with the smallest child in the centre, they walked forward and the eldest placed the flowers amongst the others. Tucking the notice into her purse, the somber service left Fanny and Bridget feeling melancholy, something that had taken until evening to pass.

Today, people were in a hurry to get everywhere. The morning was bright, and the coolness lingered longer than Fanny would have liked. Along with Bridget and Art, the trio set out to take their daily stroll.

There were people of all colours in the town, and the caste system was very much the same as in England. The abundance of slaves was startling. Fanny had knowledge of black slaves from discussions overheard back in the club, from members who had completed their Grand Tours but here there were slaves of all colours, some even as white as she was. She was confused as to what made one man free over another, especially when no crime had been committed.

Fanny was fascinated by the Indians and their distinctive, simple clothing. She was struck by the beauty of their darkened skin, some weathered by the sun, and the shiny blackness of their long hair. The overwhelming sadness she felt witnessing a small group of Indians being herded along the main street was something she had never experienced before. The clinking of the iron chains and the fear in their eyes made Fanny feel sick. Many of the townspeople stopped to watch the group pass by, some yelled, others threw food at them. She could not fathom what crimes the group, especially the women and children, could have committed to warrant such humiliation and cruelty.

She had heard many stories of the Americas before coming, how it was different, yet so very much the same as England. There was a familiarity in the way some people spoke and went about their day, but with a newness of change.

With Art leading them, they left the main street behind. In just a short time, the runty boy had grown as tall as some men, taller than Fanny. His cheeky, crafty nature had matured into a serious side, although the rascal with the easy smile was always there to make her laugh.

They were heading to a coffee shop and passed through a parkland, growing in infancy, that would one day become a fabulous garden. Many people strolled along the earthen pathways and very few took advantage of the benches that stood in the morning shade of some old and exceptionally large trees.

Despite her beautiful surroundings, Fanny's thoughts would not rest. There were plans to make, responsibilities to continue – namely Bridget and Art. Would they want to continue along with her? And where was she continuing to, she had no idea. Lost in thought, Fanny was surprised to discover they had arrived at the coffee shop that had become her favourite. She could smell the scent of the roasted beans from the street.

With Art opening the door ahead of her, he nodded that all was well, and she followed him in with Bridget close behind. Art wordlessly made his way to the hearth and Fanny and Bridget sat by a small, windowed table and waited for their breakfast to arrive.

They had almost finished their meal when a commotion outside had others crowding around them to peer through the window.

"Bar the door!" The man over Fanny's shoulder shouted as Art and two other men were already lifting the timber into place.

Fanny gasped, holding Bridget's hand tightly as she watched uniformed men firing their weapons across the street. There were many of them, both on foot and horse, chasing down a small pack of dirty, unshaven men.

A kindly, older gentleman made his way to her side, placing a reassuring hand on her shoulder. "Don't you worry, my dear. This happens every month or so when there is a big night at the saloon. These boys are probably runnin' from the tables."

From outside, someone had tried to force their way in, causing a few of the women to scream and one to faint. With the only door closed, the air in the shop was warm and stuffy now. Fanny looked around to see that the locals were not fussed by what was going on and the people gathered around her were moving away.

"It'll pass soon, Miss." Art spoke calmly, raising his voice just enough to gain Fanny's attention.

Sure enough, the shouting ended and upon hearing cheers from the street, the nervous silence lifted in the coffee shop and the door was unlocked. Fanny smiled at Bridget, relieved that nothing more had come of the commotion. Today was a busy one for them, for tonight they would be attending a dinner at the Hamilton estate in Lady Mary's place. An invitation extended via Miss Rosie, had been handed to Bridget with strict instructions to give to Fanny upon their first night in the colonies. With everything needed already packed, a coach would be collecting them just after noon and they could not be delayed by unruly men on the street.

Later that day...

"Lady Howarth, may I introduce you to Lord Hamilton?"

Fanny felt the small gasp pass her lips and she instinctively offered her hand, watching intently as the white, wigged head bent before her, feeling his stifled laughter upon her hand.

"My Lady, would you do me the honour of accompanying me to dinner?"

Wide eyed and speechless, Fanny nodded her agreement and allowed herself to be escorted near the center of the table where their hostess was seated. The Dowager Duchess was a magnificent woman, almost at the edge of her prime by London's society standards, yet still very much in demand.

If the rumours told to Fanny by Bridget were true, the Duchess was once a mere governess that a Highland Lord had fallen in love with the moment he laid eyes upon her at a court picnic. The tales tell of a Lord so mad with lust that he stole her away to his castle in the far north until she agreed to marry him.

"Dear Nephew, I see you have found a companion for this evening." The Duchess asked, winking at Fanny after arriving to their conversation accompanied by three companions.

"Yes, I most certainly have. May I introduce Lady Francisca Howarth – Fanny, a friend from London." Holding his hand tightly around hers, Fanny was speechless, unsure of what to make of the relationship before her. How was it possible that Rob Longshot was the nephew of a Duchess?

Fanny watched as the Duchess roamed her eyes upon her from head to toe, lingering a little too long over her stomach. Her companions did the same.

"Now, Auntie, don't go looking like that. Fanny is a friend, is all."

"No such thing!" She lovingly admonished him, tapping his shoulder with her fan. "Forgive my curiosity, Fanny. As my husband's nephew was once thought dead and with him, the end of the Hamilton line. It was such a relief when he arrived alive and well. Although, he sadly made it two days after my dear William had passed."

With sad eyes, the Duchess clasped his hands to her breast. "He would have been so happy to have seen you after so many years apart."

Struck by the heartfelt moment, Fanny watched on quietly confused, trying to piece together what was happening. There was an obvious affection between the two of them. But the man she had met in England had no bearing upon the man here today.

A bell rang throughout the long hall, and everyone moved to stand behind their seats. Polite introductions to those seated near filled the room with an energized chatter, a distraction Fanny needed.

The Duchess, in no hurry to be seated, chatted away eagerly to all those around her. Many moments passed before the servant, eyes keenly waiting for the Duchess to sit down, rang the bell again. The guests, some already deep in their cups, were a mixture of high society, politicians, artists and more than one actress.

"Auntie likes to have dinners that do not conform to the norms of the ton." Rob grinned, watching Fanny look around the table.

Fanny shifted awkwardly as he stared into her eyes from across the lavishly decorated table. The way he smiled was so breathtaking she felt herself blushing. As she smiled back, a memory fluttered into her mind, and she recalled the last time she had seen him. Her skin grew warm, and a familiar tingle found its way between her thighs. She could almost smell the caves.

A distracting note passed along the table to Rob caught his attention and if the look upon his face was any indication, Fanny was certain he liked what was written. She watched curiously as he laughed and shared it with Lord Alex, who was sitting to Rob's right, he then pointed down the table where a woman raised her glass to him. And then to Fanny.

"She likes you," Rob smiled pleasingly, passing the note to Fanny.

The writing was machine printed in French. It was a calling card of sorts. One word she knew meant 'her', and along bottom *Fais ce que tu voudras*, was printed with four symbols furnishing each of the corners. Made from stiff card, with a border of gilded gold and smelling of a floral scent, it was unlike anything Fanny had ever seen.

Fanny looked up at Rob who was watching her intently, "My Lord, unfortunately my French is a little hazy, perhaps you could offer some guidance?"

A bright smile filled his face and as he was about to reply, Lord Alex boyishly interrupted, much to Rob's displeasure.

"Lady Francisca, I would be delighted to give you all the help you require and…" A fast elbow to his side cut off what further he had to say, and he spluttered to catch his breath

"I will be the one helping Fanny with everything she requires," Rob stated, his voice heavy with agitation as he held Fanny's eyes with his. A knowing tingled tickled along her spine.

The moment was lost with the food being served, far more than Fanny had ever seen at one table. As Fanny's guest for the evening, Bridget, had been seated on the opposite side at the far end of the table. From where she was sitting, Fanny could keep an eye on her friend although after several glances, she could see Bridget was having a joyful time.

Fanny had dressed her in a gown of crushed velvet in the burgundy colour, which she had especially made for Bridget. Every fitting at Elizabeth-May's shop had been under blindfold. The richness of the gown looked magnificent against her pale, Irish skin that she took so much pride in. Bridget had cried when Fanny had unveiled her in her dress for the first time earlier today. So much so that they were almost too late in their arrival to dinner.

Fanny had been pleasantly surprised by the different fabrics available from the traders, some who had journeyed from places she had never heard of. The oriental brocades with silver and gold threads were breathtaking. Fanny's reminiscing ended with the clinking of glasses and watched as Rob rose to give a speech.

"My dear Auntie, honoured guests, family and friends, I would like to give thanks to you all for not forgetting about me. It has been many years and most thought I was long dead when in fact, a childhood escapade left me captured in the hands of a travelling merchant, who upon finding a dirty, lost boy with a stutter in the forest, thought him to be an orphan who would make a grateful servant.

"I spent many years travelling, working my days away for as long as there was light. My master was a hard man, ill-equipped to raise a boy, thankfully his wife, Carys, who was found the following summer, was a kind soul who cared for me."

Fanny narrowed her eyes at Rob after noticing his deliberate pause, his steadying breath, and his targeted eye contact with the women most moved by his story. His eyes watered up when he settled them upon the Duchess, and with extended arms he opened his palms towards her and smiled.

Placing his right hand over his heart, he continued, "My Aunt, the finest woman I have ever known, and along with my dear Uncle William, never lost hope of finding me. It was as if God himself guided me to one of the men they had searching for me.

It was a chance meeting that led me back to where I belong. Back into the bosom of my family after being raised in the wilds for so long. My only wish would be that it had happened sooner so my uncle would have known his searching for all these years was not in vain."

The room was quietly engrossed in his heartfelt speech, a few sighs could be heard. Many men nodded their heads when Rob spoke of his uncle, one even called out in support.

Fanny was not sure what to believe. She looked towards Bridget who was as caught up as everyone else. Perhaps she did not recognize him after all this time. Here he was clean and wearing a wig, not the grubby stagecoach robber who made her stand in the cold night air holding the horses.

The Duchess raised her glass, and three cheers rang out for the miracle of the little lost boy coming home.

Fanny was almost too deep in her cups by the time she made her way to the twin staircases in the east wing. With the event being held at the Hamilton country estate, Fanny was grateful not to have to leave and spend the night in the large village nearby.

Tired, she paused to look out the window and catch her breath after the partial climb. Her dress was feeling quite snug. The gardens on this side were lush and featured a large maze. Servants with their sconces were standing at various points guiding people around the vastness. A shining fixture deep within the maze caught her attention with its whiteness gleaming against the night sky. It was half in the shadows and light appeared to flicker around it. Curiosity won out and Fanny made her way back down the stairs and out through the side doors into the crisp late-night air.

Two servants stood at the gateway to the maze, opening the heavy, ornate gate to allow Fanny through. She had once been told that every maze had a secret code, and it was as simple as making all left or all right turns. The trick was to choose the correct way at the start. She was not sure if she believed it and only chose to go left as it was less dark.

Walking fast to warm herself against the damp air, Fanny took the paths along where she could see the best. A mix of both left and right turns. So far, she had passed three light bearers, quietly standing in small alcoves in the hedge. The deeper she went into the maze, the quieter it became, and she made it to a dead-end in a far corner and rested upon the bench. A sconce that had been placed in the small square let her know a servant would not be far away.

Hearing a small animal scurry about, Fanny leapt up and started towards the sound of distant laughter that was being carried on the gentle breeze. Twice she thought someone was following her, so she stopped and listened, but no one was there. She could see the subtle glow of light floating just above the hedge and made her next turn in that direction.

Three more turns and the lively sounds of sex brought her to a standstill. The rhythmic sound of flesh upon flesh was close by. As she walked, the moaning grew louder, the sound of a man reaching his peak aroused Fanny and her skin grew prickly. Silently she took the pathway towards the deep, husky grunting and there the lights grew brighter, luring her in like a moth to a flame.

Fanny turned a corner and came upon a courtyard in the deep center of the maze. She came to an abrupt stop, admiring the beautiful surroundings. It was a large, square space filled with people, all in varying stages of undress. Around the edges, alcoves had been cut into the hedge rows and long benches covered with bright rugs filled the spaces. There were no curtains and Fanny could see many people in the depths of pleasure.

To her left, she watched a man on his knees, suckling at the breasts of a Lady sitting on a bench covered in blue. She was dressed in a shift with the front unlaced, gathering at her waist. Her body exposed; the candlelight reflecting upon the beautiful darkness of her skin. Her face glowed as she smiled, watching the man in front of her.

The man, with lily-white skin and hair as red as the flames, made a stark contrast to the woman as if they were night and day. Shirtless and with his trousers opened, Fanny could see them catch on the rise of his buttocks, only staying in place because of his parted legs. She could also see the head of his cock he was fisting slowly as he licked the woman's breasts. His teeth caught the light as he grazed gently upon her flesh.

Another man, with long black hair and still fully clothed, soon joined them, taking the woman's other breast roughly in his hand. The Lady gasped loud enough for Fanny to hear, and she grabbed the man by his hair, forcing him to let go. Holding his jaw in her other hand, she admonished him with a shake of her head and waited for his nod of understanding, and then hurriedly brought her mouth upon his.

Fanny watched the playful exchange, feeling the sensitivity of her own breasts from these past two days increasing with her arousal. The wearing of clothes fit for polite society were sometimes unbearable, especially when her flux was due. It was these times that she longed for the clothes from her time spent with Miss Rosie.

Nymphs dancing around firepots caught her eye and Fanny gazed upon their lush, naked bodies without a care of who might see her. Their laughter was infectious, and their bodies shone with oil. They twirled and jumped, bumping into each other their bodies jiggled as flesh met flesh. Many taking advantage and stealing a kiss or a touch.

As she moved further into the courtyard, Fanny walked towards the gleaming white statue of Venus. This is what she had seen from the window. Fitting in with the flamboyancy of this part of the garden, it was not a simple statue. No, this was magnificent.

Venus was sculpted from the whitest marble that glittered in the night. She stood in the center of a matching squared pool, legs apart, her back was arched as she stared into the stars. One hand deep in her cunny and the other gripping her throat, her mouth was wide open as if she was screaming her pleasure for all to hear. Freestanding, decorative iron sconces held enough candles to light the dark around Venus and cast long shadows upon the walls of the hedges.

On the lawn at the far side of the garden, an orange rug and colourful pillows had been laid out over the grass and was now covered in amorous bodies, enjoying each other with their mouths. Whilst Fanny had learned about this at the club, she had never actually seen this type of sex.

"Are you enjoying your first orgy, Fanny?"

The voice from behind startled Fanny and she spun around and into Rob, who caught her with steadying arms. She gazed into his eyes and instantly felt her heart flutter. Her mouth opened and she quickly forgot what she needed to say when Rob took her in his arms, crushing his lips against hers. Joyous moments passed and Fanny started to sway in his arms, she turned away to catch her breath.

"Rob," she gasped, her voice sounding far too husky for her liking. It was bad enough her body ached for him; she did not need to lose her senses as well.

He grabbed for her again, this time cradling her high in his arms and walking towards a near-empty rug on the grass. No one around them seem to notice as Rob placed her down and began the arduous task of unlacing her clothes.

Soon they were joined by a nymph, and then another. The first reaching in to kiss Fanny gently on the lips. Oh, how this livened her and she leaned in, opening her mouth and wanting more. Lost in the tender moment, Fanny gasped the instant the cool night air covered her aching breasts, now free of the confines. Piece by piece, all her clothing was removed.

She had never been undressed in a way that made her pussy ache before. Hands caressed her, fingers danced over her breasts and down between her wet lips. Rob walked behind her, shortening his height just enough to press his hard cock between her bottom. He then reached around to offer Fanny's breasts to the mouths of two hungry nymphs. They latched at the same time Rob's fingers found their way inside her body.

"Is this what you want?" He whispered into her ear, his breath warming as it flowed down her neck.

"Yes!" Fanny yelled as she started to grind against Rob's cock, squeezing her buttocks around it, and shifting her hips back and forth. She could feel the wetness grow between her thighs and enjoyed the noises his fingers made as they delved in and out of her body. The nymphs pursed their lips around her nipples and suckled greedily. . It was almost too much for her to take.

Fanny raised up to her tiptoes, trying to lessen the overwhelming release that was close. Strong arms wrapped around her thighs, keeping her grounded as a mouth claimed hers. She grunted her frustration and slammed her head into Rob's chest, rocking her head from side to side, watching the lights begin to blur, she closed her eyes and climbed to her pinnacle with a scream that pierced the night. They all fell with her, cradling Fanny gently onto the cushions.

Opening her eyes, Fanny kissed the nymph closest to her and then lowered her mouth down to her breasts, pushing them together and kissing both nipples as one. She felt her legs open and a hungry mouth lapped at her wetness. Fanny knew instinctively that this was a woman for it was far too gentle to be a man.

She placed her legs up onto the shoulders of her lover, crossing her ankles to bring the head closer to her pussy. Writhing under the mouth, Fanny reached for Rob, lifting her head to lick the tip of his already moist cock.

"Harder!" Fanny demanded; her body was winding tight again, and her hands fisted in the hair of the woman between her legs. Thrusting her pussy into the mouth, she needed more. Fanny's mind climbed higher and higher. As Rob moved deep into her throat she lapped hungrily and found her release again.

Fanny woke the next morning to Bridget opening her window coverings. Bright light flowed into the room, blinding her and she buried her head in the pillows, pulling the bed covers over her head so she could ignore the now muffled sound of cheeriness from her maid. Her mind was lingering on the events of last night. Or was it this morning? She was sure the day was breaking when Bridget had escorted her from the maze to her room. A smile settled inside of her like a secret that only she knew, but it was not just her, it was many. She felt happy and alive.

Silence loomed and Fanny, believing Bridget had left, peaked out from the covers only to find her maid waiting patiently seated in the chair near the dressing mirror. Before Fanny could retreat, Bridget was upon her, pulling the covers back to expose Fanny's still naked body.

"Miss, it is time to get going or we will miss breaking our fast at this late hour. Your dress was returned a while ago although no one can find one of your slippers." Bridget's voice was full of determination. She always got a little short when she was hungry.

Fanny sat up; her nakedness did not bother either of them. "What time is it?"

"Almost noon, Miss. Cook said she will keep breakfast for the stragglers but won't keep it all day. She's a bit bossy that one."

Fanny bit back a laugh at her maid calling someone else bossy. Bridget was born bossy, she was sure.

"And what about that Rob Longshot, being the long-lost heir of the Hamilton. What a story that is, mind you, not sure if I believe it myself. Seems too good to be true. Things like that just don't happen, not with the lad being lost in the wilds and all," Bridget blathered.

"I was wondering the same. What are the servants saying about him?"

"You wouldn't believe it, Miss. They think he is the king himself and go on about how happy the duchess is now he has been found. They say the duke looked for the boy all his life and never even came close to finding him. He had men searching all over the highlands, even searched my homeland for him, going village to village. Word had been received saying the boy was being sold off on the docks. The duke left as fast as he could and found the boy stuffed in a cage with many others. He thought him familiar in many ways to his deceased brother and his wife except for his dark eyes and seeing this knew he could not be of Hamilton blood. Still, they say, the duke was kind enough, and bought the boy's freedom and returned with him and put him in the stables."

Fanny sat quietly, taking in all Bridget had said as she was laced into her dress. The questions that slipped her mind last evening filled her mind now and she was tempted to skip breakfast and find Rob. Although, judging by how quickly Bridget was lacing her, food was needed before anything else.

Their last day had been filled with a picnic laid out under the old oak trees next to the winding creek, situated amongst the rolling hills of the estate. They had missed breakfast when being caught up amongst a small group of guests about to stroll to the creek. Fanny had spent much of the day lazing around on the pillowed rugs, gorging herself on food and wine, and listening to the *Ode on the Spring* by Thomas Gray being read by the duchess herself.

As the afternoon drew cold, people slowly departed, leaving a small group, many chatting away with loose tongues from being deep in their cups already. Fanny had waited all afternoon for the right moment to speak with Rob and after watching him walking towards the creek, it seemed like the perfect time. She had become sober long ago and her mind was clear with what she wanted to ask.

"Why, Miss Fanny, you do look a treat today dressed in yellow, you remind me of the summer skies of home."

Fanny was glad to hear the slight slur in his speech and see the sway in his stance – not too much, just enough to loosen his tongue. His smile had her lost in the memories of their time together last night. Oh, how he had filled her many times. Pushing it out of her thoughts, she sat down on the grass and removed her bonnet, patting the space beside her. Rob stumbled as he sat down, bumping her with his shoulder, causing them both to laugh.

They sat in quietness as Fanny tried to organise the questions in her mind. She did not know how to ask someone if they were a liar. Rob laughed again, swigging on a flask of wine he had pulled from his coat. He certainly was deep in his cups.

"Thank you, Rob. Yellow is my favourite colour. I am happy it reminds you of something special, like home. Where is home?" Fanny could have rolled her eyes at how lame she sounded and was not sure Rob would take the bait.

He had finished downing his wine and threw the flask into the creek. "Home is a little spec of a village in the highlands, nestled between two hills that block the sun for half the year. When the sun comes, it is as if life comes with it along with the brightest shade of yellow there ever was. Just like your dress."

He laid back on the grass, arms flaying out to the sides and sighed deeply. Frustrated by the need for answers, Fanny watched him closely, certain he was sleeping. She poked at his side, and he did not move so she poked once more, only harder this time. Rob sat up so fast she let out a squeal of fright, closing her hand over her mouth, and only relaxed when he started laughing.

"I was moved by the story you told last night. You must have been so frightened as a little boy. What ever happened to that awful man who stole you?" Fanny was surprised to feel hurt for a little boy and his life she was certain could be a lie."

"I killed him."

Not an ounce of guilt was carried in his words and for the first time Fanny questioned if she needed to know the truth. It was not her business after all. She owed no loyalty to any person of the Hamilton linage.

"I killed him and made him suffer after he beat my ma dead. You see, I was not stolen, that part of the little boy's story was a lie. That little boy was me and the man was my father though. A horrible brute with fists as big as an axe. He would make me work all day long, even in the snow from the time I could walk. He beat my baby sister to death, so he did not have another mouth to feed. And my ma, one day she just did not wake up. Her face was all bruised and bloody and I..."

Fanny felt the tears slide down her cheeks and reached out to place her hand on Rob's arm. He turned away from her, but not before she could see the wetness of his eyes. Her answers were not needed anymore. Her privileged life often made her oblivious of other people's hardship. She sat quietly, giving Rob time to compose himself.

"I had to bury my ma in the same grave I buried my sister in the summer before because my father said the ground was too good to waste on two graves. That night, I killed him with his axe and left his body for the wolves.

"I left my home the next day and have never returned. I was found about a year later by a merchant and his wife, they talked a little strange and had a different god that they kept hidden away from everyone. I had never been so well cared for in my life. They died of fever about two years ago."

"So how…" The words caught in Fanny's throat. More curious than anything, she knew it was none of her business.

"How did I come to be the missing heir to the Hamilton fortune?" Rob asked the question for Fanny, intently staring at her before his faced quirked into a lopsided smile. Something he did when he was deep in his cups.

"It is quite simple really. Meeting you, Miss Fanny, changed my life. You see, the night I robbed the mail coach and went through that lawyer's papers; I found all the information I needed to become one missing blue-eyed, Robert Alexander William Hamilton. In amongst the letters was a detailed description of the orphaned son of the duke's deceased sister and her husband, the report from when he went missing, all the searches and, most importantly, information about the duke's failing health."

Fanny stared wide-eye, aghast at how simple it really was. A child no one had seen for many years would be easy to pretend to be. Rob's story of growing up in the wilds accounted for his lack of refined speech and the ways of the high-born – even if only a child, although Fanny had noticed that he had become a quick study on that front. He was every bit the Lord now. Fanny was lost for words.

"And best of all, there was enough muck about many well-to-doers in that lawyer's packet that I will never be found out. With the right information, I can even pretend to be the bastard son of the Grand Master himself. As for the fat lawyer and his runt of a clerk, well…" Rob swayed and fell flat on his back, passed out cold.

Fanny gasped and placed her hand under his nose to feel a steady breath and at the same time Rob started to snore. She could not decide if she was annoyed by not finding out what had happened to the lawyer and his clerk. Maybe she did not want to. Maybe it was safer to let Rob think he had told her nothing at all. One thing was for sure, she needed to leave Charles Town sooner than she had planned.

Later that week, after a lengthy silent walk through the streets, Fanny's plans to leave Charles Town along with Bridget and Art were firmly set in her mind. Thanks to Uncle Harry, she had funds to support the three of them and to open her own gentleman's club. She had missed working at Rosie's and longed for the friendships and fun of living a risqué life. The day-to-day life of a Lady was not for her.

Fanny was keen to leave for several reasons, one being the increasing stories of sickness. It seemed there were always people with yellow fever or smallpox or some new illness that no one had seen before. She had overheard some men saying it was due to being a port town with people arriving from faraway places, especially with all the slaves being traded. Others were saying it was the soldiers who fought the Cherokees in Governor Lyttleton's expedition that had brought smallpox back with them.

She had walked all morning, with Bridget patient and quiet at her side, and Art close behind. The day was humid and when they had passed one of her favourite buildings, a rundown pink tavern made from Bermuda stone on Chalmers Street for the third time, she decided enough was enough, and made her way to her favourite place by the river. They stopped for a picnic of cornbread, cold meats, cheese and iced tea under a grove of oak trees overlooking Folly Island. Fanny reined in her excitement and then passionately laid her plan out for Bridget and Art to hear.

"Boston!" Fanny blurted out. It was not the most ladylike way to propose how to uproot their lives, but Fanny couldn't contain her enthusiasm and hurried on breathlessly.

"I have heard it is a much bigger city than Charles Town. There are many opportunities to start a new business, even for women. My plan is to open a tea shop and once that is successful, a gentleman's club. With Uncle Harry's generous gift and a lot of hard work, we should be thriving in a year's time. I recall Sir Francis saying Boston's weather is akin to home. And I know we all dearly miss those cold winters and snow. Sir Francis also has business there, as well as Rosie, and I'm sure they would be only too happy to write a letter of introduction to help us get started."

Finally speechless, Fanny picked at a small wedge of cheese to eat. She was nervous about what Bridget and Art may have to say about her plans. Their continued silence made her twitchy. How could they sit there, casually eating without giving any indication as to what was going through their minds? Fanny was not sure if what she was asking was selfish of her. She knew Bridget still had a fondness for

Mr Evans ever since their first meeting at the Hell Fire caves, and Art, he had grown into a smart young man who had a longing to be educated.

Her heart sank a little when Art motioned to speak privately with Bridget and they walked to the river edge, keeping their backs to Fanny the whole time. Fanny craned her neck, hoping the breeze would blow their conversation her way, but it did not. Tears pricked her eyes and she quickly blinked them away, ignoring the doubt niggling in her mind and reached for a Bene wafer, another new dish that she had become quite fond of since arriving in Charles Town.

Bridget and Art returned, both looking quite forlorn, and Fanny's heart sank as she watched Bridget ballooning her skirts to gracefully sit down on the rug. Bridget reached for Fanny's hand and suddenly her corset felt too tight, and she felt lightheaded.

"Breathe, Fanny!" Bridget demanded tersely, yanking on her arm. "We're just having some fun."

Art's laughter bellowed about them, and Bridget's look of stern Irish concern broke into the most beautiful smile. In an instant, Fanny's worries disappeared.

"Of course, we are with you, Miss. Where else would we be?" Art said gently, kneeling beside them, and taking their hands in his.

Tears of relief flowed down Fanny's cheeks as she looked upon her friends, feeling their bond into the depths of her soul. After hurriedly packing up the picnic, they made their way back to the hotel, excitedly discussing their journey ahead.

"Pardon me, Miss Howarth, you have a visitor in the private parlour," the manager announced discreetly as Fanny and Bridget walked into the foyer.

A little surprised, Fanny made her way towards the small room located at the side of the hotel. It was her favourite place here as it had an exquisite window seat that looked out over the small garden. It was beautifully decorated in feminine hues of blue and yellow and felt very peaceful - like an inside secret garden. Fanny entered and shock held her in the doorway.

"Girl, where have you been? I've been waiting all day for you!" A gruff voice announced loudly to an empty room.

It took several seconds for Fanny to find her voice. "Lady Mary?"

"Sit down, Fanny. We have much to discuss and I've already wasted too much time travelling to this English backwater, even if it was to finalise the purchase of an estate. Why they call this uncivilized place the New World, I'll never know," she huffed.

Fanny flopped on the settee and watched as Bridget slowly poured the tea. She knew Bridget was deliberately taking her time so that Fanny could catch her thoughts. The low afternoon sun was seeping through the window, and Fanny looked around to observe how the afternoon light deepened the colours of the room. She was not sure if it was the semi-darkness or the fact that Lady Mary was here, but she could now imagine the room functioning as a private place for gentleman to indulge in their ways.

Silently they sipped at their tea. Fanny discreetly watched Lady Mary and was relieved when she saw the tension finally relax her shoulders.

"Rosie sent word to you a week after you departed Bristol, and then again, one month later. Have you not received them?" Lady Mary asked, the irritation fading as she stared directly toward Fanny.

Fanny reached for her tea and quietly shook her head, unsettled as to where this may lead. She knew Lady Mary liked to sail, but was still surprised that she was in Charles Town. She was suddenly a little afraid of why she was here.

"I thought as much. Drink up, you're going to need it." Lady Mary stated bluntly, motioning to Bridget to refill their cups with a brisk wave of her gloved hand.

"There is no good way to say this so you will have to excuse me if I appear rude. Your uncle is dead. The drunken fool lost a duel at dawn three days after your departure from Bristol. The family property is yours. Matter of fact, it always was because your mother had willed it to you."

Fanny's shocked gasp was loud. She stared back at Lady Mary, mouth wide open and it wasn't until the dish of tea she was holding started to rattle on its saucer that she found her voice.

"I do not understand," was all that she could stammer, annoyingly so. In an instant, Bridget came to sit at her side, smiling calmly and taking hold of Fanny's hand for the second time that day.

Lady Mary softened her voice. "I don't know the full story myself yet. Rosie didn't have all the details when she hurriedly told me at the pier. What I do know is Harry was making some enquiries before he passed, and he had mentioned something wasn't right with it all. When word of your uncle's death reached Rosie, she sent Annie back to Langston to sort the mess out. It was Annie who discovered your mother's box of papers hidden in the safe."

"You see, your grandfather willed the property to you mother and upon the passing of your father when you were a babe, your mother was too bereaved to take care of the estate, and that is when your uncle stepped in as conservator. Although he is not really your uncle either. What I do know for sure is that Lord Compton has stepped in to oversee the investigation."

Fanny could not find her voice and so much of what Lady Mary was saying was new information to her. She did not remember her father at all, just that her mother had loved him deeply and forever felt his loss. The staff would gossip that they had been one of the great love matches, just as her grandparents had been. As for her uncle not being a blood relative, she felt more content than bereaved.

"Drink your tea up, girls. It'll help with the shock, especially as there is no time for anything stronger. You've got some packing to do, we sail before noon tomorrow."

A year later…

Fanny looked around the cellar decorated in all its hedonistic flair, ready for her first Hell Fire celebration. *Fais ce que to voudras.* Fanny smiled, staring at the wall above one of the roaring fires in the large cellar. Reading the letters carved into the stone made a shiver of anticipation for tonight's events flicker down her spine. This would now be a place of true pleasure, having burned all her uncle's torture devices in a big fire in the courtyard recently.

She had arrived back to find Langston Hall in a state of upheaval. Some of the staff had already moved on and those who stayed had been relieved to see Fanny. Even her old horse neighed excitedly from the barns when Fanny approached. She was happily surprised he was still alive.

Her memory of the Duchess's party and the discovery of Rob's true colours were very distant now. She had been only too happy to dump his ring in the Ashley River and along with it, any sense of affection she had for him.

Oh, how fickle the first feelings of love and lust could be, and in her case, potentially dangerous. Fanny had recently heard that he was favourite to be elected to parliament. Having met a few politicians, she knew his deceiving soul was suited for the job.

Uncle Harry had certainly been on the nose for something not being right. Fanny's mother was indeed the owner of Langston and some smaller family estates. Her uncle was her mother's adopted brother and therefore had no right to the estates at all. The documents in the safe detailed that he was adopted as a newborn, to cover up the death of a much-wanted son of Fanny's Grandparents. Unsurprisingly, there was no other information about him, not even a birth name or parish as to where he may have come from.

Thank goodness Annie had discovered the secret drawer in the safe, if not, Langston and Fanny's mother's possessions, would have been sold before Fanny could intercept its sale by the government under the debt laws. The thought of what could have been had given her many restless nights, it was finally all sorted by Lord Compton and his associates shortly after her return.

Laughter from the end of the room snapped Fanny out of her memory and she turned to see Mr Evans vying for Bridget's attention with a kiss on the hand. Fanny smiled; her heart full at seeing her friend so happy.

It was near time for her guests to finish arriving. The cool evening air had her donning a cloak over her nun's habit and Fanny walked up the servant stairs towards the side entry, in time to see the last of the carriages enter the restored carriageway. Her uncle had certainly not invested any money into upkeeping the property and it had taken many months of people working very hard to make it right again. Thankfully, because of the large inheritance her mother had hidden away for her, Fanny was able to have all the work completed in time for tonight's final event before winter settled in.

She watched as a hurried Art, fresh from his daily studies, made his way towards the entrance for the last of the arrivals. Fanny could not convince him to take a more senior position within the household, instead she employed a tutor to teach Art and other members of her staff to read and write.

A hooded Clarita, led by a well-disguised Lord Harmsworth, stepped from their all-black carriage and quickly make their way in through the main entrance foyer where they would be greeted by the Grand Master himself. The stiff breeze caught under Clarice's habit and allowed Fanny to see a peek of the daring red negligee hiding underneath.

When Art rang the hand bell that echoed throughout the night, all Fanny's guest made their way down into the cellar. They were all eagerly gathered around the altar at the far end of the room when Fanny made her way through the crowd.

Prickles of awareness made the hair stand up on her nape and Fanny turned to find the cause of this sudden sensation. It was not a bad feeling by any means, it was something familiar, something that brought her body to life without being touched.

Fanny's breath quickened as she cast her eyes over the elaborately dressed guests, many wearing hoods, some with excited eyes peering out to meet hers, others choosing to remain hidden at this early hour. She glanced towards Rosie who smiled and raised a glass of champagne to her, nodding for Fanny to turn around. Raising a quizzical brow across the room in reply, Fanny turned and came face to face with a man in a silver half-mask complete with a single red ruby. Stunned. She stared up into eyes that she had first seen so long ago in this very room.

"Hello, little one. Do you remember me?" His voiced purred as he took her in his arms, leaning her back, his mouth mere inches from her ear.

"I told you I would return," he whispered, tightening his grip on her waist.

Fanny instinctively arched against his body, shocked and delighted, she hungrily kissed him, feeling the burn of passion ignite through her as she wrapped her arms around his neck.

Fanny shivered as her cloak fell to the ground and she broke the kiss, allowing herself to follow this man to the altar. As she walked through the crowd, she glanced around, and upon seeing Rosie's beaming smile, she instantly knew that this was her doing. This man, whose name she did not know, touched the very heart of her.

Side by side, they climbed the two steps and he turned Fanny to face their audience. From behind, his strong fingers caught the hem of her habit and he quickly whisked it over her head. The crowd cheered and staffs began a cadence in the stone floor.

Fanny was swept up into his arms and laid bare upon the fur covered alter. He leaned down and whispered, "Are you wet for me, little one?"

Fanny nodded eagerly, her lips were moist and swollen and she yearned for his hand to part them and be inside of her. Her hips arched towards him, and a moan escaped when she squeezed her thighs around her arousal.

"Tonight, you will finally be mine."

The crowd hushed as the Grand Master made his way through the room to take up his position at the head of the altar. Fanny arched her neck to look up at him and he winked at her.

"You're supposed to be timid and just a little unsure of what is happening as we sacrifice you tonight." He said with a sly wink.

Fanny laughed. Oh, how far she had come. The time spent with Rosie and the girls at the club had turned her into a woman with great desire, and here, amongst her friends, she felt their acceptance and feared nothing.

"We are gathered here tonight, not to sacrifice but to worship. For this woman who lays upon this alter has already been our sacrifice once before. I'm sure you all remember it well," Sir Francis roused, smiling at his own memory.

Staffs struck the ground in appreciation, with many men and women yelling out in agreeance. "We do love our Fanny!" a man yelled from the side. The whole room erupted into laughter.

"So, on this night, we worship...our Fanny...indeed we do. And I gift her to the one who claimed her first in this very room so long ago, Sir Hugh Churchill." Sir Francis placed his lips upon Fanny's and then moved to take up his place at the front of the crowd.

Fanny's body tingled from head to toe. She finally had a name for the man who first allowed her to feel pleasure. Hugh...his name echoed in her mind and she smiled. Farewell to the stranger she first knew as having obsidian eyes, and hello to Hugh, the man whose passion matched her own.

"Are you with me, Fanny?" Hugh said sweetly, looking down upon the woman who seemingly disappeared from England nearly two years ago. He brushed the hair from the side of her face, admiring the smile of distant thoughts.

"I'm with you, Sir Hugh," she let it hang in the air. A private first introduction of sorts. He had barely touched her yet already her whole body was flushed with arousal. Her breasts, in particular, were heavy and her nipples ached to be suckled.

"Then up with you. Up on your knees, facing everyone so that I may drink at your altar."

Fanny gasped as Hugh assisted her in moving briskly to her knees.

Once again, the staves pounded the ground in anticipation of the commencement of tonight's debauchery.

She gazed out over the crowd, nuns and monks smiling and cheering. Already some were near naked and there were many monks with tented robes, clearly aroused by the environment in which they stood.

"Spread your thighs for me, Fanny." Hugh demanded, in a gruff tone that captured Fanny's full attention. He had removed his half-mask and now she could see what a truly handsome man he was. His golden-brown eyes were sparkling in the candle light, and his wide smile broadened his square jaw.

Fanny did as asked, assisted by two nymphs also kneeling to her side. Their fingers ran up the inside of her legs and tested the moistness of her cunny. Thankfully, the thick furs underneath her knees cushioned her against the stone slab for she felt sure that she may pass out before too long. His mouth latched hard between her wet lips, indelicately sucking at her clit with such power that she grabbed fistfuls of the white fur so as not to collapse upon him. Her climax came so fast that her sudden scream echoed throughout the cellar, much to the bawdy cheers of all in front of her. Lightheaded, Fanny swayed and almost begged him to stop, fearing she could not take anymore.

The nymphs took to her side, supporting each arm and began to rein kisses upon her shoulders, neck and mouth, distracting Fanny just enough to take the edge off her arousal. Fanny's head lulled forward and her husky moan grew into a whine as soon as her arousal started to peak.

Strong fingers dug into her bottom, Hugh's stern voice left all sweetness behind, "Not yet, Fanny. You come when I say you can!"

Through gritted teeth Fanny nodded her agreement. The pain in her bottom was enough to subside her arousal, but not for long. The air had grown warm and many people were as naked as she was. They watched her high upon the altar as a man ravaged her cunny and a nymph suckled each breast.

Fanny opened her eyes; her hands were now clenched into Hugh's dark curls after she had dislodged his wig some time ago. She looked around the room, making eye contact with many, including the Grand Master who stood off to the side with Lady Mary and Rosie.

Her release was too close to ignore. With her whole body stretched tight, she pulled tighter on Hugh's hair. Her clit was overly sensitive and beginning to hurt when she pounded Hugh on the shoulder and begged, "Now?"

He snickered into her cunny, sending a cool breath over her heat, "Now, little one. Let it fly." With his fingers grasping her bottom tightly, Hugh delved into Fanny's lips, latching onto her clit as she began to buck into his mouth.

Once again, Fanny screamed her release to the room, closing her eyes she gave way to the comforting darkness and fell into his arms. Waking a short time later to see that she had been moved to one of the beds, and now laid with Hugh at her side.

Life had come full circle and Fanny could not be happier.

Hello Simon,

Well…there you go. Was that as good for you as it was for Fanny?
Do I get bonus points for keeping Rob alive? I initially had thought to do away with him as well – and it would have been somewhat gruesome but that was about three years ago. I've mellowed.
I cannot believe we have finally made it to this point, some 5ish years later of toing and froing and life intervening and, in a time where at the beginning of writing, the T word was more distasteful than the C word that has upended all our lives these past two years. And now parts of the world are at war. I didn't see that coming.
Where to now? Ah, yes, editing. That time to print a (seemingly) million pieces of paper and smother it in red pen corrections. I know my mind has bookmarked a few things along the way, like my initial introduction of Mr Obsidian Eyes and if I confused/combined him with Rob Longshot's character. I feel there is something untidy there that I need to fix. I'm hoping I have all my notes and research in the one place with me at home, especially as I was still living in Australia for the first two years of writing Wish me luck.
Speaking of Australia, I am now back for a short while for medical treatment and after dodging Covid for two years, I have contracted it. Although I cannot say "Thanks for the germs, 'Stralya," because I am unable to pin down when I was exposed. Thankfully, symptoms were mild, but it did give me many restless nights of worrying if my surgery would go as scheduled. So far so good.

Oh, how different it is to fly in the post-pandemic-panic environment. Flights are all over the show, every tray table is suspect, and travelling is no longer enjoyable for me. Not yet, anyway. But it could always be worse, as we have learned.
Now, onto editing!
Debb.

Debb,
Well, after an indecently long break, I sit down to complete our story. And the first thing I find is that the girls are apparently homeless. Where have they been living? I did search your last chapters and could not find a reference. Perhaps I did not look hard enough.
No problem. As new but respectable visitors to town, they have taken lodgings. And as one of their first calls would have been to Mr Burridge's business contact, William Williams Esq., they found comfortable rooms at the back of his house, overlooking the garden. They will have their meals at the family dining table and the protection of staff if a certain ratbag comes to call. Mr Williams' house is on Longitude Lane, a narrow alley running back from the waterfront. It is unpretentious but has a large garden devoted mostly to vegetables.
So; here goes…

Simon

Debb,
Aargh! Another disaster! I was just re-reading that part of our story that has Fanny writing in ledgers in the club when something struck me. I have her writing with ink and a dip pen, like the ones I learned to use in school, way back in the mists of time. Would Fanny have used the same pens? A quick rush to Uncle Google says "In 1792, The Times (London) advertised 'New invented' metal pens. A metal pen point was patented by English inventor and entrepreneur Bryan Donkin. In 1822, John Mitchell of Birmingham started to mass produce machine-made, steel pen nibs and their popularity took off."
So no modern dip pens for Fanny in 1760. She is stuck with goose quills which must have been a nightmare to use. And I have to go back through our text searching for any reference to writing and eliminating all metal pen nibs. Damn.

Simon

Simon,

Well picked up on the fact that I had in fact left them homeless, or in non-descript accommodation that had a wonderful parlour. I guess with all the excitement of change, I forgot they needed their own bed as well.

I must confess to loathing those quill pens. A primary school I attended had an 'old fashion' farm and for one week a year, we got to turn back the clock and dress up and live like a colonial, including writing with quills and ink. Mighty messy business, although I am sure a Lady would have mastered the blotting much better than a group of grade six students.

It is interesting to pick up little tidbits that are not suitable to use in our timeframe. Amazing Grace was one I thought would be definitely a no brainer, but as we know, this was not the case.

Now on to your ending. I eagerly await to see where you take us.
Debb

Chapter Twenty ~ Simon's Ending...

Election Day in Charles Town ~ Longitude Lane
~a tea shop for Charles Town? ~ The London Teahouse
~ Rob Longshot on the hustings ~ jacks-in-office
and indentures ~ a letter from Lord Compton ~ Rob Longshot pays a
visit ~ thoughts of home ~ speaking frankly

They walked back to Longitude Lane, avoiding the crowd either helping to clear the debris from the tavern opposite or possibly looking for a free beer.

"I have never seen an election," said Fanny "They seem very noisy here. I don't think they're like this in England."

Art looked at her in surprise. "Beg pardon, Miss, but I've seen a good deal worse at home. This is nothing, anyways. They're just warming up. The real fun starts Tuesday fortnight when they hold the vote. All the country folk will be coming to town and the candidates will be giving away beer and pies. Anything to build up their share of the poll."

"He's right, Miss," said Bridget "I was in Langport one year at election time and it wasn't safe for a woman to be outside. There was beer everywhere and the candidates had bands marching up and down the High Street. Every other man was stupid with drink and I stayed indoors until the wagon was ready to go home again."

"But – but that's not right. It's like buying votes. I'm sure that's against the law."

A man was coming towards them, carrying a placard on a pole.

The Right Honourable Robert Dashwood will attend Mr McCrady's Rooms on East Bay Street this evening to meet the electors of Charles Town and discuss their manifest concerns. Refreshments will be provided.

The man was poorly dressed and showed no interest in the election he was advertising. Dashwood, thought Fanny, and Robert too. I suppose England is full of Dashwoods, but I wonder… and they turned into Longitude Lane.

Where their progress was blocked by a wagon wedged into the narrow lane. Mr Williams had run short of warehouse space again and his stables were having to accommodate the overflow. Men were rolling barrels down from the wagon and through the stable-yard gate. The sweet smell of rum hung in the air, and the horses would have to tolerate it until Mr Williams arranged a passage for the barrels to Bristol and Mr Burridge.

Once the last barrel had been rolled away, the wagon moved off and they could reach Mr Williams' front door. The house was modest, a brick built terrace whose front door opened straight onto Longitude Lane, and that lane was small and modest enough in its own right. Charles Town was no more than a village compared with the grandeur of Bristol, and it was clear that Mr Williams could not be compared with Mr Burridge. Longitude Lane in Charles Town was interesting, even quaint, but nothing like St Stephens Street and Mr Burridge's elegant house.

Fanny wondered if the difference reflected an imbalance in trade between the two ports. Perhaps the interchange of goods between the two generally favoured Bristol, and the old lady on the River Avon simply became richer and richer. She supposed that farm produce such as tobacco, indigo and cotton could not compare in value with fine manufactures from England.

Whichever way the advantage lay between the two ports, Mr Williams was certainly profiting. He had told them himself that he had arrived in the Carolinas as an indentured servant with nothing in his pockets. All he owned now had come from his hard work and, Fanny suspected, from a reluctance to spend on what he called fripperies. Which meant the three Williams daughters had no piano and certainly no dancing master. They were expected to help their mother run the household, making and clearing away breakfast before attending school.

Fanny had not seen much of Mrs Maria Williams, an imposing Creole lady. Fanny had certainly heard her; she might not say much in public but her own domain was full of noise. Her conversations with her servants rang through the house, as did their singing as they worked. It must be a happy house, Fanny and Bridget decided. The servants at the Priory had not been permitted the slightest noise and actual singing was unthinkable.

The girls could not help wondering what sort of marriage Mr and Mrs Williams shared. It clearly worked, for Mr Williams had an uncertain number of sons working for him and learning the factoring business. Fanny had once summoned the courage to ask him how he had met his wife and instead of describing a meeting, he simply said "Maria? Marrying her was the smartest thing I ever did in my life."

Today they found him sitting on a shaded cloister behind his house, sipping tea and watching the workers in his vegetable garden toiling between rows of beans, peas, potatoes, and Indian corn. He jumped up as they came near.

"Miss Fanny, Miss Bridget. Do you come and sit here, and I'll have the girls bring some compote for you. You take the chair, Miss Fanny, and Bridget will sit along with me on the bench. I shall be back directly…"

"That's a proper vegetable garden, isn't it, Miss?

"Bridget…"

"I mean, isn't it, M- Fanny? Oh, it's so difficult to call you Fanny. I'm sure it'd be easier for a frog to learn to fly. And I can't imagine what Miss Hodges would say if she heard me, if I ever make it home."

"Except Annie Hodges will never be a problem for you again. I'll always remember her dressed in only stays and stockings, ordering Lord Compton upstairs for a thrashing. And if you can call her Annie, you can call me Fanny. We're in the new world now and it's time for new ideas."

Mr Williams returned, leading a daughter with a large jug of compote and two plain earthenware tumblers. The punch was cool and very dilute. The girls sipped it gratefully.

"And how are you making your way in Charles Town, Miss Fanny? A bit quiet for you, I'm sure. Nothing like Bristol, nothing like so grand."

"I believe Charles Town suits us very well, Mr Williams. The climate is gentle and the people are friendly. What more could you ask for?"

What indeed? Fanny sipped her compote and thought about her life in the Carolinas. In truth, she had nothing to complain of except… they did not seem to be doing anything worthwhile. Her time in London had given her a completely new outlook on the world, especially with regard to money. She was spending money every week on rent for Mr Williams, and for their food and upkeep but she had no income to balance the expenditure. Back at the Priory, money had been no concern of hers. In London, the absolute importance of money had shocked her. She had peered over the precipice of poverty, and thank God for friends like Rosie Palm and Lady Mary. And Uncle Harry too, of course. They had helped her, but she was no flighty girl who could live without a thought for the future. She needed to command her own life, and a secure income was essential.

"Mr Williams, I would ask your advice. You are a man of business and understand such things so much more than I."

Mr Williams looked flustered at the thought. "But I'm sure I couldn't advise a lady such as you…"

"I don't see why not, but let me ask you a question. Why are there no tea shops for ladies in Charles Town? There are taverns and rooms for men to meet and gossip, so why is there nothing for women?"

Mr Williams thought for a moment. "I don't suppose Mrs Williams would go to a shop to drink tea with her friends. She visits them in their kitchens mostly, when they ain't busy. Or they might come and sit out here, just as we're doing. I don't see them paying good money for tea. Not when they can have it gratis here with Maria."

"I have seen well-dressed ladies at the shops. Perhaps they would like a tea shop to visit."

"That's as may be and I'm sure you know more of these things than I do. But you'd have to make your own, for I'm sure there's not one for sale."

"I was rather hoping you would help me find a suitable shop. It doesn't take much of a kitchen to serve tea and perhaps coffee – I'm sure you could find something for us…"

Now she had Mr Williams' interest. He might not know much about tea shops but business was the sea he swam in. She could see him thinking.

"I can't say as I have a shop for you, but I do have a place round the corner on Church Street that might suit. But you're a lady – do you think you could run a shop? Ain't easy, you know, dealing with all the money coming in and going out. I doubt I could manage here without I have Maria and the girls managing my books.

"But I ain't sure it's a job for a lady, and Miss Bridget there don't look like she's done that sort of thing before."

"You'd be surprised, Mr Williams. I've managed business at home and in London. I even went over Captain Luxton's ledgers on the *Hispaniola* and they were no picnic, believe me. And when you come to us for a cup of tea, come with a full purse because Bridget will be doing her best to empty it.

"When can you show us your shop? If it's just around the corner…"

Fanny had to admit that Mr Williams knew how to get things moving. Scarcely two weeks had passed since she had sat with him overlooking his vegetable garden and planted the idea of a tea shop, and now Fanny was standing in it. So much had been done – the tarred weatherboard warehouse had been transformed. Everything was new, and the smell of damp whitewash filled the air.

The painters had turned black exterior walls to white, and the bare wood interior into a pleasing cream. Carpenters had worked as men driven by dreams of a large payment from the mad lady from London and quickly replaced the wide double doors with a shop front. Now the building had neatly glazed windows either side of an inviting entrance, to tempt and welcome customers.

Already the shop was attracting attention and a small crowd had gathered on the other side of the road to watch the name board being lifted into its place above the door. *The London Teahouse.* That should attract the local ladies.

But there was so much still to do. The back of the building – the kitchen - had yet to be screened off with a curtain. The kitchen furniture would be coming that afternoon, and the customers' chairs and tables tomorrow. Fanny really wanted to open her doors for the first time on Saturday, so they would have Sunday to straighten out anything that had gone wrong initially. And then they should be shipshape on Monday, ready for the busy streets of election day on Tuesday. Not that many ladies would be on the streets at that time. Already the town was plagued by roving bands of men drinking and shouting in support of their candidate. The streets were no place for a lady. Nonetheless, people would see the shop and perhaps talk about it when they returned home.

Bridget pushed in through the carpenters working on the front door. "Miss, Miss, I've just seen him! Rob Longshot. He's in the election, except he's calling himself Robert Dashwood now, and he doesn't have his earring no more."

"You saw him? Where is he? Did he see you?"

"On Broad Street, opposite the Jewish orphanage. He's making speeches – you could catch him if you hurry."

Fanny could hear the drums beating as soon as she stepped out onto the street, and a crowd had gathered at the junction with Broad Street. She hurried on to the town centre with its substantial stone and brick buildings. The crowd was large and noisy, and some men were noticeably drunk. She caught glimpses of the speakers' platform, a farm wagon adorned with ribbons and posters. In front of the wagon, a band of drums and fifes were playing the new song *The World Turned Upside Down* as loudly as they could, loud enough to draw in more people and to drown the shouting from the crowd. Fanny pushed on, trying to see more of the men standing on the wagon. They seemed to be waiting, talking amongst themselves and paying no attention to the crowd.

"Mind where you're going, Miss," protested a solid man in a frayed top hat. "Stand on your own feet, not mine." Fanny pushed on wriggling through the crowd, apologising as she went. The music was very loud now and she was close enough to make out the faces of the men on the wagon. Rob Longshot was not there. The band changed to *Over the Hills and Far Away*, played with even more gusto. The crowd was expectant, waiting for something to happen.

The men on the wagon reached an agreement and one of them stepped forward and waved at the band. The music trailed off with a last rattle of drums and quiet spread over the crowd. The man waited as the last voices died away. He made an impressive figure, tall and beautifully dressed in a dark green tailcoat and breeches. A neatly tied jabot and a Ramillies wig marked him out as gentry, a cut above the people he was about to address.

He took a deep breath and shouted, "Carolinians!' He was forced to wait as the crowd cheered; they approved of their name. "Carolinians! Why have you come here?" and again he waited as the crowd assured him that free beer was their major concern. "You are come, of course, to elect a new council member. This is a very responsible position and you need a very special person.

"And I'm here to tell you – Carolina has been lucky. In a moment I will introduce to you a gentleman recently arrived from England. Not a lord or baron sent to exploit the riches of our beautiful country, but a gentleman who is truly one of the people. A gentleman who cares for you and your families. He sets no store by position and friends in London. He cares nothing for money or patronage. He thinks only of our home here and us, the people.

"So, I introduce to you a leader to take us forward to a freer future. A man who has advised the king and regularly dines with the highest in England, but retains the spirit of the ordinary man in his heart. I give you … Mr Robert Dashwood!"

Fanny found herself standing on tip-toe, trying to a glimpse of Rob as he climbed the steps to reach the speakers' platform. The crowd had begun to shout and clap as soon as his tricorn hat appeared and – there he was. Not Rob Longshot the Highwayman, and certainly not the deviant monk who had celebrated her entry into the Hellfire Club. This was the perfect English gentleman in breeches and stockings, a smart riding coat and fine white lace at his neck. He stood in front of the cheering crowd, scanning the people from side to side, basking in their welcome.

And she recognised him! In this strange town, dressed in strange clothes, she recognized a man with whom she had exchanged so few words. That was Rob, the only man who had ever taken her, but what had happened to him? He stood alone, wooden and uncertain. He was not the man she had known. He reminded her of a liveried footman at the front door of a big London house.

The crowd was quiet as he looked from one side to the other, and then something touched him. He stood taller, broke into a smile and spread his arms wide. "Hello, Charles Town!" he shouted, and the crowd shouted back, aided by the fifes and a flourish on the drums. This was more like the Rob she remembered and she joined in the clapping. Rob let the cheering continue and then waved the crowd down. "Thank you, thank you – how are you all doing today? How's the beer? Good? There's nothing I like better on a fine day like this – the sun on my face and a mug of beer in my hand."

The crowd agreed with that, and the beer had made them boisterous. "You all know who I am, and you all know why I'm here…" Rob knew the crowd, and he led them on. "I'm a candidate for council. What do you think of that? That's right. Someone has to tell those jacks-in-office it's time to pack their bags and take the next ship back to England."

Fanny looked around her at the people – mostly men – cheering and shouting. They were strange to her, loud and brutal, braying like jackasses. If these were the electors of Charles Town, she was surprised the town survived. Were elections like this back home? She had never dreamt of attending election hustings and her only contact with the political life had been through the members of Rosie Palm's club. She could not imagine any club member ever standing before a crowd like this. Not even to wish them good day.

Rob was in his element. "And talking of jacks-in-office, what do you think of the Governor? There's a man who knows which side his toast is buttered.

"What? No, shooting is too good for him. And besides, lay a finger on a King's man and we'll have redcoats all over us. That's not the way. You've got to petition the King. I know about these things. I've sat at the King's private dinner table. He's a good man, I tell you. A great man. But you can't say the same about his advisers. Privy Councillors they call themselves, and that's where they belong. In the privy, head first and kicking. You should see them. Bums a mile wide from stuffing themselves with pies and puddings every day, and you can guess who pays for them. That's right – they've got their slaves back home, for all those slaves ain't black. They're white folks, slaving away to support Lord This and the Earl of That. Don't see a scrap of bacon from one end of the year to the next, and their lords are in London dining on larks tongue pies.

"Except when they get short of guineas. Then they're off to the King to beg a position as a governor somewhere. *Oh, Your Majesty, pray allow me to be Governor of somewhere. I have to pay my gambling debts, you know. Doesn't the money fly away... but a fine rich colony like the Carolinas, that would set me up again quite nicely.* And you know who'll be filling up his treasury for him? You will! Taxation, that's what it's all about. A little bit of money for the King – I don't begrudge him that – and a very big heap of money for the so-called Governor. He lives here, next to us, but does he do any work? Can you imagine him hoeing a row of beans or driving a plough? Why should he, when he can trick you into doing it for him?

"We need a Council and a Governor for the common man, like you and me. Men who get their money by working for it!"

Rob had succeeded in exciting the crowd and they were shouting agreement. Fanny found herself wondering about Rob's money. He'd earned it on the highways, with horse and pistol. And if that was not enough, his father would surely help with some more. She doubted he had ever earned a penny by hoeing beans or driving a plough.

Confused shouts were coming from the back of the crowd, shouts about blacks. About there being too many of them. About them being worse than animals. About blacks working for nothing and leaving honest men to starve. The shouts coalesced into a chant of *Blacks out! Blacks out!*

The chanting increased in volume until it drowned everything.

Where had that idea come from? Fanny was used to the world treating Negroes as little more than animals; she might have thought that way herself if she hadn't shared a cabin with Sally. Denigration and mistreatment of any of God's people upset her, even people as strange and foreign as the colony's slaves, and now this mindless, wicked chanting had taken over the crowd. Where had it started? Had someone prepared a claque for the crowd? Who would do such a thing, and why?

Rob waited minutes before calming the crowd. When he judged his shouted word would carry, he began again. 'Exactly, Friends. Why do we see them in town at all? Blacks belong on their plantations. And do you know why they're here? Because your masters want things so. They don't want to pay an honest man to do work when they can have their slaves do it for nothing. Picking tobacco out in the sun is one thing; no-one wants to do that sort of work for a penny a day, but blacks do it whether they will or not. But what place do they have in town? Charles Town was made by white people and for white people. Blacks should live and work where they belong – on the plantations."

"What about indentures? Down with indentures!" The chanting started again but this time it was *No more indentures! No more indentures!* Rob smiled and let the crowd continue until he cut them off. "Yes, my friends, what about indentures indeed. Ask yourself – really, ask yourself – who holds these indentures? Do you? Of course not. Indentures are just a way for the rich and powerful to turn white men into slaves. That's right – there's many a man come from England and now in chains of servitude. Why? Because that's where your masters want to keep them. Do you think those poor men will ever go free? No, not while they can still work. Every year their work grows harder and their debt grows larger. And I tell you – they'll wear those chains until death carries them off.

"No, my friends. It's time to put a stop to the rich who run this place and get richer by importing indentured white men. If they want people to work for them, we have people a-plenty. Why should they be allowed to import white slaves to take your work away? You'll work an honest day for an honest wage, and that's what they must pay."

As the crowd cheered its approval, Fanny pushed forward through the men standing nearest to the platform. She wanted to see more. She wanted to see this new Rob who no longer spoke like an uneducated thief with a gold earring. He spoke with the accents and confidence of Sir Francis's son, a man of the ruling class – the class that ran England and the colony. The class he was now attacking.

"Excuse me, Sir, excuse me. I can't see..." Surprised to find a lady burrowing through the crowd, men moved aside and made room for her, and she reached the front of the crowd where she could see the platform, and be seen in return.

Rob continued to provoke the crowd. "And I'll tell you what I want to know – I want to know what happens to all the customs and excise money. I'll lay there must be barrels of it, every year. Every time you buy a shirt made from good Scotch cambric, His Lordship the Governor takes a share of your money. I want to know how much he takes, and how much of it he passes on to King George. You're not stupid and neither am I. You know a good deal of that money never travels further than the Governor's palace – of course you do."

As the crowd responded with shouts and cheers, Rob stood confidently and surveyed his supporters, from the claque at the far edge of the mob and right down to the front where Fanny stood. Their eyes met and she saw the shock on his face. He tried to smile, but turned to speak to one of the men behind. They were both looking at her as the noise lessened and Rob had to return to his speech. "And I'll tell you what we're going to do," he shouted. "First of all, you're going to give me your votes. And then we're going to roll up our sleeves and start demanding answers! Are you with me?"

Suddenly, the noise was simply too much. Fanny began to push her way out of the press, easier now because the mostly male crowd could see her coming and tried to stand aside. Although they were willing enough, it took Fanny five minutes or more to disentangle herself from the crowd and reach Church Street and safety again. She needed to hurry back to the tea house and sanity; she needed to think.

"Miss, Miss!" a young boy's voice was calling her. She stopped and turned to see a youth in fine clothes hurrying to reach her. He took off his hat and said, "Please excuse me, but I am told you are Miss Fanny?" She must have nodded because he continued "Mr Dashwood sends that you may attend on him at Shepheard's Inn after eight o'clock."

Oh, may I? she thought. Does he think I'm the sort of woman who wanders the streets at night and 'attends' on gentlemen in strange taverns? The youth stood uncertainly, half expecting a sharp reply. She looked him up and down. He had brought Rob's message but had nothing to do with its content. "You may inform Mr Dashwood that should he wish to attend on me, I may be found at the London Teahouse. Good day."

She hurried back towards the tea shop, her mind whirling. Rob Longshot had been at the back of her mind since she had first met him – of course. Who could forget the man who first took you? And she suspected the thought of meeting him again had brought her to the Americas. A chance without chance, she told herself. And yet, here he was, but not as she remembered. The old Rob, Rob Longshot the highwayman, had been a rogue but – he had been so interesting. She had never met anyone so far from her own world of gentry, tradesmen and farm labourers. No-one who shed morals so easily, who could smile and rob a lawyer of his gold at the same time. Or a girl of her virginity, she added to herself, although... She had not struggled, but that was because she did not realise what was happening until it was too late. But would she have struggled if she had understood? She was no longer sure.

She shook her head. She had behaved exactly like a stupid young girl, swept off her feet by a handsome but worthless rogue. She told herself she was older now, with more experience of the world. And Rob appeared to be older too; he had changed his coat and was now a politician. She was not sure his new profession was any better than the old but at least it did not bring the risk of being hanged. Dictionary Johnson had defined a politician as a man of artifice and of deep contrivance, which might be truthful but was far from flattering.

She hurried back to the Teahouse to find Mr Williams waiting with a letter in his hand and all thoughts of Rob left her. News from home! She wanted to hide away immediately and read but she must entertain Mr Williams first. She drew him inside and sat him at a table by the window where he could be seen by passersby.

"Our first customer, Mr Williams. Please sit down and I will see what Bridget can manage." Behind the curtain dividing off the back of the old warehouse space, Bridget and one of Mr Williams's daughters were already preparing a tray with a tea pot, two cups and a small plate of biscuits. "Another cup, Bridget. You have to celebrate as well. Mary-Anne can serve us, once we've sat down."

Mr Williams sipped his tea, looking around at the furniture and new paint. "You've done a proper job here, Miss Fanny. A proper job. Who'd have thought this old shed would polish up so fine? I lay you'll have it full of ladies come Monday. Will you be allowing gentlemen to come along too?"

"We were wondering about that. I don't think so – the men here are too wild and they would frighten the ladies away. Perhaps gentlemen will only be allowed if they are accompanied by a lady. And we're not serving rum at all. There are enough drunks on the streets without us adding to them."

Mr Williams nodded. "That's the way. I shall have to ask Maria to bring me – she'd like that. Do you want me to put a word in the newspaper for you?"

"Would you? That would be so kind. And people might listen if it is coming from you. I'm going to put a note on the door saying we will open properly at nine o'clock on Monday morning. Mary-Anne, do we have any more biscuits? Your father seems to have finished them."

Mr Williams had enjoyed his visit and stayed far longer than Fanny wanted. The letter was on the table between them, unopened. She wanted to hide away and savour the news from another world. As soon as she could, she left Mary-Anne and Bridget to tidy up and hurried off to her room. Sitting at the window, she broke the seal and carefully unfolded the contents. It came from Lord Compton, in his chambers.

Dear Miss Howarth,

Firstly, I must thank you for your letter. I received both copies, one from Mr Burridge and the other by hand of a young seaman who refused payment, saying he owed you too much to take anything. I had one of my clerks take him off for a good dinner instead. It is certainly a good idea to send more than one copy, and may I counsel you to number your letters so we will know if any have gone astray. You will see this letter is numbered 1.

Now, much has happened since you left England. Most importantly perhaps, on the 4th of May you were made a Ward of Chancery. Perhaps in your exotic retreat you woke feeling a little different next day? If I explain briefly, being a Ward means that you and all your affairs are now under the

308

supervision and protection of the Lord Chancellor. Your uncle can no longer touch any inheritance you may have or the money Lord Beaconsfield left you. I have been appointed as your guardian until you come of age and are able to handle your own affairs.

Your uncle has been a problem. I began searching for him through local lawyers in Langport and Whealdon and it turns out that you have already met your uncle's lawyer, and he remembers you very well. His name is Higgins and he was travelling with you when your coach was robbed by the infamous Rob Longshot. Mr Higgins apparently lost a good deal of money that night before he ran away, leaving two innocent girls to the attentions of a ravenous highwayman. I called him to a meeting in The George at Whealdon but he was very reluctant to tell me anything of your uncle and his affairs. By the way, the host and servants at The George remember you very famously; the girl who drove a coach and four into their stable yard as cool as a cucumber, and then ate devilled kidneys for breakfast.

I did discover one valuable source of information on your uncle – Miss Annie Hodges, who arrived at Mrs Palm's about the time you left. She is an intelligent woman, and business-like. As you know, she was previously your uncle's housekeeper and I believe she knows more about his rents and income than he does himself. Annie says that your mother left the Priory and lands to you in her will, passed on from your father. Your uncle owns the adjoining lands known as Bedwith Hollow which are apparently productive farmland but do not have a grand house to match the Priory. So your uncle moved in and treated all the lands as a single estate. That is important, and I will explain why.

Your inheritance was left as a trust until you come of age. It belongs to you and there are limits to what your uncle may do with it. For instance, he will have access to rents etc. but may only use the funds to support you and for the betterment of your estate. He is certainly not able to sell the land or use it as security for any loan or mortgage.

After spending some time with Annie, I had a reasonably clear picture of your uncle's situation, so I called the lawyer Higgins to meet in my chambers at Lincoln's Inn. Once I had put the fear of God into him with Annie's information, he became much more cooperative and confirmed that, yes, a mortgage had been taken against the value of the estate. I'm sure it was negotiated against the value of both the Priory and his own Bedwith Hollow, but that does not concern us because he had no legal right to encumber your property. If the worst comes to the worst, his creditors will be free to plunder Bedwith but your inheritance remains out of reach and safe.

I have, of course, put out the word against your uncle's behaviour and took the liberty of telling the secretary of one of his creditors, a man with the most to lose. As a result, your uncle has now retired to Langston and no longer goes out in public.

If I might advise you, I suggest you should make a will immediately and send it to me. Perhaps in three copies sent by different vessels. If you send them to Mr Burridge in Bristol, he will forward them to me immediately. Once I have that document and have informed your uncle and Mr Higgins, you may return to England in safety.

I do not know what your plans are for the future. I understand the climate in Charles Town is mild and fruitful, so once you have set your affairs here on a proper footing, you may choose to return. However, it is most important that you are in London in person while we settle your affairs, and I look forward to seeing you then.

Mrs Palm and Annie have asked me to send their love, along with best wishes from all your friends,

Yours respectfully,

Compton

Fanny stared out of the window as thoughts raced around her head. She had expected something stiff and austere from Lord Compton and instead she held a letter from a friend giving both good news and good advice. Suddenly she wanted to go home, back to London and her friends. She wanted to see the Priory again, as long as her uncle had been permanently removed. Lord Compton had said little about Annie Hodges, even though he must know that Fanny understood exactly how she entertained him upstairs in the club.

The Teahouse had filled her time for the past weeks and on Monday they were due to receive their first customers. It had been all she thought of, but now she had other things on her mind. It would be good to talk to Cook and Mr Fearnley again, and to walk in the walled vegetable garden and see how things were growing.

But what about Bridget? Would she want to go home too? Back at home, she would be no more than a servant. Here she would soon be manager of the fashionable London Teahouse, a much more substantial person. Fanny rushed to find her, and give her all the news. And then she must find Mr Williams and ask for a trustworthy lawyer who could write a will that would stand up to scrutiny by

Lord Compton.

Rob Longshot appeared at the teahouse on Saturday evening, as the sun was beginning to fade. The girls were doing the last minute things needed for a smooth opening on Monday. Fanny had hoped to be at home by now but there had been so much to do that she had seized a mop and helped Mary-Anne and Bridget. The three of them worked steadily, saying little and focused on cleaning, arranging, preparing. Tomorrow was the Sabbath, so everything must be completed tonight.

Fanny answered a knock at the door still wearing her apron and a cloth about her hair. She had her mop in hand and showed no sign of elegance or even propriety. Rob stood in silence.

"Rob – what are you doing here?"

"You didn't come. Waited all evening but you didn't come."

She suddenly realised he was drunk. His speech was hesitant, his stance uncertain. "Rob, you're drunk. You shouldn't let your voters see you like this."

"Not properly drunk. Old Hamilton has been buying ale for the voters all day. Good ale, too. Most of our people are sleeping it off, but I'm still walking and talking. Do you live here? Can we go upstairs?"

"Certainly not! You're drunk – go home and sleep it off. I've got cleaning to do." She went to close the door but he pushed her back.

"Let me in. I know what sort of woman you are. No matter what – no matter… I've seen you. Let me in."

Fanny felt the girls come up behind her as Rob continued. "Let me in, you bitch. You've no right…"

"Shall we push him out, Miss?" asked Bridget.

"Miss! I know you and your servants. I know how you earned your money. On your back in a brothel, fucking half of London." He was shouting now and no doubt half of Church Road would be listening in. "I'm Robert Dashwood an' I'll be Sir Robert when – in time, I'll be Sir Robert. What do you think of that? You think you and your sluts can stand up to me?"

The three of them were pushing on the door now, struggling to get it shut. Rob continued shouting, but they were winning. The door was inching closer to the jamb when Rob must have slipped. He lost his footing and fell, the door slammed shut and Fanny shot the bolt.

"You bitch – that was my fucking knee." They stood with their backs to the door, frightened and trembling. The door shook as Rob gave it a heavy kick. "I'll be back and burn your bloody shop down. See if I don't. I'm going to find a proper woman." They heard him move away and soon the street was full of Rob's singing, a bawdy version of *The Seven Merry Wives of London*.

"You're well rid of him, Miss" said Bridget. "There's nothing like drink for showing a man's true colours."

"Fanny," said Fanny.

"I meant Fanny. Sorry. But he's not worth the dirt on your shoe. All smiles and gold earrings, but scratch the surface and he's only fit for the honey cart."

The image made Fanny smile. "Well, I daresay he'll find his way there without our help. And I'm sure he won't go around making up stories about us. Not when he sobers up and remembers what we know about him. Now, Mary-Anne, I'm sorry about Mr Dashwood's behaviour. I'm sure he won't be back but, just in case, I'm putting a notice on the door for Monday saying gentlemen will only be admitted if accompanied by a lady. That should keep the trouble makers away. Now, let's finish up and go home. A good rest tomorrow, and we'll be fresh for our new venture on Monday morning."

Next morning, after church, Fanny and Bridget took a walk, for health and to give Fanny a chance to think. Meeting Road showed many families, all dressed in their Sunday best, taking the air and enjoying the sun. They walked in silence past the shops and fine houses. Fanny glanced at her companion. She loved the way Bridget could relax. She worked hard when there was work to do, and when there was not, she relaxed completely. Of course, she was relying on Fanny to do the worrying for her and she had a child-like confidence that whatever Fanny attempted would turn out the best for both of them. Fanny felt she had always muddled through, and she had been lucky. Lucky in her friends here and back in London. Lucky in her enemies too – her uncle had not succeeded and her erstwhile enemy Annie Hodges was now an admirer. Rob Longshot, now there was a thorn in her shoe. She had lain in bed for many hours thinking of their two brief encounters, and she knew she had been lucky – again – that Rob had shown his true colours on the electoral hustings and his attempt to force his way into the teahouse.

They took Amen Street towards the waterfront and turned for home. Here was a street devoted to the business of Charles Town, lined with warehouses and offices, almost deserted on a Sunday. On a whim, Fanny carried on to The Battery to enjoy the sight of the ocean and the wind in their faces. They sat on the seawall and watched the restless water.

"Are you liking the Carolinas, Bridget? Better than home?"

She thought for a moment. "I think Charles Town's a very fine place. Not as grand as Bristol, of course, but what do you expect? Everything so new, even if it's a bit gimcrack to begin with. But the weather's fine and the people are friendly. Back home, I'd be the servant and you'd be the lady. Here, things are a bit different. I can be whoever I want to be – with your help, of course. No-one knows me or judges where I came from, and that's nice.

"All the same, it's not home. I don't know if I shall stay here forever. I've little enough in the way of family in Ireland but I suppose it won't hurt to write and see how they're doing. Not that I'd ever go back there. I'm living like a princess today compared to the girls in my village. And you? You're not thinking of Rob Longshot, I hope?"

"What? Him? No. Definitely not. We've both moved on a long way since we met that highwayman. There's no going back and I don't want to. Yesterday – I suppose yesterday just confirmed it. I didn't like him when he was speaking to the crowd. I liked him even less when he was trying to push his way into the teahouse. Perhaps I've grown up."

"Not too much, I hope. We're still young enough to have some fun before we settle down."

On Monday Fanny had little time to think about the ugliness beneath Rob Longshot's façade of lovable roguery. The London Teashop had opened its doors to the curious and fashionable ladies of Charles Town and the girls were as busy as bees on a summer's day, bringing cups of tea and plates of cakes to the tables promptly and with a smile. The smile became more difficult as the day wore on, especially when the cakes and fresh milk were running low. One of the three of them had to go for more, putting extra work on the shoulders of the other two.

A young man from the *South Carolina Gazette* newspaper, well-spoken but with ink-stained fingers, came on the first morning and Fanny had charmed him into writing a very favourable mention of the Teahouse. She thought his style of writing would sit better with a retired parson than a near youth, but his recommendation was generous and seemed to bring in more customers. Most of all, they were the talk of the town. Charles Town was well known for its gossip mills and they worked feverishly to spread the story of The London Teahouse and its respectable hostess but recently arrived from the Old Country.

Fanny did eventually find time to obtain a will, in five copies; one for her, one to be lodged with Mr Williams and the remaining three for Lord Compton. In the copies travelling to England, she included a note saying she would sail for Bristol in three months' time, unless she heard anything to the contrary. Which would mean Bridget would have to manage the teahouse on her own for a while. Why not? She had a good head on her shoulders. She would manage, but Fanny would have to make her sit down with the books. You cannot make money without good book keeping and she decided to start Bridget on them immediately. Better for her to make mistakes or have difficulties while Fanny was still beside her.

The London Teahouse thrived. Although the men of Charles Town had a wide choice of places to meet their friends and share a drink together, the ladies had been left behind. Now they seized the chance to meet like the sophisticated ladies of Europe, and drink tea with delicate cakes from a Belgian baker in Chalmers Street. Without intending to, the London Teahouse had become the centre of Charles Town's female society. It was quite as fine as anything London itself had to offer, run by a genuine English lady. By all accounts, Fanny was rich and had an estate in the country near London. And it was the talk of the town that she had written letters to Lord Compton – think of that! A real lord!

Even more intriguing were the letters she had written to the famous society beauty, Lady Mary Montagu Wortley, no less. And she had addressed the first ones to both London and Constantinople, wherever that was. As if Lady Mary might be found in either place. And Lady Mary had replied! From London, as it happened. Charles Town wondered what Fanny might have to discuss with such a high born person, and her stock in local society soared.

The gossip reached Fanny from Mary-Anne, and her source was her father. Fanny supposed that Mr Williams' business depended on knowing the latest news from England and the Caribbean. And one particularly tasty piece of news in the Williams household was that one son - Ben - was attempting to court Bridget. The poor boy must be suffering agonies from all the interference and advice coming from his sisters and mother.

Bridget had become used to balancing the books. She had been terrified at first, imagining book keeping to be a magical process far beyond her ability, but now she felt much more confident. The ledger had clear entries in her fine round hand and Mr Williams had offered her a position in his business should she become bored with serving tea. Bridget had even taken over their weekly banking, aided by Ben Williams for protection. The business would be in safe hands, and Fanny had arranged her passage to Bristol without worrying about the teahouse.

Sunday found them sitting on the sea wall again, looking out over the ocean. It should have been the height of summer but there was a cool breeze blowing into their faces. Two small schooners were headed to port, probably carrying cargo from the islands. And the cargo would almost certainly be rum. Fanny's thoughts were an ocean away when Bridget asked, "Which way is England?"

Fanny pointed out over the ocean. "About that way, I think."

"Would those boats be coming from England, do you think?"

"Too small. I expect they're just traders from the islands. Bringing in rum and carrying off the best goods they can afford from men like Mr Williams."

"I'd like to go to the islands one day. We could visit Sally. I wonder how she is going – whether she has her house surrounded by coconut palms. I'd like to see proper palms, after all the fine things she said about them."

Fanny often thought about Sally. "I expect we would find her with a baby or two. It's been long enough. And I expect Captain Beardsley has set her up very nicely. Apparently he has an estate outside Kings Town. I wonder if he has relatives there – he certainly has friends. And he doesn't keep slaves which makes it a better place than Charles Town, in my mind anyway.

"But what about you, Bridget? Are you thinking about babies?"

Bridget looked at her feet and Fanny thought she saw a blush.

"Perhaps. I suppose it will happen one day. But not now. I'm too busy with the shop."

"You've seen a bit of the world, Bridget. You can get married, have babies and still run the teahouse. And don't let anyone say you can't. If Rosie Palm can run the club, you can run a teahouse. And Ben seems to be a good young man."

"And you, Miss? You're well rid of Rob Longshot, but you're not looking for a beau? Perhaps you're waiting for London and you'll bring one back with you."

"Oh, I don't know. I'd like children, of course, but you have to start by finding a good man. I suppose it will happen soon enough. I'm in no rush.

"We've done some things together, haven't we, Bridget? I still think about Langston Priory – but just the good times. Not my uncle. Certainly not about my uncle and Annie Hodges. But I supposed they got us started on our adventures, so we should be a little bit grateful. Do you remember Mrs Bones of the Bull and Mouth? I still haven't made my mind up about her."

"Oh, she was alright. She was honest, more or less, and I heard later she often helps lost girls. You know, runaways. People send them to Mrs Bones and she helps them on. And gets paid for it, I'm sure. She doesn't sell them on to the bad houses, you know. Most of them end up with a maid's position, working all hours but staying alive. She must have been pleased to have you drop into her lap. I wonder if Mrs Palm paid her anything for finding us."

"I never asked her. I liked Rosie Palm. She wasn't born a lady but she's worth a lot more than many women who were. The club runs very well, and that doesn't happen by accident. She knows her business, but she's kindly with it. It looks as if Annie Hodges has found a place with her. I doubt you'd drive Annie out of the club if you used a whip." Fanny paused. "Especially if you used a whip. I don't think I could ever get fond of being whipped but from the way Lord Compton writes, he's perfectly happy to have Annie polishing his bum. She helped us a lot, you know. She gave Lord Compton all sorts of information about my uncle and his money.

"Do you remember Cousin Clarence? Or should I say, Clarita? I suppose I must visit him when I get to London. Give him the latest news about his father. I wonder what he'll say. He told me he never wanted to see his father again. You know he has to make his own way in the world. He lives on Lord Harmsworth's generosity. And now I don't think his father could take him back even if he was kind enough. According to Lord Compton, my uncle has serious money troubles.

"You didn't come with Lady Mary to Lord Harmsworth's grand display. I wish you had seen it – everyone looked wonderful and the girls would put any real woman to shame with their fine gowns, and powder and rouge done so well… I felt like a church mouse."

"I heard you didn't behave like a church mouse…"

"Who knows what church mice get up to when no-one is looking? Anyway, Clarita put me to shame, I'm sure. I danced with her – or him. Clarita danced the woman's part and I was all over the place trying to dance like a man. You know, the hall they held the dance in was *really* impressive – like a small cathedral. I'd like to go back there in daylight one day."

"And the Hellfire Club," said Bridget. "I enjoyed myself there. I believe I had more fun than you on your altar slab. I was dressed as a nun – half-dressed anyway – and the gentlemen… They were so energetic. I've never done so much in just one evening, and I doubt I ever will again. I don't know how I got back to my own bed, I'm sure."

Fanny remembered that evening very well, the ceremony, the heady atmosphere, the frantic desire of both men and women to misbehave. "Yes. My second time, and it was with Rob again. I don't know what to think about that now but it was wonderful at the time.

"You know what? We've seen a lot of things and done a lot of things and we owe it all to Uncle Harry. Yes, other people have been kind to us but Uncle Harry was generosity itself. Such a kind man. I miss him dreadfully."

"And the *Hispaniola*. I never would have got onto a ship if you hadn't taken me. I almost died from sea sickness but after that, just sliding through the waves with porpoises and flying fish…"

"And pirates –"

"Well, yes. I didn't enjoy them. Poor Captain Smollett. Or showing my bum to all those disgusting pirates. And Captain Beardsley rescued us. I thought it would be really difficult to sit down for dinner with him afterwards, but he's a perfect gentleman."

"I dare say Sally's bum helped make him choose her," said Fanny.

"No – that was love, pure and simple. It could happen to anyone

I suppose. But it hasn't happened to me yet. You know, Miss, er – Fanny, I'm so glad you saw through Rob Longshot. That sort of man would be off with all your money as soon as you said 'I do'."

At least Fanny had avoided being named Mrs Longshot. "I wonder what he's doing now he's won the election."

"You didn't hear? He has a position in Governor Greville's office! After all those nasty things he said so he could get elected... I suppose he has to earn his bread and butter somewhere, and the Governor took him in. You know he put the bad word out about us, saying we were whores back in London, well, it didn't work. No-one believed him. All the ladies who have come to the teahouse and met you, have gone home and told their husbands it was all stuff and nonsense. Anyone can see you're a lady."

Fanny thought about that for a moment. "You know, I don't think we did anything wrong. Do you? I know the vicars wouldn't approve but what do they know? Rosie Palm runs a club that is kind to its members and kind to the girls that work there. No-one is hurt, nothing is stolen. It's good for the business of London. The members have somewhere pleasant to sit in the evening, and the girls have paid work and someone to take care of them."

"Will you go back to the club?"

"Certainly to visit Rosie and our friends, but if Rosie has Annie Hodges checking her books, she can do without me! Perhaps I'll join as a member, if they'd have me. Or perhaps they will make allowances for a single woman who lives out of town. I don't think the members would favour allowing married women to join. Half of them go to the club to get away from their families."

They sat and watched wavelets lapping at the sea wall, thinking about London and all they had left behind. Bridget had no doubts. "Well, I have a better life here. London's very grand, but I'd always be just a maid there. Here, things are different. Thanks to you, I'm managing a teahouse. That has to be better, quite apart from the weather."

"Yes, Charles Town has many things in its favour. The people are more friendly, and they get things done. I suppose that goes along with being a new colony. But I still miss the club. All those important men and their talk about politics and parliament. And I'd like to see the Priory again. I hope the staff are still the same. I'm going to hurry up there as soon as I can. I suppose I'll have to set the bailiffs on my uncle first. Or perhaps he'll just leave when he hears I'm coming."

"But where will he go?" asked Bridget. "You said Bedwith Hollow would probably be taken by creditors. He won't be able to live there. He'll have to take his bag and start walking, because I'm sure the sort of friends he has will not take him in without money."

Fanny looked out over the sea towards England. Soon she would be sailing over the horizon, on her way to London and Lord Compton. As soon as she could, she would be off to Langston Priory. She felt no sympathy for her uncle. He had never been a loving man and the things he had tried to do to her had driven her away. As he had driven Cousin Clarence away. And he had come looking for her because he wanted to sell her and her inheritance to one of his shady friends. The hard truth was she did not care in the least what happened to him. She could support herself and, most importantly, she had friends in London and here in Charles Town. And – unlike his friends – her friends could be trusted. She simply did not care.

"Ah, my uncle. Frankly, my dear Bridget, I don't give a damn."

Debb,
Ta-dah! The 29th of December 2021 and I have reached the end of my bit. 132,000 words, although that will change a little as we get into the editing. That's a sensible sort of length for a romantic novel. Unfortunately, it will be a little too fat to be accepted as a letter by Australia Post. A \$9 parcel rather than a \$5 letter, but that just means I will have to think twice before sending copies to friends and potential reviewers
I struggled a bit trying to work out an ending. It seems to me whether Fanny settles in England or Charles Town or both, she has ended one life and will be starting another so I pinched something from Gone with the Wind *(also set in that part of the world) and just ended. I hope you approve.*
And then we can start on the interesting process of editing. We will be coming down with questions and loose ends for months… but it's all worth it if our readers enjoy it.
Regards,
Simon

Hello Simon,
Well, what an enjoyable and very different way to end your part of our story. You have a knack for writing the ways of politics of the day, although one might say that some places may still be the same.

A Gone with the Wind ending is a perfect touch. Why should Fanny's story finish with ours, she can have whichever life she chooses.
Argh, editing. Truly torture by words and grammar and punctuation. I have already discovered what I thought was a missing storyline, was only a thought inspired by research that never was written down. Something about a pink house in Charles Town.
Let the torture begin.
Debb.

Hello Simon, or should I say goodbye?
The time has come, and we have now finished our labor of love, frustration, annoyance, distraction, inspiration, challenge, enlightenment – maybe just all the words.
What started as a request to co-write ended up being a wonderous 5 year-ish journey, back and forth, through the highs and lows of life – with a pandemic thrown in. For me, it was a life crowded with relocating overseas to a third-world country with the world's dodgiest wifi, multiple surgeries, deaths and births of loved ones, and a world that just stopped and trapped people where they were.
As a writer, the challenge of never really knowing what you would create was enjoyable. I have admired the way in which we have been able to massage each other's ideas to make our story whole. Often, I have found a reply humorous and laughed aloud in a quiet place. There have also been days and weeks of contemplation (and baking brownies), as you have taken Fanny in a new direction. In the end, all roads lead to a fork in the road, and we both found a different direction to take, which I think is very fitting.
It has been a pleasure to write with you. Thank you.
Debbie.

Well, Debb,
It has been an adventure, hasn't it? I was thinking just yesterday that it has taken a very long time to get our job done, but consider the context. We have had a global pandemic in the middle of our efforts. You have moved out of Australia and become an expat, a representative of the colonial class. I'm a little surprised you haven't started writing like Kipling. Or Conrad (a better writer, I believe).
During those years, both Jana and I lost our mothers to old age, and my younger brother was taken by cancer. Jana now has two titanium knees and I have one – but we still went on a cycling holiday every year even when we were confined to the Atherton Tablelands instead of old, worn, cheap and

comfortable Europe.

During those times, I met a friend I had last spoken to in our University days – a mathematician called Jill Jones who is today happily playing matriarch to a large family in Cornwall. As you know, she volunteered to copy edit our book and I have to say her mathematical mind is ... incisive. Plus she seems to be as happy to inflict pain on poor authors as, say, Miss Annie Hodges would be. Our text would be stuffed with typos and clumsy English if it had not been for her efforts and those of Jacqueline George-Phillips from Canada.

I am happy with our book. I feel we were able to produce a story that is richer than it would have been if either of us had written alone, and whenever I scroll through looking for edits, I inevitably slow down and just read. Because I enjoy it.

But now I am on tenterhooks; will our readers like our story? Will we even have any readers? Will they like Fanny and the woman she has become? Will they demand to know more about her future (as I'm sure my daughter will). What can I say? We have folded up a big sheet of stiff paper into a boat and will soon push it out into the stream. Let's all wish for a happy voyage and, as paper is not very strong, I will have to share the launching bottle of champagne with Jana and Rudy the cat. Please join us in your colonial hideaway...

Simon